THE WORLD *of* THE END

THE WORLD
of THE END

OFIR TOUCHÉ GAFLA

Translated from the Hebrew by
MITCH GINSBURG

A Tom Doherty Associates Book | New York

THE WORLD OF THE END

Copyright © 2004 by Ofir Touché Gafla

English translation copyright © 2013 by Ofir Touché Gafla

Originally published as *Olam Hasof* by Keter Publishing House in Jerusalem.

A Tor Book

Published by Tom Doherty Associates, LLC

175 Fifth Avenue

New York, NY 10010

www.tor-forge.com

Tor® is a registered trademark of Tom Doherty Associates, LLC.

Library of Congress Cataloging-in-Publication Data

Gafla, Ofir Touché
    ['Olam ha-sof. English]
    The world of the end / Ofir Touché Gafla.–First edition.
        p. cm.
    "A Tom Doherty Associates Book."
    ISBN 978-0-7653-3356-8 (hardcover)
    ISBN 978-1-4668-0320-6 (e-book)
    I. Title.
PJ5055.22.A338O4313 2013
892.4'37–dc23

2013003719

Tor books may be purchased for educational, business, or promotional use. For information on bulk purchases, please contact Macmillan Corporate and Premium Sales Department at 1-800-221-7945 extension 5442 or write specialmarkets@macmillan.com.

First Edition: June 2013

Printed in the United States of America

0 9 8 7 6 5 4 3 2 1

Acknowledgments

I wish to express my thanks to those who provided support and joy over the years:

Biological family: Menachem and Hadassa (parents), Atzmon, Gil, Orit, Dalia, Noa, Omer, Yamit, Yaniv.

Other family: Ori Brenner, Lior Elbo, Lior Gefen, Eitan and Racheli Shavit, Gil & Moti, Shay Leon, Dganit Saar, Renana Sofer, Ran Meirovich, Noam Shavit, Dan Morgenstern, Avshalom and Clarissa Caspi, Koby Israelite, Idan Talesnik, Orna Shamia, Christopher Kloeble, Saskya Jain, and Chandrahas Choudhuri.

Feline family: Pele, Pupu, and their whiskered posse.

Many thanks to Shimon Adaf, the man and the myth.

Thanks to all IWP members, staff, and dreamscape.

Thanks to all at Keter Publishing House.

Thanks to Iris Mor.

Thanks to Adam Friedstein.

Thanks to Norbert Pariente and the angels from France.

Thanks to all at Tor Publishing House.

Thanks to my wonderful agents, Deborah Harris (Israel) and Kathleen Anderson (United States).

Thanks to Katharine Critchlow for such a warm welcome.

Thanks to Stephan Martiniere for the gorgeous cover.

Many thanks to Lisa Davis (production editor) and Edwin Chapman (copyeditor) for their dedicated work.

Big thanks to my extraordinary translator, Mitch Ginsburg.

Special thanks to Marco Palmieri, my excellent editor, for his superb work and for being there.

Every ending is arbitrary, because the end is where you write The end. *A period, a dot of punctuation, a point of stasis. A pinprick in the paper: you could put your eye to it and see through, to the other side, to the beginning of something else.*

−Margaret Atwood, *The Robber Bride*

THE WORLD *of* THE END

1

The End

Some fifteen months after Marian lost her life under bizarre aeronautical circumstances, her husband decided to celebrate her fortieth birthday. Their old friends, well aware of the couple's love for one another, were not surprised to find, amid the daily monotony of their mail, an invitation to the home of the live husband and the late wife. They also knew that he had yet to have his final word on the matter, and that, beneath the emotional prattle and the love-soaked murmurs, Ben Mendelssohn was a man of action. His friends, put at ease by the invitation, saw the party as classic Mendelssohn, which is to say a come-as-you-are, be-ready-for-anything affair. After all, Ben paid the bills with his imagination, crafting surprise endings for a living. Writers of screenplays, writers at the dawn and dusk of their careers, letter writers, graphomaniacs, poets, drafters of Last Wills and Testaments—all used the services of Ben Mendelssohn, righter. In intellectual circles he was known as an epilogist; among laymen he remained anonymous, never once asking for his name to appear at the close of the work he sealed for others. Over time, experts were able to recognize his signature touches and, within their own literati circles, to admit to his genius. Marian, who recognized his talent from the start, had a keen distaste for her husband's enduring anonymity, but he, chuckling, would ask, "Do you know any famous tow-truck drivers? All I do is drag miserable writers out of the mud."

After his wife's funeral, Ben asked his friends to let him be. At first they ignored his requests, stopping by his house and leaving messages on his machine, even though he had made clear, from the moment his wife had been tucked into the folds of the earth, that he had no interest in salvation. He lived reclusively, and they, in turn, stopped harassing him, convinced that he meant for his mourning to be a private affair. At their weekly get-togethers, they would bring him up and discuss his antics in the past tense of the posthumous, occasionally wondering what he was up to in the present. It took some time before they realized that they were, in a sense, simultaneously mourning both Ben and

Marian, who, in death, had stolen the refreshing animal blue of her husband's wide eyes. The day she died, his enormous pupils narrowed, his eyes dimmed, and his muscles seemed to release their hold on his frame, sinking his shoulders, curving his back, pointing his forehead downwards. His hands, limp at his sides, told a tale of detachment. Their friends tried to bring back the old Ben, the live Ben, but were forced to make do with alcohol and nostalgia, trudging down the alleys of memory and avoiding the cross streets of today, which were guarded by a mute wall, a wall of no-comment.

And then, out of the blue, the invitations arrived and put an end to their exile. A sign of life! Ben was back from the dead. They met immediately to discuss a delicate question—what to get a dead woman for her birthday? The poetic friends pushed for something Marian would've loved; the practical ones advocated for a gift for their cloistered friend. After three packs of cigarettes, twenty-six bottles of beer and fifteen variations on the word idiot, they arrived at a decision. No gift could make Ben happier than a painting by Kolanski.

Kolanski's lovely wife turned out to be the perfect hostess. She did not ask for their names or their intentions, led them to a living room lined with artwork, served fruit and soft drinks, and then excused herself to call her husband from his backyard studio. His arrival brought Ben's friends to their feet. The great Kolanski had put his work aside, crossing the room quickly in his electric wheelchair.

His black eyes filled with disgust. "Who are you and why are you eating my fruit?" he boomed.

His wife told him to settle down, but he lashed out at her. "What do you want from me? Maybe they're murderers. She opens the door for anyone. What would you do if they were terrorists?"

His wife smiled tenderly. "As you can see, my husband suffers from paranoia."

"When we're butchered, will you still call me paranoid?" he barked.

"Can't you see that these people are harmless?" She pointed to them, rolling her eyes to the ceiling.

"We are . . . ," Kobi, the self-chosen representative of Ben's friends, began, before losing his nerve at the sound of the artist's hate-doused voice.

"Art students? Art teachers? Art critics? Artists? I can't stand any of them."

Tali, Kobi's wife, cleared her throat. "Mr. Kolanski, we have nothing to do with the art world."

The artist swiveled in her direction and shouted, "What do you want?"

"Mr. Kolanski, we have a very close friend; his name is Ben. He has always admired your work, never missed an exhibition. A year and two months ago his wife Marian died. They loved like children. The kind of love you don't see every day. Ben mourned her so intensely he severed ties with the outside world. Till yesterday. Yesterday we were all invited to her birthday party. We thought about what would make the best present and came to a decision that nothing would make him happier than a portrait of him and his wife, drawn by his idol. . . . We know that . . ."

"Okay, I've heard enough," the artist said, "You want me to paint your wacko friend and his dead wife. Love conquers all and all that shit. She's dead, he's alive, and they're still in love. Kitsch. Camp. Colors. Romance. Get out of my house or I'll vomit on you."

"Rafael!" his wife called, giving his chair a kick and stiffening her lips.

"Oh, of course," he mocked, "you're probably moved by this nonsense, right? Think about it, Bessie. If I were dead, would you be happy to get a portrait of the two of us?"

She responded at once, "Absolutely."

"Absolutely," her husband mimicked, "but not for one moment do you consider what he will do with this portrait? Shove it up his ass? Stare at it all day? And since when do I paint portraits? I've never done a portrait. I don't believe in portraits. They stifle creativity. They habituate the mind to a single paralyzed expression, and over time your loony friend will look at the portrait and forget, more and more, what she really looked like. All he'll have left of her is a single, awful expression. Listen to me—don't document a thing! Not a thing! The more a person documents, the faster his memory betrays him. He knows he can rely on his wretched little photo album. You follow? You've all grown accustomed to indulgence! You can keep everything, everything, up here!"

Ben's friends huddled together, exchanging bashful glances. Tali, summoning her courage, pulled out a picture of Ben and his wife and extended it to the artist. She whispered, "Just in case you change your mind . . ."

The artist snatched the picture, glanced at it, and nodded. "Hmmm . . . your friend was a lucky man. The woman, on the other hand, must have had some trouble with her eyesight. Or maybe there's really something special. This is good, like me and Bessie—the flower fell in love with the thorn, that's the strongest love. The thorn pokes the flower and the flower drugs the thorn. Awake and asleep. Clamorous and quiet. No other love can endure. Two flowers bore each other to death, two thorns prick each other to death, and all the rest are just weeds. I'll give you some free advice. You say the thorn is celebrating the flower's birthday? If you love him, ignore him. After all, it's the woman's birthday, right? Hers! Any present for him will carry the mark of unnecessary pity, as though you know the present is for him since she's dead, and in a failed attempt to make things right you've tried to skirt the problem with a present that ties the two of them together, like the portrait. Think of the woman, eh? Get something she would like if she were alive. And try to find something she would love and he would hate. As far as he's concerned, she still exists, so if you get him a present that hints at death, he'll be offended. That's my advice. If you take it, great; if you don't, go to hell!"

As they reached the door, he charged after them. "What do you think you'll do about your friend?"

Tali smiled, "Why do you ask?"

"It's not me, it's my ego."

"We'll have to think it over."

The old man growled and slammed the door.

A month later, Kolanski's ego chalked up a victory, which its owner, having suffered a sudden stroke and slipped into a coma an hour after the guests left his house, was regrettably not aware of. Bessie, despairing, took up permanent residence at the small hospital, never once straying from her husband's side, refusing to heed doctors' advice and get on with her life, shuddering each time she heard the vile e-word spoken.

During the first nights, she curled up next to the artist and whispered in his ear the kind of syrupy sentences that, had he been alert, would have won her a sharp slap in the face. By the following week, the syrup had dried up and all that remained was a gummy abrasiveness in her throat. Tired, drained of all hope, she looked at her husband with a distant stare and prayed that she, too, would be stricken. The stroke never materialized and the kindhearted woman, in her third week of waiting, was seized by an unfamiliar rage. She began hurling insults at her husband—chastising him for all lost time, for his appalling selfishness, for his unfinished paintings, for the disappointment sprawled across the empty white plains of canvas, for his devastating laziness, his unconvincing simulacrum of a corpse—a somber flower next to a withering thorn. Certain that the change of tack would help her words pass through the hidden currents of the mechanized life-support apparatus, Bessie launched into long, fertile monologues, tyrannizing him, vowing that if he let go, she would wipe away all traces of his existence, destroy his work, and spread abhorrent lies about him. Seven days later, when she realized that her threats were not bearing fruit, she turned to her husband and said, in a conclusive tone, holding her voice flat, "Rafael, you remember the Edgar Allan Poe story about that cursed house, I can't remember its name, the one where the owner couldn't escape, until, in the end, it drove him crazy? You remember what he did? How he and his friend buried his sick sister and how, a few days later, the friend realized, to his horror, that the sister hadn't been dead and that he had helped bury her alive? I'm sure you remember the story. I say this because, as time passes, I'm beginning to feel like the crazy owner of the house. What are you asking me to do, bury you alive? Because if that's what you want, I'll see it through. But I don't want your death looming over my conscience. The doctors say you won't wake up, and I don't know, it's hard for me to believe them but I'm starting to. Oh hell, Kolanski, it's your sleep and my nightmare. What do you want? Their hints are getting thicker by the day. I keep hearing that word. Euthanasia. They say you're suffering; that with the flip of a switch I could deliver you from this torment. I can't stand the idea, but maybe they're right. . . ."

The ward's head nurse, eavesdropping at the doorway, smiled contentedly. She knew these monologues by heart, knew where they were leading. Within a week and a half at most, the woman would come to her senses and, after walking the weathered track of deliberation, would ask submissively to grant him eternal rest. If unexpected signs of optimism arose, the nurse would gently explain to her where true hope resided. She had, over the past decade, already nudged the spouses of ninety-nine men and women into proper bereavement, and it was now

Kolanski's turn. After all, ever since she first experienced the wonders of euthanasia, she had vowed that after the hundredth death she would opt for early retirement, secure in the gladdening knowledge that her calling had been answered in full. The fifty-year-old nurse saw herself as an angel of salvation, delivering the comatose from the anguish of their loved ones. The other nurses dubbed her The Angel of Death, a nickname that clashed eerily with her frail and fragile bearing.

She left the hospital early in the evening, in no rush to get home. As always, she walked the city's main streets, perfuming herself with the pulse of everyday life, drinking in the notion that all the people in the cars, stores, cafes, restaurants, movie theaters, and on sidewalks, this mass of mankind, was not, at this very moment, engaged in the act of love. She walked her usual route, pleased by the sight of mortals immersed in their affairs, urban men and women of the cloth, who, for the time being, kept their chastity belts clasped tight, as did she. Her mind, at this point, still shied away from her sanctum sanctorum. Five minutes away from her house, she crossed the street and approached the final bend in the road, where an untamable, feral pounding erupted in her chest. The rational part of her mind stabbed at her repeatedly, for her childish excitement, for the crudeness of the whole affair, for the fact that a geographic Spot could charge the dusty battery of her heart and fill it to the point where she could almost hear the growl of an awakening engine in her ears, causing her to scan the street, to ensure that no one else had heard the ghastly noise. But no one heard and no one knew.

Two years ago, the bend in the road was just another curve on the way home from work, and she had no reason to believe that a health club would be built right there, firmly and unavoidably in her way. And then it happened. Since then, had anyone noticed her, they would have had some trouble interpreting the expression draped across her face—a lethal concoction of embarrassment, paralysis, disdain, attraction, disgust, agony, excitement, jealousy, resentment, indignation, pretension, and happiness. For the past two years she had been shuffling past the club, feigning nonchalance as she glanced through the front window, behind which sweaty and sleek men and women exhibited their bodies' achievements. For two years she had been experiencing a tiny pleasurable heart attack, averting her eyes whenever they happened to meet those of any male club member. For two years she'd endured tedious, ten-hour shifts at the hospital in order to reap the reward of five blissful minutes on the walk home. If she could have it her way, she'd be way-laid for a while longer, but she feared that her sinewy heroes would spot her and creep into her forbidden thoughts. So, after five probing min-utes, she marched on. Every once in a while, with the arrival of a new member or the disappearance of a regular, a wild sheen invaded her eyes, as if her mind had, with secretarial diligence, filed away every possible twist in the usual plot. A year before, she chose her protago-nist. She had been tracking him since then, focusing on his mute attri-butes. The man frequented the gym every evening, never mingling, devoutly safeguarding his privacy. She was reminded of her first glimpse of him: tall, well-groomed, in his early forties, with brown hair cropped close to his scalp, whimsically spiked; blue, void and immobile eyes; a thick nose, thin lips, and body language that spoke of firmly harnessed sensuality. Over the course of the year, she wondered why the once-scrawny man distanced himself from the humming social scene at the health club, especially as his body revealed its clear intent to join the gym's pantheon of well-defined Herculi. To her delight, he did not turn into one of those formidable monsters that treat their bod-ies like a sacred temple. He kept his humanity, immersing himself in his demanding workout, determined to carry on with the addictive mis-sion, as though he expected some great reward at the end of the road.

Taking the bend, her eyes widened in surprise. Tonight, for the first time, he was not there, his absence creating a chasm between the perky-breasted blonde to his right and the expressionless blind man to his left.

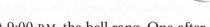

At 9:00 P.M. the bell rang. One after another, Ben's friends, heavy with longing, poured into the house that had been off limits for a year. Be-yond the dozens of balloons, wall decorations, overflowing plates of food, blaring dance music, and the enormous sign for Marian, the guests had no trouble recognizing the familiar guest room and were delighted to see that the owner had made no changes—the overloaded shelves still groaned under the weight of books, CDs, LPs, and videos, and the works of art, so loved by the woman of the hour, were still immaculately strewn all over the house.

Still, his friends struggled to make sense of their old friend's new appearance, wondering what stood behind the dramatic shift and whether it conveyed a specific intent. The masculinity gushing out of every pore of his hardened body did not suit Ben, and not for aesthetic reasons. They circled around him relentlessly, hugging him, treading carefully around the thin ice of Marian's name. Yet Ben, the life of the party, threw his head back and laughed, open-mouthed, constantly bringing Marian up, signaling that he was aware of the delicate situation and eager to put everyone at ease. With each passing moment it became clear that Ben refused to accept even the slightest gesture of pity. The blood that drained from his friends' faces—when he joked that Marian had perfect timing, leaving when she did in order to avoid having to deal with a midlife crisis—slowly resumed its normal course as they began to realize that Ben could only relate to the crushing loss with humor, and so they played along, chuckling on cue when he announced that his wife had found the most original manner in the world to leave a man without hurting his feelings. After an hour of verbal ballet, Ben suggested opening the presents. He failed to conceal the moistness in his eyes when he ripped open the wrapping paper, revealing the newest works from his wife's favorite writers, musicians, and fashion designers. But before the evening was stained with melancholy, he brought his palms together, rubbed vigorously, and said it was about time he revealed his second present for his dear wife. When one of them asked what the first present was, he posed for her, struck a male-model pout, and pirouetted three times, arms extended, enchanted by his own inane performance. "This body—Marian always wanted me to put some work into it."

His friends, rejoicing at the simple explanation, rose out of their chairs and clapped him on the back, some of them wiping away tears.

Ben waited for them to settle down and then repeated his earlier statement. He walked over to the window, pulled the curtain aside, and nodded. Before his friends had the chance to fully interpret his actions, their ears picked up the crack of gunpowder from outside and, at the sight of Ben, smiling, nodding his head toward the door, they rushed out and stood dumbfounded in the front yard, their eyes tracing the arc of the fireworks in the sky, the wealth of stunning colors crowning the night with festive circles of light. The eye-and-soul pleasing shades flared across the night sky, drawing hearts and roses, baby blue fountains and emerald gardens, orange suns and regal purple stars. As Ben's friends oohed and ahhed, the neighbors came out of their houses and joined them, enjoying the breathtaking pyrotechnic display on the eve of an ordinary day.

But it was not, the friends learned, a regular evening, nor was it an ordinary day. Twenty exhilarating minutes later, they filed back into the house to thank Ben for the generous display but were rudely denied the chance. Ben lay in a puddle of blood, seeded with parts of his brain. In his right hand he held a warm gun, and in his left a note asking them to open the fridge and take out the towering birthday cake with the maple syrup script that read "And They Died Happily Ever After . . ."

2

Other World Orders

Welcome to the Other World. First, we would like to extend our deepest condolences to those you have left behind. We sincerely hope they realize that no harm will be done to you here. If they think otherwise, they will simply have to wait their turn and see the error of their ways. Surely, you will be pleased to note that, as opposed to the previous world, which you entered without any instruction or orientation, we offer several prefatory comments as you stand here at the gates of your renewed existence. We promise not to carry on at great length, offering merely that which is essential for you to get the most out of this world, to suck the marrow out of death.

Two brief clarifications before we commence: For those of you worried about scars, souvenirs, or remnants from the events that brought you to this world, allow me to ease your minds. When the light goes on and you look at your body, you will, I assure you, be pleased with its fine state. All praise to our reconstructive surgeons and various somatic artisans. Each and every one of you has come through the Other World's O.R. on your way here. You've all been outfitted with a brand new immune system and undergone a full-body tune-up, including repair work on defects and disabilities. Unfortunately, we are not able to fully repair birth defects; those suffering from congenital deformities, however, will be happy to hear that we have installed microscopic tactical devices that will allow you to dispense with your disabilities for the duration of a year. At the end of the prescribed term, we ask of, say, the blind, to report to the See No Evil clinic in their city, where their artificial eyes will be replaced with a new pair. The deaf will report to the Hear No Evil clinic, the dumb to the Speak No Evil clinic, the anosmic and the tasteless will report to the Different Strokes clinic, the mentally challenged and disabled will report to the Artificial Intelligence lab, and those suffering from physical disabilities will report to the Spare Parts lab. As for all of the others, shed your worries. Any disease you suffered from in your life, congenital or acquired, has been excised from your system with death. In our world, disease is nonexistent, and health is no cause for concern.

Our apologies to doctors, nurses, researchers, and others in the field of medicine, but if you wish to continue practicing in your respective fields, you'll have to take a series of exams, after which, if you pass, you will be posted at one of the six aforementioned clinics, or at one of the many thousand reconstruction labs described earlier.

The second clarification pertains to language. Since you speak so many different tongues, we have installed a microchip in your brains—Babel—which contains more than one hundred languages and a thousand dialects. Whenever you feel like speaking with someone in a once-foreign language, you will find that you are fluent, even eloquent. Owing to our belief in candor and honesty, we've not forsaken the crasser trends of the tongue, offering a series of twenty curse words which will be at your disposal during rare moments of rage. Do not deduce from this that we support verbal violence. We simply prefer you swear rather than strike. It's your responsibility to visit the multilingual labs once a year to update your chip, lest your vocabulary in the unpracticed tongues dwindle and your circuits start to short out your conversations.

Apologies to the translators, transliterators, language teachers, and others in the field, but if you wish to continue practicing in your area of expertise, you will have to take a series of tests, which, if you pass, will enable you to work in the multilingual labs, making the necessary updates in language, particularly in the realm of slang, and keeping abreast of the changes instituted by the academies of language.

And now several facts pertaining to our world:

1)   In light of the devastating results of the financial system in your previous world, it has been decided that here, in this world, currency, in all its forms, be abolished. We urge you not to seek it out. It simply does not exist. If you are interested in acquiring a certain item, go to the nearest store and ask the "salespeople" for assistance. They will provide whatever it is you seek, for free. Fear not, there is enough to go around. If it is hard for you to accept the system in our world, we shall clarify and elucidate: Those of you who choose to work in your fields, or to undergo a career change, will not be receiving monetary compensation

for work performed. This ensures that your occupation will be a labor of love. Soon enough, you will realize that the rewards in our world are great. The nonmonetary system spawns creativity and, since you have all the time in this world at your disposal, there is no choice but to engage in activities that compensate you with, well, love.

To the merchants, bankers, entrepreneurs, economists, brokers, mint workers, banknote printers, counterfeiters, misers, rainy-day savers, big spenders, materialists, and others in the field—our apologies.

2) In accordance with our devotion to candor, purity, and maximum freedom, all residents of this world are naked. When the exposed outweighs the concealed, people are infinitely more trusting, developing a reputable, honest society where costumes, masks, and other props are unnecessary. Moreover, studies have proven that nudity markedly reduces the rate of violence. Before moving on to the next matter at hand, we have a simple request, which will not be elaborated upon due to security concerns: Now and again you will bump into people who are clothed; please do not mingle with them or disturb them. To the fashion designers, models, tailors, cobblers, seamstresses, kings and queens of haute couture, and all other members of the garment and shoewear trade—our apologies.

3) Good news for the vegetarians among you: Since in our world everyone has successfully undergone the death stage, there are no bodies, no carrion, no roadkill. From this you can safely surmise that the only type of food you will not be eating here is flesh. Hunting is absolutely prohibited. Bon appétit.

4) Housing. As you will soon see, the contours of this world are not easily grasped. In order to avoid a population explosion caused by a dizzyingly large aggregation of the dead, the Other World has been built in four dimensions. You are familiar with geographic parameters that measure length and width. This world is characterized by retroactive time dimensions, enabling it to house all of the world's dead since the dawn of humanity. Place is time, confusing as that may sound. Simplifying matters, all of the dead people in this room, 9,568 in number, passed away on June 21, 2001 and therefore live on Circle 21, in the city of June 2001. Each and every one of you has been provided with living

quarters in the skyscrapers on June 21 Circle, which serves as a type of neighborhood. Each skyscraper has 1,000 housing units, divided into twenty-four floors. Each door bears your initials. The hour of your death determines your floor. For instance, someone who died between one and two in the morning will live on the first floor, someone who died between two and three will live on the second floor, and so on. You are not obligated to live in your specified quarters, but if you do, order will prevail. In general, even if you do decide to change your place of residence, your address will be yours forever. At the close of the lecture, as you leave the room, a guide of ours will escort you to the circle and assist the bewildered in finding their new quarters.

5) Transportation. In our world there is but one kind of mechanized vehicle: the multi-wheel—a five-hundred seat bus that will take you from the central station in your city to the destination of your choice. In order for our paved roads not to be overburdened, all other vehicles have been banned. To the drivers, chauffeurs, mechanics, grease monkeys, off-road enthusiasts, and Formula One fanatics—our apologies.

6) Entertainment and Recreation. At your disposal is an awesome array of entertainment options, including plays, movies, concerts, operas, galleries, libraries, indoor courts, outdoor courts, grassy fields, playgrounds, restaurants, cafés, pubs, and nature reserves. We direct your attention to the video rental shops across town, where you can find, along with the usual selection of movies and TV shows, a series of special tapes chronicling your former life. If you want to watch them, you must use your personal identification code—in other words, your thumbprint. Upon arrival at the window of the Vie-deo, you'll be asked to push the request button. Present your thumb. Within ten seconds you'll receive your selected video. Each year of your life is documented on a different tape. If, for instance, you'd like to watch your twentieth year, then push the button marked twenty on the console's calendar. There's no need to return the tape of life to the shop. Since we support each person's right to privacy, the Vie-deo will bar all attempts at identity theft. Our apologies to the peeping toms and those who lived dull lives. Moreover—and this next comment is directed at the fingerless or the thumb-less—your artificial thumb is equipped with a unique print that will be considered your identification print, and yours alone.

7)   The godget. You wear the godget around your neck. It is the size of a calculator and it resembles a remote control. The godget has six buttons for your convenience. Each button has a function that allows you to determine the conditions of your renewed existence:

BUTTON 1–Day and Night, determines your favorite part of the day. One click–dawn. Two clicks–morning. Three clicks–afternoon. Four clicks–dusk. Five clicks–evening. Six clicks–night.

BUTTON 2–Weather, setting your preferred climate. One click–zero degrees Celsius, snowy. Two–ten degrees, cold but not rainy. Three–ten degrees, cold and rainy. Four–fifteen degrees, chilly with a stiff wind. Five–fifteen degrees, chilly, no wind. Six–fifteen degrees, drizzling. Seven–twenty degrees, warm with a gentle easterly. Eight–twenty-five degrees, warm and dry. Nine–twenty-five degrees, warm and humid. Ten–thirty degrees, desert-dry. Eleven–thirty degrees, a wet sauna. Twelve–other.

BUTTON 3–Sleep, determines your preferred mode of sleep. One click–eight hours of dream-free sleep. Two clicks–eight hours of sleep plus dreams. Three–catnap. Four–two hours of light sleep. Five–twelve hours of stone-cold dream-free sleep. Six–twelve hours of sleep with dreams. Seven–eternal sleep.

BUTTON 4–Daily updates from the previous world on matters of: One click–news. Two clicks–art. Three–sports. Four–science. Five–other.

BUTTON 5–Daily updates from the current world on matters of: One click–news. Two clicks–art. Three–sports. Four–science. Five–other.

BUTTON 6–The telefinger, similar to the telephone you all know, is operated by fingerprint. It is endowed with an enormous amount of memory and can collect up to one hundred thousand potential fingerprints. If you'd like to call a certain individual, all you need is for that person to leave his or her fingerprint in your device and it will remain in your contacts page forever.

It's important to recall that each godget responds only to its owner.

8)   Last comment. In two minutes you will hear the public address system. Its job is to inform the citizens of this world that new citizens of

the old world have arrived. The Announcer calls the names of the newly arrived so that veterans of this world can meet their loved ones, if any such exist. We request that you stay in the room for two additional hours in order to allow the old timers ample opportunity to make it here and welcome you. We truly hope that our comments have been helpful and illuminating. We wish you a happy and satisfying death. Welcome to the Other World.

When the screen darkened and the naked girl faded from view, the room filled with light, forcing all present to rub their eyes and blink repeatedly. 9,568 naked people lay on the floor, stunned into deathly silence. Ben was the first to come to his senses. Like everyone else, he was surprised, electric with anticipation, but unlike the other 9,567 freshly dead, he was not in shock. He smiled, content. He knew it. Well, part of it. Even in his wildest dreams he hadn't imagined any of the shades of details that had been laid out by the gorgeous woman in the introductory talk, but what he had known—that death was not the end—sufficed. Pulling the trigger was like an express ticket to the other side of life. To Marian. All he had to do now was wait for the doors to open.

A metallic voice came over the loudspeaker and began intoning the names of those present in alphabetical order, its diction sharp and precise. It was funny, Ben thought, to look at the thousands of naked bodies, speechless amazement stamped on their faces. Funnier still were their bewildered awakenings and the way the PA system triggered a laughable herd mentality. As their names came over the loudspeaker each person in turn nodded and said "yes" in an array of languages, as though the Announcer had come to take attendance in school, summer camp, or a military barracks. Shock was still apparent. As far back as any of them could remember, they had been taught to expect to reach one of two places or none at all. Anything but this strange place. The more Ben tried to bottle it up, the more the laughter tickled his insides and climbed toward his vibrating Adam's apple, until, at last, their goggle-eyed expressions made it spring forth. Ben rolled on the floor, reveling in the disappointment of the heathens and the greater astonishment of their sworn foes, and, had a fifty-year-old woman not shattered the silence, shrieking that, "you can see my everything," he would have continued laughing for a while. Luckily for her, her best friend was partner to their final journey. She soothed her, hugged her close, and pointed all around, intoning, in extreme momminess, "It's okay, everyone can see everyone else's everything. . . ."

Ben examined his body. A warm wave washed over him as he considered the thought that in less than an hour he would see Marian, and probably the rest of his family. When he heard the Announcer call his name, his heart shifted gears, keenly aware that she waited on the other side of the doors.

As the last of the names was called, Ben was first to his feet, his eyes boring into the white double doors as if the intensity of his stare alone could pry them open, his hands rubbing one another in mounting joy, his body alive with surging enthusiasm. Another minute passed before everyone realized the magnitude of the moment, calling at the doors excitedly, huddling and pushing as though only some of them would be allowed to leave. Ben turned his head and was about to hammer the guy next to him, who was relentlessly jostling for position, when the doors opened with a soft wheeze. Turning back around, his eyes widened, his smile shriveled, and the tremor that had been coursing through his body went limp.

3

A Spot of Bother

Ann hated the world. Not with a burning jealousy, not with raging passion, and certainly not with much interest. No, her hatred was moderate, calm, and accepting. From a young age, she had understood that she could see people but they did not see her. The world blatantly ignored her. Waitresses forgot to wait on her in restaurants, receptionists continued to talk on the phone in her presence, and everyone cut her in line at the movies, post office, and supermarket. At ten, she came to terms with society's attitude toward her presence, accepting her inferiority as a congenital aspect of her personality. The understanding that her most striking characteristic had developed in her mother's womb helped explain the relief that coursed through her as she examined her dwarfish reflection in the bathroom mirror and whispered, with equanimity, "inferior."

The diminutive, mouse-faced woman blamed no one for her condition. She had always believed that she was unnecessary to the world, conducting a clandestine affair of what she believed to be mutual animosity. "Why argue with the truth?" she thought, remembering the dark days of her youth in a rundown orphanage. At eight, the kindhearted orphanage director turned to her with a yellowing picture of a couple on their wedding night and asked if she recognized the young bride and groom.

"The two ugliest people in the world," the girl scowled and spat. The director, appalled, informed her that those were her parents and that they had been killed in a car accident a year after she was born, not long after they moved from England to Israel, but Ann, smiling, said it was too bad they weren't killed much earlier, and then she ripped the picture to shreds.

The director took the melancholy child under her wing, privately meeting with her in her office every day for three months, befriending her and soothing the embittered girl's self-hatred with positive reinforcement. Yet just when it seemed that the child had finally begun to like herself, the director made an awful mistake. She left her office door open while speaking to a close friend on the phone. "I have no idea why she bothers to go on living," Ann overheard her say, "her existence is flat-out pointless." The troubled girl had no way of knowing that the director was referring to Anita, a battered woman who had, for the twentieth time, returned to the now-loving arms of her husband. Certain she had been referring to her, Ann avoided the soul-lighting smiles of the director and other staff members, convinced that her parents had taken their own lives because they were unable to stomach their revolting daughter. The accident story, she was sure, had been concocted by the pitying hypocrite who spared her feelings and insisted on protecting her from the cruel truth.

Ann excelled in school, she reckoned, because life had taken no interest in her, and while her classmates dedicated their lives to wooing the boy with all the right bulges, she sat on her bed, shut her eyes, and tried to disappear. She never took this tactic to its extreme end, fearing that her body would go undiscovered and be left to rot in the fields where the scavenging birds would find her, pick out her eyes, and feast on her innards.

Ann was certain she belonged to a rare strain of human, the kind that was supposed to be born invisible but, due to a biological fluke, had emerged barely noticeable, stuck between two phases of existence, making their lives far more complicated than that of their peers. It goes without saying that she was the last girl in her class to require a tampon, further proof that nature, in its own way, ignored her. When at fifteen she felt the first drops of blood trickle between her legs, she looked down, then up, stuck her tongue out, and groaned, "I don't need any favors from you."

Late puberty did not rattle her apathy toward boys. In her mind, the opposite sex was childish, brute, swaggering, competitive, garish, selfish, stupid, hairy, and repugnant. In the same vein, she saw her own gender as talkative, annoying, gossipy, compulsive, self-absorbed, and shallow.

The college scholarships, which came in droves, only served as kindling for her raging self-hatred. She reasoned that they were part of the education system's overarching conspiracy to convince her that she was not worthless. Her loathing for the world played a crucial role in her choice of career. On the threshold of adulthood, she vowed to spend her life avenging the glaring injustices done to her: She would dedicate herself to healing the sick, forcing them to continue to suffer the bland burden of existence. Hating people, she sought with all her might to prolong their lives. All those who, in their blindness, stamped her inferiority with their approval could live forever as far as she was concerned. She privately congratulated herself on devising such an insidious scheme, which no one in the world could recognize.

Upon completion of her studies, summa cum laude, she joined the nursing staff of a private hospital in Tel Aviv and, within a month's time, even got used to the nickname her jealous coworkers gave her. "Anntipathy" felt great elation when the nurses watched in awe as she, a glum loner, cared lovingly for her patients. They failed to piece together the two jagged edges of her personality. The more she exhibited her intolerance for her coworkers, the more her shining attentiveness to her patients' needs skyrocketed. Although she never exchanged so much as a "good morning" with her colleagues, she chatted incessantly with her patients, smiling and doting on them. The staff, failing to break through her chilly wall of estrangement, decided that her unblemished professionalism was yet further proof that she lacked any type of life beyond the hospital walls. Still, they struggled to make sense of this strange woman in their midst. She was the first to volunteer to cover for a coworker and, over eight long years, she had never once taken a day off. She had been sick on eight different occasions, but she had still come in, scooting between the beds as her body burned with fever.

Ann was desperately invested in her patients' rehabilitation, sending them back to their lives with a sly smile. Deep down, she knew that their praise, which bordered on adulation, was nothing more than the natural and temporary condition of a dependent person. Every time one of her patients checked out of the ward, she felt like an inconsequential servant. So long as they were in good health, they were the same people who cut her in line, walked all over her, ignored her.

For her existence to be palpable, theirs had to be in jeopardy. In her eyes, that was the root of inferiority—to be seen, not as a human being but as a service provider. A hefty middle-aged patient dealt her the worst blow when, after two months of constant care, he passed her on the street without so much as a nod. She laughed at the sound of hundreds of patients' voices reverberating in her ears, pledging to stay in touch, to come by and visit from time to time. Not one had kept their word. They had all managed to forget. She no longer held a grudge.

She just learned to ignore them to nearly the same extent that they ignored her, pretending to be human.

She wakes at five, showers, has coffee, leaves the house at five forty-five, gets on the bus at five fifty, arrives at the hospital at six twenty, puts on her white uniform, reads the night's charts till seven, then attends to her patients till one, at which point she has lunch—the same two triangles of egg-and-potato salad sandwich with a glass of mineral water—and at one thirty, returns to the ward till six, tending to her patients, new and old, galloping like a possessed woman from room to room, solving all problems, calling the right doctor when necessary, and filling out the daily chart ten minutes before leaving the hospital. At six twenty in the evening she boards the bus. At six fifty she gets off, basking in the time she allows herself to roam the streets. At eight, she returns home, eats dinner, showers, watches TV, and crawls into bed. At eleven she shuts off the light and falls asleep in three minutes flat.

Ann's robotic life afforded her no pleasure, stimulation, or satisfaction, but she refused to allow the dreariness to deflate her. Lacking an alternative, she simply continued living. It was so decreed, and she complied with dull obedience. The same dull obedience she showed when told by the director of the hospital that she had been promoted to head nurse. She didn't bat an eyelash at the news of her promotion or the small pay raise. A simple calculation revealed that she would, barring a miracle, pay off the monstrous mortgage on her small house by the age of sixty.

When Ann turned forty, the miracle arrived. A complication during surgery left an elderly woman, who had been in her care for six months, in a vegetative state. The woman, Hanna, had taken the possibility of complications into account, and had told Ann that if she were to emerge from the surgery, held in this world by the thread of life support, she should wait no more than a month. If, after that, she saw no changes, she should disconnect her from the tubes and turn off the machines. A moment before entering the Operating Room, she smiled and patted Ann's hand as though she knew that her life would end with the touch of the scalpel as it carved the tumor from her brain. Ann spent every spare minute of the next thirty days by her side, coaxing her back to life. On the thirty-first day, she gathered herself and went to see the hospital director, laying out the story of the old woman who had no next of kin. The director weighed the matter and said he trusted her instincts. At 12:45 that afternoon, Ann, in the presence of two doctors and three nurses, disconnected her from life support, kissed her on the forehead, and left to go eat her egg-and-potato salad sandwich. Two days later, for the first time, she attended a patient's funeral, alongside a rabbi, and a lawyer who came over to her afterwards and informed her that the deceased had left her a palatial house in Kfar Shmaryahu. Ann stared at the lawyer till he smiled and said that Hanna had lost her family in the Holocaust and had not borne children. Ann knew the details. Hanna had told her everything, aside from the will and the fortune.

After checking her options, Ann sold Hanna's house and covered her own mortgage, surprised to see that there was a hefty sum still left over in the account. Then she started to save. Each month she deposited the excess from her salary in a savings account along with the inheritance money. Her future plans did not involve traveling around the world or laying the foundations of her dream house; her sole desire was to ensure financial independence through the prairies of old age. Dependence disgusted her. (Over the years she also cultivated a cautious distaste for love and its legions, convinced that the matter was nothing more than an ensnarement meant to deny people their independence.) To her dismay, she learned with time that her new job responsibilities called for counseling and other skills she had never considered acquiring. She read several books about bereavement, fished out a few hollow clichés, and kneaded them into a single truth. Over time, she learned to polish her words, lending them a professional gleam. Listening to her, the widowers-to-be were under the impression they were being counseled by a woman deeply familiar with the workings of the unconscious mind. They were unaware that her arguments had been drafted in the distant realms of her imagination, and that, more importantly, she had been profoundly changed.

Hanna's death heralded the start of a new chapter in Ann's life. She embraced the burden of disconnecting people from life support and, along with that, slowly relinquished her grip on revenge—she had nursed enough of the infirm back to life; now was the time to send her patients to the kingdom of eternal rest. Hanna taught her something about human kindness and, had she stayed alive, she would surely have said "hi" as she passed her on the street. Ann felt she owed her a favor in return, and asked the hospital director to be charged with caring for the patients on life support.

Ten years passed as Ann eased the comatose into even deeper sleep. During that time, her reputation grew until, at age forty-six, after her forty-ninth departed patient, she decided that she would retire after one hundred. The director of the hospital, perhaps assuming that round numbers hint at rationality, agreed to her terms: the hundredth deceased patient would ring the freedom bells for the "Angel of Death." He even promised her an enhanced pension package and took an interest in her post-career plans.

She shrugged and said, "All my life I've cared for others; when I retire I'll care for myself." Beyond a vague feeling in her gut, she had no idea what that meant. But then, two years later, she came across the health club and felt her stomach twist into knots. The Spot. During that year, Ann feverishly surveyed several candidates. Each lingering glance she allowed herself made the rest of her walk home an uncomfortably wet affair. The following year, she chose her Romeo, the man whose name she didn't know, who wreaked havoc inside her. The harder she tried to banish him from her mind, the more entrenched he became. Those five intoxicating minutes in front of the health club window so dominated her mind that only as she stared at the wall at night, a moment before disconnecting herself from the animated world, was she able to recognize her menacing addiction.

With each new morning came fresh denial. She sailed past the window without so much as a glance in the direction of the orphaned machines, emerging empowered and inoculated against the club's clawing gravity. But one December day, when her guard was down, just as she was contemplating how to convince the relatives of a comatose patient to authorize his inevitable transformation, the Spot emerged in her mind, sprouting into reality, spreading the dark gravitational force of physical attraction, a corrupting power that yearned to drag her headlong into the thick of a wild frenzy, pulling her face-to-face with a beautiful, sculpted body, which scrubbed her senses clean of all thoughts beyond the small drops of sweat that slid down an athletic chest, over the hard boxes of his stomach, pausing for an interlude at his belly button and thieving their way directly down the wet slopes of her desire, slipping under the elastic band of her panties, making it difficult to walk. He turned around, steel and flesh melding as his bottom rhythmically rose and fell, and Ann's pupils were riveted to the image, refusing to believe that winter could bring such throbbing heat, as she hid under an increasingly concave umbrella, letting, at last, the cascading water wash the scum from her feverish mind. Ann ran for her life. The umbrella flew out of her slippery hand and bounded gracefully over a stretch of film-coated puddles. When the nurse's feet came to a stop in front of her door, she knew she was sick. Out of work for four days on account of the flu, a collaboration of the pouring rain and the Spot, she vowed, on the fifth day, to shake the addiction.

For a full grueling week, she came home from the hospital and didn't dare raise her eyes as she passed the health club, pushing her feet past the Spot, repressing the familiar sensations of pleasure. On the eighth day, she allowed herself a glance. Once again, six months passed during which Ann succumbed to the Spot and returned to her sordid ways. Luckily, her frozen features masked her private turmoil. One time, in the eye of a sexual storm, she met a colleague from the oncology ward and was able to hold an agreeable conversation, as though her athlete's tongue wasn't lapping at her insides, shocking her to the core. Although Ann enjoyed every moment, she never grew accustomed to the notion of the stranger inside of her, and deduced that her sudden licentiousness was a result of the deep change within her—from an inferior, invisible woman to a woman who controlled the fate of others, a woman treated with reverence by those around her, a woman who, despite her continued adherence to her most exceptional characteristic, spread fear among the young nurses that joined the staff. These days they looked at her admiringly, most assuredly noticing her existence. Now that her humanity had been confirmed, her body started to seek out her femininity and found it in the world of make-believe—Ann's favorite fantasy entailed a slightly different take on *Sleeping Beauty:* The handsome man from the health club, who has fallen into a vegetative state after an accident, is cared for by the devoted nurse. She tries to bring him back to life in every way, but when there is no other choice, she puts her hands on the plug and brings her lips to his in farewell. The patient opens his blue eyes, draws her close, and thanks her in the most appropriate manner. Ann fed off the fantasy for months, enriching it with speculation regarding her dreamy partner's life. One time, he's an accomplished scientist conducting complex experiments in his lab; another time he's an impulsive artist overflowing with fresh ideas; but at all times, he's a shy lover who has eyes for her and her alone. The first time she saw him from the Spot, she swore her allegiance. A year later, her mate was still the one. Soon she would unplug her hundredth patient and get a life, which would, one way or another, involve her athlete. Maybe she'd even summon the courage to walk straight through the door of the terrifying place and ask to sign up for a membership. She laughed and dismissed her frivolity as nothing more than a ridiculous fantasy. Ann loved no one, certainly not a nameless sweaty someone. And the Spot? The Spot sat on the rift between true and false. When she was overexcited she told herself that her athlete played but a minor role in the creation of her fantasy, and that if he didn't exist, she'd find a substitute.

Yet for all her self-assurances, she was proven wrong on the third evening since his disappearance. Ann looked up, discovered his absence once again and didn't know whether to be happy or sad: the Spot had lost its power. She felt nothing, her body sent no objectionable signals; the engine was dead. The debate had been resolved; the man, in his absence, had stolen the pleasure that had been reserved solely for him. Ann was finally willing to admit that his sudden disappearance saddened her. There was a bland taste in her mouth. She bought her favorite chocolate bar, and the bland taste remained. A soft sorrow rose within her. Shoot, she thought and bought another candy, he's turned invisible. Just like me. She tried to relax, to explain his absence as a vacation or a work-related trip, encouraging herself that he would be back. Then she dismissed the thought. Deep within, beneath the calming voices, she heard a voice say, "He won't be back. He's gone. Left you for good." She moaned, looked at her reflection in the display window, and hissed "inferior."

She didn't sleep all night, bemoaning the bitter end of her fabricated love story. Throughout the next day's bus commute, she strained to find a plausible excuse for her tardiness. She couldn't say that she was three hours late because she spent the first five hours of the night crying and only went to sleep at four in the morning. She decided to say that the bus was in an accident. She arrived at the hospital, her story tightly stitched and perfectly packaged. The director swerved past her in the hall and the nurses were dashing about, attending to their chores like industrious ants. Ann bowed her head and smiled sadly. She had no need for an excuse. No one noticed she was late.

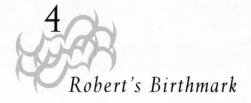

4
Robert's Birthmark

The immaculate lawn stretching from the white room to the station was all but empty. A lone figure sat in a wheelchair at the edge of the grass, hidden behind an enormous sign adorned with the words CATHERINE DUMAS. At first, the newly dead thought the man was aflame, but as they drew close they saw that the acrid smoke swirling out from behind the sign emanated from the stout cigar jammed between his lips.

Before the 9,568 inductees had the chance to voice their disappointment at the well-manicured lawn, which, despite the assurances offered at the orientation, was barren—no friends, no relatives, no acquaintances, no lovers—they heard a deep male voice call to them from the far end of the path. "Welcome to one and all. We'd appreciate it if you could board the multi-wheels so that we can take you to your new homes on Circle 21 in the city of June 2001. The multi-wheels will depart in ten minutes. We request that you not push; twenty multi-wheels await you. As your guide, I'd like to wish you a bon voyage and a pleasant death." A second or two later, a stampede began, the herd of people charging toward the blue vehicles at the far end of the lawn. The guide, standing in front of the vehicles, brought the megaphone to his lips and announced through a spreading smile that there was "No need to run. And, please don't step on any bodies."

Only Ben stayed put. Rather than ignore the cigar-smoking cripple like everyone else, he looked him over carefully until, feeling the warmth of Ben's curious stare, he called out in a thick French accent, "You are going to miss the bus." Ben smiled apologetically, sorry that he had not listened to Marian and found the time to learn the language of lovers. But then, his eyebrows perking up at the sound of his own voice, his lips opened, and he said, in perfect French, *"C'est d'accord."*

A moment after the newly dead stormed the twenty-wheeled multies, they set out, leaving a wave of roiled air behind them. Ben took an admiring look at the tracks—the multi-wheels were a strange crossbreed of bus and train, with special rails and smooth humps that mysteriously rose each time the multi-wheels approached, pushing the surging vehicles forward at the speed of dueling race cars. A moment later they were part of the horizon and Ben was alone with the cripple, who shifted in his wheelchair, pulled a gold box out from under him, opened it, and offered it to Ben.

Ben nodded his gratitude, but said, "I don't smoke, and anyway it's your last cigar."

The smoker curled his upper lip and returned the box to its place. "You're right," he mumbled in a charred voice, "and congratulations on your reasoning."

"Excuse me?"

"You didn't take the cigar because it was the last one. If there's one thing I hate, it's people who refuse for the wrong reason."

"What reason is that?" Ben said, eyes fixed on the strange birthmark on the smoker's left nipple.

"Cancer . . . ," the cripple said, wheezing out a laugh. He spread his arms out to either side of his chair and said, "You only live once. . . ."

Ben joined the burst of laughter.

The smoker shook his hand, "Robert."

"Ben. Can I ask you something?"

"You want to ask why no one came to greet you and the others?"

"How did you know?"

"It's simple, *mon ami*. I've been coming here every day for ten years. Ten years of shock, day-in, day-out, on the newly dead's faces. The speaker promises, but doesn't deliver. You have no idea how big this place is. Who's going to make it to the lawn within two hours? Don't forget, people are busy and they usually don't hear or pay any attention to the PA system. In ten years, I've seen maybe six emotional reunions. Six, friend, that's it. And between us, all six were relatives of terminally ill patients, if you get my drift. . . ."

"You said you've been coming here every day? For the last ten years?"

"Yeah," Robert sighed, tapping the sign, "ten years I been waiting for her. I won't take the chance of missing her when she arrives, so I show up at opening time every day. I never stray too far from the area."

"I take it she's not terminally ill."

"Like an ox," Robert said, shaking his head. "She's sixty, and you know what that means? That I might waste the next twenty years, easy. But I haven't given up. We'll meet yet."

"Hats off to your determination," Ben said, trying to raise the man's spirits.

"I hope she feels the same way," he mumbled, bringing his cigar back to life.

"I think every woman would feel that way if she knew her man waited for her for ten years."

"And what if she doesn't know that you're her man?" Robert's voice rose from behind a wall of smoke.

Ben caught his breath, just barely keeping his peace with the stench of the cigar. "She doesn't know?"

Robert closed his eyes, sucked long and hard on the cigar, and growled, "She knows nothing, that foolish woman. Nothing." After an uncomfortable silence, he added, "So long as she doesn't fall in love with another woman. That, I could not handle."

Already feeling the pull of the hopeless romantic's tale, Ben urged him on. "Why would she fall in love with a woman?"

Robert flicked the cigar a good distance away and let out an anguished moan. "Because that's what always happens to them in prison. Five hundred women in one jail. How could they not fall in love with one another? All that beauty in one place . . . you could lose your mind. And imagine if a diamond like my Catherine arrives. They probably started circling as soon as the guard shut the gate."

"I don't understand. She's in jail? She's a prisoner?" Ben asked petulantly, sitting down on the grass.

Robert pointed at the birthmark—a brown star crowning his left nipple—and then whacked it hatefully. "It's all this thing's fault. This fucking mark ruined my life."

"I've never seen such a unique birthmark. Usually they're like stains—plain, boring, and shapeless. But that star . . . it's art."

"Eh, what have I not heard about this fucking star? A perfect five-point? A fantastic pentagram? In school, I told the kids I was from another planet and the pentagram was the proof. From the first moment I saw it, I felt that fate had marked me, planned great things for me in the future. That, plus the fact that I dreamed of being an actor . . . when you're young you let mysterious signs lead you down the most optimistic paths. And you know why you find all of these idiotic signs? Because you're looking for them. It's simple. And I, I was a magnificent imbecile, drawing a connection between this shit on my chest and my future.

This mark sure hasn't made me special. It makes me, if anything, miserable. Fucking miserable."

Ben didn't take his eyes off the birthmark. "Why is she in jail?"

Robert pointed to the white doors. "How do you think I got here?"

Ben looked at the doors, and turned his head back toward Robert, surprised. "She killed you?"

"I'd prefer if you chose your words with greater care." Robert smiled. "She murdered me. In cold blood. Emptied an entire magazine on me. Pumped me full of lead. I'm sure the good doctors in the reconstruction rooms were shocked when I arrived. Robert, the human cheese grater."

"But why?"

"Some would say hate. I assert that the true motive was a rigid unwillingness to acknowledge love. A denial of emotions. From the very beginning she played hard to get. I had no problem with this. Everyone has their fun with foreplay. Between us, who wants a girl that gives it up on the first date? They have to make us crawl so we can feel what it's like to fly. But what would you do? You're a twenty-year-old who, if you'll pardon my French, makes Alain Delon look like Louis De Funès. Sexual innuendo surrounds you. Women throw themselves at you, but you're crazy in love with your woman. You live under the same roof, know you were meant to be together, but there's one small problem—she isn't willing to give of herself, if you know what I mean."

"How long were you together?"

"One year," Robert said, dragging the two syllables out of his mouth, as though they could connote the true duration of the term. "One year I lived with the most beautiful woman the human race has ever known. The woman who makes all others pale in comparison. The woman who, with one look, makes you think all her peers are a genetic scam. That she and she alone was what God had in mind when he used the rib. Ah, *mon dieu*, but this is the catastrophe. Every day I sang her songs of praise, saluted her beauty. Even when I knew I'd gone too far, I couldn't stop. She laughed at me, said Paris is full of beautiful women, and retreated to her room."

"Hold up, what do you mean to her room? You lived under the same roof, you were in love, and you're telling me you had separate rooms?"

Robert smiled bitterly. "We were platonic lovers. We never touched. She said she was saving herself for someone else."

"Someone else?"

Robert raised his finger to the heavens, waiting for the nickel to drop. Ben held his belly and laughed. "God? Catherine was in love with God?"

Robert tried to stifle his own laugh, which was a hoarse echo of Ben's. "What did you expect? A whole year I told her that God had created her in his image, I called her divine, begged for a piece of paradise, and she . . . what is she up to? Locking herself up in her room all night with her dildo, moaning with the wild passion of a Georgian monk in the throes of religious ecstasy. I'm talking about the pinnacle of spiritual life—in the morning a theology student, in the afternoon caring for a sick priest, and at night Mary Magdalene."

"God," Ben said.

"Don't mention him. You tell me, how can I, flesh and blood, compete with Him? Just try to imagine the torment: Day after day I gaze into that stunning face. A year slips by and I can't be sure if she's real, if she was born this way, or if she is just an evil plan hatched by her true love who created her just for Himself."

Ben smiled. "And what about other women? I'm sure that at some point you let nature run its course and . . ."

"I had no natural needs!" Robert said, slamming the armrest of his wheelchair. "None but her. She was all I needed in life. I knew you wouldn't understand. As soon as I met her—that was it! All else was dead to me! The entire female sex! It's as though I had seen the master plan . . . her very existence negated the existence of others. And the more she held out, the more feverish my love became."

"Rejection is the ultimate aphrodisiac, everyone knows that."

"Oh, how I was drawn to her room at night and how soundly I was denied."

"Excuse me?"

"She used to lock her door at night. 'So that I wouldn't get in their way,' at least that's what she said."

Ben, recognizing the potential in the cripple's life story, the man who waited on the arrival lawn of the Other World for ten years, knew that they had reached the pivotal moment.

"And then?" Ben cradled the words on the way out of his mouth. He used them often, in fact, when squeezing the life out of false plotlines.

"You remember I told you how I dreamed of being an actor? There wasn't a show in Paris I didn't audition for. Two weeks before the event that changed my life, I auditioned for a small part in a movie rendition of *The Miser.* Molière. It was the worst audition of my life. I was wound so tight that instead of playing the part of the well-mannered gentleman, I came off as a tic-ridden madman. After a minute of reading, I dropped the text and walked out of the room. It was clear I'd missed another opportunity. Two weeks later I got a call. The casting director was on the line. She wanted me back for another audition. I was shocked. The next day I showed up for the second call, still sure I was auditioning for Cléante, but the director asked me to read Harpagon's famous monologue. You know, Act Four, Scene Seven: 'Thieves! Thieves! Assassins! Murder! Justice, just heavens! I am undone; I am murdered; they have cut my throat; they have stolen my money!' I thought the director had made a mistake, but he insisted, saying my neurotic behavior made him think of Harpagon. My heart was thumping; I closed my eyes and thought of Catherine and the way she had wronged me. I had her stand in for the miser's stolen money and screamed out the monologue, on the verge of tears. Two days later I got the good news: I'd been chosen to play the lead role in the movie version of *The Miser.* I felt like the king of the world. At last it was happening; my star was living out its promise. I intended to be the second Belgian in history to bring honor and fame to his country. I mean, what else do we have to be proud of besides Brel? The most famous detective in history, who was created by an English woman? At any rate, that night I asked Catherine to come out with me, but she was in one of her moods. She refused, saying she wouldn't leave the house until she found her key. Turns out she'd lost the key to her room. I couldn't see why that bothered her so much. Anyway, I left her at home and went out with friends. We drank half the night away and, for the first time since I'd met my mother superior, I managed to avoid thinking about her for a few consecutive hours. I came home at three in the morning in high spirits. I went to my room, took off my clothes, and crawled into bed. I don't know how much time elapsed while I was asleep, but when I woke up I was sure I was dreaming. I opened my eyes and saw a fully naked woman mounting me. I switched on my lamp but still had trouble believing what my eyes reported: the exquisitely naked Catherine Dumas was making love to me, eyes closed, moaning 'mon dieu' and coaxing herself down on top of me in the most glorious manner.

"I remember thinking to myself that the star was doing its thing; that everything was falling into place. We made love till first light. When I left the house that morning she was still sleeping . . . in my bed. I floated down the street, got into my car, and went to the director's house to sign the contract. When I got back she wasn't there. By nightfall, I was worried. Catherine was still nowhere to be found. The door to her room was open. Just as I considered calling her priest, four cops burst through the door. They clapped the cuffs on my wrists, told me I was charged with the brutal rape of my roommate, and dragged me to their car. I had no idea what they were talking about. They asked me thousands of questions about what happened that night. I assured them that there must be some mistake. They said they doubted it, considering the charges she'd pressed against me. I begged them to bring her down to the interrogation room so that she could look me in the eye and tell them that this whole affair was an awful misunderstanding. They refused, saying I wouldn't be looking anywhere near her eye until the trial. Trial! What the hell were they talking about? I spent a month and a half behind bars. Naturally I lost the part, but that's beside the point. My lawyer said we had no choice but to portray Catherine as certifiably insane. I didn't want to go along with it, but what choice did I have?

"I told him everything, everything. The physical love affair with God, the platonic relationship with me up until that night, the whole story. He smiled and said she would live to regret bringing charges. I waited a month and a half for the trial and believe it or not–I was more eager to see her than to discover my fate.

"When the day arrived, the police escorted me to the courtroom. I saw her sitting next to the prosecutor and I couldn't hold myself back. I called to her. She spun around, opened her eyes wide, and started to scream bloody murder, 'No! Don't come near me! No!'

"I won't torture you with the details of the trial. Just the dry facts. From the outset, it was clear that the jurors were infatuated with her. How could they not be? She looked like a wounded angel. Add a tough lady with a gavel into the mix and you start to get the picture. I suppose you won't be shocked to learn that the trial lasted less than two weeks. In her closing arguments the prosecutor contended that I had taken advantage of the fact that Catherine was a sleepwalker and raped . . ."

"Whoa, just a second, hold up!" Ben called. "What are you talking about? You never mentioned that Catherine was a sleepwalker."

The grimace spilling across the sad Belgian's face deterred Ben. "Now you see what they did to me? They pulled this story out of nowhere. They brought in an expert who testified that she's a sleepwalker. That she locked her door every night for safety reasons, so that she wouldn't, you know, wander out of her room and hurt herself. You remember that she couldn't find the key? Well, they accused me of stealing it. In fact, that was the prosecution's main piece of evidence. They found it in my pants with my fingerprints smeared all over it. It's obvious she planted it there to frame me. They claimed I stole the key, snuck into her room in the middle of the night, and, in order to make it seem like another one of her wanderings, took her to my room, where I forcefully raped her. You see what kind of deranged fairy tale the bitch cooked up?

"I took the stand and denied every word of that story, even though I knew it was hopeless. When I told them how she crept into my bed at night, she swooned to the floor and started to bawl. I remember exchanging a glance with my attorney. He shrugged and clasped his briefcase. I'll never forget that gesture. That's when I knew it was over. The key, the bruises on her body, the semen, and the Broadway swoon.

"The verdict came as no surprise. Ditto for the sentence. The beastly man who had taken advantage of the young woman's naiveté was sent to prison for eight years. She left the courtroom without looking in my direction and that was the last I saw of her until the day I died. I'll spare you all the horrors I witnessed in the darkest place on earth, save one. I spent seven years living in a jungle. If I went into what I saw there, you'd pound button three seven times just to make me stop."

"What happened during the eighth year?" Ben asked, fingering the godget, his eyes fixed on the storyteller.

"During the eighth year," Robert sighed, "a new guard arrived at the prison. Twenty-five years old, built like a brick shithouse. He always walked with his chest puffed out, like a soldier. Or a duck. The inmates called him Moulard. One day, half a year after he came to the jail, he sauntered by my cell as I was reading aloud from *The Picture of Dorian Gray*. He stopped, smiled, and asked if I was an actor. I nodded. The next day he tossed me three books through the bars. New books, not the kind you can find at the prison library. For the next two months he kept bringing me books, and we gradually became friends. He used to come by my cell and talk about literature. Everyone called us 'the scholars.' He was brilliant and sensitive and I felt that, after all those wasted years in the jungle, I had been brought back to life. I noticed that his eyes tended to stray toward my star, but I didn't think much of it. One day I asked him what an interesting man like him was doing in a heinous place like this. He looked down and said he'd tell me one day.

"I had four months left behind bars, I had a new friend, and I started to smell freedom. I couldn't stop thinking of the day I'd be let out and of my imminent reunion with Catherine."

"Catherine? I thought that . . ."

"What," Robert said, cutting him short, "that eight years in jail wipe away the memory of love? The only thing that kept me alive in there was the thought of meeting Catherine. Had we met, my forgiveness would've broken her."

"But?"

Robert's voice cracked. "One hundred and seventeen days before I got my walking papers, I went to sleep at midnight. At one thirty in the morning I woke up to the sound of whispers. I looked up and saw four guards in my cell. Before I could figure out what was going on, they shackled my arms and legs and jammed a filthy rag in my mouth. I've never been so scared. They pulled me outside and took me down the spiral staircase to the hole.

"They threw me inside, on a mattress, stripped me, and waited. They pushed my head down into the mattress and laughed. I knew something awful was about to happen. Then the door opened and a fifth man came in. He told them to give him half an hour. They left. It was just the two of us, Moulard and me. He got undressed and mounted me. I tried to break free, to yell, to fight, but he was enormous. The whole time he whispered in my ear, 'your birthmark's driving me crazy . . . I've wanted you since the moment I saw it . . . what a star, Robert superstar . . . Moulard wants you . . . Moulard loves you . . .' When he was done I wanted to retch, but the shock prevented me from reacting, especially as he continued to whisper, 'Now you see why I do this? Why I work here?'

"He got up, got dressed, and called the others. They took me back to my cell and wished me sweet dreams. I didn't sleep for three days; didn't eat, didn't shower. I just sat still and thought. On the fourth day, he came to my cell and brought me a book. Calm and collected, smiling like nothing happened. I played his game, giving him the feeling that all was good. A week went by. He brought me another book. There was a note inside: 'Superstar. Tomorrow night, you and me, in the hole. M.' The next day I returned the book with a note of my own, 'Moulard, tonight, you and me, in the shower, alone. I want to do it right.'

They came during the middle of the night. All four. They took me to the shower, threw me inside, closed the door, and waited. Moulard was ready for me, naked, his hands clasped behind his back, excited for my arrival. He asked me to get undressed. I did. He asked me to come close. My heart must've been doing two hundred beats a minute. I approached him and saw that he was holding a gun. I started to sweat, asked him what he was doing. His voice cold, he told me to get down on my knees and go down on him. I asked him to let go of the gun, said it was ruining the romance. He brought it to my head and said romance was the last thing on his mind. I got down on my knees and did as he asked. He warned me that if I made any kind of false move he'd blow my head off. When he started to move with pleasure, you know, started to lose control, I bit down with all my might. He cursed me and fell to the floor, writhing in pain. I grabbed the gun out of his hand, put it to his temple, and shot three times. That's when the four guards came in and started to beat me up. You can imagine the rest. When I was up for release, I went back to court, this time for premeditated murder. It's one thing to kill a prisoner and another thing entirely to kill a guard, especially when four other guards testify against you, saying you killed their friend in cold blood. It was the shortest trial in the history of man. Two weeks after my original discharge date, I was sentenced to twenty-five years in jail. Twenty-five more years."

∽

Ben's mouth fell slack. "Robert, I don't know . . . what to say . . . it's . . . it's inconceivable."

"No," Robert said, shaking his head. "I'll tell you what's inconceivable. It's inconceivable that a broken man by the name of Robert did twenty more years, got out at the age of fifty, and swore to do two things upon release: to surgically remove the cursed birthmark from his chest, and find Catherine in the old apartment. It's inconceivable that no matter how hard I looked, I couldn't find her. It was like the earth had swallowed her whole. It's inconceivable that on the day of the surgery, lying in a hospital bed, the upper half of my body revealed, glad to be almost rid of this badge of dishonor, a woman walks through the door, by mistake, apologizes, leaves the room, then comes back two seconds later, looks at my chest and back at me, pulls a gun out of her bag, and empties the whole clip into me. Yeah, Ben, it is inconceivable on the very day of the operation, the day I was to begin my life anew, after two months of tireless searching, Catherine finds me and kills me in cold blood. And the most inconceivable part, I suppose, is the coincidence. What the hell was she doing there, in the plastic surgery ward, on that particular day, and why in the world did she have a gun in her bag and why, why, did she not say a word?"

Ben scanned the cobalt sky in silence. "The most unthinkable part of the whole shocking story," he ruled, "is the fact that you've been waiting here for that woman for ten years, and that you've forgiven her. Not that I'd want to advocate for revenge, but how, for fuck's sake, can you possibly still be devoted to her?"

"It's my last chance," Robert said, spreading a bland smile, "I owe it to myself to ask her why. Why did she accuse me and, even more importantly, why did she kill me? But most of all, to ask her if after all we've been through, she's willing to give our relationship another chance. If she refuses, I promise to relent. But till then, I won't rest. The thought that I could spend my entire death wracked with regret is too much. You have to agree, the woman owes me an explanation. At the very least."

"Of course," Ben sighed. "You said she was in jail. Do you mean she's still there?"

Robert nodded.

"How do you know?" Ben wondered. "You've been here for ten years. Maybe she got out early for good behavior. Maybe she was never arrested. Maybe . . ."

Robert shifted in his chair, pulled the cigar box out from under him, sifted through the contents, and removed a rectangular piece of white paper. Ben looked at the business card and read aloud, "The Mad Hop—Private Investigator. Unravels Mysteries, Finds the Missing, Solves All Crimes. Address: September 1986, Circle 4, Building S, Floor 18, Apartment 45."

Ben smiled. "The Mad Hop? What kind of nickname is that?"

Robert shrugged. "Look, he's the best investigator I've ever known. He's got his share of eccentricities, but who doesn't, eh? When I got here, I contacted him. I asked him to report back about Catherine, to relay any and all information that came his way. He told me about her arrest and trial. Twenty years for first degree murder. If anything changes, trust the Mad Hop—he'll know."

Ben gave back the card, pursing his lips. "There's just one more thing I don't get. Your chair, the wheelchair."

Robert smiled. "I'll explain. But if you don't mind, accompany me to the tobacco shop. It's on the way to the central bus station, so we'll both get something out of the stroll. I imagine you're already dying to see your new apartment. . . ."

"I'm dying to see my wife's place." Ben chuckled, happy to leave the white room behind him and explore the promising new world.

As they headed toward the spot where the multi-wheels had waited two hours before, Ben said, "At the orientation they explained to us that . . ."

"Yeah, yeah, yeah," Robert said, cutting him off, "that there's a substitute for every human organ and all that other bullshit. What are you, a gullible little kid who believes everything he hears? They want to present an idealized picture of the Other World, that's all. Sure, their labs are good, they have replacement parts and immune system buffering devices, but between us, they're not Catherine's lover: There is a limit to their skills, and the proof is speaking to you. When Catherine riddled me with bullets, she did irrevocable damage to my spine. The surgeons were barely able to repair half of it. Hence, the chair. Ben, it's important you learn not to believe everything you're told. After all, we're talking about aliases."

Ben stopped walking and looked at him, bewildered.

"Forget it. I don't feel like going into it," the Belgian sighed, spinning his wheels with surprising speed.

Ben bounded after him. "It's unbelievable. You were disabled after death."

Robert nodded. Ben, sunk in thought, chin on his chest, feet marching mechanically beside Robert, thought about arriving at Marian's apartment and tried to shake the disturbing spell of the cripple's story.

"We're here!" Robert called, rousing Ben from his reverie.

Looking up, he saw a long line of people waiting in front of a giant cigarette stand. To the left of the stand, at the end of a long avenue of

people engaged in animated conversation, he saw a neon sign: 06/21/
2001–CENTRAL BUS STATION.

He spun around excitedly. "I think we part here."

Robert shook his hand. "Thanks for listening, Ben. It's always a pleasure to make new friends."

Ben smiled. "Good luck with Catherine."

Robert crossed himself and rolled toward the front of the line. The
smokers made room for him and he disappeared behind the counter.

Ben's heart quickened as he approached the flashing sign. Coming to
the end of the avenue, he heard someone call out behind him. He
turned around and saw a group of twenty kids, all around ten years old,
laughing and arguing. He wondered what kind of calamity had snatched
them from life at such a young age. The only reasonable thought that
came to mind was a bus accident on a class trip, the kind of thing that
had weaned him off newspapers back in the old world.

An hour later he got off the multi-wheel. In the middle of a giant
circle he saw a sign made of thousands of red leaves. MARCH 2000, it read.
The circle, laid with a dozen different shades of marble, was teeming
with people, and Ben squinted as though he were peering through binoculars and watched them tend to their business as he searched for
Marian. Lightheaded, inhaling the scent of the thirty-one flowered
paths that radiated from the heart of the circle, he noted the numbered
sign at the beginning of each path. Steeling himself, he strode down the
seventeenth lane. When he passed under the chosen number, he felt as
though he were entering another world, where his senses were stimulated
by each and every feature, small and large alike, from the rainbow-
colored carpet of flowers that lined the walkways to the cloud of dizzying scents they emitted; from the whirlpool of familiar and previously
unknown colors to the dazzling cross-pollination of indigo anemones
sprouting out of the sky-blue bottleneck of the orchids; from the absolute chaos ruling the flower arrangement to the fatigue of the astounded
eye and its soft, fluttering closure. Ben, forced to deal with the frontal
sensory assault, walked as fast as possible, hoping to leave the narcotic
effect trailing behind him. At the end of the path he found himself at
the foot of a long road, lined with hulking skyscrapers on either side, a

ribbon of uniformly tall silver buildings, rectangle after rectangle that, despite their identical hue, were not unpleasant, perhaps due to the queer domes that lent the arched roofs a futuristic feel.

Ben looked at the domes and realized that each of them was adorned with a letter of the alphabet, stretching from A to Z into the distant horizon. After asking a woman with tears in her eyes how to find his wife's apartment, he learned that the letters atop the buildings stood for the tenants' last names and proceeded toward the seventh building on the left.

He thought about giving Marian, a vehement vegetarian, a hard time about her building, which held aloft the immortal sign of the meat industry. Burger jokes would surely be a part of their future in this slaughterhouse-free world. He opened the main glass doors and walked inside. Astonished by the size of the lobby, he began to comprehend the enormity of the building—if each building had a thousand apartments spread over twenty-four floors, then by simple arithmetic each floor had some forty-two apartments!

"Unbelievable!" he called out, advancing toward the elevator doors. They opened, but the sight of the grand piano at the far end of the elevator, which was more like a wedding hall than a device for transporting people up and down the height of a building, stopped him in his tracks. The piano player was bent over the ivories. He played a soft tranquil melody, utterly oblivious to Ben's hesitant entry into the elevator. Ben pressed 11, recalling the instructions given in the orientation. The doors came together and the elevator sailed up. Once it eased to a stop, he prepared to step out, but taking in the vastness of the halls, he turned to the pianist who, without lifting his head, said, "What time did he or she die?"

"I don't remember the exact hour. A little before noon," Ben said.

"You need the left wing," he said, motioning him out of the elevator.

Ben thanked him and stepped through the open doors. Following his instructions, he scanned the numbered and initialed brass plates, which were positioned right in the center of the gleaming steel doors. Suddenly he realized the final detail. The jumbled numbers on the left side of the hall all shared a common trait: they were more than thirty, (and less than sixty) except for the last one, nearest the elevator.

Ben smiled in recognition. The apartment numbers marked the exact minute the person had passed away, which was why some doors had the same number but not the same initials. The statistical principle of standard deviation worked in this world, too, Ben noted, considering amusedly the chances of two people with the same initials dying on the same day, at the exact same time. Ben, figuring that the right wing started with 1 and ended with 29, ran full throttle down the hall, delighted to discover that only one door had the initials MM. He filled his lungs with air, let it seep out for a long moment, and then knocked on the door. The creeping fear that Marian wouldn't be home was stilled by the sound of advancing footsteps. A soft feminine voice cooed, "Arthur, what took you so long?"

Before Ben could process the question, the door opened, revealing the last woman in the world he expected to see.

5

A Thousand Words: A Picture's Monologue

You nasty, crude, insensitive humans! Allow me to protest! Years have passed since the initial daguerreotype, and I, in my innocence, believed that you had evolved along with the apple of your eye, your raging technology. But to my chagrin it seems that each new breakthrough has only set you back a square. The unbearable contempt, ungratefulness, and despicable ease with which you treat us—as though we shall eternally serve you!

Sometimes, in my wildest dreams, I wish that all of the world's camera lenses were encased in a permanent fog. Perhaps then you'd show some contrition, perhaps even take a vow not to maltreat us, even though you, me, and my band of sisters all know the worth of a human word, which brings me to my point of contention: I don't know which bastard came to the conclusion that I'm worth a thousand words, and if I did know, I'd find a way to settle the score with him in the dark-room. I do know what the bastard meant. He thought he was complimenting us. As though the comparison to a thousand words would pad our self worth and puff up our pride; as though a thousand were the ultimate number of words one could use to praise the value of a picture.

Poppycock! That's a cowpie dressed up as a chocolate soufflé. We aren't going to be taken for that ride. I demand a change in the saying, the proverb, the colloquialism, or whatever other politically correct phrasing you decide to attach to a thousand words. Henceforth, a picture shall be worth a hundred thousand words—at least!

Surely you'll agree that when humans look at photographs it's impossible to know what feelings will flood their hearts, what thoughts will wander into their heads. Perhaps, while surveying the matted or glossy evidence, unexpected sentiments, warm clouds of nostalgia, telling revelations, or a thousand and one stories will make themselves known. Their worth has no quantitative definition, let alone a word cap.

It has been my privilege to be one of those pictures—controversial, understood by some, mysterious to others. I was born in Wales, thirty minutes drive from Bangor, next to a beautiful hostel in Bryn Gwynant on 8.13.89, at 11:37 A.M., to an Olympus mother and a Kodak father. Two of my sisters were amateurishly overexposed, leaving twenty-two of us in the hands of the midwife, a salesman named Kobi. He and his wife went on vacation with their good friends, a recently married couple—a righter and an English teacher. My birthplace was a deep-green pitch of dew-soaked grass, littered with three scarlet-stained ciga-rette butts. In the background, a mountain flank plunged into the sea, placing the springy grass and the water on a single plane. The sky was decorated with an armada of feathery clouds and the wind brought with it the news of a premature autumn.

The righter and the English teacher were in the middle of the frame: He—a thin man with spiky brown hair, big blue eyes, and protruding cheekbones—in faded jeans and a red T-shirt and she—a thin woman with brown hair that fell to her shoulders, slanted blue eyes, full cheeks, and a long swan neck—in a violet-colored velvet dress. They were facing my mother, wrapped in an embrace. My mother giggled naughtily just as Kobi pressed the button, perhaps forecasting what was about to take place. Moments before, a sheep sauntered across the lawn and helped herself to some breakfast while getting rid of dinner. The two people that took her spot on the lawn had no idea what they were standing on, which most likely explains why they didn't pay any attention to the joy-ous bleating from behind a large tree as the sheep watched the woman slip, the man try to arrest her fall, and the two of them tumbling to-gether on the olive-like pellets from her intestines. My mother man-aged to capture the very moment of the fall. The two of them, laughing hysterically, looking at Kobi, asking him not to take the picture as he, to our good fortune, snapped three quick shots. Two, as I said earlier, were overexposed, and only your humble servant remains. The hug that preceded me, and the buffoonery in the pellets that followed, are both gone. Only the comic fall remains. If I'm not mistaken, the couple was more than happy to leave the picture with Kobi and his wife. Maybe they had enough pictures of themselves. Maybe, since I was a product of the friend's camera, he was supposed to develop an extra copy, but due to a careless mistake, he tossed my dad into the trash and I was all that remained. All gloating aside, it would be perfectly reason-able to say that I am a natural survivor.

A word, if you will, on the matter of survival. In the moment before birth each picture is promised that she will live forever. That is the essence of our existence: immortality. We are the scraps of life you decide to save. But how, for God's sake, are we supposed to live forever if you let us collect dust, turn yellow, crumble, tear, burn, and die? In a just world, you all would have been forced to answer for criminal abuse!

This Kobi character takes the picture without noticing that a loose hair has slipped out of his slacker ponytail, swooping down in front of my mother's womb at the critical moment. That, my friends, is abuse! I'll always carry that strand of hair on my upper right corner! The bubble of perfection was popped pre-partum and I haven't even mentioned the maltreatment I received at the hands of him and his wife. You brought me into this world, thank you very much! You shoved me into an album along with my sisters: thanks again. You did not open that album once in ten years and you know what? I don't even mind the indifference, I can bear the affront, but what have you got against aerating? Let's see you live in the house for ten years without opening a window. Why can't you understand that each and every one of us needs to be framed and placed in a visible spot, like that kitschy one with you and the kid, who, by the way, is gravely undernourished, if you haven't noticed.

For an entire decade, we've been suffocating in the coffin you crafted for us, you ingenious humans, and you still don't get it. The picture of you two hugging at the castle in Cardiff, okay; the fragrant landscape shots, fine; but did you forget what the wife of the righter stepped in? All my sisters keep a more than polite distance, turning their noses, yearning for me to depart. I learned to live with the burden, and you could say that my nose-holding sisters learned to live with the smell, but then, all of a sudden, a decade later, you decide to open the album and pull me out. How exciting! Someone's finally paying attention to me. My sisters breathe easy. We all wonder where I'm going.

Shockingly, you give me to the old geezer. I don't even want to go into the insults he hurled at me; let's just say that I wish him a long life and a brutal senility. From the moment that appalling artist shoved me in his pocket, I knew I was in danger. I spent a whole month lying in his pants, dying of boredom. I wanted to scream—since when do we fold a photograph, ay?! But the fool had a stroke and I had to suffer through his repulsive shudders. Thank heavens they force patients to wear a uniform, or I would have spent a month at that depressing hospital.

Luckily, his wife took his pants and threw them over the couch in the guest room. Just like that, for a month, as if I was worthless. At the end of the month, Kobi and his wife arrived at the artist's house and asked for me back. They mumbled something about me being the only picture they had of the righter and his wife, and that they'd love to get me back in the album. The old lady didn't waste any time. She fished around in the pocket and returned me to them.

I returned to my owners with mixed feelings. On the one hand, I was upset by the way they carted me off a month before; on the other, life in the coffin was better than wasting away in a ratty pair of pants, especially if you take into account the horror stories I've heard about the washing machine. Kobi's wife put me in her pocketbook, forever changing my fate. They thanked the artist's wife and then decided to stop for coffee on the way home. After an hour at the café, pleased to have me back in their custody, about to order the check, the woman excused herself to go to the bathroom, saying she'd be just a minute. Kobi laughed and joined her. The surreptitious smiles didn't elude me. It wasn't the first time, and I imagine it wasn't the last. But it was the last time they saw me.

The shamefully libidinous couple forgot the bag under the table. Five minutes after they got up, a young woman, with the look of a starving college student, walked into the café. With truly shocking nonchalance, she spotted the forsaken bag, picked it up, slung it over her shoulder, left a small tip, and walked out. I shuddered, knowing I was in the hands of a criminal. She bolted out of the place and only slowed to a walk at the corner, where she went through the bounty. She opened the wallet and smiled. Crime pays well. She searched for other valuables and only then noticed me. She pulled me out, looked at me briefly, and flicked me to the sidewalk. I was devastated. I knew it was the end of me. A picture on the sidewalk? How can you extricate yourself from that type of situation? Desperate, I cursed the thief, lay down on my back, and waited. Shortly, any moment now, they'll step on me, trample me, throw me . . . throw?

Yes, after less than a moment the wind came to my aid. She came out of nowhere, a strong cold gust that lifted me off the face of the sidewalk and pressed me close to two intertwined plastic bags, the three of us flying as an improvised kite. I tasted freedom for the first time in my life—no albums, no frames, and, most importantly, none of you, people.

Even though I feared the fall, I enjoyed every moment. The inevitable happened in the early evening. The wind tired and I found myself torn from my random friends, landing at the entrance to the new Central Bus Station. Trying to escape the stampede of passengers, I felt a small hand lift me up. I looked at him and screamed. A kid. A kid. They're the worst. Wild, cruel, dirty, heedless. His fingers were oily and I remember how disgusted I was when he smeared my edges with lamb- and onion-smelling paws. I almost barfed. I wanted him to get rid of me so bad, but the little idiot just folded me up and stuck me in his pocket. The woman by his side hustled him along. The two of them entered the station, got on the down escalator, and waited for the bus. While the louse petted me inside his pocket, I cursed Kobi with everything I had. They got on the bus, paid, and sat down. The bus pulled out of the station. He took me out of his pocket and looked at me covertly, like some kind of spy. Then he picked his head up and stared at the woman sitting opposite him. The woman next to him, most likely his mother, asked him a question, which he didn't answer. She turned back to him and said it was impolite to stare.

He whispered something in her ear and showed me to her. She looked at me, looked at the woman opposite them, turned to her, and said something like, "I'm sorry but I think you may have dropped this. . . ."

The woman smiled bewilderedly, took me in her hands, arched her eyebrows, and thanked her. The kid started to cry like mad, "It's mine! It's mine!" The blushing mother asked him to calm down. The bus came to a stop. The woman got off, looked at me again, this time intently, bent over, opened her bag, and threw me inside. Two days have passed and I'm still in the dark. I hope with all my heart that she'll be kind to me and, for heaven's sake, will pull me out of this gloomy place.

6

Dead Prefer Blondes

Ben couldn't decide what shocked him more: the fact that the woman who opened the door wasn't Marian; the fact that she flashed him the most famous smile in the history of womankind; the fact that she had dyed her hair a charcoal black, taking away her hallmark; or, perhaps, the sudden realization that she wasn't who she pretended to be. She sighed petulantly and signaled him to wait. Then she took off down the long hall of her apartment, disappeared into a room, rattled and rummaged, finally returned with a Polaroid camera, bent down, pressed her face against his, called out "cheese!" and pushed the button. Embarrassed, Ben looked at the photo she shoved his way. The frozen and forced smile on his face lent him the expression of the ultimate idiot. However, he made up his mind not to call her bluff.

"Here," she said, "you can show everyone you had your picture taken with me. What more could you want? Please, sir, please, just take it and leave. Arthur is supposed to be back any minute now."

He furrowed his brow, thinking about the prosperous industry of look-alikes in the previous world and wondering whether "Arthur" was "the" Arthur Miller, or, strangely enough, a look-alike of the famous playweight, then handed back the picture. "I've got no use for it," he said, shrugging.

"Marilyn" smiled faintly. "Do you know how much this picture is worth?"

Ben snatched the picture, glanced at it, and stared at her condescendingly. "I'm sorry, Ms. Monroe. I'm of the mind that you earned every compliment you ever got . . . but I swear, I am not a fan. I came here with one thing in mind, to find my wife."

"Your wife? Why did you think you'd find her here?"

Concentrating on her face, he responded with a question. "Why do you live here? Shouldn't you be living in 1962?"

Her face soured. "Don't you think I'm tired of moving from place to place? I have no choice. They always find me. They always find their way to my new apartment and force me to move." After a ponderous silence, she asked in astonishment, "You're really not a fan?"

Ben shook his head. "This place belongs to my wife, Marian Mendelssohn. I actually still don't understand why you took her apartment; it seems a lot like trespassing."

"You think I need to trespass? I have a good friend who finds abandoned places with my initials for me. I move every year. And before you even ask, yes, a lot more people loiter around apartments with the initials N.J.B., thinking I'm undercover with my old name."

"Did you ever consider changing your name?" Ben asked, immediately regretting the question.

A tremor of desperation slipped into her gleaming smile. "Even if my name was Florence Nightingale they'd find me. The move just buys me two or three months of quiet till they come again."

"If your fans find you everywhere, why don't you just go live with Arthur? The way I see it, all your problems would be solved if . . ."

"Marilyn" raised a finger to her lips. Her face dull with boredom, she answered in a sleepy voice, as though she were saying this for the thousandth time, "because of the AACM."

She groaned at the sight of Ben's blank face, and said, "We'll make this short, okay? As I'm sure you know, in the Other World you can change your name in one direction and one direction only. You can cut it short but you can't make it longer. I'm talking about the name you had when you left the previous world. Mostly it's for people who had three names and more. Like Wolfgang Amadeus Mozart. He, for instance, had no intention of changing his name in any way. And from what I hear, he led a fascinating death until the Association for the Appreciation of Classical Music caught up with him. The AACM is full of musicologists, amateur composers, musicians, and just ordinary aficionados. Fanatics all. If you're a famous composer, they'll do anything to convince you to keep writing music. They'll never let you be. Their love for music borders on a pure hatred for musicians. They decided they wanted Mozart to finish the *Requiem*, as though he'd never gotten sick. He refused outright; said he was happy with Süssmayr's work and that no one would convince him otherwise. But that didn't make much of an impression on them. They wrote petitions, staged protests, hounded him wherever he went. But he stuck to his guns. The real victim here is actually Süssmayr, who couldn't handle their insults and, despite his teacher's praise and encouragement, punched in a seven over three. Mozart was crushed. He blamed the AACM for his student's eternal sleep, but they just brushed it off, and as if that wasn't enough, later that day they went on the air, on the evening news, and urged him to write a brand new requiem, because "now more than ever," he had the best possible reason: He could compose a requiem for the composer who had finished his own requiem! Naturally, Mozart refused . . . He said nothing would sway him. Everyone thought it was over, but they wouldn't let him be. They came after him everywhere, harassed him constantly. He moved five times and they found him each time. Mozart thought about going back to his original name, but like I said, you can't add names, you can only subtract. Think about it, with a name like Joannes Chrysostomus Wolfgangus Theophilus, who would find him? Anyway, he decided to drop Wolfgang. You know, just keep the essence. Amadeus Mozart. I don't know what he was thinking. They've been combing the world for him for two hundred years and now suddenly it's over? The truth is, he almost pulled it off, would have actually, had it not been for Salieri, the tattler, who bumped into him at a Beethoven performance, the *Tenth* I think, and then followed him back to his apartment where he uncovered the ruse.

"Since then, the poor guy's been on the move, darting from place to place. Anyway, my Arthur's borne the brunt of it. You know how many times they've come to his place by mistake because of the initials? And these aren't sane people, mind you. Even when they see they've made a mistake, they ask permission to search the place. These loonies think Arthur's hiding Mozart in his apartment. He moved eight times before he took my advice and moved in with me. Sure, I'm harassed, too, but not with the same intens—" She yawned and covered her mouth. Ben promised to leave soon; he just wanted to know how she ended up in his wife's apartment.

She stretched and sleepily repeated what she had said earlier. "I have a good friend. He finds abandoned places. No one's lived here for at least six months."

"Six months?" Ben asked. "But she only came here a year and three months ago. You're saying Marian only lived here for nine months?"

"I have no idea. I've been living here for three months. That's when I was able to set this up."

"But this is an eternal address, no? This will be Marian's address a thousand years down the road, too. That's what they said during the orientation."

"That's what I meant when I said I was able to get this thing set up. My friend works in the thumb center. So, you know . . ."

"No, I don't."

"Look, you think I died yesterday? I know you're just buying time," she said.

"No, no, no," Ben said, "I'll be out of here in a second. Just so you know, though, I did die yesterday. I hardly know anything about this world. Like that thing with the thumbs. As far as I know, all you use it for is to take out tapes and . . ."

"Alright, rookie, alright," she laughed, opening the door and pointing to an elliptical, thumb-shaped hole. "You see? We don't have keys or locks. We have the thumb hole. You recognize your apartment by the signs—date of death, initials—and your apartment recognizes you by your thumbprint. In the whole history of this world there's not been one recorded break-in. You come to your apartment, put your thumb by the door, push lightly, and in you go. Simple, easy, and spares you the sorrow of carrying keys."

"But," Ben said, enchanted by the simplicity of the idea, "this hole is supposed to recognize Marian's thumb, not yours."

She agreed and hurried to explain. "Every time you come and go a blue light goes on in the thumb center HQ. If six months go by without any movement, a red light goes on. It means that the resident either left or went seven over three. Ninety-nine percent of the time it's the former. Once someone's left, a resident can come and ask the center to move in. The higher-ups in the center have you sign a piece of paper that says that if the initial resident returns you have to pack up and leave within three days. As I said earlier, Arthur and I have been living here for three months and no one has asked to move back in."

"And the fingerprint?" Ben asked.

"Switched!" Marilyn's copy announced, raising her thumb. "This is my thumb print and my thumb hole. If your wife comes back, I'll have to leave and take my thumb hole with me."

"What about Marian?" Ben asked childishly. "Where is she?"

The woman rolled her eyes. "Sorry, I left my crystal ball in the previous world."

Ben gave her a look.

"I don't mean to sound cynical, it's just that your wife could be anywhere."

"What about at the HQ? Would they know there?"

"The center gives out info about original residents in their given apartments, that's all."

Ben nodded pensively and said, "Can I ask you a favor?"

"You want to leave your fingerprint in my telefinger so that if your wife turns up at my place I'll let her know that you're looking for her."

Ben placed his finger on number 6 in her godget. "Push!" she said. He obeyed, raising an eyebrow as she held out her hand. "Nice to meet you, Ben." Reading the astonishment on his face, she smiled and touched her ear. "News and telefinger services are fed straight to the ear . . . as is the name of the person you are about to call, so there's no mistake in identity."

Before he had the chance to thank her, she offered some more helpful advice. "Take your godget and push number two four times. You're sweating like a racehorse coming around the final stretch."

Ben smiled bashfully. A chilly wind parted the curtain of sticky humidity, and for a brief moment he managed to escape the chaos churning in his mind.

"How can I thank you?" he asked.

She stepped back into the apartment, smiled, and shooed him away playfully. "Go. That'll do the trick."

On his way to the elevator, he remembered he had forgotten the picture of the two of them. He pivoted, made his way back to the front door, raised his hand, was poised to knock, and then heard "Marilyn" say "Leave it for Marian."

7

The Defect

About a year and a half after the Y2K farce fizzled, Yonatan laughed, remembering the night all four digits changed. As the world toasted the historic date with a rousing symphony of sound and color, Yonatan finished reading Salman Rushdie's book, *The Ground Beneath Her Feet*. A surge of adrenaline coursed through him as he read his favorite author's final words. Unable to sleep, he sat down at the computer and sneezed seven times. Despite the flu, there was much to be thankful for, seeing as the sickness got him out of making the rounds through Tel Aviv with his friends, celebrating the most egocentric birthday party humankind had ever known. Going back into the kitchen, he made himself a cup of tea, splashed in a lug of whiskey, and went back to his seat, heart pounding expectantly, nostrils quivering with germs. He sneezed again, moaned, cursed the fucking virus, and brought the computer to life. It complied, earning him a quick 2,000 shekels. He had bet four friends 500 shekels each that the bug was a sham, spread by twisted minds who enjoyed toying with people as they teetered on the cusp of a new millennium.

Yonatan didn't believe in the end of the world. He believed in the end of man. He scoffed at the idea that one day a hidden hand would wipe all humans away. He also had nothing but scorn for people that heeded the foolishness of seers, openly wishing that their worst fears materialize posthaste, if only because they were so wrapped up in their own demise they never started to live their lives. His close friends resented the outrageous simplicity with which he lived his life, taking him to task for his dizzying carelessness. Yonatan smoked three packs of Gitanes a day, drank three bottles of Guinness a day, was a regular at Pizza Hut and McDonald's, slept with strangers without protection, flew once a year to sunbaked beaches and turned his body over to the sun's rays, had no familiarity with the seat belt, tended to start the week with a few lines and end it with a few light blue pills that sent him straight to the dark side of the moon, put good money down on good-for-nothing soccer teams, and turned his computer on at the stroke of midnight.

Yonatan will get the money the next day and take his friends out to a feast, after which he'll insist on driving home drunk to the south side of town. Roni will clap him on the back and say you can't drive like this; Yonatan will ask why not; Daniel will laugh and say what will you do if you run into a cop; Yonatan will shrug and say it'll be an honor to puke on a man of the law; his friends will say he's impossible; Yonatan will respond that he's improbable, and drive home, zigzagging moderately. After parking the car on a diagonal, he'll stagger inside, hold on to the staircase railing, fight the lock and key, enter his apartment, shut the door, and collapse on the rug into a long, deep sleep.

Only the following night, after coming back from the bookstore, will he turn on the computer and see, to his delight, that a woman left him the following message: "Dear Grimus, I was moved by your words. If you feel like it, drop me a line. Vina." Yonatan will recall the eve of the millennium. He turned on the computer and went to the Salman Rushdie fan site, wrote that he just finished reading *The Ground Beneath Her Feet* and described how touched he had been by the Indian master's mythical story of rock and roll:

> The ground beneath Vina Apsara's feet is the only holy ground I know—the ground of love. The only ground worth fighting for. Ormus fought, Rai fought, Vina fought, each in their own way and each simultaneously won and lost. When the ground opened beneath Vina's feet, she disappeared. Love swallowed her whole. And then she rose again, like a second sunrise, in a different place, on different ground. And disappeared again. And rose again. Vina reinvented herself, the masses reinvented her, her lover invented her and her friend as well. Vina is the quintessential heart that keeps on beating after every crisis, attack, or shock, the heart that refuses to bow before a quake. With her heart Vina Divina drove everyone mad, especially Ormus. The Goddess made the God crazy and their madness made the ground shudder, claiming lives. That's true love. Demanding, selfish, cruel, larger than life, undaunted by death. Because like the song, it, too, survives the end of life.

Rushdie's latest work finds me in a sentimental state of mind, at the height of an annoying period—the world blabbing about the end of days, apocalypses, and phobias. The color black rules the roost. The world doesn't understand that fear of death is as irrational as fear of earthquakes. I don't fear death. My close friends warn me with the worn cliché "you think it won't happen to you." Bullshit. I'm sure it will happen to me. I don't believe in caution—I have to be impulsive, careless, unencumbered by considerations. They say I'm suicidal. I say at least I'm enjoying the suicide—slow, systematic, pleasurable. They fear the end as though it's a surprise. I'm not scared, because I'm ready for its arrival at any given moment. I'm not worried that the earth will open wide and swallow me whole. Who ever said you need to die in ripe old age? Between us, most of the elderly are overripe. And if by some miracle I make it to old age, I'll know I marked my days with inconsequential sins; and if my lifestyle managed to strip away some of the frailer years, so be it. I can puff out my chest and flaunt my accomplishments. It is I who shake the ground beneath his feet, not God, not fate, and not some tired tectonic fault. I, Grimus. And like Vina, dread is foreign to me. I have nothing but envy for her. For the great love. Not the love of the adoring masses, nor that of the photographer who provided human warmth, but for Ormus's love, which bounded across the borders of logic and emotion. Ormus looked under ground. Ormus, who warned against quakes and becomes addicted to the quaking of his sad soul, finds Vina between the fault lines. Many Vinas. A million. How many of you have experienced love like that? How many of you have experienced love at all? I imagine very few.

I know it's very few.

And I know that despite the cynicism that controls my life and the lives of those around me, it would only be fair to admit my desire, just once in my life, to be Vina or Ormus. Not out of modesty, but because I don't believe in the multiplicity of great loves within a single life. Either the ground shakes beneath your feet, or it doesn't. I'd like to know if all of Literature's loves are the imagined fruits of feverishly romantic minds, or if they are the rare, authentic, sublime variety. I hope it's the latter.

Grimus.

~~

"Vina" was a real Midnight Child. Her mastery of Rushdie's work paved the way to camaraderie and then true friendship. At first they reveled in competitions, testing each other's knowledge of Rushdie's tales with riddles, trivia, and anagrams of even the most minor characters' names (as inspired by the Magister Anagrammari). Beneath the surface of things, the two of them knew that their literary gamesmanship spanned two simple feelings: pride, regarding the depth of knowledge and understanding; and slight resentment, toward the other person, who bored deep into the rich works but also managed to make them part of their own private life. The first sentiment stemmed from the intellect's need to boast; the second from childish possessiveness. The twin emotions, shared by the two of them, spawned a new one, which excited them no end. A month into their nocturnal chats, it was clear that the two of them were of one mind. They cleared the hurdles of competitive knowledge, successfully passing each other's tests, and then began picking apart the major issues of their favorite works, two minds wedded at the hands of a mutually admired third. When "Grimus" labeled *The Satanic Verses* the intellectual status symbol of a society intent on impressing itself, "Vina" knew exactly what he meant. She derided the fact that so many people bought the book because of the ignorance of a few deranged clerics rather than for its brilliant ideas. They agreed that the consumers, who bought the book in order to lay it on the living room table, turning it into a piece of fashionable furniture, and flaunting it in social gatherings were garishly hypocritical. "Grimus," the manager of a bookstore on Pinsker St., told "Vina" that over the past decade he had met thirty-five people who had bought the book because they "need it at home," and then when they came back to the store and were asked whether they had read it, responded with a rainbow of excuses, including "I haven't had the chance," "I'm waiting for the right time," "I bought it as a way to show my support for the freedom of speech—isn't that enough?" "I couldn't get through the first thirty pages," "I only read the part about Mahound, because that was the part that really drove the fanatics crazy." "I only read the Return to Jahilia part, because that's the part that really pissed off the Iranians," "it's a tome," "it's fiction," "it's too dense," "it's too demanding," "it's not him, it's me," and "I'm not much of a reader."

In another chat, that spanned eight fascinating nights, they analyzed the matter of rivalries, which are at the root of all Rushdie's work. The perpetual rivalry between good and evil, the angel and the demon, the divine and the devilish, the sacrifice and the sacrificer, the rooted and the uprooted, the modern and the primitive, the accepted and the rejected, the strong and the weak, the free and the shackled, the terrestrial and the heavenly, the honored and the mortified, the crooked and the straight, the hidden and the seen, the religious and the secular, the constant and the ephemeral, the winner and the loser, the past and the future, the unresolved conflict between the Saleems and the Shivas, the Farishtas and the Chamchas, the Auroras and the Umas of our world, and they sadly surmised that the silk curtain of tranquility would never fall on a world so utterly constrained by self-interest.

But the conversation that clarified how deep-seated their mutual understanding had grown was born of something that was far from a learned discussion and actually came as a surprise to both of them.

GRIMUS: "You know, Vina, we've been blabbing about Rushdie for a month already and I just realized I don't know why you love his books so much."

VINA: "I can't believe it. I swear I was about to ask you the same question."

GRIMUS: "Then why didn't you ask?"

VINA: "Don't know. We were so wrapped in analysis and . . . I really don't know."

GRIMUS: "I promise to answer after you do."

VINA: "Okay. I think that . . . no, no, Grimus, let's not do it like this. Let's make it more interesting. I'll try to guess why you love his books so much and you try to guess why I do, okay?"

GRIMUS: "Sounds interesting. Let's give it a whirl. I, Vina, love Rushdie's books for the writing. I love the fascinating mix of soaring prose and Salmanian jargon, the blend of learnedness and down-home wisdom, the word play, the humor, the metaphors, the breathtaking completeness of his melded Englishness and Indianness that has reached the boundary line of a new language—Rushdish. Something like that, I would say, no?

VINA: "How did you know that his writing is what does it for me?"

GRIMUS: "Because you never quote lines that relate directly to the plot. You always focus on his devastating way with words. You really love

Virgil, especially the line about language making concepts and concepts making chains."

VINA: "I, Grimus, love Rushdie's work because of the way he spins his wild yarns. I'm crazy about his associations, his unforgettable characters, but more than anything else, I'm a slave to his imagination. He is the one and only!"

GRIMUS: "Insightful, well done, but I think we're both flatulent fucks."

VINA: "I don't smell anything."

GRIMUS: "But I hear it. Vina, it doesn't take much to say we love Rushdie for his style or his imagination. What about us? When you love someone, that person probably fills a need deep within you. My question isn't why do we love *him* but why do *we* love him."

VINA: "Dear Grimus, you're being a smart ass."

GRIMUS: "You think?"

VINA: "A lot of people love his books."

GRIMUS: "We're not a lot of people."

VINA: "So what are we?"

GRIMUS: "A guy asking a question and a girl trying to get out of answering."

VINA: "I'm not trying to get out of answering."

GRIMUS: "I'll make it easy for you. This is something I wanted to ask you a long time ago. Vina, in what language did you read his books?"

VINA: "In the original."

GRIMUS: "Which explains your elegant English."

VINA: "I could say the same about you."

GRIMUS: "True. I don't trust translators and I know you don't have any issues with them. But you chose to read him in English, even though we both know how lush the language is in the original."

VINA: "I like the language. And anyway I've always advocated reading in the original."

GRIMUS: "I agree and would like to tie that commendable position to what interests Rushdie the most—roots, belonging, home, and the lack thereof. Is it possible, Vina, that you feel like you don't belong?"

VINA: "To what? People often mistakenly believe that belonging relates only to a place. One can't fall into that popular trap. There's belonging to a place, to a time, to a language, to a people, and probably a few more I forgot. I don't feel any belonging to the country in which I live, and the fact that I am comfortable with computers does not mean I'm interested in the modern period. I prefer English to my native French, I have no idea why, and as for people . . . let's just leave that be."

GRIMUS: "Is there a historical period you'd like to return to?"

VINA: "History is too dark for me."

GRIMUS: "And the future?"

VINA: "Too bright."

GRIMUS: "Where does that leave you?"

VINA: "Waiting for Rushdie's next book."

GRIMUS: "I'm happy to learn new things about you . . ."

VINA: "What about you? Where do you belong?"

GRIMUS: "Nowhere. The fact that I was born forces me to belong to this world, other than that, it's all nonsense. And let's not get started on politics . . . .so I was born in this godforsaken place, so what?"

VINA: "And time?"

GRIMUS: "I wouldn't mind being a Caesar in ancient Rome. But without all of the diplomatic shenanigans, the wars, the religious rites, and the silly senate."

VINA: "Hedonist!"

GRIMUS: "What else can we do? Cry about how life is too short? Complain all the time?"

VINA: "You never thought about moving?"

GRIMUS: "A million times. But my short trips abroad taught me the secret."

VINA: "Every new place is Eden for a week."

GRIMUS: "Exactly. I never could stand that feeling, you know, when after a week you start to feel like less of a tourist and begin to mimic the locals. Seems to make much more sense to come back to this cursed land and cultivate my familiar and treasured lack of belonging."

VINA: "I agree. I think. I'm a bit tired, but I'd just like to ask you one last question."

GRIMUS: "???"

VINA: "You don't have to answer right away. Just think about it. Grimus, if someone offered you the opportunity to board a spaceship and fly to a populated planet far away, but you knew you could never come back to this one, would you do it?"

GRIMUS: "You know the answer."

VINA: "You think?"

GRIMUS: "I'm sure, about both of us."
VINA: "I guess you're right."

Yonatan didn't tell "Vina" that the spaceship question had crossed his mind dozens of times since he'd been a kid and that he couldn't believe he'd finally "bumped into" someone who wasn't critical of his reckless lifestyle. Yonatan liked the Frenchwoman's warm indifference when he told her about the bad trip he'd been on last Sunday. He liked the equanimity of the art and culture reporter who'd seen it all and had long ago stopped being impressed by passing trends, fly-by-night fads, and pseudo-cultural gimmicks. More than anything else, though, he liked the fact that "Vina," like him, wasn't enamored of her own existence and that she had no fear of death, or, for that matter, an absolute departure from the known world in the belly of a spaceship.

Maybe she shared his birth defect, Yonatan thought. One day he'd tell her his most guarded secret. But not now. She might think he was an idiot. No, not Vina. She'd understand. She'd understand that his life philosophy stemmed from the dark shadow he'd been born into. He had a heart defect. He hadn't even had a chance to live and already the partitions between the right and left chambers of his heart had been breached. The hole, however, was small and the operation was successful. The doctors inserted a small plastic stent that enabled his heart to function at a normal capacity. The surgeons eased his parents' minds and told them that the defect would not influence their child's life, but Yonatan didn't believe them and continued to treat his heart like a weak and untrustworthy organ. Certain his heart could betray him at any moment, he preferred to stop it on his own terms. At age twenty, he began waging a full scale war on his heart, pushing it, testing its outer limits. Twenty years later, he was surprised to find that the little bastard wasn't showing any signs of submission or quit. He was sure that that blemished organ was directly responsible for the romantic moonscape that was his love life. What sane woman would ever fall in love with a guy who lived like there was no tomorrow? The only woman that had ever deigned to conduct a love affair with him left in a fury after a month of passion as soon as she realized that her self-destructive drive was peaking and that two self hatreds don't equal love.

When he and "Vina" started chatting, she was in the midst of separating from her husband. Six months later, they were divorced. "Vina"
described the heartbreak and anguish to "Grimus." He tried to raise her
spirits, but she swore that no love was worth that kind of searing pain.
Six months after the millennium, the two gave Rushdie a rest and
started to cover new ground. Two people from two separate continents
sharing ideas, experiences, and feelings, reveling in the notion of the
kindred eye, cradled in the certainty of unconditional friendship. After
six more months of chatting, they summoned the courage to reveal a
fraction of what they held in their hearts.

Instead of "Grimus," "Vina" mistakenly typed "Ormus." Yonatan
was amazed. Throughout their time together he hadn't dared let the
rather likely scenario cross his lips, fearing that it would, perhaps, tunnel under the fortress of their friendship and scar the beautiful thing
they shared. "Vina" apologized and wrote "Grimus." Two weeks later
the incident had been buried under the normal nightly chats about
work, friends, and other humdrum affairs. And then came Yonatan's
turn to make a "mistake." One winter night a friend came over to his
apartment and after hours of drunken talk, teased him to bed. Yonatan
thought he was pleased. It was the perfect sexual arrangement. Once a
year the woman would appear out of nowhere, get drunk, sleep with
him, and make haste in the morning. But that night, looking at Talia-
the-Grunter's breasts sway, he felt cheap and lowdown and asked her to
leave before she had the chance to rake her fake nails down his back.
She was stunned. He reiterated his request, and when she asked if there
was another woman, he nodded and pointed at the computer, avoiding
the inebriated hail of obscenities she directed at him. The unbearable
weight of betrayal overwhelmed him and, with his head spinning, he
typed, "Vina, call me Ormus." He apologized the next day, explaining
that the whiskey had been dripping from his fingers the night before.
"Vina" wrote back that she understood.

The next night she addressed him as "Ormus." Delighted, Yonatan
recognized that their relationship was hurtling toward a strange and
exciting love—epistolary love. By the weekend he had already written
her that the thought of the coming night keeps him alive. "Vina" wrote
that her days were suddenly doused in color and that she walked
around in a daze until she sat down at her computer and saw his name.

The next two months were devoted to virtual love games in the belly of a spaceship. The two space travelers landed on a faraway star called "Gorfik" and slowly unraveled, each for the other's eyes, a series of adventures on the fascinating star. "Vina" and "Ormus" met a host of outlandish characters who gave them magical and mysterious gifts in return for human lessons on love. On their one hundred and fiftieth night on the star, Prolificus—a creature as towering as a Sequoia tree, who widened when excited—gave them a pill that enabled the body's organs to multiply infinitely, and the two of them conducted, to the tune of rousing applause from the Gorfikers, humanity's first two-person orgy. A week later the two spent some time in PARADICE, the largest casino in space, and won a mind-reading competition. The prize was an organized trip to Venus. "Vina" and "Ormus" spent four nights on the love planet as guests of the Cupids, ace archers who made their stay special by teaching them to shoot at targets and hunt lonesome meteorites. The queen of the Cupids, Artemis, arranged a dazzling gala for them and invited thousands of stars and starlets that met and fell in love thanks to their marksmanship. The residents of the lonely meteorites thanked them and begged them to stay, but the couple smiled and said they would like to continue touring the galaxy. Artemis nodded in understanding, wished them eternal sweetness, and sent them off the next day at noon to tour the Honey Moon, the temple of kitsch and all things saccharine, where the two whispered a sticky stream of sweet nothings and, under the influence of the viscosity of the whole affair, decided to proclaim their imperishable love in the way of the locals of Uranus.

For the first time since they began playing their game, Yonatan shuddered at one of "Vina's" inventions. According to "Vina," Uranusian couples show their love by exchanging hearts. Once the man has given his heart to the woman, he passes away for a short period of time. The two-hearted woman examines the heart and decides that the display of chivalry and self sacrifice, and the faith in her faithfulness, are worthy of her love. She pulls her own heart from her chest and dies. If their love is true and honest, a Uranusian cardiologist from the celestial board of eternal love will do a simultaneous double transplant so that the lovers will wake back to life at the same moment and, from that moment on, the two will be inseparable. They will carry the scars of the other's heart as though it were their own. His soul torn, "Ormus" agreed to "Vina's" proposal and the two took the Uranusian coronary oath, even though Yonatan hated the idea of "Vina" serving as the receptacle for his treacherous heart, furious with his imagination and the way it had thrust him back to the daunting present.

The couple's love odyssey lasted five months, five hours a day, during which they were continually impressed by the savagery of their shared hallucinations. The rest of the time "Ormus" lived as Yonatan Gur, a forty-year-old man who split his time between the bookstore he owned and daydreaming about a woman whose real name he didn't even know. He did not feel obliged to get acquainted with the mysterious figure he had fallen for. After all, her identity was no secret—he knew what she did for a living, what she loved and hated, the texture of her most intimate thoughts, her strengths and weaknesses, her opinions and worldviews. She had even swapped hearts with him in a dubious ceremony. The rest he filled in, pleasurably focusing on the aesthetic rind of the fruit of imagination. After five months of studying the taste and licking the core, he relished the thought of the peel. His mind's eye painted her hair blond and combed it down to her shoulders, slanted her blue eyes, filled her cheeks, thickened her lower lip, rounded her face, elongated her neck, colored her body an ivory white, traced her hips and filled them, padded her stomach with a slight pouch, stretched her legs to the arc of her hips, measured her at five foot seven, weighed her at 130 pounds, and smiled. He pulled her posture straight, lent nobility to her movements, peppered her expressions with kinetic intelligence, softened her speech, lowered her tone, harmonized her heavenly laugh, and sprayed a sweet floral scent on her neck. He didn't want to give the woman of his dreams his flawed heart, fearing that it would exact its revenge on her even as he mocked himself for the devout seriousness with which he addressed their nocturnal escapades, light years away from his real life.

It's just a game, he thought, sparking a third joint. The light mist resting on the windshield of his mind turned to a thick fog when, sitting at the computer, at the usual hour, he went online, typed in the code, asked whether they were going back to Gorfik or continuing on to a different star, and got no response. After an hour, he left her a short message: "My Vina, where have you gone? Looking for you. Ormus." With night threatening to release its grip and dawn peeping behind its back, he

pounded the computer, not knowing what to make of it. After another
Vina-free night, he flooded the site with messages and begged her to
make contact. On the third night of her absence, he called up the neighborhood dealer and asked for the good shit. On the fourth night, he
drank himself sick. The fifth night brought with it a shocking realization. Yonatan understood that the earth had swallowed "Vina," just like
in Rushdie's book. By the weekend, he was asking himself whether
"Vina" was a figment of his imagination and, no less importantly, whether
he was losing his mind. After another week without "Vina," Yonatan let
loose with three straight days of mayhem. He got drunk, got high, got
laid by two prostitutes, trashed his apartment, and thrashed anyone who
came close to him. Tearing through town, driving like a madman in
the dead of night, two policemen doused his orgy of destruction. Yonatan spent the night in jail. The next day, he was let out, his license
suspended. The return home was unsettling. Nothing, save the computer, which blinked in the darkness, had survived his wrath. Utterly
drained, he dropped himself into a hot bath. Two hours later, feeling
mildly human, he started to pick up a week's worth of debris. Carting the
shards of a television screen and other trash, he noticed the computer
screen flash. He brought it to life, sure of the disappointment that awaited
him. Yonatan couldn't believe he had mail. He tossed the shards away,
practically crushed the mouse in his grip, and clicked nervously until
his eyes hit the following, "Dear Ormus, Sorry to have disappeared. I
was way busier than I had ever anticipated. There was an insane mess
here. Hope all is good with you. If by chance you are home and not in
the store, let's chat at four. If not, then at the usual hour. Love you more
than Rushdie. Vina."

Flabbergasted, Yonatan looked at his watch and waited out the next
hour nailed to his chair, simultaneously reviewing their visits to Gorfik
and the hellish week he had been through. In his mind, creatures with
twenty arms merged with the anguished cries of a masochistic prostitute; red spaceships and howling police sirens bled into one; cold-
blooded archers picked off hot-headed drug dealers; and, above all of
the chaos, a Viennese strudel floated, batting its wings and screaming
"Zogoiby, Zogoiby." He woke up at one minute to four, wiped the drool
from the corner of his mouth, tapped a knuckle against his pounding
head, and met "Vina" online.

VINA: "Ormus how are you?"

ORMUS: "Okay, where were you?" (Yonatan: Where did you go, you bitch?)

VINA: "You won't believe it."

ORMUS: "I will." (Yonatan: You found someone else?)

VINA: "My boss called me into his office and made me a very tempting offer."

ORMUS: "Regarding?" (Yonatan: Son of a bitch.)

VINA: "Our arts and culture correspondent in Israel committed suicide. He offered me her position for a year."

ORMUS: "Her position?" (Yonatan: What's going on here?)

VINA: "Yeah, to cover cultural events, whatever happens in the shadows of national news."

ORMUS: "Arts and culture?" (Yonatan: Dear God, tell me you turned him down!)

VINA: "Yes, sweetheart. I knew you'd be surprised. You know what I said, right?"

ORMUS: "Not really." (Yonatan: You said no! You said no!)

VINA: "I had only one thing in mind."

ORMUS: "What . . . what do you mean?" (Yonatan: What in God's name are you saying?)

VINA: "That soon we will meet, my love. I've never been this excited in my life."

ORMUS: "Me too, my Vina, me too." (Yonatan: Are you dead set on giving me a heart attack?)

VINA: "Now you see where I went? I wanted to surprise you. I took care of all the arrangements, found a place to live and started work yesterday."

ORMUS: "Yesterday?" (Yonatan: Why do I not smell that sweet floral scent?)

VINA: "Yes, honey. It's perfect. I mean, it's not London, but I think I'll like Tel Aviv just fine."

ORMUS: "What? You're here . . . in . . . Tel Aviv?" (Yonatan: Oh God, you're so close, you're . . .)

VINA: "You hungry, Ormus?"

ORMUS: "What?" (Yonatan: How could you possibly be talking about food right now?)

VINA: "I'm sorry. I shocked you. You have every right to be annoyed

with me. I just thought you'd get a kick out of the surprise. It's not
Gorfik or anything, but it's right here, right now. Don't you think it's
time we met?"

ORMUS: "Of course, sweetheart." (Yonatan: Hell no! As soon as you lay
eyes on me you'll beat the Concord back to Paris.)

VINA: "That's why I asked if you were hungry. Do you want to go to
dinner? If I'm not mistaken, you like Indian food. I hear there's a
great place on Dizengoff Square."

ORMUS: "It's great, but you have to have a reservation there. There's a
funky little place on the south side of town" (Yonatan: What are you
doing? What are you doing?), "on Florentine Street."

VINA: "Sounds great. Should we say nine?"

ORMUS: "Nine's great." (Yonatan: What's so great?!)

VINA: "I'll wait outside."

ORMUS: "How will I recognize you?"

VINA: "Say my name."

ORMUS: "Vina?"

VINA: "Not my nickname, Ormus, my name."

ORMUS: "Which is?"

VINA: "Same as Robin Hood's love. See you soon, my love."

Three hours later and Yonatan still couldn't remember Robin Hood's
love's name, but that was the least of his concerns. The fact that she was
just two hours away paralyzed him. The man staring back at him in the
mirror looked miserable and indistinct, bowed and diminished, surprised and alarmed—a man who never dreamed of fantasy and reality
meeting, who feared that the latter would demolish the former, and
would, as usual, exact its price. Yonatan nodded his head sullenly—the
man looking back at him would never be Ormus. Ormus isn't bald,
isn't fat, doesn't have watery eyes framed by heavy black rings; his nose
isn't reminiscent of a trunk; his lips aren't paper thin; he has a discernable neck; he isn't short; no moles dot his cheeks; and his teeth are
straight and white.

Yonatan thought about "Vina" and the way she would be blindsided
as soon as she laid eyes on him. In one stroke, his belief that the soul
projects its beauty onto the exterior was erased: Even a good soul's
warm glow has its limits. He knew how the story of their great love
would end—Vina would want to keep him close as a friend and would

berate herself for embracing such cheap superficiality. The last thing
Yonatan wanted was for his love to look at him and be wracked with
guilt by the fact that nature had reared its ugly head. Even he was deterred by his own reflection. No. He would stay home and spare her the
terrible punishment that falling in love with him had entailed.

The black pants, blue button-down shirt, and brown blazer clothe the
sobbing yet dry-faced Mr. Gur. His burial gowns mock him, make him
laugh, and raise the obvious question of why he chose to shed the moth-
balls if he had no intention of meeting the woman. Yonatan doesn't respond. He's preoccupied, diligently brushing his teeth, cursing the
toothpaste glob on the front of his jacket, then washing it off. He's certain that this night will go down as the most supremely pathetic of all
and that it's merely for the sake of marking the milestone in the extem-
poraneous history of his life that he is scrubbing the back of his neck
and face, daubing the area behind his earlobes with cologne more
suited to slaying insects than women. He leaves his apartment at eight
thirty, planning to head down to the neighborhood café and forget the
entire affair. He hails a cab and asks to be taken to Florentine Street,
trying to keep his cool in the face of the cabbie's diatribe. After ten more
minutes of steady one-way talk, during which the driver never once
stops kneading the issue of the terrible terror attack that had killed
dozens of people only an hour before, Yonatan apologizes and says his
head is exploding.

The driver shuts up but keeps a hostile eye on him. Yonatan doesn't
care. Curiosity has killed his pride and he is going to see her. Not to
meet her. Just to satisfy a childish desire that a bigger man would have
been able to squelch. When they arrive, Yonatan feels sick. His con-
torted features wipe the hostility from the driver's tired face. He asks if
he's alright. Yonatan nods, gets out of the cab, and looks at the restaurant from the far side of the street. Three women are reading the menu
hanging in the restaurant's front window. It's hard for him to tell which
one of their backs belongs to "Vina." He coughs and remembers her
name isn't "Vina." After a minute of consultation, two of them enter the
restaurant, leaving the third behind. Yonatan waits for her to turn
around. She's burrowing into the menu. She'll probably order the chicken
tikka massala, he thinks, and hides behind a tree. A minute later, he
gathers some strength and, in an act of cowardice, yells "Vina" and
then ducks down, his eyes devouring the sight of her as she turns

around. Yonatan pinches his arm, forcing himself to believe. The strip of asphalt between them can't hide the smooth blond hair, the slanted blue eyes, the full cheeks, the thick lower lip, the round face, the long neck, the rounded hips, and the nobility of her bearing. She still doesn't see him. He yearns for her to spot him and strains to remember her name, but his thoughts abruptly trail away. The sharp tightening in his chest doesn't let up, and even when he's ready to stand up and show himself, his body maintains the upper hand and hurls him to the sidewalk. He clutches his heart, begging for air. Shocked by his own helplessness, he sneers, cursing the mutant son of a bitch, which has picked its moment perfectly. He closes his eyes, then remembers, and whispers, "Marian, Marian."

8

Father Tongue—A

Ben knew he was right as soon as he set foot in the multilingual labs. For a woman like Marian—who helped the foreign diplomats' kids through the deep sands of English in the morning, coached local actors hell-bent on Hollywood through the labyrinths of diction in the afternoon, and drafted the hardest crossword puzzles she could muster in the evening; a woman who went dictionary shopping on a regular basis; a woman who freely admitted she violated the vows of marriage with Shakespeare; a woman for whom there was no better place than these rooms, which housed every possible constellation in the universe of language—this was heaven. As soon as Ben realized that his wife, who had something akin to an allergic reaction to procrastination, would have chosen the labs as her place of employment, he recalled the orientation speech and beamed with pride, certain that she aced the requisite exams. She must have blown them away with her knowledge of, and sensitivity to, the nuances that divide and link the different languages. He imagined the ongoing, interdepartmental quarrels over Marian's services and was awed by the range of possibilities that must have been set before his intellectually curious wife. Unsure of which department she had chosen to endow with her skills, he decided to poke around all five departments.

His first stop was the main department, where the long line of people snaking down the corridor made him cringe. Raising his head, he understood why the dead kept coming en masse, and why, despite the thoughts perched on the tip of their tongues, to judge from their troubled gazes, they waited in silence. The floor-to-ceiling sign read: BABEL—DON'T BE LATE OR YOU'LL DISCOMBOBULATE. Ben had a hunch that these tongue-tied dead brought the nasty habit of perpetual postponement with them from the old world. He assumed these dead were in a silent race against the clock to have their microchip updated before a full year of sand ran through the hourglass, forever trapping them in a languageless wasteland. Ben, at first, had a hard time imagining what would happen to a dillydallier; two hours later, the vein in his temple threatening to explode, his curiosity was more than satisfied, and he was left longing for a handful of extra-strength aspirin. But before witnessing the communication meltdown, he visited the second department, where the sign read LIFE AND DEATH AT THE HANDS OF THE TONGUE. Here, too, he was greeted by a divine hush. He turned to one of the dead and asked in a whisper about the department. The man smiled, opened his mouth, and pointed to the gap between his top and bottom teeth. Ben looked at him perplexedly and whispered, "I don't . . ." Before he had a chance to complete his thought, Ben felt the mute's dainty fingers clasp his tongue.

Coming out of the elevator on the third floor, he felt a rush of longing for the speechless. The This-and-That Department surged with unprecedented verbal activity. The thin dividers between the ten different lines failed to contain the ghastly commotion, and Ben, who had taken it upon himself to stand in each line to see if his wife was one of the verbal therapists receiving the loquacious patients, had to shield his ears from the tumult. For her sake, Ben hoped that Marian wasn't a staff member in the cacophonous department but, spurred on by the steady drum roll of his own curiosity, he tamped down his rising aversion and waited patiently for five hours till he reached the front of the line, where he could inquire about his wife. While waiting, he endured a conversation between two former mutes, who, after a lifetime of silence, were so eager to make up for missed time that even when they tried to slow their chatter, they found they had lost control of their tongues. Ben was surrounded by people in the throes of their own personal Babel story. They were plagued by an array of disorders, the result of their dalliance: some people's lips formed sentences that came out in a dozen different languages; some had voices that produced a disharmonic blend of languages and accents; some stirred a disorienting brew of the chip's one-hundred-plus tongues, produced in a single sputtering stream of gibberish; some had an obsessive need to rhyme; some spoke in a sped-up pattern of speech that operated at three times its normal pace; some in a slowed down version that came out at half time; some could only make palindrome-ridden conversation; some dropped vowels, consonants, and letters; and, strangest of all, some exhibited an awful lack of synchronicity between their flapping lips and their voices.

In the elevator on the way up to the fourth floor, the throbbing in his temple spread down to the back of his neck. He couldn't bear the thought that the next floor might be equally nerve-wracking. He closed his eyes, imagined his wife massaging his temples with one of the many aromatic oils she kept on hand for steamy nights, and left the elevator with a smile.

To his surprise, the hall was empty, and he made his way slowly, soaking up the silence. Soon enough, he learned that the hallway's thirty-two doors were part of an academic maze of etymologists, philologists, and phoneticians who bored into the irregularities of language. Finding no trace of his wife in any of the rooms, he bounded up to the top floor, a trace of tension in his stride. The fifth floor, known as The Uppertongue, held thousands of experts, bent over tomes, engaged in fierce arguments in a multitude of languages. When Ben tried to ask about the department's specialty, he was sent to the lab director's office. The jovial and effusive old man explained with mounting zeal that he and many of his colleagues, dead and alive, felt humanity had no need for such a profusion of languages, especially in the current age of technology. Now, through the sheer brilliance of their communication programs, they were able to create a Father Tongue, a meticulous gleaning of words from all known languages, melded into a single, new language that would house all the needs of expression under one roof. Suppressing the urge to engage the professor in a Socratic conversation about the distinct advantages of each and every language, Ben muttered something about being in a rush and did an about-face. He walked into the elevator and pressed the basement button, deflated but unwilling to yield.

The sign on the green basement door made him laugh. He had spent the better part of a day in the lab's different departments while, all along, just beneath him, in the basement, was the Human Resources Department. He sat down opposite a bespectacled woman, who asked how she could be of service. He wanted to know if there was a Marian Mendelssohn in any of the Other World's several thousand labs.

She typed in the name, waited thirty seconds, and shrugged.

"None?" he whispered, his voice caught in his throat.

"There are twenty-seven Marians," she said, pulling out the computer printout, "but none of them are Mendelssohns."

"And Corbin?" he asked, "Might there be a Marian Corbin?"

Her eyes flitted across the page. She shook her head. "Sorry."

Ben scanned the printed page, his fingers twitching with the urge to shred it. He got up, thanked her, and left. Fatigue tugged at his shoulders. Since he arrived in this strange world, he had managed to hear the life story of a bitter Belgian, meet a Marilyn Monroe look-alike, and tour every corner of the Multilingual Laboratories' departments. But he had yet to justify his decision to come to the Other World. No one told him that if he ended his life he'd still have to search for his wife. He was sure she would be there, without strange announcements, mathematical living arrangements, and disappointing laboratories. No one prepared him for this wholly unnecessary surprise.

On the way to the nearest bus station, his thoughts were truncated by a kick in the ankle. He smiled at the bowlegged kid who had bumped into him and then continued chasing his ball. Turning toward the young boy, he wondered how it was that the beautiful park to his right was so full of young children. The child, in the meanwhile, let his ball go, stared straight at Ben, and marched toward him with remarkable determination. Ben couldn't understand why his heart was pounding so, as if he feared harm. He flashed an innocent smile at the child, who returned a smile, continued toward his right leg, let out a long gasp of wonder, and latched on. Ben wanted to pat the five-year-old's head, but something about his viselike grip made him flinch. Meanwhile, the child buried his head of thick brown hair in Ben's leg as though he were trying to dig himself into his thigh. Ben had no idea what he wanted from him. The boy just held fast to his leg and made *Y . . . aaah* noises as though he had found a treasure whose worth only he knew.

Ben looked up and surveyed the park. Panic made its way into his throat as he looked at the kids and grownups frolicking only a few yards away. What would they think of him if they saw him like this, in the middle of the street, a naked kid clutching his leg? He chuckled and stuttered, "Hey, little guy . . . I gotta go . . . could you . . . l-let go of my leg?"

The kid ignored him. Ben prayed for the ground to open up and swallow him. He tried nudging the kid off his leg. Realizing, though, that if he didn't use some force there'd be no end to this bizarre act of magnetism, he pushed him away with both hands. The kid looked up at him, hurt, and tried to get close to him again. Ben raised a finger in the air and said, "Don't! I'm very sorry, kid, but I don't want to be accused of God knows what kind of perversions. Promise me you won't do it again, okay? It's not alright to run around and hug strangers' legs, you know."

Realizing that the kid was gearing up for a third charge, Ben took off, only to find that the kid had the acceleration of a salivating cheetah hot on the heels of a well-haunched antelope. Ben stopped four hundred yards from the improvised starting line and, as the kid approached, warned him in the sternest voice he had, "Go away! Get out of here, kid! If you come near me now, you'll be sorry!"

The kid ground to a halt. Ben gesticulated wildly, shooing him away. "Get out of here! I'm not in the mood for this crap!"

The kid didn't move. He just continued to cast his uncomprehending eyes at the man, who, for his part, sighed in relief when a multi-wheel arrived. He found a seat and watched the kid run back to the park, sit down next to an elderly woman, and hug her. The multi-wheel pulled away from the stop and Ben leaned back, closed his eyes, and decided it was high time he headed home. Maybe the next day would bring a fresh idea about how to find Marian.

9

The Sleep of
the Guillotinesse

For five full weeks, Bessie hardly slept. The few times she succumbed to exhaustion were brief and she dreamed of guillotines. The severed dreams looped back and forth over the same awful ground. She escorts her husband to the decapitation device, raises a beguiling eyebrow, says there's no choice, asks him to place his head in the proper spot, trumpets the start of the execution, and lowers the glinting blade on his neck.

Yet again, she woke from the chilling three-minute vision, and glared at her eerily tranquil Rafael. He had no idea how many times she had calmly gone through the motions of killing him, as though she truly wanted to see him dead. She hated the dream and even more so its meaning. She treated the pictures of the execution like a violent rape of her mind, perpetrated by her swirling conscience. Then she was forced into open-eyed vigilance by her husband's comatose state. The recurring nightmare was nothing more than the ring of her alarm clock. Yet the abiding pattern surprised her each time anew. She fell asleep, she saw the guillotine, she woke up. Aside from the short bursts of sleep, she was awake at all times. She talked to Rafael, she went down to the cafeteria and ate, she went home for a shower and to change her clothes, she returned to his bedside. Three days ago she heeded the nurse's advice and left the hospital for a night. She stepped into the bedroom, yawned, and lay down on the bed with obvious delight. For the past fifty years, the bed, which welcomed her with open arms, had known all of her secrets. She stretched her back pleasurably, in a way she had managed to forget since the stroke. The bed moaned beneath her, and Bessie felt herself merge with mattress, a wondrous sense of comfort engulfing her. The sweet sensation didn't last long. Bessie stole a glance in the direction of her husband's side of the bed and wondered how she could allow herself to rest in a double bed that had never known loneliness, a bed that in a single solitary instant made her feel like an invasive miscreant. After all, it was impossible to ignore the riotous absence at her side, the sheet was too taut, the pillow too chilled, and all she could hear was the sound of her own breathing. She tossed and turned, all too aware of her ears and the way they rejected the silence. She tried to conjure Rafael's nighttime wheeze, that agitated donkey braying that had faithfully escorted her into a less clamorous world thousands of times before, but wasn't surprised when the silence proved too loud. "How can you possibly expect to remember the wheeze of a man who can't breathe unassisted?" she asked out loud, getting out of the bed and calling a cab to the hospital.

"The prunish nurse will be back soon," she said, looking out the window at the early light of dawn rising out of a thick fog, and then whispered, "Rafael, I don't like her. She hasn't done me any wrong and she always asks me how I'm doing, but there's something about her, not sure what, maybe it's just her size. She's tiny and she leaves the impression of a frail woman, but she isn't what she seems. She won't stop consoling me, as though you were already gone. She says that medically speaking you're almost entirely dead. She explained something about the brain. You'll be fully dead when all of your brain dies. Looks like you just can't stop yourself from rebelling, ah? You're keeping us all guessing with the living part of your brain." She held her silence for a while and then resumed speaking, enthused. "You're not going to believe who came to visit you. Yehoshua Dolev, the owner of that gallery that had your exhibition up five years ago, remember? Anyway, the gall on that guy. He came up here to ask me who you were leaving your work to, as if I care, as if I had any idea, as if you were already gone. I asked him to leave, but he said he'd be back. Next day Rafi was here, you know, from the museum. He also wanted to talk wills. Look how popular you are. For five years you didn't exchange a word with them and now all of a sudden you're a star. In this country, you've got to be unconscious to regain recognition. Not that you need any of that business. Okay, I won't bother you. I'll go out and get some air. Just pray she doesn't drive me crazy again today. Even though I think she's bound to relax a bit. There's someone new on life support. Came in last night. His wife needs a lesson or two. She comes and goes all the time. Never stays for more than two hours. So, you see how it is? With my luck, he'll probably wake up, and you? You'll probably wait till they bury me and then you'll get up and go look for some young girl, ah, Kolanski?"

"Good morning," a small voice behind her said. Bessie stiffened. The nurse always managed to creep up and surprise her. She greeted Ann similarly, her eyes glazed with resentment. Ann approached Rafael's bed and purred, "How are you today?"

Bessie shrugged. "I think I'll go down to the cafeteria. I'd like a cup of tea."

She walked out of the hospital and sat down on the front steps, gazing at the quiet street, watching it rise to life until her weighted eyelids were pulled close. Another guillotine came crashing down on her husband's neck. Jolted awake, she checked her surroundings as though a blindfold has just been removed and put a trembling hand on her chest right after the small voice worked its way into her ear canal.

"Nightmare?"

Again she hadn't noticed the nurse, who sat down beside her two minutes earlier and was getting ready to wake her.

"Yes, nightmare," Bessie affirmed, preparing to change the subject.

"Bessie, I think you need to let go," the nurse said.

Bessie didn't turn in her direction. "I'm of a different mind," she murmured, her eyes fixed on the trickle of traffic.

The nurse's voice went up a notch. "Bessie, Rafael's chances of awakening are negligible. Infinitesimal. I don't want to mislead you. How old is he again?"

"Eighty-three next week."

"You really think a man of his age has any chance of awakening? He's already . . ."

"Reached old age? He can keep on going."

"Not in his condition. He wasn't in good health in the first place. Bessie, for over five weeks he's been lying there lifelessly. I have no problem artificially respirating him for several more years, but logic dictates a different course of action."

"I'm expecting a miracle. Don't taint it with logic."

"But you're not a young woman either. This type of grind will take a toll on your health, too."

"My health is not up for discussion right now."

"Your health depends on his. You need to understand that your situation is not going to improve because his is not going to."

"From where, exactly, do you draw that kind of certainty?"

"Experience. Rafael could lay there for a month, two months, a year and . . . nothing. Then, one fine day, the machine won't help anymore . . . and, you know."

"I don't."

"Bessie, have you given some thought to your life after he's gone?"

"No."

"Really?"

"It's always been clear to me I'd die before him."

"Clear?"

"When you live with someone for so long his presence becomes as permanent as nature. The trees are always there, the sky's always there, Rafael's always there."

"You can't imagine the world without Rafael?"

"I don't want to imagine that kind of world."

"Bessie, excuse me if what I'm about to say sounds rude, but he's not going to wake up. And worse still, he's suffering right now for no reason."

"Suffering? How do you know he's suffering? You've been in his condition?"

"I've seen dozens of people in his condition. People who were so close to death but due to some sort of complication remained suspended between heaven and earth. As far as I see it, he's stuck in the throes of death. Your husband's been suffering for over five weeks because he's not being released, not being allowed to rest in peace and quiet. True, no one can guess what's going on in his mind, but one doesn't need to be a mind reader to know with near certainty that if all he's left behind is his shell, a body without life, then he's probably not interested in staying with us."

"So you're saying that my childish insistence is making him suffer?"

"I wouldn't put it quite that way. But I'd say that when the fate of a loved one is at stake, we need to take ourselves out of the equation. Bessie, this delay is fundamentally unnecessary."

"Alright already. Enough. You're stuffing me to the gills with guilt."

"I'm sorry."

"Don't be sorry, we're talking about the biggest disaster of my life, all pleasantries are off the table. I'm losing my mind. He survived the Germans but he can't survive this damned stroke?"

"It's not a storm you can weather. You either snap out of it or not."

"Don't you understand that I know all this baloney? I don't want to hear what I already know. I just don't want to kill him and then discover that there was a chance he would've woken up, even a whole year later. Ann, I've got all the patience in the world, but then you come along and tell me he's suffering, in the throes of death, stuck in limbo, and that's not helping me at all. Not in the slightest."

"I'm being of service when I tell you that the chance you're talking about doesn't exist. And that all the patience in the world won't bring Rafael back. Bessie, Rafael's dead. You need to face that fact. And another thing, Bessie. No one's killing anybody."

"Euthanasia?"

"What about it?"

"It's not sanctioned by the law. I'm just asking because I want to make sure we're not, God forbid . . ."

"Bessie, the only crime we're committing is that we're allowing him to suffer. Let's send him on his way."

"On his way?"

"Yes, Bessie. I'm sure he lived a full and honorable life. Let's make sure he'll stay true to that in death, too."

"And what about doubt?"

"I think you've enjoyed its benefits long enough, no?"

Bessie accepted the insult. The fact that she had to balance her hostility toward the frigid nurse with the undeniable chinks in her own arguments infuriated her. Ann mumbled something about being on call in a certain room and, as she turned back toward the gloomy building, asked her to consider what they had discussed. Bessie watched her retreat. "Who do you think you are?" she hissed under her wisp of a mustache. "Rafael doesn't even know you. You're going to kill my Kolanski? A small, superfluous woman like you?"

When she came back from lunch, a piece of yolk stuck between her front teeth, the small, superfluous woman handed Bessie a medical form in quadruplicate. Bessie asked what the papers were for. Ann fished through her pockets, pulled out a pen, and extended it to her. Bessie's eyes wandered between the lines, ever downward, to the bottom of the page, where they stopped at the thick black line. With practiced tactfulness, Ann slipped out of the room, leaving the sorrowful old woman to deal with the sickening formality of death. Bessie wondered if the nurse's muted action was yet another stage, bolder than its predecessors, in the nurse's systematic campaign. She held the pen with the tips of her fingers, as though it were a bloodied blade, finding it hard to believe that such an innocent object could stir up such real and immediate danger. This pen was to seal the fate of a man who had always been repulsed by signatures, a man who claimed that anyone who saw his paintings should recognize that he had created them. Even when presented with bank forms and the like, he would make an offended face and scribble *Fuck You* in the looping shape of an impressive signature. Bessie was the only one who knew that he never signed his name. When one day she remarked that a time would come when someone noticed his little stunt, he narrowed his eyes and said, "This from the mouth of a woman who used to fill entire notebooks with her ridiculously expressionistic signature attempts? A woman who hoped that she and her girlfriends would find the perfect shape for their names and that their personalities would follow suit?"

Weighing the irony of the moment, Bessie grimaced—her clean, pedantic signature, which was always a target for her husband's loving arrows, might now prove to be lethal. She read the form until she knew it by heart, as though dressing and undressing each word gave her control over it, enabling her to water down its malice.

By early evening she was forced to admit that the words had gotten the better of her. Her head spinning, she got up and left the hospital, passing by Ann's smiling face and trudging to the nearest bus stop. The ride lasted an eternity. All she wanted to do was sleep. Her eyelids toyed with her sadistically, rising and falling, enabling her to see her fellow passengers as blurry dots of liveliness and then giving in to the comforting darkness of improvised night for a brief instant. But how could she sleep without Rafael's soundtrack? For some reason she was sure that the solution to her problem could be found in the archives of her shared life with the artist, whose cavernous nostrils, filled with stalagmites and stalactites that hindered the flow of air, made him snore. Somewhere, in one of those drawers, she was sure she would find a way to sleep again. Still caught up in the thought of Kolanski's old lullabies, her gaze settled on the young man sitting opposite her. The pleather and chrome he was wearing emitted a slight whiff of Gestapo, but his expression softened the effect and she stifled a smile at the sight of him. There was pleasure scrawled across his face as his head bobbed. That's when she saw the tiny headphones buried amidst a row of a dozen identical earrings. His head gyrations came to a stop, his fingers stomped on the appropriate buttons, and he pulled out the disc and inserted a new one. Bessie's gaze followed the disc and just like that she wanted to press her gratitude on the young man with a kiss.

Half awake, she got off the bus and hustled home, Rafael's fifty-year-old voice careening down the halls of her memory, defending himself. "You're talking nonsense. I snore?"

She ran to the kitchen, snapped open cupboards and drawers, seeking hungrily, smiling at the sound of her own answer. "One day I'll record you and then you'll believe me when I say you sound like an asthmatic dragon."

She ran to the workroom, flipped through the overflowing drawers of paint, laughing at the mental picture of the artist's face, when the screeching sound of his trunk came over the tape. She smiled triumphantly as her fingers grabbed hold of the dusty cassette in the bottom drawer. She wiped it clean, brought the equally dusty tape recorder from the studio, laid it on Rafael's side of the bed, put the tape in, turned off the light, and pressed PLAY. Forty-five joyous minutes of sharp snoring filled the room with miraculous life and Bessie fell asleep, her face lit with tears.

But, in sleep, Bessie went to the familiar site. Rafael was marching erect as a battle horse, the hunchbacked, downcast executioner behind him, the guillotine waiting ravenously. The bucket at its feet craved his splendid head. Bessie was buried in her robe, cloaked in shame, yearning for the end of the despicable ceremony. Rafael was already standing on the platform, his head ready for decapitation. But when the guillotinesse hesitated, he whistled to her just as he did the first time he laid eyes on her virginal beauty, on the secluded beach in Brighton, a rosy-cheeked girl who had unknowingly infiltrated his landscape portrait. Excited, she advanced toward him, a straight line spanning the space between four loving eyes, and now Rafael was the one smiling victoriously. The lady executioner wasn't sure of his intention, and he nodded in the cramped quarters afforded his head, as though he were urging her to lower the blade. She asked, "Are you sure?"

His smile widened. The guillotine fell.

Six hours later, at noon of the following day, Ann walked out of a room at the end of the hall just as Bessie stepped into the hall's opposite end. Their eyes met and they approached each other in measured paces, nodded, and carried on.

When the nurse turned and called out to her opponent, the latter looked straight at her. "Yes?" she asked.

Ann scratched her forehead in false embarrassment and coughed up a weak giggle. "Did I, by any chance, leave my pen with you?"

Bessie giggled back. "I think you did." After a minute of simulated searching in her bag, she pulled out the pen and gave it to her.

"Well," the nurse ventured, "did you use it?"

Bessie nodded.

10

The Mad Hop

Ben found his apartment with ease. City of June 2001, Circle 21, Building M, Floor 24, Apartment 7, BM. Pressing his thumb to the hole in the door, he tried to shake the image of himself as a burglar. The door popped open and he walked in, closing it quickly behind him. Groping through the darkness, he found the light switch, flipped it on, and leaped back in surprise, throwing a consoling hand to the back of his head where he had smacked into the door.

Marian stood in the center of the apartment, beautiful and radiant as ever. "Hi, sweetheart," she said.

Ben stared at her in disbelief.

"So," she said, striking a come-hither pose, "did you come all this way just to get clocked on the back of the head?"

Ben walked straight toward her, holding her gaze, eager to verify with his hands what his eyes had registered. Only when he caught the raspberry scent off her skin did he know for sure that she was there, in the flesh, a step away. For the better part of an hour, the two of them hugged and giggled, like kids who had pulled off the ultimate practical joke. Marian bit his ear lightly. "Mmm, how I missed this little lobe . . ."

Ben arched his neck in the direction of her mouth, offering more skin, and then, as though unsatisfied with the intensity of her emotion, he asked dryly, "How did you know I was here?"

Her lips sought his, and between long pulls she whispered, "The Announcer."

Ben smiled knowingly. "You heard the announcement?"

Marian didn't answer. Busy reacquainting herself to his new and improved form, kissing every old nook rendered fascinating by time, she accompanied each kiss with a metallic intoning: "John Dart, Mahmud Davul, Svetlana Devchokshenski, Francoise Deveroux . . ."

"Just a second," Ben said, pushing her away. "Marian, what's going on? Why are you saying all of these names?"

She smiled angelically, continuing, "Deidre Didskin, Bernie Dole, Manny Dole, Sam Dole."

"Marian, stop, please," he said before being hit with another wave of names.

"Marian, I'm begging you, please stop. Stop right now or I'm leaving."

His threats making no impression on her, he walked to the door, stunned by the sheer number of Doles in this world and by the amount of them that had left the world together. He swung it open, went outside, heard seven more names, and slammed it behind him.

The noise shook him and he opened his eyes. In the background he heard the lifeless voice of the Announcer reading the list of names in a monotone and he knew that there was no way Marian had heard his name, even if she had been listening for it. Ten names and the brain sealed itself off. Ben got off the floor, exhaled as he stretched, wandered around his empty apartment, and considered his next move. The Announcer's voice, which was still ringing in his ears, and his vivid memory of the dream, brought a resolution to mind: from now on he'd hit 3 once on the godget each time he wanted to sleep. He'd also get a radio to drown out the jarring intonations and the inevitable headaches that accompanied them. For now, though, a shower would suffice.

A hot shower always had a soothing effect on him. Under the warm stream of water he thought of the moment he pulled the trigger and retraced his steps to see if he had missed anything. As he finished his mental checklist, he turned off the faucet, remembered he had no towel, and rushed out of his apartment, pushing 2 on the godget ten times as he stepped into the elevator. For twenty-three floors he was subjected to the fat sax player's wanderings up and down the musical scales. Ben preferred the piano player at Marian's building; when the doors opened, at long last, he charged out of the elevator and boarded the nearest multi-wheel heading in the direction of the central bus station. Ten minutes later, he thanked the driver as he got off, and, in his haste, while crossing the avenue, got run over twice, recovered both times, sprinted through a gaggle of kids, and pulled to a stop at the edge of the crisply manicured lawn leading to the doors of the white room.

Thousands of moonstruck dead, fresh out of the white room, stumbled to the multi-wheels waiting behind Ben. They cast quizzical looks in his direction, trying to figure out why a dead man was walking against the flow. Had Ben been in a more playful mood, he would have told them he was tired of being dead but, in need of the love-struck Belgian, he pocketed the idea. Four hundred and seven plane crash victims later a smile came to his lips. He threw a hand in the air and hollered, "Robert!"

The Belgian, surveying the crowd with weighty eyes, swiveled his wheelchair and smiled back.

Ben walked up to him and clasped his hand. "How you doing?"

"Not bad, *mon ami,* not bad," Robert said, "how 'bout you?"

"Could be a lot better."

"Hmm . . . ," Robert said, sucking his cigar and pursing his lips knowingly. "I see you haven't found her yet."

"No." Ben winced. "I need a favor."

Robert extended his hand. "Help me up? His card's in the cigar box."

"You have no idea how grateful I am," Ben said, smiling, as Robert produced the card. "Is there anything I can do for you?"

Robert grinned. "Find her and bring her by for a visit. I could use a shot in the arm."

"She'll come," Ben said, placing an assuring hand on the Belgian's shoulder, "I'm sure of it."

Robert shut his eyes. "That's all I wanted to hear."

Just before they parted, Ben suggested they exchange thumbprints on the telefinger. Robert shook his head. "You won't be coming to see me again."

At seven of noon, Ben reached his destination and knocked on door number 45 three times. The door opened to reveal a short, moonfaced pudgy man with quick blue eyes behind thick glass lenses, puffy, protruding lips, and a squeaky clean, hairless scalp. The man looked forward and twisted his lip, his chin quivering in disgust. His head was level with Ben's belly button. Ben took a step back and cleared his throat.

"I'm looking for the Mad Hop."

The small man looked up, suspicion draped all over his face. "What do you want with him?"

"I'm told he can track down missing people, and I can't find my wife."

"You should have kept a better eye on her," he spat.

Ben, chastised, kept his mouth shut, appraising the sixty-year-old man in silence. After a moment of mutual inspection, Ben smiled. "You're English, right?"

"And you're Israeli," he said flatly. "Even Babel can't kill that accent."

Ben, miffed that the strange man had not yet invited him in, took a step forward, amused by the midget's quick retreat. "I thought . . ."

"Who gave you this address?" the man cut him short.

"Robert," Ben responded, his brow wrinkling at the man's condescending chuckle.

"Oh . . . *Le Malade Imaginaire.*"

"I think you're mistaken," Ben said. "That was *The Miser.*"

"Forget it," he said, chuckling again as he put a hand on his invisible neck. "Small man, big mouth."

"Robert?"

"No, me" the pugnacious host said, shaking Ben's hand with paternal might. "Samuel Sutton, and I'd appreciate it if you refrained from making jokes about the initials."

"Ben Mendelssohn, nice to meet you."

"Before you ask any questions," Samuel said, raising his index finger, "I'm the Mad Hop to clients and Samuel to everyone else. Now, let's go inside before I strain my neck."

Ben followed him into the apartment, which had been converted into an expansive office, furnished with three oak desks, each with a computer, four bookshelves lined with files, two faxes, a Xerox machine, and several towering stacks of paper. Sitting down, Ben's feet encountered some more packages of paper under the Mad Hop's desk, filling out the kingdom of office equipment he had established.

"I got to tell you, this place reminds me of the previous world more than any place I've seen," Ben remarked.

The Mad Hop smiled. "I hope that's a compliment." Without further ado, he pulled a brown pad out of a drawer and cleared his throat.

"How old are you, Mr. Mendelssohn?"

"Forty, and call me Ben."

"Where do you live?"

"June 2001. Circle twenty-one. M building, twenty-fourth floor, apartment seven."

"You don't waste time."

"True. My wife and I are in love and I need to find her."

"When did your wife arrive?"

"March seventeenth, 2000."

"How did you come to this world?"

"Shot myself."

"Hmm . . . courageous lad. Why'd you do it?"

"I wanted to join Marian."

"Marian? Your wife. Marian Mendelssohn. Maiden name?"

"Marian Corbin."

"And I thought the days when love could kill were long gone."

"You were wrong."

"Why did you wait so long?"

"At first I was in shock. I didn't know what to do. Slowly, a decision took shape. Six months after her death, I had already decided what to do."

"And still you waited another year . . ."

"Marian always wanted me to work out. She claimed my body had great potential but I was lazy. I didn't have the patience to go to the gym. The whole thing seemed ridiculous. A few months after she died, I remembered that on our last night together, we were in bed, and as she ran her hand over my chest, she asked, "Will you think less of me if I call you Van Damme in bed?" I worked out for a year. On her last birthday I committed suicide as a present to her. I'm sure she'll be shocked when she sees me."

"Just a second. I want to understand this. All of the beefing up was for her? For the suicide?"

"Yes, and before you ask, I don't know why, but I was sure that life continues."

"Did you consider what would have happened if you had been wrong?"

"Nothing. I would've died in good shape."

"I've got to say, I've heard my fair share of stories but this one . . . how long were you married?"

"Eleven years. Happy ones."

"And in the previous world, what line of work were you in?"

"I was a righter. An epilogist. I wrote endings for books, screen-plays . . ."

"Interesting. I'd think someone like you might take death as something absolute. The grand finale, if you like."

"Bit simplistic, don't you think?"

"We'll only be able to know that in the future."

"Look, I've come to you because in the two days I've been in this strange place, I've tried desperately to find Marian and failed. I went to her apartment; she doesn't live there anymore. I went to the multilingual labs; she doesn't work there."

"The labs?"

"She was an English teacher. She was . . . she's in love with language."

"I see. Kids?"

"No."

"Sorry to hear that."

"Under the circumstances I suppose it's for the best."

"Because if you had a kid you wouldn't be sitting here opposite me, asking for help?"

Ben nodded and watched the quick strokes of the Mad Hop's pen across his pad.

"How did she get here?"

"Sorry?"

"How did your wife die?"

"An accident."

"Could you be more specific?"

"A car accident."

"A car accident. I see."

Ben heard a strange purring sound emanating from under the desk. He bent down, expecting to find a cat, but saw nothing. The deep purr only got stronger and, as fear started to whirl inside him, he watched the Mad Hop's facial muscles quiver like jelly. Before he could make any sense out of the situation, the investigator's cheeks inflated like Dizzy's before a long blue note, and in front of his disbelieving eyes the fat man broke into laughter, shaking the desk with his full-bodied cough, pounding it with his fleshy fist, while he kicked the horrified righter's armchair.

Ben shot up from his seat. "Samuel, is everything alright?"

The Mad Hop, his flabby cheeks coated in tears of mirth, pointed to a drawer by Ben's side and rasped "Take it . . . take it out."

Ben opened the drawer and stared at the gun. He pulled it out and set it on the desk.

"No," the Mad Hop yelled, his voice rising, the color of his cheeks deepening from crimson to purple, "Pick it up! Fire it . . . fire!"

Ben took the pistol and aimed at the Mad Hop's feet. Groaning, choking on his own laughter, he said, "The head, you idiot, the head."

Ben set the pistol's sights right between the Mad Hop's wispy eyebrows and pulled the trigger. His fat head hit the table with a thump. Ben threw himself onto the armchair, let his head fall back, and closed his eyes.

Less than a minute later, the bass voice resurfaced from the opposing couch. "I apologize, Ben, for the poor taste I've exhibited."

Ben opened his eyes and sighed. He thought his rest would last longer than a minute, but the Mad Hop shoved the gun across the desk and ordered him, in a dry voice, to put it back in the drawer.

"What was so funny?" Ben asked.

The Mad Hop sighed, too. "The human soul has its way. When you grow up in a conservative home, terrorized by your parents, who have given you nothing but a strict diet of discipline, you develop certain habits that come back and bite you in the ass. You asked why I laughed. Ever since I left home on my twentieth birthday, I've picked up certain neuroses, such as uncontrollable bouts of laughter. Are you with me? From me you can expect devotion, attention, understanding, but not, alas, tact. You'll tell me that your wife died in an accident, and I'll cackle like a poop. You have no idea how many times I've been thrown out of funerals, booted out of weddings, tossed out of beds. At least here there's a way to put an end to these attacks . . . till the next time."

"Have you tried to get treatment?"

The Mad Hop blinked twice, flipped through the scribbles on his pad, and answered without raising his head. "Too late. Ben, last question. Do you by any chance have a picture of Marian?"

Ben smiled. "I wish."

The Mad Hop raised his head slowly, pinning him with a grave look. "I apologize up front for the cliché," he said, "but she's a needle in a haystack. It's hard for me to turn down this kind of challenge, but I'm not making any promises. Finding missing persons in this world is ten times harder than in the previous one, which is precisely why I'm willing to take this case."

After a brief pause, he continued, "Back there, in the old world, I worked for thirty-seven years as an investigator, and the truth is, despite all the experience, I never really made it up to the Premier League. I had a job, a small office in Manchester, a moderate caseload, mostly dead boredom, the dullest cases imaginable. When I moved to London, I couldn't compete with the big offices. The clients started to thin out. From eighty-three to eighty-four I didn't have a single case, believe it or not. I learned my lesson well. When I got here, I vowed to myself I'd be the best private investigator the Other World had ever seen, and, over the past fifteen years, I've established a reputation most wouldn't even dream of. I unraveled cases where the victims had no idea who would ever want them gone; I found missing persons in places that nobody–alive or dead–would ever consider; and I changed my name. Few people know that Mad Hop is actually an acronym, comprised of my favorite detectives–Marple, Dalgliesh, Holmes, and Poirot."

"I had no idea" Ben said.

"What's important," the Mad Hop said, getting up and walking toward the door, "is that money never meant much to me. I've always investigated for the right reasons, unadulterated curiosity. Nothing satisfies me more than the clean annihilation of question marks. The path from question to answer, though, winds through a dark and bewildering forest. Every good investigator needs to take his cues from the helicopter."

"From the helicopter?"

"Yes, to hover above, to see the full picture. To see the forest and not just the trees. . . ."

"I get it, I get it." Ben smiled. "So is that how you plan to find my Marian?"

The Mad Hop opened the door and pulled the godget out of a side drawer nearby. "For starters let's exchange prints."

After they'd done so, he put a fat finger to his lips and hummed an unrecognizable tune. Then, speaking authoritatively, he said, "You said you're forty and that she died a year and a half ago. I want you to go to the nearest Vie-deo, take out tape thirty-nine and come back here. We need an updated picture of her."

"When do you want me back?"

"As far as I'm concerned, come back here in three hours. You can do that, can't you?"

"I suppose."

Noting the haze of confusion settling on Ben's face, he smiled and pointed down at the godget. "If you press the telefinger once, you'll get the time."

"Hold on a second, I thought it was noon now . . . ," Ben said, staring at the little screen, which posted the time as a quarter to eight.

The Mad Hop giggled, a cuddly form of malice. "And I thought the dead don't lie."

Ben left the office, pretending not to have heard the Mad Hop's remark. "So we'll see each other in three hours?"

The Mad Hop nodded and shut the door. All the way to the Vie-deo, an inner voice nipped at Ben's mind, wondering, "How, in God's name, did he know I was lying?"

11

Extracted Wisdom

"What are you doing?" the tall uprooter asked, taking in the hideous gyrations of his coworker's behind.

The short uprooter soured his face and pulled his head up from the ground. "It's none of your business."

"Like hell it isn't . . . ," the tall man said, stomping his foot. "I never seen you move around like that before. Looks like something's stuck. . . ."

"Don't say it," the short man said, cutting him off and resuming the side-to-side motion, his eyes locked in concentration.

"Why you moving like that?" the tall man repeated.

"I told you it's none of your business!" the short one said, making sure his hips kept time. His colleague stomped down the first row of plot 2,605,327, pulled binoculars out of his backpack, surveyed the path, and spat, "nothing."

The short uprooter waddled up the opposite path, inspected it through his own binoculars and said softly, "nothing here either."

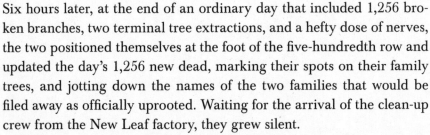

Six hours later, at the end of an ordinary day that included 1,256 broken branches, two terminal tree extractions, and a hefty dose of nerves, the two positioned themselves at the foot of the five-hundredth row and updated the day's 1,256 new dead, marking their spots on their family trees, and jotting down the names of the two families that would be filed away as officially uprooted. Waiting for the arrival of the clean-up crew from the New Leaf factory, they grew silent.

Silence, though, was rare and short lived in this dynamic forest, which was alive twenty-four hours a day with the slow crackle and pop of branches tearing free of their trunks, hanging at impossible angles, dancing in the toss of the hollow wind, linked by an unseen string—a strand of a spider's silk, a filament of lace, a filigree of sorts—to stronger, intertwined branches that, stooping, yearned to graze of the earth and yet still craved another last drop of life, draping the uprooters with the dying throes of tens of thousands, who clung, just barely, to the cords of their existence.

The tall uprooter never got used to the screeching music of disengagement. More than anything else, it reminded him of a jungle predator's padded shuffle as it prepared to pounce on its prey. He always talked, whistled, or hummed something to himself, in the vain hope that the ceremony of decay, which he witnessed daily, would not infiltrate his mind. Today, too, he had a song in mind. He was ready to mangle the tune when he realized there was no way he could get into it with his buddy gyrating his hips like a girl in a hula-hoop trance.

He knew his curiosity would never be satisfied if he approached his buddy through the usual channels, so he looked to both sides, made sure the horizon was clear of clean crew workers, and began swiveling his hips, perfectly mimicking his colleague's charm-free performance. The short uprooter noticed what he was doing, froze, and asked, "Why you ridiculing me? What kind of an alias are you?"

"Who's ridiculing you? Look how nicely I can spin it . . ."

"Spin it? What are you talking about?"

"I'm spinning an imaginary hoola-hoop around my waist."

"Why would you be doing something so silly?"

"Because swinging your hips without one, like you're doing, is way worse."

"But I have a reason."

Finally.

"Well, why you been shaking your butt like that all day?"

The short man buried his face in his hand and burst into tears. The uprooter lay a knobby hand on his friend's shoulder and asked softly, "57438291108, why are you crying?"

The short uprooter raised a pair of moist eyes and in a crushed voice said, "I hate him. He'll ruin everything."

"Who?"

"Elvis."

"Elvis?"

"Presley."

"The singer?"

"The singer!"

"What do you want with him?"

"You seen him dance?" the short one said, kicking the ground hard.

"You seen the man dance? You're lucky you weren't at the show last night. He moves his hips in a way that makes the ladies lose their minds. They went wild, pulled their hair, cried, screamed, hit; I thought I wasn't seeing straight. As soon as he started to dance the women in the crowd lost it. Totally! The aliases guarding the stage had to keep an inflamed group of savage women at bay, but one of them managed to break free, got to him, and wrapped herself around him. He laughed and sang her "Love Me Tender." When the song was over, he tried to break away from the yellowish woman. No dice. The crazy woman had rubbed something like ten jars of peanut butter all over her body. When he realized there was no shaking her free, he started to lose it, scream-ing at the aliases to get her off of him. In the end, he went backstage with the groupie still stuck to his body. Broke the show off early. I couldn't stop laughing, but 88888888 whipped around and scolded me, 'When you can move like him, then you can laugh all you want!' She told me I was immature and then gave me that iceberg-melting glare of hers. 'And you never take me out dancing anymore . . .' An hour later I found myself in some funky club with the hottest alias in 2000 shaking her thing in my face as I bopped from side to side like a robot in need of recircuiting. She forced me to dance the whole time we were there and then sprang an ultimatum on me—learn to move like Elvis, by next week, or be gone forever. In the morning I woke up and saw she had left."

The tall uprooter's smile held shades of compassion and jealousy. "Look, 57438291108, what are you going to do? You picked a tough alias. If she was just an ordinary alias, maybe, but 88888888 is amaz-ing. I don't want to hurt your feelings, but the fact that she left you twelve times over the course of the past decade is flattering."

"Flattering?" he squawked.

"Of course. She came back to you twelve times. There's no doubt about it. If she ever goes for good, she'll be turning her back on a super alias."

"There's something to that," he said, his eyes coming back to life. "The first time she left me it was 'cause I couldn't swim. The second time was 'cause I didn't know how to paint. After that it was cooking, chess, massage, the tuba, mimicking animals during sex, meditation, flo-ral arrangement, ambidexterity, effective use of metaphors, and now dance."

"And, since you were able to master the others, you'll do the same with dance."

"I don't think so," the short one said, shaking his head. "You saw how ridiculous I looked. I'll never manage to dance, not like the King. She's not coming back this time."

"You love her?"

"You know I would live for her."

"Then don't say you won't learn to dance."

"Who's going to teach me to dance?"

The tall uprooter smiled. "My alias has a friend who teaches a two-week course in lower body dance."

"Lower body dance?"

"Yeah, I think it's called Bootyriffic. My alias says there's this guy, Ricky Martin, that's been driving the women in the old world crazy and that he's got this new technique for shaking the bottom half of the body. From what I understand, half the course is devoted to his hip-thigh connection. I'll get you the rest of the details tomorrow."

"Thanks," the short one said, spreading a smile over a layer of anxiety. Worried about his noncooperative pelvis and dreading the thought of returning to an apartment without 88888888, he obsessed about his silent telefinger, longing for the sound of her fabulous voice in his ear.

"She's harassing me," he said out loud.

"What did you say?"

"Passive harassment. That's what she's doing to me. She's not calling, despite, and maybe because, she knows how badly I want to hear her voice. She'll disappear now for a week or two until I prove to her that I know how to dance. Then we'll have a happy period where all seems wonderful, and then she'll come up with a new requirement. I live in permanent fear of the next ultimatum. Maybe we weren't meant to be together. She's perfect and I'm in constant need of upgrading like some sort of defective alias."

"You think my alias doesn't try to change me? Like hell she don't. Only difference is she's not trying to turn me into a copy of herself. I think 88888888 might be a little too in love with herself. Who can blame her, right? But instead of arguing, you're always off trying to add another link in your long chain of skills. What I don't get is, why you don't ask her to put some new links in her own chain."

"She gives me her love . . ."

"Ha!" the tall one cried, lifting a satisfied finger in the air. "And you give her your love. But you know what the problem is with your love? It's unconditional! Maybe it's about time you lay down some conditions."

"Conditions? What kind of conditions am I going to lay down on perfection!"

"There ain't no perfection. And even if there was, you got to put some holes in it."

"How do you put holes in perfection?"

"You look for a weak spot and zero in on it."

"And in the meantime?"

"In the meantime?" the tall one said, flashing a toothy smile. "You need to teach your ass how to dance."

The short uprooter nodded sullenly, surveying the busy horizon. The clean-up crew arrived, packed the severed branches and the two additional trees onto their electric wheelbarrows, and hovered over to the next plot.

"Okay, we can go now," the tall one said, striding out of plot 2,605,327. Thirty seconds later he noticed that only a single shadow accompanied him. He furrowed his brow, turned around, and called out in surprise, "What's keeping you?"

12

The Charlatan

Turning the tape over to the Mad Hop, Ben couldn't rid his hands of apprehension. The investigator, all too aware of the repercussions of what he was about to do, pointed Ben in the direction of a nearby room, showed him to the sofa, and Ben, lowering himself, stared blankly at the widescreen TV.

The Mad Hop sat down beside Ben, ran his hand over the smooth surface of his head, and cleared his throat. "Any questions before we begin?"

"You bet," Ben said, pulling his eyes away from the screen and toward the small man's somber face. "During the introductory lecture they mentioned these life tapes. If you were alive for forty years, you have forty tapes, right? So, one tape contains a full year of my life?"

"Each tape documents a full year of your life," the Mad Hop said dryly, "except for your final year, unless of course you died on your birthday."

"I don't get it. How do you chronicle a full year on a single tape?"

The Mad Hop rolled his eyes and groaned. "You still haven't managed to grasp that this world is a little more advanced than the one you left two days ago? In the previous world, could you dictate your own weather? Could you decide on nightmare-free sleep? Could you speak a hundred different languages? Don't worry your pretty little head, you'll get used to all of their technological advances in due course. Think about it, Ben, how many TV addicts actually understand the process that brings the picture to their tube? I'd be willing to bet that a lot more people know who shot J.R. or why Jerry, Elaine, George, and Kramer were locked up, than how it works. . . ."

"What do you know about Seinfeld?" Ben asked. "You died in eighty-six, way before . . ."

The Mad Hop raised his right palm, stopping Ben in mid-speech. "You reckon the Other World deprives the dead of the fruits of the previous one? If that were the case, most of the residents here would be entertaining themselves with bonfires and wheel design. And if it's gossip you're after, then I'll have you know that Bach's crazy about techno, da Vinci advertises his inventions online, and Curie never misses an episode of *ER*. After you die, you get the best of both worlds, terrestrial and post-terrestrial."

Ben asked, "You said that in due course I'd get used to all of their inventions. What'd you mean by 'their'?"

"The aliases," the detective said, his face brightening.

"Oh, well that explains that," Ben said.

The Mad Hop laughed. "Sometimes I forget what a novice you are. The aliases are the ones in charge of the Other World. In effect, they control it."

Ben bit his lower lip. "What do you mean by 'control it'?"

"They run the show, might be a better way to put it," the Mad Hop said, lighting a Benson & Hedges. "Don't worry, you haven't arrived at some godforsaken galaxy. They're human beings, same as me and you. The only difference between us and them is in the way they got here."

"But why are they called *aliases* and, if we're already at it, how did they get here? You're not talking about a different life-form, are you?"

"Ben, I could go on forever about the aliases. But what's the point? You don't bother them and they don't bother you."

"And yet there's some sort of delineation, otherwise there wouldn't . . ."

"True, but it's meaningless. Believe me, Ben, they're the loveliest creatures I've met in my death. . . ."

"You're driving me nuts," Ben said childishly. "I want to see them!"

"You've seen them aplenty," the Mad Hop said, picking a piece of errant tobacco off his tongue. "The girl from the orientation lecture, for instance."

"She's an alias?" Ben asked, summoning a visual of the cold beauty. "She looked like a normal human."

"She is a normal human."

"And now you're going to tell me that they're responsible for the tapes," Ben said, narrowing his eyes.

"That's right. They film everything."

"How the hell do they film a person from his first moment till his death?" Ben cried.

After a moment, the Mad Hop inquired, "You settled?"

"Sorry for yelling. I just don't like this whole Big Brother thing, especially as it turns out he documents as well. It gives me the creeps."

"Ben, it isn't espionage. It's a bloody brilliant initiative. You can rewind your own life and understand all kinds of things you could not previously, because you were too engaged. Now you're on the outside looking in."

"Are you saying that the tapes help people look back at their old lives and soul search?"

"Yes, but for themselves, I should say, before you get carried away with deep religious ruminations."

"Oh, on the matter of religion, what about . . . ?"

"He wasn't revealed to you in life; no reason for Him to be revealed to you in death."

"So the unanswerable . . . ?"

"Remains so."

"You're saying nothing's changed?"

"True enough. Don't look for explanations. There are none. You'd do better accepting the unknowable and investing your all in the pursuit of happiness."

"You sound like you swallowed a barrel of fortune cookies."

The Mad Hop smiled and, looking at Ben's troubled face, sighed and asked, "What?"

"Did you ever ask them? How they film us, that is?"

"The aliases get insulted if you imply there's any difference between them and us. They'll just stay mum if you ask them how they manage to document our entire lives. But I've got a mate, an astronomer by trade, who's looked into the matter. He says he's got it figured out."

"Well?" Ben nudged him.

"His theory's quite simple. And crazy. He's sure every person's got a satellite star that follows them from birth to death. On the star there's a special camera that tracks the individual's life. On the day he dies, the star falls. You know, like a meteor. That's why, as he sees it, so many stars dot the sky."

Ben scowled. "Let's watch the tape," he said.

The Mad Hop nodded, shoved the tape into the mouth of the round machine, and hit PLAY. Ben leaned forward, his eyes boring into the giant television screen. On the upper left corner the date read 05.18.1999, alongside a running clock with hours, minutes, and seconds.

Ben remembered well what was being replayed on the screen. Twenty hours before they celebrated his thirty-eighth birthday, he tried to get his wife to disclose a few details about his upcoming surprise party. She lay in bed, engrossed in Rushdie's *Haroun and the Sea of Stories*. He lay by her side, trying to read her mind.

The Mad Hop said, "I now believe you when you say you spent a full year getting in shape."

Marian, smiling, doesn't take her eyes off the page. "Stop it," she says.

"Stop what?" Ben asks.

Her smile freezes on her lips. "Stop looking at me like you've never seen a woman read before."

"I've never seen a woman pretend to read before."

Marian turns toward him. "Excuse me?"

Ben smiles. "You're running interference."

Marian: "Interference? Interference for what?"

Ben: "For the thoughts racing across your mind. Did I invite everyone? Will they all come? How will I keep it a secret?"

Marian cracks up. "Benji, for the thousandth time, there's no surprise party this year."

Ben: "You say that every year."

Marian, getting serious, puts the book facedown on her night table. "But this year I mean it. Kobi's in Glasgow, your mom's in America, and if my memory serves me right, we have movie tickets."

Ben: "What are we seeing?"

Marian: "A special showing of Prospero's Books."

Ben: "What, Greenaway's insane adaptation of The Tempest? *Haven't we seen that already?"*

Marian: "Not with the director."

Ben: "I bet they'll be there tomorrow."

Marian: "At the theater?"

Ben: "Or at the restaurant after the movie."

Marian: "You're nuts."

Ben: "You're my inspiration."

Marian: "Don't kiss ass just to try and get info."

Ben: "I'm right, then?"

*Marian: "Not even close. We're going to have a great night together, just the
two of us." She kisses the tip of his nose.*

Ben: "Now who's kissing ass?"

*Marian: "If you call that ass kissing wait till you see me grovel." She pushes
up against him and puts his earlobe in her mouth.*

Ben sighs. "Interference, round two."

*Marian kisses him, takes his hand, puts it on her belly button, and turns off
the light.*

The Mad Hop froze the picture. "Right, then. So, what happened in the
end?"

Ben said nothing. Rigid shock was written all over his face, and his
hands, fidgeting around his mouth, covered his lips. For a few long minutes he looked at the screen, taken hostage by the sight of the woman that
still glowed in his mind's eye, desperate to crawl into it and disappear. He
squeezed back tears and pointed at the screen with a crooked finger,
speaking with difficulty, "It's . . . so real." After a short silence, he scooped
his chin in his hand and whispered, "You know how long it's been since
I've heard her voice? How long it's been since I've seen her move?"

The Mad Hop smiled. "Well, was there or was there not a surprise
party?"

"There was not. We spent an amazing night together. Just the two of
us. As promised."

"I see."

The Mad Hop, trying to stir the silence that hung between them,
made a show of reaching for the remote control, and asked in a casual
tone, "Remind me, when did Marian die?"

Ben responded mechanically. "March seventeenth, 2000."

"Did you see her that day?"

"Yes. In the morning."

"And after that?"

"No. She left the house at ten thirty."

"So, ten thirty in the morning on March seventeenth, 2000 was the
last time you saw your wife?"

"Yes. Why are you asking?"

"I want to get an up-to-date as possible a picture of her."

The Mad Hop fast-forwarded and stopped a minute later: 21:40,
02.01.2000—*Ben's sitting in his study, writing furiously.*

The Mad Hop hit the button again and stopped: 08:57, 02.23.2000—*Ben showering.*

The Mad Hop hit the button again and stopped the machine for the third time: 12:00, 04.16.2000—*Ben lying on the couch, dead eyes staring at the ceiling.*

The Mad Hop hit rewind and stopped: 10:38, 03.17.2000—*Ben's in his study reading a journal. There's a coffee mug in clear view.*

The Mad Hop moaned and hit fast rewind. *Ben closes the journal, spits in the coffee mug. He gets up, walks backward to the kitchen. He puts the water back in the kettle and the coffee back in the jar. He smiles and walks to the door. It opens. Marian walks in, hugs him, kisses him on the lips.*

The Mad Hop stopped.

Ben: *"Too bad I can't come with you."*

Marian: *"Too bad is right."* *She kisses his lips, hugs him, and leaves.* The Mad Hop rewound again and put it on frame-by-frame advance. *Marian walks in, a big smile on her face.* The Mad Hop stopped. Her face filled the screen.

After three minutes of intense staring, the detective decided it was time to get the ball rolling. He turned off the machine.

"What are you doing?" Ben yelled.

"Come," the Mad Hop said, getting up and making his way to the door. "You need to get some air."

"I don't want to get any air."

"What you want doesn't really concern me. I've got a missing person. Don't worry, the tape isn't going anywhere, which is something we sure can't say about your lovely lady."

"Where do you want to go?"

"You'll see soon enough."

But Ben did not. He didn't see why they were going to 2001, and when he asked the Mad Hop, he cut him off with an angry wave of his hand and requested a few minutes of silence. By the time they got off the multiwheel, the little man had a mischievous smile on his face. He asked Ben if he was hungry.

"Hungry?"

"Yes, Ben, hungry."

"That's really weird. I just realized that since I died I haven't eaten a thing. And I don't feel even the slightest twinge of hunger."

"Death satisfies all human needs," the Mad Hop announced.

"Another fortune cookie?" Ben asked.

"Simpler than that. After death, the body relinquishes all of its needs. But I urge you to eat. Otherwise your appetite will just wither away and you won't be able to eat even if you want to. Same's true, by the way, for drinking and sex."

"You're saying that if I don't have sex for a while, I'll lose the drive entirely?"

"More like, if you don't *think* about sex for a while, you'll lose your drive. That's why I urge you not to forsake hunger and lust just because you can."

"What about you? You eat?"

The Mad Hop patted his stomach proudly. "Three hours after I arrived, I found 1986's best pizza parlor."

Ben laughed, feeling a swell of endearment for the investigator, who continued listing his favorite foods until they arrived at a place called Ambrosia. "Let's go," he said.

"We just drove fifteen years for a restaurant?" Ben asked.

"Not *a* restaurant," the Mad Hop said, walking in.

The restaurant stretched the length of a city block, or at least that's how it seemed to Ben, whose senses were assaulted by the myriad seating sections, the gluttonous, screaming swarm of eaters, and the striking colors of the different dishes. Ambrosia was split into dozens of rooms, all teeming. From amid the metallic gnash of the silverware, Ben was able to make out the major characteristics of the largest vegetarian restaurant in 2001. Each room held about a hundred diners. They chose their dishes with great discretion from the circular buffet table in the center of the room. Neither waiters nor chefs played any visible role in the feast. The food, Ben surmised, was prepared by chefs in a hidden part of the labyrinthine restaurant and then passed forward on an unseen conveyor belt to the dining rooms.

"Well, starting to feel hungry?" the Mad Hop asked.

"No, Samuel, and to be honest, I'm still not sure why you brought me here."

"We need an up-to-date picture of Marian, yeah?"

"Yeah, and you're running a tight race here for the non sequitur of the century," Ben snapped.

The Mad Hop, issuing Ben one of his all-knowing grins, palmed his shining head and asked, "Notice anything off, Ben?"

"Off?" Ben looked around calmly and twisted his lips. "Aside from the fact that everyone is stuffing their faces like they've never seen food before?"

"Interesting," the PI said, crossing his legs. "The optical illusion got you, too."

"What illusion?"

"Like selective hearing, the eye also chooses what it wants to see. Your eyes chose to see faces stuffing and . . ."

"Oh my God, how did I miss that?" Ben cried, covering his crotch. "We're the only two naked people in the restaurant! They're all dressed!"

He surveyed the diners, only now noticing that they all wore the same blue one-piece work suit, like a chain gang or a group of prisoners on lunch break.

"More like mummified," the Mad Hop corrected him.

"Preserved? As in ancient Egypt?"

"No, as in unable to disrobe."

"Yet again I'm reminded of that book set seventeen years ago."

The Mad Hop took a step back, cupped his hands together behind him, and began speaking like a tour guide pointing out an obscure local phenomenon. "Presenting the Charlatans! They've got nothing to do with Orwell, and I'd caution you to avoid voicing the kind of literary associations that demonstrate your love of strange and peculiar dystopias. The Charlatans are as their name implies. Their deaths are an act of deception, of fraud, of first-rate charlatanism. That being said, we must not judge them too harshly. Their chicanery is not of their own choosing. Their hand was dealt in the previous world and I'm happy to say it's temporary. Call them transient guests, unbidden visitors, personae non grata, but know that they're scared of you. You're dead, Ben. No one can do you any harm. They, on the other hand, are only dead for now, meaning that fear plays a major role in their existence.

"The aliases don't want the Charlatans to go back to the previous world and report to humanity what awaits them when they go the way of all flesh. The natural separation between the two worlds would be irreparably breached. They're put in those one-piece suits so that the dead can easily recognize them. Nothing can cut them off, so there's no mingling among us before they return to their tedious old lives. That's where you and I come into the picture. Every Charlatan's deepest wish is to return to the world he just left. I brought you here to help pick the best candidate for the job."

The Mad Hop picked up the pace and made his way over to the fourth room of the restaurant. "Wait up," Ben said to the slightly humped, receding back. "How do you know we'll find him here?"

The Mad Hop turned toward him, the edge back in his voice. "Ben, this place is the Charlatans' meeting spot. As opposed to us, they need food to survive. And I need a novice Charlatan, otherwise I would have taken you to Ambrosia eighty-six. You must understand, the longer a Charlatan stays in the Other World, the mistier his mind becomes. He turns into a rather lackadaisical character."

"I have no idea what you're talking about," Ben said, despairingly. "What do we even need a Charlatan for?"

"He'll help us get an up-to-date picture of Marian. If we just snap a photo of the tellie, it'll be blurred and won't resemble her in the least. Luckily, I've got a mate who took a bullet in the head and is still holding on. He's a forensic artist from Manchester, an expert of facial composites. Usually eats in the ninth room, which is where we're heading."

"He's already done this for you in the past?"

The Mad Hop answered with a smile. Ben responded in kind. "And what does he get for his efforts?"

His voice a whisper, the Mad Hop said, "A promise that I'll return him to his native environment, and before you ask how it's done, let's just say I've seen a drunk alias do the trick."

Ben gnawed his fingernail. "Samuel, how many times have you used this forensic artist already?"

"I don't remember," the Mad Hop mumbled.

"And what makes you think he'll agree after such a string of false promises?"

"He's got no choice. I'll promise him it's the last time I'll use his ser-vices before . . ."

"That's awful Samuel. You're abusing . . ."

"Woah, enough," the Mad Hop cut him off. "You think death makes us holy? If I had the necessary skills, I wouldn't have to take advantage of innocent Charlatans."

"And you can't just find a *dead* portrait artist?"

"I've got nothing to give them in return."

In the ninth room, the Mad Hop pointed to a side table, flaunting his familiarity with the subject matter. "That's where he sits. Between Michael and Ahmed. Come."

But when he asked, the fat American smiled and said Nigel had left.

"Bloody hell, found himself a convenient time to wake up, did he?"

"At least you won't have to go on lying to him," Ben offered.

The Mad Hop pointed to two empty chairs to the left of Ahmed. "Let's eat."

"I'm not hungry."

"Yes, you bloody well are," the Mad Hop said. "Wait for me here."

Ben obeyed and took a seat beside Ahmed, trying not to stare at the blue-suited people stuffing themselves with dozens of different dishes. A tired voice to his left said, "You mind moving to another table?"

Ben, embarrassed by his nudity, responded with his head bowed. "Excuse me?"

The tired voice became thorny. "It's hard for me to eat in peace when just a few feet stand between me and a naked guy."

Ben looked away from him and found a small table on the other side of the dining room. Thankfully, the four chairs tucked in by the table were unoccupied. However, less than a minute after he sat down, a finger drummed his right shoulder. An aged and cantankerous voice said, "Sorry, sir, but you're in my place."

Ben thought that if he ignored the voice the pest would move on and find a different table. To his chagrin, the finger drummed his shoulder a second time and the voice only got louder. "Excuse me. You're in my seat!"

Ben closed his eyes, only to feel warm rancid breath in his right ear. "Are you deaf or are you just pretending not to hear?!" the man yelled.

Ben whipped around, pounced on the old man, pushed him to the floor, and screamed. "Listen to me you rancid old fuck, what the hell do you think . . ."

The old man's plate flew out of his hands and he shielded his face. "Don't hit me," he cried.

Ben looked down, sure he had made a mistake. "This can't be. I'm mixing you up with someone else."

The old man screeched. "Don't hit me, you scum."

Ben yelled hysterically, "Just let me see your face. I'm not going to hit you. Just let me see your fucking face."

The old man refused. Ben pulled the pair of gnarled hands apart and then brought his own hands to his face. "I don't believe it. I don't believe it."

The Mad Hop walked in, carrying two plates of steaming vegetables. "I leave you alone for one second and the first thing you do is accost an old man? Ben, you have any idea how bad you look right now, with all your bulging muscles on top of this old geezer?"

"You don't understand," Ben sang out. "Do you have any idea who this is?"

Before he got an answer, Ben gave the old man a hand and helped him to his feet. "You have no idea how excited I am to meet you," he said, introducing the man to the Mad Hop with great pride. "This exquisite man here is my favorite painter, Rafael Kolanski."

"Painter?" the Mad Hop said.

"If this is how you show your veneration . . . ," the artist mumbled, bringing his face close to Ben's shocked features.

"What, what are you doing?" Ben asked.

"I know you," Rafael said authoritatively, and then, allowing some scorn to enter his voice, "You're the husband of that woman . . . The one who threw a birthday party for the dead woman. I remember you from the picture."

Ben's face blanched. "How do you know I threw Marian a birthday party?"

Rafael kept the scorn in his voice. "Your friends came to me, said they wanted to surprise you. They asked me to draw a portrait of you and your wife."

"What?"

"Yes. I told them I don't do portraits. And if you're really a fan of my work then you know I'm not lying. Now leave me alone."

"Not likely," the Mad Hop said, turning away from his food. "Ben, this must be your lucky day." A jack-o-lantern grin on his face, he turned to the artist. "Mr. Kolanski, you're going to stray from your usual routine and draw a portrait."

The artist opened his eyes wide and asked Ben, "Who is this ridiculous dwarf and why is he insisting on making me laugh?"

"This ridiculous dwarf is Samuel Sutton, the famous private investigator, and he's helping me look for my wife and, as far as I can tell, he's asking you to paint her portrait."

Rafael seethed. "Over my dead body!"

The Mad Hop maintained his smile. His voice sugary, he said, "Mr. Kolanski, I wonder, have you any idea where you are?"

The artist answered with a rebellious shrug. "Not where I belong. I know what's going on here. It's some kind of sick hallucination. Something to do with the dead."

"Something to do with the dead," the Mad Hop repeated. "Mr. Kolanski, this is the world of the dead. And you were absolutely spot on when you said you didn't belong here. It's not yet your time to strip off the blue suit. But bad luck has it that you're stuck here with us."

"What am I supposed to make of that little sermon?"

"That if you don't lend a hand, you'll be stuck here for some time."

Seeing the disappointment smeared across the artist's face, the Mad Hop winked at Ben. "Right then, Ben, seems we've got a mule on our hands. Let's go. I suppose he really doesn't have all that much to go back to. There are enough talented artists around that actually miss life."

Ben nodded and the two of them started across the hall. The old man's refusal lasted for seven strides. "Wait!" he called out.

The Mad Hop turned around, a warning finger raised. "I've got no time for mucking about. If you promise to draw Marian, you're back to your life tonight. If you change your mind, I swear you'll never see . . ."

"Bessie," the artist said, "Sweet Bessie. You promise I'll see her tonight?"

The Mad Hop extended a hand and proclaimed, "Mr. Kolanski, I promise you, you'll be in your beloved Bessie's arms tonight."

Rafael succumbed to his outstretched hand.

⸎

Four hours later, the three of them sat opposite the Mad Hop's TV, nailed to the frozen image on the screen. Rafael asked them to leave the room

while he worked, and they happily acquiesced. His voluminous demands had already taken a toll. Only after going into half a dozen
shops, looking for the proper brushes, paints, canvas, and easel, did they
return to the Mad Hop's house, at which point the artist announced that
he must eat. After feasting on the vegetarian banquet the Mad Hop
prepared for him, he made Ben swear that he would tell no soul, living
or dead, that the portrait was a Kolanski. Then he booted them out of
the room.

Waiting in the adjacent office, the two sunk into the couch and woke
up thirty minutes later to the sound of the Announcer. Ben signaled to
his friend to keep quiet as he crept toward the room, put his ear to the
door, and listened to the artist kvetch. "Prostitution. That's what this
is, Bessie. I swear, prostitution. Only for you would I do this vile work.
Portrait! They have no shame."

The artist kept his complaining up for hours, jabbing the canvas
with a particularly limp brush, dunking his fist into the color palette
and knocking his knuckles against the canvas, dotting it as he perfected
his despised work of art. When he felt that Marian's eyebrows had become too sharp, he spit right between her hairy arches, softening them,
and when it seemed her smile was overly sweet, he scratched the scarlet
lines around her lips with his sharp nails. Done at last, he peeked at the
TV screen, then back at the canvas, and grimaced. After swearing he'd
never undergo this type of humiliation again, he opened the door and
called them.

Deaf to the two men's appreciation, Kolanski allowed a smile only
when Ben pointed to a small beauty mark above her left nostril. "What's
this?"

The artist clarified. "Since we're dealing with a particularly amusing case of *cherchez la femme*, the portrait will now entice you to look for
her. The painting is meant to remind you that your real wife cannot
be captured by any painting. The slight lack of accuracy is meant to
spur you to find the real thing. This loathsome portrait is a replica
with a tiny unreliability that will temper your excitement each time
you look at this face. It's functional art at its lowly nadir. The beauty
mark will keep sleep at arm's length until you find the wayward lady
and then, I hope, you celebrate with pure vandalism and trash this
painting."

Ben nodded. "Samuel, we should get going."

The Mad Hop mumbled affirmation, left the office, pulled a pen out of one of the drawers, and invited the others to join him.

For over an hour he led them far from the ornate circles at the city center, through back alleys and hidden lanes, explaining that they were heading to the borderlands between his city and the one beyond it.

As they passed the last building in December 1986, Ben asked what they were doing along the borderlands. The Mad Hop said they were looking for the edge.

The threesome stood before a long white path, dividing 1986 and 1987. The Mad Hop claimed it was the border between cities and that all they had to do was follow it to the end. They walked along the white asphalt path for a long time. When at last the Mad Hop told them to look back, they were surprised to see that the skyscrapers had disappeared and that the old surroundings had been replaced by a broad field of cotton.

"What the hell?" Ben asked and then fell silent. A thin black line dawned in the distance.

"What's that black line?" the artist inquired.

"That's the horizon," the Mad Hop responded, "and if you cross it there's no way back."

"What's over the horizon?"

"A void," the Mad Hop said, giving the word a chill.

Forty minutes later, the Mad Hop stopped the artist five steps shy of the black line. "Your left hand please."

The artist agreed, not sure why the weird PI was scribbling a few words in his tickled left palm.

"Don't read what I wrote. Not now. Wait till you get there safely. And, at any rate, know one thing for sure, as soon as you leave this world, you won't remember a thing about its existence."

Rafael looked across the line. "These white things," he asked, his voice wobbling, "are they . . . ?"

The Mad Hop came close. "Clouds," he said dryly.

Rafael refused to move. He wouldn't jump without knowing what awaited him beneath the clouds, without a guarantee of his safe landing, without being certain that the midget wasn't up to an evil trick.

The howl he emitted when he realized he was not on safe ground rever-
berated in their ears, even as they covered them and looked at each
other in horror.

Ben yelled, "I think I'm deaf."

The Mad Hop apologized. "It'll go away soon enough. We should've
picked cotton balls. They always yell like that when they start to sail
into the unknown."

"Why the hell did you push him?"

"Because if we waited for the gentleman to do the honors himself,
he would've gone to the white room first."

"And had I jumped?"

"You wouldn't have been able to."

"And what did you write on his hand?"

"I'll tell you later. Let's head back to the apartment. I reckon the
canvas has dried and you need to take it back to your place."

"To my place?"

"Yes."

"You said it would help us search."

"Mentally."

"Excuse me?"

"Don't tell me you thought we'd reproduce the portrait and hang
it up in trees all over town. Kids would rip it right off. And I imagine
you understand that if we put it online we'd be swamped with messages
from bored psychopaths all over the Other World. We're not running
a police investigation here. I've got my own ways of finding a missing
person."

He stopped and surveyed Ben's face.

"Don't look at me like I've gone mental. Ben, go home and hang
that picture on the wall. That way you'll have a palpable reminder of
the woman you're looking for. Without the picture you'd be a full-on
addict for the tapes and you'd never leave the house. Can't have that.
You see?"

"I'm not sure. You're telling me that all that mess in the restaurant
and with Kolanski was just so I could hang a picture of Marian up on
my wall?"

"So that you don't come back home from a long day of searching and spend the night in front of recorded memories. That temptation must be obliterated."

"But how the hell do you plan on finding my wife?"

"Come over tomorrow afternoon and we'll talk about it. I've got a few other clients, you know . . . ," he said, yawning.

"Okay, so what now?" Ben asked.

"Now? Now you go home, hang the picture on the wall, and stare at the artist's brilliant beauty mark," the Mad Hop said, tossing the pen off into the dark horizon.

13

Stigmata

"Ormus, I mean, Yonatan. It'll take me some time to get used to your real name. It's only been two days since our first date and I'm still trying to calm down. I found you flat on your back. A major heart attack. I called an ambulance but the big hospitals were full because of the bombing. That's why you're here, at this small hospital. Truth is, I have no idea what they did. All I know is that when you came out of surgery, they hooked you straight up to life support, and now everyone's just waiting for you to wake up. I wonder what Rushdie would say—even he never dreamed that when Vina and Ormus finally meet, Ormus would be unconscious. It's strange, but when I first saw you, I wasn't surprised. I had a strong feeling that you didn't look the part of the knight in shining armor. But it felt good. I already had one of those guys—looked like a million dollars but wasn't worth a penny. Anyway, what am I blabbering about? You know all about him. What else do I have to report? As you can imagine I haven't totally acclimated, although on Tuesday I interviewed Gabriel Din, the plastic artist whose work is going to be exhibited at the Biennale. Fascinating guy. Apart from that, I've been getting calls every couple of hours from my friends back at the Paris office, checking that I'm still alive. My boss's been asking where I disappear to twice a day. Obviously I don't tell him. It's like those stories I used to read in the papers and crack up. I couldn't believe they actually happened. And it's not just us, Yonatan. You wouldn't believe what happened here two hours ago. Really intense drama just over on the other side of this room. So, I guess you have no clue who's lying in the other bed, also hooked up to life support? Rafael Kolanski, the famous painter. From what I understand, he's been here for the past six weeks. He had a brain aneurism of some sort. They were supposed to disconnect him this morning. They'd given up hope. His wife was here and the weird nurse who's been caring for you, and the hospital director, a lawyer, and two other nurses. I peeked through the curtain that divides the room. I had to see it. The scene reminded me of Greenaway. Or

Polanski. The lot of them huddled around his bed like some kind of mystical sect, everyone saying a few words, except for the wife, who stood there in silence, shaking. The plug was to be pulled at ten. When they were done, the small nurse made her way over to the side of the bed and put her hand on the switch. The time was one minute to ten. The artist's wife took his hand in hers and continued to tremble. I swear I could hear the rattle in her teeth. Other than that there was total silence in the room. I don't know how many seconds passed but all of a sudden we heard a giggle. Rolling and cute, girly. Everyone looked around trying to discover who was behind the tactlessness, only to find that the old woman, twenty-five seconds short of widowhood, was giggling like a little girl who had just pulled off the most delightful of pranks. For a second I thought that, you know, she had lost her mind. The hospital director asked her why she was giggling, and she said, 'He's . . . tickling . . . me.' Of course I didn't understand what she was saying but they explained it to me afterwards. Then she went stiff, stopped laughing, and called out, bemused 'he's tickling me.' The thick-headed nurse must have been daydreaming or something, because she still had her hand on the switch and was ready to flip it. The doctor shouted, slapped her hand away. She turned from the machine and, like everyone else in the room, stared at the old man's hand. After that I had a hard time telling what was going on, but there was plenty of hooting and hollering and I was able to tell that his pinkie was moving. Amazing, no? A man's life was saved because his pinkie came back to life and at the perfect time. After that they started to celebrate, even ordered champagne. Bessie, the artist's wife, asked me to join them.

"His awakening was thrilling. When he opened his eyes, she went wild, crying, laughing, letting out all that had been bottled inside for weeks. I drank the bubbly wine with them and heard the doctor say that what happened was a medical miracle. Everyone started to trickle out and I told Bessie I was really happy for her. She thanked me and listened to the doctor's orders. He told the artist to take it easy, saying he would have to run a few tests and that in the meanwhile he may have trouble speaking. The old man was so cute, he acted like he'd just come back from Mars, smiling with half his mouth at his happy wife. Once the doctor left, only the nurse remained in the room with Bessie and the old man.

"Yonatan, I really felt sorry for her. She went up to Bessie and tried to shake her hand but she ignored her. The nurse couldn't take Bessie's withering looks any longer. She left the room. I came back to you, sat by your side for something like five more minutes, and then heard a sudden shriek. I ran over to see what had happened, scared he had fallen back into a coma, but it was nothing like that. I asked Bessie why she looked so ghastly. She said that if she could kill the nurse, she would. I smiled knowingly, even though I didn't really understand what made her yell like that. Then she shrieked again. 'Look, look what that needless piece of trash did.' She raised the artist's left hand and asked me to look at it. Yonatan, it was so weird. Right in the center of his palm, in blue ink, it said 'There's Life After Death.' In English. Under different circumstances, I would've burst out laughing. But just then I understood why the old woman was so angry. She says that the nurse wrote those words on his hand because, as someone who thoughtlessly pulls the plug on human lives, she wanted to soothe her own conscience, and also, to raise Bessie's spirits, so she'd know that she'd be with her man again, you know, like in all those ridiculous stories about lovers reuniting in paradise. I tried to calm her down, but she was furious. She said she was going to talk to the hospital director. An hour later she came back into the room, a Napoleonic smile spread across her face. The director suspended Ann, that's the nurse, for a week without pay. A slap on the wrist to appease the artist's wife. Bessie said that at first the director didn't believe her and that he called Ann to his office and questioned her. She swore she had nothing to do with it. Bessie pointed to the pen Ann had in her hand and asked what more of a smoking gun he would need. Ann looked baffled and said that everyone has a blue ballpoint pen. Between us, Yonatan, this is no Minette Walters story. It's obvious she did it, although I should say that my gut feeling is she had an ulterior motive. At any rate, the director apologized to Bessie and asked for her discretion in the entire matter. He said Ann was one of the best, most devoted nurses he had and that he didn't want a one-time slip to tarnish her reputation. Bessie agreed and the controversy passed. Small, sweet doses of revenge always help settle things down. Bessie went to freshen up and Ann was sent away for a week. I guess one of the other nurses here will replace her and take care of you for the time being. Actually, Ormus, Vina's got to go, too. Got to bang out an article on the reading habits of children in the age of Harry Potter. Seems like an interesting thing to look at—do Israeli kids read other

14 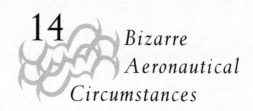 *Bizarre Aeronautical Circumstances*

For the third time in the past three days, Ben found himself sitting opposite the smiling midget, wondering what it was about this supremely confident man. "Quit looking so worried, Ben. I guarantee you that within several months at the latest you'll be back with your wife again."

"Why such confidence?" Ben asked.

"Why such doubt?" he answered, smiling and pouring himself a glass of wine.

"Sorry to disappoint you, but I'm finding it hard to be optimistic when my wife has disappeared and I don't have a clue where she is."

The Mad Hop sipped the wine, shut his eyes, and purred, "There's always a clue."

Before Ben had a chance to figure out where his friend was going with that last morsel, the latter opened his eyes, licked his lips and asked, "What kind of music does Marian like?"

Ben smiled. "She likes it all. Operas, jazz, country, punk, world music, trip-hop . . ."

"Rock. What about some old-fashioned rock 'n' roll—does she like that?" the Mad Hop cut him short.

"Sure! She's crazy about rock."

"When you say crazy . . ."

"I mean she was always buying CDs, never wanting to miss a new album. She was . . . she is enormously curious. If you haven't picked this up already, Marian was a culture fiend, went from one thrill to the next, movies, books, discs, plays, exhibits, shows. One time I asked her why she buys so many CDs, and she smiled and said it was all part of her retirement plan. Eyes glistening, she said, 'Ben, think how much fun it'll be. We'll have time to listen to everything, see everything, get to know everything . . . .'

"I laughed and asked her if she thought that at age sixty-five we'd be listening to The Smashing Pumpkins. She nodded and whispered, 'Yes, albeit at a lower volume.'"

The Mad Hop poured some more wine, his face shining with satisfaction. "Told you there's always a clue."

"Once again you insist on opacity."

"Not at all," the Mad Hop said, fitting his fingers together. "I know, for example, where Marian is going to be during the coming three days."

"Excuse me?" Ben said, his body coiling.

"It's a safe bet to say you know nothing of the Forever Young Festival, eh? Every year, between the twenty-fifth and twenty-seventh of June, the Other World has its biggest rock concert. Three straight days of gigs. It's the big event for rockers. Morrison, Lennon, Joplin, Mercury, Hendrix, Buckley, Drake, Cobain, Bonham, Curtis, and friends all share the same stage. Fifty brilliant artists that ended their lives under tragic circumstances but never lost their hunger for music. Your wife will definitely be in the mix with all the rest."

"Where's it held?" Ben asked.

The Mad Hop smiled forlornly. "I wouldn't get excited. Park 1945. Nine million fans attended last year. Could be a bit tricky spotting a woman in the middle of nine million revelers."

"So what do you suggest?" Ben asked.

"Such a shame she died in a car accident," the Mad Hop said, lighting a cigarette.

Under his appraising gaze Ben started to blink at a rapid rate. "What do you mean?"

"Had she died in a less common manner, it might have been of help."

"In what way?" Ben asked, unable to keep the tremor out of his voice.

"What does it matter, she died in a car accident, didn't she?"

Ben was ready to respond, but he held the words on his tongue when the private investigator dropped the chattiness from his voice and said, "Or are you finally going to tell me how she really left the previous world, a fact that may well help the investigation get off the ground."

"How did you know?" Ben asked, evading the quick hunter's eyes.

The Mad Hop stretched, outwardly pleased. "Remember when you told me that your wife died in a car accident and I had one of those uncontrollable laughing fits?"

"How could I forget?"

"Good. You may not believe me, but I wasn't laughing because I lack tact."

"Why else would you laugh?"

"I laughed because you lied."

"How did you know I lied?"

"I laughed."

Ben chuckled. "Clearing the lines of communication between us wouldn't hurt."

"I already mentioned you might not believe me, but still I wouldn't want to deny you this piece of information. At a young age I realized I had a special radar. You could say I'm a walking, talking polygraph machine."

Ben sat at attention. "Polygraph? You're telling me you can detect liars?"

"Lies," he corrected. "One lie doesn't make you a liar, otherwise I never would've taken on your case. You see what I'm saying? The bursts of laughter are my needles, dancing to the tune of someone's lie. You've the right to regard this information as you see fit, but I ask that you not test me on purpose—I'm not a toy."

"Samuel, hold on, what you're saying is sensational. As soon as someone lies your body reacts with uncontrollable laughter. How does it know?"

"That's the gift, my mysterious talent, I reckon."

After a silence, he added, "And now if you'd be so kind as to explain why you lied, I'd be ever so grateful."

Ben sank deep into his chair. "I was afraid you wouldn't believe me."

"Why?"

"Samuel, the cause of my wife's death is so strange it seems to defy human logic . . . it . . ."

"How the hell did she die?" the Mad Hop yelled, cutting him short.

Ben answered with an equally angry scream. "She fell off the fucking Ferris wheel."

Twitches and ticks spread across the Mad Hop's face like a crack through ice, his body started to palpitate, and he hammered the table with his fist. Had Ben not seen the strange nature of the private eye's laugh before, he wouldn't have known how to put an end to the fit. He snapped open the drawer, pulled out the gun, aimed at the Mad Hop's head, and squeezed the trigger.

Between heaves of laughter, the private eye sounded jovial. "Ben, I forgot to get bullets. . . ."

Ben tossed the useless weapon back in the drawer and slammed it shut. "You still don't believe me?"

The Mad Hop shook his head vigorously. "No, this time it's just funny! Woman flies off Ferris wheel, perishes. God, just when you feel like you've seen it all, death does you one better. Ben, wife or no wife, you must admit this is hilarious."

Although, after fifteen months of captivity, there was a giggle squirming to get out, Ben pursed his lips and kept it caged. The Mad Hop showed no sign of relenting, tapping Ben's arm, growling, "Ben, please, don't be such a self-important old fart, and show me you're human. I know it's your wife, and she's the most precious thing in the whole world, but look me in the eye and tell me that if this happened to someone else you wouldn't be bent over with laughter. Ben, your wife flew . . . off the Ferris wheel. That's the most slapstick death I've ever heard of . . . We've seen this kind of thing in the cartoons, but in real life . . . oh, my jaw's breaking . . . imagine what would have happened had she lived through the whole thing. What would she tell people when they asked her how she'd been paralyzed? I flew off the giant Ferris wheel and into a wheelchair?!"

Ben covered his mouth, his hand shaking, his head bobbing in abrupt bunny hops, and gave in to the contagious laughter. The two cackled for a while, wiping tears from the corners of their eyes, enflaming the atmosphere with nasty jokes about Marian's flying abilities, her hidden wings that didn't pass their big test, the smash of impact, and the shock of the kids who witnessed their teacher disengage from her seat and plummet to her moronic death.

The Mad Hop sobered up first. "What kids?" he asked.

Ben explained, his voice still carrying traces of giddiness. "I told you, she was an English teacher . . . that morning she took her students, the kids from the consulate, to the amusement park, and that's where it happened."

"How the hell does something like that happen there? The rides are supposed to be perfectly safe. How does one go from an immobile, seated position to a freefall?"

Ben shrugged. "No one was able to explain it. Maybe she wasn't seated. Maybe she was standing. When they asked the kids, they were too shocked to answer. They were pretty self-involved."

"Who was sitting next to her?"

"Some old guy she invited to join them. One of the kids said she saw him next to the ride and that he looked like a homeless guy. She must've felt sorry for him, wanted to give him a few minutes of fun. It's so like her. But the police couldn't find the guy for questioning. Too bad. He could've solved the mystery."

"Did she die instantaneously?"

"Luckily. Even though the damage was permanent."

"What a strange comment."

"If you'd seen her face, you wouldn't say that. It was totally disfigured. . . ."

"She was identified by her dental records then?"

"Yeah. And by a beauty mark."

"Don't tell me Kolanski got it right."

"In all but location. It was between her big toe and the one next to it on her right foot."

"I see. I'm sorry to raise such sore points."

"Don't be sorry. The woman lying on that bed in the morgue only symbolizes Marian for me. Nothing more. Her smashed face, surprisingly, didn't make much of an imprint on my memory. Marian remained, and will always remain, the same beautiful woman that left the house at ten thirty that morning."

"And with the reconstructive surgeon's full overhaul upon arrival in the Other World, you can take it easy. The Marian we're looking for is not the woman you lost with the smashed face."

Ben's smile slackened. "Oh my God, she's probably paralyzed!"

"What are you talking about?"

"You know, like Robert. The reconstructive surgeons weren't able to fix . . ."

"Forget it," the Mad Hop said, rising to his feet. "Marian isn't a cripple, trust me. Now let's get going and stop wasting time."

"Where we going?" Ben asked.

"I'll explain on the way."

The Mad Hop explained during the hour-long trip to September 1980: "Ben, in the Other World I've come across a phenomenon of 'anti-phobia' quite a few times. People who perished under tragic circumstances are often drawn to the type of environment in which they died so that they can confront the now-entrenched fear. A bloke who, say, drowned can spend an eternity at the sea until he can get the best of his phobia and, trust me, it takes time."

"So, what are you saying? Marian is out wandering like some freak through amusement parks?" Ben asked.

"I suppose," the Mad Hop said.

"Okay, and how many such places are there in the Other World, Samuel?"

"Loads, Ben. But I'm not really interested in them."

"Why not?"

"Because we're going to *the* amusement park, a kind of Disney World for the dead."

"Don't get upset, Samuel, but I have a hard time believing that Marian's spending all her time on Ferris wheels."

"And yet you don't seem to be hopping off the multi-wheel. That's the beauty of the doubt nestling inside you, the paradox of your certainty. She could be anywhere and nowhere. So long as that doubt lingers, you'll keep looking. But enough with shallow pep talks. You need to know that the people in the park can be divided into three easily discernable groups: kids, grown-up couples, and druggies."

Ben laughed. "Drug addicts?"

The Mad Hop smiled patiently. "I think it's some kind of new trend. I've seen it mostly over the past two years. People roll up to the park with their heads completely lit, take one of the rides, and scream like children. Someone told me their high takes on a new dimension."

Ben felt a tepid disappointment wash over him as he looked out at the masses of people roaming the park, which stretched out before them like a long highway dotted with games and rides. "We'll never find her with all of these people," he said.

The Mad Hop offered a sideways glance. "Ben, it only seems complicated. All we have to focus on is the Ferris wheel. I suggest we split up. The park's built like an estate. Cut into twenty-six plots. Look to your right and you'll see a large gate with the letter A above it. Look to your left and you'll see a similar sight with the letter Z. We've got to cover all of the plots—thirteen for each of us—and meet in the middle, at M Gate. Don't worry, we won't need to backtrack. You can exit the grounds from any one of the gates."

"Hang on a minute, I see the big wheel in area A."

The Mad Hop pointed over to the left. "And what do you see over there?"

"Another big wheel. Please, Samuel, don't tell me that . . ."

He nodded. "Each section's got a big wheel of its own. Let's say five hours from now at M Gate, alright?" He turned, started to walk, stopped, and turned back. "Remember, don't pay any attention to the kids and the druggies. Focus on the adults walking on their own. Good luck."

Ben reached the meeting point forty minutes late. The investigator, shifting his weight from foot to foot, was in a foul mood. "You're late and empty-handed?" he called out.

Ben disregarded the comment. "It was madness. I kept looking for her, afraid I'd miss her in the crowd, or on the wheels, till my eyes registered nothing. Unbearable commotion. When I got to the sixth area, I even thought I saw Uncle David, but when I got near . . . ."

"Uncle? You have a dead uncle?"

Ben sounded indifferent. "My entire family is dead. But . . ."

"Halt!" the Mad Hop commanded, his face stern. "What did you just say? Tell me I misheard you."

"What do you want?"

"Did you just say your whole family is dead or am I suddenly the only deaf person in the Other World?"

"Yeah," Ben said, "no one's left of my family in the previous world. They all died. I was the last of the lot."

The Mad Hop fixed his gaze on a faraway spot on the horizon, examined it for some time, and then hightailed it over to a waiting multi-wheel, hopped in, and disappeared into the belly of the accelerating vehicle, which left in its dusty wake a shocked and downtrodden righter, who sat down on one of the big stone blocks outside the gate and dropped his head in his hands.

15

The Element of Surprise

Once a week the current forest director met with the former forest director in the latter's luxurious wooden cabin. Sipping schnapps, they regaled each other with tales from the field. The host, who retired after one hundred and five satisfying years, offered sage advice and urged his successor, who was only three short decades into his term, to come to him with any professional queries. At this week's meeting, the former director took immediate notice of the shadow hovering over the young director's ordinarily sunny face.

"What's on your mind?" he asked him.

The youngster leaped at the chance to explain. "There's something that's keeping me up at night. I'm sure I'm just getting carried away, but I can't get this out of my mind."

Billion leaned back and threaded his fingers together. "I'm listening."

Halfabillion didn't let his smile intrude on the sincerity of his question. "In your day, what was the highest rate of expiration you ever saw?"

"In times of war or peace?"

"Peace. War's another story altogether."

"Good. I always said you were a quick learner. Let's see. In 1906 we had one family totally wipe out another one."

"No, no, no. I mean naturally, under normal conditions."

"Till uprooting?"

The youngster nodded, flicked a playful red curl out of his line of vision, and sipped the plum schnapps while his furrow-browed friend mumbled a few names that mingled with an unrecognizable tune, squinted, sunk his teeth in to his lower lip and, his face bright, called out in restrained triumph, "I recall a Dutch family whose uprooting dossier was sealed in 1973. The Van Der Lockes had a very high rate of expiration, as far as statistics go. Eleven months between deaths if I'm not mistaken. It played out like an arithmetic progression. The oldest granddaughter was the only one who deviated from it, being the last of the line."

"When did she die?"

"A year and two months after her brother died. She hung herself."

"Not surprising. The last survivor almost always seems to take his own life."

"True. The survival instinct is worn down when you have no remaining blood relatives, even though, evolutionarily I'd expect it to be the opposite. Still, I guess she didn't want to perpetuate a dynasty of corpses."

"Maybe she was scared that even though she'd made it over the eleven-month hurdle, death would snatch her when she wasn't ready."

"Maybe. I'd have been happy to see her pass at old age and not at twenty-four."

"That's the part that fascinates me, Billion. Do you think she would have lived to old age had she not used the rope?"

"The dog's collar, my friend, not a rope. And yes. I have no doubt that had she stood firm in the face of the pain and the hounding of death, she would've reproduced and the whole story would've ended differently."

"By the way, did the rest of the family die under ordinary circumstances or . . . ?"

The former director smiled playfully. "Same as the granddaughter, they all used the dog's collar."

"They all committed suicide?" Halfabillion asked.

"Yes, which I suppose explains the precision of the expiration rate."

"And it explains why the granddaughter waited three extra months till she could gather up the courage to carry out what sounds like a pretty mysterious family ceremony."

"Or rather that explains her courage during the time she refused to enter the family tradition, until cowardice or despair got the better of her and she put an end to her life."

"Okay. But I was asking about the expiration rate of a normal family. An entire family that systematically kills itself off doesn't exactly qualify, does it?"

"They were a normal family until the granddaughter's younger sister, a girl of nine, started off the chain reaction. Before that the family's rate of expiration was thirteen point seven."

"The young granddaughter started the whole thing off?"

"Yes. She lost her dog and then hung herself with his collar."

"Unbelievable. A whole family was wiped out because of a lost dog?"

"The first suicide was because of a lost dog. The second was because of a hanged granddaughter."

"Hmm, the domino effect."

After a weighty silence the young director asked the older man if he recalled any other naturally brief death spans.

"Why, what kind of strange bird have you come across?"

"A strange bird indeed. An Israeli family, the Mendelssohns. From grandfather to grandson, who was the last of them and of course ended his own life, the entire family drifted into extinction with somewhere between a six and twelve month expiration rate. From 1994 to 2001, the last eight of them died and the tree was uprooted."

"I see we're dealing with a pretty small family."

"Yes. But before the nineties the last death in their family was in 1970."

"I see. So, like with the Van Der Lockes, you're wondering if something happened in 1994 that triggered the whole thing?"

"Exactly. Except that as opposed to the Van Der Lockes, the Mendelssohns all died in different ways. Accidents, diseases, murder, suicides. Were it not for the strangely high expiration rate, I wouldn't even pay any attention to the case. All told, we're looking at a good, reasonable, well balanced mode of departure from the world."

Billion shrugged. "I know this isn't the most convincing answer, but I think what you've got is just a particularly cruel coincidence."

Halfabillion twisted his lips. "That's what my deputies said. Quarterbillion used the old argument."

"Trunk degeneration. A tree whose branches are detached too frequently is sapped of its strength and its limbs lose their purchase on the trunk."

"I don't know," the young director said, his face clouded again. "I have a hard time with those explanations. Think about it, Billion, such a high death span, such diversity in manner of death and . . ."

"A minute ago you mentioned a good, reasonable, well balanced division."

"True. But some of the deaths were so bizarre."

"Bizarre in what way?"

"One was eaten by a leopard. One drowned when his plane went down."

"Excuse me?"

"The plane went down over water. He miraculously survived the crash but his swimming technique left something to be desired. . . ."

"I see."

Halfabillion laid his cup on the table, leaned forward, and said in a stage whisper, "I think I've got an explanation."

Billion mimicked his friend and whispered back, pleased with the surreptitiousness of the affair. "Do tell."

"I'm almost certain there's malicious intent behind the Mendelssohn case."

"Malice?"

"Yes, maybe the family had enemies that wanted to destroy them."

"No," Billion said, wrinkling his forehead. "I don't think so. Say such an enemy existed and say he reached this world before 1994, what could he do? The paths to the forest are sealed. Only workers are permitted into the forest, and all the workers are aliases."

"Are you saying that there's no way that a non-alias could sneak into the forest? Don't forget, they're known for trickery and slow-burning vengeance."

"Luckily, all the trickery and vengeance in the world aren't enough to get past the ring of guards around the forest. As you well know I, em . . . you employ over a million aliases."

"I know the numbers, but aren't we being a little narrow-minded if we completely rule out the possibility, however insane?"

For the first time during their conversation, Billion's face wore an unfamiliar anger. He folded his arms across his chest, leaned back, and began to speak, his voice loud and flat, "You're looking in all the wrong places. The possibility you raise is negated by logic. They don't even know about the forest, let alone sneaking into it. On the other hand, accidents happen. Sometimes rushed uprooters can mistakenly yank out a dangling branch. Terrible, awful, fateful mistakes, but human nonetheless."

"Mistakes don't repeat themselves eight times in a row," Halfabillion said.

Stone-faced, Billion summed up their meeting, "Aren't *you* being a little narrowminded if you completely rule out the possibility, however insane?"

But the other possibility, the horrifying alternative that he preferred to keep to himself, seemed a whole lot less insane the next morning.

~~~

Late at night, Halfabillion left his mentor's cabin and wandered the
streets aimlessly, hoping not to bump into any of his employees. Feeling
inexplicably parched, he decided to quench his thirst at a faraway pub.
He knew the forest workers didn't tend to frequent 2001 and made his way
in the direction of the new city. After a bout of deliberation, he thought the
better of it and walked into a small pub in May, took a seat by the bar, and
ordered a whiskey. Watching a group of Irishmen dance themselves into
oblivion, he heard a soft warm voice to his right, ". . . ey . . . rea . . . ny."

He turned and looked at a tall woman, sitting upright in the adjacent
chair. Moving gently in her direction, he asked, "What? I can hardly
hear over all the noise they're making."

She brought her lips close to his ears, "They're really funny. What's
the deal with the nudity?"

"I'm not sure I understand you," he said, looking her over and decid-
ing that the impressive woman had died in the fifth decade of her life,
perfectly timed if one wants to preserve the most profound feminine
maturity.

She took him in and repeated her question. "Why's everyone naked? What's the deal? The girl mentioned something about it at the
lecture but I was too deep in thought. What, am I in heaven? Or hell?
Or is it someplace in between?"

He smiled and tried to sound convincing. "It's much easier and more
comfortable to be naked. And I can assure you, you aren't in heaven or
hell. You're, you know, in the Other World."

"And in this Other World all men hold lively conversations with the
breasts of the women next to them, or is that just your specialty?"

Halfabillion blushed, apologized, and ordered another drink.

She laughed playfully. "It's alright, even nice considering I spent my
first few hours here certain I'd arrived on a giant porn set, which I wasn't
so happy about."

"First few hours?" he asked. "How long ago did you get here?"

She raised a sculpted eyebrow. "I'm not exactly sure. All I know is
this morning I was still in Paris. Between us, I'm still expecting to
wake up."

"It's not a dream." Halfabillion smiled. "You'll just go through a
short adjustment period and then it will all seem normal to you."

"It already seems normal to me. I'm just not sure what I'm doing here, how I got here in the first place, and what's the meaning of this weird thing hanging off my neck."

"You don't remember how you died?"

"I don't remember *that* I died," she said, nibbling a fingernail. "I took a taxi to the airport and then I don't know what happened, but now I'm sitting here naked, chatting with a naked guy who can't take his eyes off my chest, in a pub full of cute drunk Irish men in the Other World, which sounds to me like a funny Kevin Costner movie, and I haven't a clue what to do. . . ."

"I told you, after a short adjustment period everything will be cleared up and you'll find where you belong."

"I hope I'm able to find my apartment first."

Without thinking twice, Halfabillion offered his assistance. The woman warned him not to expect anything in return.

They spent four hours walking around June 2001 until they found the right apartment. She placed her thumb on the hole and asked if he'd like to come in.

"You said I shouldn't expect anything in return."

She laughed and pulled him close. "I'd be a selfish bitch if I didn't offer you a little something after all you did for me. You listened to me for hours, then looked all over for this apartment, and even promised to pull a few strings to find out how the hell I died. It's really just like me to find the perfect guy on the day I die."

He left her apartment in the early hours of the morning and arrived at his office three hours late. His deputies, picking up on the wild curls, the unshaven face, and the newfound dreaminess of his expression, prowled around him, demanding to know what had happened the previous night. He offered a half smile and told them to get back to work. Halfabillion breathed easy as they filed out of his office, called her name up on his screen, and waited for an explanation. A minute later, the complete death report of the newly released prisoner, who had killed her abusive husband with eight strokes of an ax and passed away on the day of her release in a fatal car accident, came up on his screen. After concentrating on the report for a few seconds, he raised his godget and was about to call her when a small detail caught his eye. Sandrine

Montesquieu, surprised by her own death, had a family tree in plot 2,605,327—the same plot where, until recently, the Mendelssohn tree had stood.

He recalled the lengthy conversation they had while looking for her apartment, especially the deep sadness that pooled in her face when she repeatedly stressed that she did not believe in her own death. He said she was in shock. She laughed and said all the movies always portrayed the tragic effects of death on the loved ones and family members of the deceased but never the overwhelming and exclusive shock of the dead. He asked if she thought the shock might be less intense had she died an expected death. She looked at him in silence, her face revealing that her thoughts had strayed far from the darkened street. When she took her face in her hands and fell suddenly to the sidewalk, lashing out at half the world, demonstrating distinct signs of a breakdown, he sat down beside her and said the pain would pass, not really knowing what he was talking about since he, like the rest of his kind, was an alias and had never been to Sandrine's world.

She turned her insult-ridden face toward him and shrieked hysterically. He hugged her softly, hiding his own emotional turmoil, sparked by her tirade against God, who had shown the highest form of idiocy when he killed her before she was able to keep her promise to her friend. "I'd been waiting for that moment for a year, and on the day of my release He ambushes me and snuffs me out like it's no big deal, like I hadn't rotted in jail for eight years, like I hadn't done my time. What's He trying to prove? Where does He get this infantile crap from? She'll never forgive me. What will I say when I see her? How can I disappoint her this way? Just as I was about to fulfill my promise, God got bored and decided he's sick of me?"

When he thought she had calmed down and squandered all her fury, she pushed him away from her and started pinching her arms, yelling at the top of her lungs, "I'm dead! I'm dead! I'm not there anymore, I'm dead!"

She mourned her own passing disgracefully, till she had nothing left. Then, in utter exhaustion, she whispered, "I never got to see New York."

The words stuck in his mind. Sandrine never got to see New York. Death took her by surprise. Came out of nowhere. He wondered if he'd ever find a logical explanation for the element of surprise and the way it always managed to roil the tranquility of the dead.

With evening darkening, he went to inspect the problematic plot. Finding the Montesquieus' tree without any trouble, he caressed the trunk and looked around for the name of the surprised dead woman. He found the miniscule sap mark labeled Sandrine at the nub of branch three hundred and sixty-eight. He came close, put his finger on the spot where the branch had once been connected to the trunk, and looked down, surprised by the thin scratch across the pad of his fingertip. The lacy fibers in the stump left no room for doubt. The branch had been brutally severed. Stunned by his discovery, he called Billion and told him about the fibers. The former director gave him a hearty laugh. "Well, didn't I tell you that sometimes a branch is cut?"

Halfabillion stood his ground, saying it seemed the branch had been cut on purpose. Billion laughed again. "You're talking about illicit behavior again. You simply have no way of proving that a branch was cut out of malicious intent. I imagine this is nothing more than an ordinary accident. I'd suggest you just let it be."

Halfabillion thanked him for listening and decided to heed his advice. He had more important things to deal with, like his pressing workload, the construction of his new house, and the incredible woman who freed him from his thirty-year-old romantic slump. During a single enchanting week the two fell under each other's spells and he managed to forget his new love's death and all the other things that had been nagging him of late. The element of surprise disappeared. For now.

16

Father Tongue—B

The Mad Hop showed no signs of life. Ben realized something was wrong after two days passed and not one of the dozen messages he had left had been returned. He went down to September 1986 with a gloomy feeling, hoping to find the investigator in his apartment or at least to slip a note under his door. But to his amazement, the Mad Hop refused to open the door, yelling at him to get lost.

Ben pounded the door, rasping, "Samuel, what's wrong with you? Why won't you open the door?"

The Mad Hop yelled back, "Ben, do us both a favor and go away!"

"Why?" Ben asked, banging his fist against the door. "What did I do that's making you act as if . . ."

He didn't get a chance to finish the sentence. The door opened, revealing the red-faced investigator. "I'll tell you what you did, you bloody idiot! You sabotaged my case by knowingly withholding crucial information."

"What are you talking about?"

"Apparently you're an even bigger idiot than I thought. Think it through on the way back to your flat."

"I'm not going anywhere," Ben said, marching defiantly through the door.

"You will not force your presence on me!" the Mad Hop said, walking out.

"You don't want to help me find Marian? That's what you're saying?"

"*You* don't want to help yourself! How dare you not divulge that your whole family had died?"

"What's your point? It never even came up."

"As opposed to your record-breaking imbecility, which has come up so often it could fill an entire book. Mr. Mendelssohn, I hereby terminate our agreement. . . ."

Ben covered his ears and shouted, "You're not terminating anything!

You're the only person who can help me find her and I'm not submitting to your insane whims."

"My whims?" the Mad Hop cried, pushing Ben farther inside and slamming the door behind himself. "My whims? You think I don't want to find her? You think I like seeing that hangdog expression on your face each time you come into this apartment? You've got some bloody nerve calling me whimsical when anyone with even a modicum of sense can see why I'd like to boot your concrete-filled arse the hell out of my apartment and never hear from you again. Please, be so kind and explain why you chose to utterly ignore the matter of your family in our floundering efforts to find a woman that so far no one has seen?"

"My family's got nothing to do with it," Ben said, trying to ward off the investigator but blushing a deep red when he asked him whether his family knew Marian. When he nodded, the investigator started yelling again, his anger tenfold. "Now you see why you're an idiot? An entire family lives in the Other World—an entire family that knows Marian, an entire family that could help us find her, a family that may well already have found her and, more importantly, an entire family that has no idea you're dead!"

Ben mumbled, "I didn't think about them. I was caught up in Marian."

"Typical," the Mad Hop said. "You see, Ben, the egocentricity of two lovebirds can blind them to their deepest needs."

"Can you give the fortune cookies a rest and just say what you mean?"

"You're so caught up with your wife, you ignored those who can help you the most. . . . Don't expect any sympathy from me if you carry on charting your course like an emotionally blind bat. . . ."

"That's exactly why I can't let you go. Samuel, you're my guide dog in this strange world. . . ."

"On a different day, I'd take offense, but right now I'm too angry to care what you say. Answer me two questions. Are you at odds with your family?"

"Not at all. Ours is a small family. I'm an only child. I have several uncles, but I've only kept in touch with my Uncle David."

"And what was Marian and your family's relationship like?"

"Very loving," Ben said. "Do you think anyone from my family met her?" he asked after a brief pause.

"If she got on so well with them, it makes perfect sense that she'd want to go and see them."

"Especially since she's alone. She's alone in this world! How did I not think of that before? Her parents are still alive, just like me she has no brothers or sisters, and she hates the only member of her family who's here, some shrew of an aunt. You're right, she must have made contact with them."

"You've got to make a list. . . ."

"Forget the list, Samuel. I know who to talk to."

"In other words?"

"My dad. Marian was crazy about him. And he about her. God, how did I not think of this myself? Samuel, you're a genius!"

The Mad Hop let the exasperation fall from his face. He folded his arms, smiled, and said, "That, or you're just an idiot."

"Guilty as charged," Ben laughed.

The Mad Hop escorted him to the door, shook his hand, and in a lower than usual tone said, "Good luck with your dad."

On the way to February 1994, Ben slipped into the warm pool of reminiscence, recalling how his dad, who issued bizarre insurance policies for a living, died, ironically, by drowning. He had been on his way back from a meeting with Indian pop star Ishkapar Matuli–the man wanted to insure the magic udders of New Delhi's most famous cow, which, thanks to some genetic mystery, supplied deliciously rich coconut milk– when his plane went down over the Indian Ocean. Mr. Mendelssohn had garnered quite a reputation by then. His livelihood rested on his unrivaled efficiency, his freshman enthusiasm, and his unusual patience for deals that, at best, reeked of wealthy eccentricity gone wild and, at worst, of an acute idiosyncrasy akin to lunacy. It goes without saying that the energetic Menachem Mendelssohn made most of his fortune off the former group's permanent quirks. By the age of twenty-five he'd secured an American partner, Justin Case, to co-head the successful insurance agency, which specialized in handling the degenerate needs of the harebrained and cash-addled aristocrats who wanted to insure their every asset, material as well as spiritual, in order to keep their peace of mind and the feeling of supremacy that the object afforded them once it was insured. When asked about the secret of his success,

Menachem always emphasized people's fear of the unknown and his willingness to address his clients' most deeply entrenched anxieties. As evidence he admitted that he had drafted a water policy for himself. He'd always harbored an inexplicable fear of water. His parents were made aware of the problem when they first took him to the beach and he screamed so loud and so long at the prospect of swimming in the shallow water with the other kids that he fainted. Twice. By his eighteenth birthday he had seen twenty-five highly competent lifeguards fail miserably in their attempts to teach him the basics of buoyancy and swimming. The three psychologists his parents hired didn't do any better, unable to find any hint of trauma in the lively boy's past that could explain his hydrophobia. Therefore, when he got older and found his path in life, he drafted an insurance policy that stipulated that if he was fatally injured in any sort of body of water his wife would receive twice what she would get if the scythe of death was wielded in any other way. Moreover, since he was adamant about proving the depth of his fear, he stipulated that if it could be proven that he had approached the offending body of water of his own volition and choosing, the policy would be revoked.

As soon as his wife, Deborah, heard about the accident, she hoped he had died in the air, well before impact with the water, but the pathological report was definitive. She assembled the family, told them what had happened, and then got on a plane along with the rest of them and flew abroad, where they cremated him, as instructed, and scattered his ashes on the bobbing water of the sea, convinced that there was no better way to portray the soul's ultimate victory over the fears of the flesh.

When Ben reached his father's apartment, he was certain he'd made a mistake. The woman who opened the door looked nothing like his mother. He uttered an apology, but the woman smiled and said, "You've got the right address."

He smiled back at her. "Excuse me?"

She shook her head in disbelief and laughed. "I know who you are. You're Menachem's son. Ben, right?"

He nodded, slightly confused.

She giggled warmly. "I know you from your father's tapes."

After a short silence, she shook his hand cordially. "Nice to meet you.

My name's Anifried Balaksen Dortmunsgund, and I am a rude woman, otherwise I would have invited you in long ago."

Ben entered, noting in a single glance the heavy wood furniture so loved by his father. Anifried showed him to the oval couch and asked if he'd like something to drink. Ben declined. She went over to the bar, poured herself a brandy, sat down opposite him, looked him over, sighed lightly, and said, "Yes."

"I didn't ask anything," Ben said.

"But you meant to ask if I'm your dad's girlfriend."

"On second thought, I will have that drink," Ben said.

She nodded, got up, and promptly returned with a glass of brandy. Before she even had the chance to sit back down, Ben threw back the amber liquid, cleared his throat, and asked, "So, where's your boyfriend?"

She leaned back, crossed her legs, and looked at the godget. "He should be back soon. He went to the multilingual lab to get his chip fixed."

"I see," Ben said, trying to mask his turmoil.

She peeled the façade away with her penetrating stare and said, "I know this is difficult for you, Ben. Maybe it would be a bit easier to swallow if I told you about Menachem and me. We met on the plane that went down. He was sitting next to me, and trust me, there are few ways to get to know a stranger quicker than spending your last minutes on earth with them. At takeoff, we were two cold-blooded businesspeople on their way home. When it became clear we'd never see home or our loved ones again, we held hands, hugged, and cried like little kids. As you can imagine, we found one another in the white room and among the thousands of confused and scared people, we no longer felt like strangers, but like the only two people who knew each other in this mysterious world. I know it sounds like a Hollywood movie, but it was only a matter of time till we fell in love. Before we even had the chance to grasp each other's personal tragedies, we had forged an indelible bond. Menachem and I discovered a new world together and we were dizzy with excitement. Sorry for the cliché, but he was the hand to my glove."

"I thought my mother was his glove," Ben whispered.

"People have two hands," Anifried said.

"Meaning?"

"Oh, at long last I detect a trace of hostility. Ben, don't be embarrassed. You're allowed to hate me. After all, as far as you're concerned,

I'm the other woman, the one who took your mom's place. I just want to make one hundred percent clear: that wasn't the case. When I met Menachem, she was still alive. She came here five years late."

"Late?"

"Yes, if the plane hadn't gone down, your father and I wouldn't have met. If your mother had been on the plane, I would have come here all alone and, it stands to reason, you wouldn't be sitting here wishing me all the bad luck in the world."

"I don't even know you. Why would I wish you any harm?"

"Because of my current status, dear. I'm your father's significant other now."

"And what about my dad? He's happy?"

Anifried closed her eyes. "He's like a schoolboy in love. Calls me his happiness policy."

Ben pursed his lips and swallowed hard.

"What's wrong?" she asked, opening her eyes.

"That's what he called my mother."

"Look, Ben, this is all a lot simpler than it seems. Monogamy is a charming idea and it often simplifies matters, but not when you're facing an eternity . . ."

"What do you mean?" Ben asked.

Anifried laughed. "Had your parents died of old age, they could well have said they'd beaten all the statistics and made their love last for fifty or sixty years, but even then, neither of us could possibly guess what was next. They'd come here and realize they have an eternity to spend together. An eternity, Ben, do you follow? Would you still think they'd never part? There's no end to the time we have on our hands, so there's also no end to our romantic options."

"Perhaps then one day you and my dad will part ways? Is that what you're saying, that you may cease to be like a hand in a glove?"

"It's possible. We've only been together seven years. Who knows what will happen in another five, fifty, hundred years? I believe every love comes to an end. Then comes new love."

"And that's an opinion my dad shares?"

"If he didn't, he'd be with your mother."

"Has he met her?" Ben asked, his voice giving out at the end of the question.

Anifried bowed her head and, in a commiserative tone said, "He hasn't, but I have. She came to our doorstep one day. He was out visiting a friend. She asked me who I was and then stormed off."

"They haven't met?" Ben roared.

"She said she didn't want to see him. Menachem was depressed for two weeks. He said he didn't even know she had passed away. It took a few days but then he settled down. I pointed out that the ball was in her court. She could come see him whenever she wanted. And anyway, no offense Ben, but he has moved on."

Ben ran his hands through his hair. "I can't believe this. This is insane. This cannot be happening."

"This happens all the time. And listen, you must keep in mind that these two worlds are radically different. No one can guarantee that a love that worked there will work here. You say this can't be happening because you think the two people who brought you into the previous world were meant to stay together in both worlds."

"I'm sorry, Anifried, I have to go," Ben said, getting up suddenly and heading for the door.

Anifried followed him. "You're not going to wait for your father?" she asked.

"I'll see him another time," Ben said, opening the door. "Do you happen to know, though, if he met my wife, Marian?"

"I have no idea."

She cast a light hand toward his shoulder. "Maybe just wait a bit more for him? If you'd like, I could give him a call."

"That's okay. I'll come back another time."

"It was a pleasure to meet you," Anifried called after him, even though he, like his mother before him, marched out of her apartment, down the hall, toward the elevator and the undulating music of the perfumed sitar player.

For the first time since he'd arrived, Ben made some room in his mind for something other than his missing wife. Concern for his mother overwhelmed him. He abandoned his original plan and headed toward December 1999.

❧

Knocking on the door and hearing the limp female voice from within, he felt a tightening in his chest.

"Leave me alone," she said.

Ben banged harder. "Mom, it's Ben."

There was a long moment of silence. He put his ear to the door and said, "Mom, please, open up."

The door opened, revealing an ashen woman, robbed of her former vibrancy. The two exchanged alarmed glances, stunned by the effects of time on their faces. Deborah, a vivacious woman who had died after having suffered a sudden cardiac arrest, took a step back, leaned against the wall, put a hand to her disheveled hair, and whispered, "I think I'm going to faint."

Ben wrapped his hands around her and led her to the king-size bed in the middle of the living room. He sat her down, noted the strange clay ornaments surrounding it, and got her a glass of water, smiling lovingly as she gulped it down, her eyes riveted on his, unwilling to waver. "Sorry for the surprise. I didn't mean to shock you."

Deborah started to cry, caressing his hair, whimpering, "Ben, sweetheart, my Ben, you're dead, nothing's left, everyone's gone. I thought maybe death would skip over you . . . that you'd reach old age . . . Ben, honey, I don't know whether to be happy or . . . I missed you so much but I didn't think you'd get here so fast."

"I missed you, too, Mom."

"Of course, sweetheart," she said, kissing his forehead and smiling. "I don't remember you ever being so big. Did you do something to your body?"

"I worked on it a bit. You changed a lot, too. What happened to you, Mom? Why are you so skinny?"

Her response amazed him. She pulled away, wiped the trail of tears from her face, blinked several times, and burst into husky laughter. "You want to know what happened to me? I'll tell you. Your father is what happened to me! The idiot has a Norwegian girlfriend, this unbelievably annoying woman with a name that you have to be Scandinavian to pronounce. Turns out they met on the plane that went down."

"I know, Mom, I met her two hours ago."

"They have been together for seven years. When I died and came to this place, the first thought that crossed my mind was to see how Menachem's doing. After all, we had a lot of years together. I just wanted to see how he is, but he wasn't at home. The great belle of the fjordlands opened the door, said I had every right in the world to be angry with her, and all kinds of other garbage. Obviously, I was upset, so I left. A week later I came back. This time he was there. Alone. Oh, Ben, the man issued every kind of insurance in the world, but he never came up with one for brain tissue gone flabby."

"I don't think I get it."

"I thought that with death something would change—in the man, in his perspective, in his beliefs; I don't know, something along those lines."

"But Anifried says that . . ."

"I know, I know. She fed him all that crap about love in the face of eternity, and how can two people stay together for that long, and why should we restrict ourselves to one person, and all the rest of that rubbish."

"You don't buy it?"

"Forget me, Ben—turns out your father doesn't buy it either."

"He doesn't?"

"You should have seen him the first time we met. He wouldn't stop apologizing, begging me to forgive him. He started blabbing about Phase II and saying that he still loved me but was *in* love with the Norwegian. That the last thing he wanted was to hurt my feelings. Ben, you wouldn't have believed it. Your dad, obsequious, hysterical as a teenage girl, devoid of any sense of humor."

"Didn't you expect an apology?"

"For what? For the fact that his plane crashed and he fell in love with another woman when I was nowhere to be found? Sweetheart, I got used to living without a partner. I'm sure you remember that during the first two years I was devastated, but after that I got the hang of it and really started to enjoy the whole thing. I missed him, of course, and not a day went by that I didn't think of him, but when I came here I felt like I'd been reborn. I felt like a girl discovering everything all over again, on my own! You know what I mean, Ben? Being single has upsides that I'd already forgotten about."

"And what about love?"

"Love? Who says it needs to be shared? I love Deborah Mendelssohn and I don't care how that sounds. I go out, travel, meet new people. I don't need to sit around for weeks and wait for my husband to come back from some faraway business trip. I meet my family every once in a while, just like we did in the previous world, and I recognize

that life is just the prologue, the introduction to the real thing. Ben, I'm
happier than I ever thought possible. I've never felt as alive as in death."

Ben stared at her in silence.

She lay down on her back and took his cold hand in hers. "I sound
like a nut job, ah?"

Ben smiled. "Forget about how you sound . . ."

"But what about the way I look, right? You remember how each
death in the family took a few literal pounds of flesh? Well, by the time
I arrived here I was pretty darn skinny, and then the business with Menachem took another twenty-five pounds. As for the bird's nest of hair,
don't think I don't realize that I look like someone on the way back
from a Salem witch convention. I just make it my business to look this
way when I know your father's coming over."

"Coming over?"

"Yeah, Benji. In fact, he left about an hour before you arrived."

Ben took his hand back. "But she told me that . . ."

"Yeah, yeah, that his Babel was broken and that he was at the labs
getting it fixed? Ever since we met up again, he's had to get his chip
fixed about two dozen times, if you know what I mean."

"He lies to her?"

"All the time. Each time he wants to come see me, he starts speaking a mix of Esperanto and Sanskrit and says he has to race to the lab.
I feel sorry for that Norwegian girl. The first lesson in a relationship is
to know when your partner's lying to you. Otherwise, how will you
ever know when he's telling the truth?"

Ben nodded. "But Mom, why does he come visit you so often?"

Deborah tapped her temple. "Because he's acting like a child, that's
why. From the moment I told him I wasn't interested in having a romantic relationship he's changed his skin, courting me like a man possessed. Typical male behavior—something is taken from you and you'll
go through the trials of Hercules just to get it back, even if you don't
want it! Now you see why I look like I do? He always calls before he
comes, which gives me a chance to make myself as unattractive as possible. Not that it helps. . . ."

"Maybe he just loves you and isn't willing to let you go?"

"Honey, he just can't stomach the thought that I might fall in love
with someone else. It's possessiveness, competitiveness, jealousy—but

it's not love. Imagine the excitement he must feel each time he lies to his lover and goes off to try and woo his ex-wife. . . ."

"You were never divorced. . . ."

"Have you forgotten that death nullifies marriage?" Deborah asked, leaning forward, flaunting her perfect diction. "'Till death do us part!'"

Noticing the frozen look on her son's face, Deborah asked, "What's wrong, Ben? Did I say something?"

"Mom, I didn't tell you how I got here, or, more importantly, why."

Deborah covered her open mouth. "Ben?"

"It's Marian, Mom. She died a year and three months ago in an accident. . . ."

"Her, too?" Deborah said. "And then you followed her here. . . ."

"Only I haven't been able to find her," he said, head down, "and judging by your reaction, you haven't seen her either."

"No, honey. Nor has your father. If he'd seen her, I'd know."

Ben nodded.

"Ben, I'll do anything I can to help you find her. I promise."

"Thanks, Mom. You won't be angry if I leave now, will you?"

"Already?"

"I've got a lot to do."

They exchanged fingerprints and he promised her they'd meet again soon. After trying to get him to stay one more time, she walked him to the door and rocked him in her arms. "You'll find her, honey."

Ben kissed her on the cheek and said, "Unless death *did* us part."

Three hours later he was still roaming the streets, Anifried and his mother's words tumbling around in his head. Even if he found Marian, her love was not guaranteed. Maybe she found new love, like Anifried; maybe she's loving her newfound freedom, like his mother; maybe she'd just lost interest in him. Dejectedly, he came to the realization that there was only one place where he'd be able to verify Marian's love, one place where he'd find solace, a place that the Mad Hop had warned him about time and again.

17

Les Enfants Terribles

Adam and Shahar lived in a private house on a small side street in the heart of the Bavli neighborhood in Tel Aviv. They inherited the place from their wealthy industrialist father, who, in death, bid them to maintain their fraternal loyalty and continue sharing their home. The old tycoon's final instructions were not difficult to adhere to. The brothers had been watching each other's backs since childhood and had sworn to live under the same roof till death came between them.

Their mother, who recognized their unique bond at an early age, figured that it was the product of shared blood, and not, in fact, the result of a soul searing experience. After Adam, nine, and Shahar, eight, lost their mother—a claustrophobe, whose heart stopped when she was locked in the basement of their villa—they grew even closer than before, much to the fresh widower's delight. Their relationship to their father, though, hit rock bottom when, as young adults, they made clear that they had no interest in the family business. Both planned to pursue more creative endeavors. Their father, who dreamed his sons would reinvigorate the business he had started on his own and devoted his life to, felt sufficiently betrayed to banish them from his inheritance.

The brothers left the family villa in Klil and moved to the big city, where, for the first time, they saw how the other half lived. Scraping by with random jobs, the two of them, without ever uttering the family name, rose to the top of their respective fields, each a success in his own right before the age of forty.

Adam was a leading game designer. Thousands of hyperintelligent kids eagerly awaited each new edition of Cryptograph, his series of questlike games. The series was inspired by his romanticized vision of the Middle Ages, a time when monarchies, parliaments, ministers, and mere political agitators communicated via encoded messages, plotting coups against the rulers of their day. Adam combined his love of history with his undying adoration for intellectual brainteasers, giving his young fans an opportunity to play an active role in deciphering hundreds of historical documents, ranging from the Restoration to the world wars, the fall of the Roman Empire, the French Revolution, the American Civil War, and other events that changed the face of the world. Aware of children's predilection for copious amounts of blood, he did not deny them the chance to engage in on-screen violence, allowing them to play heroic roles as a prize for solving a riddle, a formula that even the most refined parents found hard to resist. When asked how he understood children so well, he smiled bashfully and said he'd never lost touch with the child he had been.

Shahar, too, stayed close to his inner child, who used to pretend to be a cruel king, an arrogant nobleman, a captive princess, or a hunchback. When he grew up, he became a virtuosic actor, capable of taking on any part so long as it allowed him to shed his own self and step into someone else's skin. Other actors, who worked with him on stage and in the studio, said he had the Day-Lewis syndrome of always leaving his personality behind when he came to work. Everyone knew that he was consumed by each new role. The word around town was that he was so good because he himself was a tabula rasa. In his fifteen years of acting, he'd played a deaf detective, a transvestite, a male stripper, a rock star, a beggar (which earned him Israel's Best Actor award), a brain surgeon, a drug dealer, an alcoholic, a mouse, a ghostwriter, a crooked politician, a decorated general, a prince (Hamlet), a king (David), and a queen (Lady Macbeth). When asked how he understood the characters so well, he smiled bashfully and said he never lost touch with the kids they had once been.

When their father died, the brothers decided to honor his appeasing will and move in together to the posh house in Tel Aviv. For them it wasn't much of a change, having always lived together. In this new house, a red door, unlocked at all times, was the only thing that divided their ample living spaces. In the evenings, Adam sat by the fire and helped Shahar read his scripts; in return, Shahar played Adam's computer games, trying to defeat history. Nevertheless, each of them knew that they had yet to beat back their own history. Success did not erase the scars of the past. Even though they had drowned the neighbor who, back when they were kids, raped them once a week for three interminable years and forced them into silence by threatening to kill one if the other spoke, they were still, for all intents and purposes, owned by their past. The two never exchanged a word about the childhood "execution." Instead, they focused on the gloomy present of a sexually inactive pedophile who compulsively masturbated to pictures of naked children he had brought to his house, and a frigid man who despised all human touch, unless it was mandated by a script. Shahar stood watch, ensuring that his brother didn't cross forbidden lines, and Adam, in turn, guarded the soul with a thousand faces, which, all too often, stood on the brink of a breakdown.

More than a year had passed since Shahar proved the full extent of his loyalty to Adam, and the latter openly displayed his guilt for his brother's sacrifice. Shahar said he was just doing what any good brother would do, but it was clear to both of them that they were extremely lucky to have escaped the incident unscathed. Ever since that awful day, Adam had been especially cautious, swearing to himself that he would never involve his brother again in his precarious pursuits. For three full months after that day, Shahar cordoned himself off from the outside world, begging his brother not to mention the incident. Adam agreed, thanking him a thousand times for his courage. Shahar caressed his brother's chestnut hair. "Too bad I'm not thirty years younger."

"Who you trying to kid?" Adam said.

Over a year later, Shahar spun the question back at him when Adam mentioned a woman that had caught his attention. Adam swore he was serious.

"A woman or a girl?" Shahar asked.

Adam smiled back. "She's short and a little like a girl, but she has the expression of a woman. She's not particularly pretty, but when I look at her I feel the same way I do about some of the kids. Like she's never been touched."

"Adam, I've never seen you like this before," the actor said, his eyes coming to life, "she's really got you worked up."

"Shahar, I'm serious, I want her."

Shahar burst out laughing. "I don't believe my ears."

"That's not all, Shahar," Adam said. "I think she likes me."

"What gives you that idea?"

"She checks me out. Each time she passes by the health club she stops and looks at me for a few minutes. Day before yesterday, she smiled at me. I'm telling you, Shahar, she wants me but she won't dare make a move. She's just not the type."

"And you, dear brother, are the type? Or do you plan on keeping her in the realm of fantasy?"

"Apparently I am," Adam said.

"Apparently you are what?" Shahar asked.

"I followed her last night. I know where she lives. I sent her a bouquet of red Sweet Williams this morning."

"And how will she know who they're from?"

"I wrote 'have a wonderful day' on the card and signed it 'Adam, the guy from the gym.'"

Shahar chuckled. "My brother, hitting on someone who doesn't play with dolls? Too weird to be true."

"At least your brother's hitting on someone," Adam said, taking off his glasses and leaning back, spreading his hands across the couch that often hosted some of his younger guests.

"And how does my dear brother plan on continuing his campaign with the little lady?"

Adam sucked his thumb. "The little lady, I like the sound of that. Your brother will keep on sending the little lady bunches of Sweet Williams and the little lady has his telephone number. . . ."

Shahar peered at the rug.

"I know what you're thinking," Adam said.

"What?"

"You're worried she's going to be disgusted by my deformity."

"No, not even close. If that bothers her then she's not even worth the trouble."

"So, what? Why so sad?"

"I'm going to bed soon."

"I told you to turn that role down. But you're hardheaded as a bull."

"Adam, come on, you know this role is an amazing challenge. I've never played a man who . . ."

"Forget it. I don't want to go into it. Next week you finish filming and it will all be behind you. In the meantime, if you want to, I don't mind sleeping in your room . . ."

"It's alright. I'll try not to scream as much."

"The screaming doesn't bother me."

"So that's how it is when you're in love?"
"I wouldn't know."

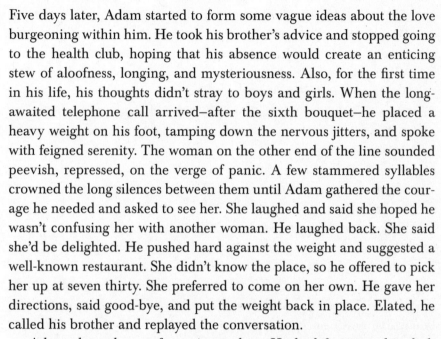

Five days later, Adam started to form some vague ideas about the love
burgeoning within him. He took his brother's advice and stopped going
to the health club, hoping that his absence would create an enticing
stew of aloofness, longing, and mysteriousness. Also, for the first time
in his life, his thoughts didn't stray to boys and girls. When the long-
awaited telephone call arrived—after the sixth bouquet—he placed a
heavy weight on his foot, tamping down the nervous jitters, and spoke
with feigned serenity. The woman on the other end of the line sounded
peevish, repressed, on the verge of panic. A few stammered syllables
crowned the long silences between them until Adam gathered the courage he needed and asked to see her. She laughed and said she hoped he
wasn't confusing her with another woman. He laughed back. She said
she'd be delighted. He pushed hard against the weight and suggested a
well-known restaurant. She didn't know the place, so he offered to pick
her up at seven thirty. She preferred to come on her own. He gave her
directions, said good-bye, and put the weight back in place. Elated, he
called his brother and replayed the conversation.

Adam showed up a few minutes late. He had forgotten his dark
glasses on his desk and had gone back home to get them. As soon as he
walked into the restaurant, he saw her, seated at a side table. Surprisingly, her face remained placid at the sight of him and he wondered if
he'd gone overboard with the gel or horribly awry with his choice of
navy blue blazer. As he headed toward her, the woman's features began
to reveal the distorted signs of comprehension. When he spread his se-
ductive, kid-friendly grin, the color drained from her face, she blinked
furiously, and bit her lip like a kid caught red-handed. When he came
to the table and apologized for his lateness, she glared at him with
muted embarrassment. And when he stretched out his hand for her to
take, she stared hollowly at the open palm, coming to her senses only
after a full thirty seconds. He sat down and smiled at the scared girl,
who had the incontrovertible expression of a trapped mouse.

"You still haven't told me your name," he said, the smile constant on
his lips.

"Ann . . . Ann Dolington," she said, her little lips flapping.

He considered asking about the origin of the foreign name but decided against it. "Ann, finally, I get to see you without the big plate of glass between us and, I must say, the distance does you a disservice."

"Thank you," she said, hiding her face in the menu.

"Do you want to order?"

"Sure, I guess. I'm a little thirsty."

"What would you like?"

"A glass of white wine."

Adam signaled for the waitress and ordered a glass of white for her and a glass of red for himself. Looking back at Ann, he read the shock on her face like large print.

"What's wrong?" he asked.

"A minute ago you said you're finally seeing me."

"Yeah?"

"How exactly are you seeing me? You're . . . ah . . ."

"I'm what, Ann?"

"You know, with those dark glasses . . ."

This time Adam went pale. "Oh my God, you think I'm blind."

"No, no, I mean you never take them off. They're so dark and, you know, I've never once seen you without them at the health club. I'm sorry. I'm so sorry."

"Don't be."

Ann cleared her throat. "If you can see, why do you wear them all the time?"

Adam glanced sideways, made sure no one was watching them, took off the glasses, and smiled his apologies. Ann steeled herself, but as soon as he bared his eyes, the most cross-eyed pair she'd ever seen, she released a soft, surprised grunt and then nodded. "Strabismus." Before he had the chance to ask, she said, "I'm a nurse."

Adam gestured at the glasses. "If it's okay with you . . ."

"Of course," she said, "although it doesn't bother me."

"Liar," he said, and they both laughed.

At that exact moment, just as the bobbing iceberg between them submerged and well before he told her about the five failed surgeries he had as a kid, the waitress swung by and placed a glass of red wine on the table. "Here you are," she said.

"Excuse me, what's this?" Adam called after her.

The waitress smiled politely. "You ordered a glass of the house red, no?"

"And the lady?"

"The lady?" the waitress said, flipping through her memory as she stared at Ann's lowered head.

"The lady ordered a glass of the house white."

"I'm so sorry, I must have forgotten the lady."

Adam leaned forward, speaking between clenched lips. "Listen to me carefully. Now you're going to get the lady exactly what she asked for and if you forget again I guarantee you that I'll make it my business to ensure that this is your last evening on the job. Are we clear?"

Ann smiled at him when a few seconds later the wine arrived. "That was very chivalrous of you. . . ."

Adam softened his gaze. "No more than your act of chivalry, Ann."

"My chivalry?"

"This whole evening. I'll understand if you get up and go."

"I don't understand."

"It's not me, right? You came here thinking you were going to meet someone else. You were looking at someone else at the health club and that's why you had that expression on your face when you saw I was walking toward you earlier. Ann, I'm terribly sorry for the misunderstanding. I was sure it was me. Especially after what happened six days ago. You smiled at me and I thought you were giving me the green light to . . . God, what an idiot."

After a long silence he asked indignantly, "Why did you smile at me if you weren't interested?"

The straightforward question earned him a similarly honest answer. "I smiled in longing for the guy who used to work out next to you."

Adam stared at her and mumbled, "I've never felt more pathetic in my life."

At that moment Ann knew she'd fulfill every wish of the man seated opposite her. For the first time in her life, she was able to shirk the paralyzing feeling of inferiority. Instead, she felt pity toward the bespectacled suitor, who misinterpreted her behavior and striped her dreary week of suspension from work in a wealth of colors she had never dared to dream of. Moreover, he had done what no man ever had. He noticed her. During the past week, her presence in the world had been verified, and even when the waitress reminded her of her absence from the consciousness of others, the precious man came along and reproached her for her attitude, shining a light on what was ordinarily hidden from view. And if that didn't suffice, the wonderful man was at her mercy, shifting in his chair, aware that he is a mere substitute for the true man of her dreams. Ann still refused to believe that she divulged her secret with such atypical ease. Perhaps it was sheer gratitude. Perhaps it was the flowers, the lazy eyes, the way the man writhed around in his chair, the unfamiliar sense of compassion. Perhaps all of the above rose to the surface as he stood and offered to call her a taxi as penance for the dreadful mistake, and she shook her head, touched his moist hand tenderly, and asked him to please stay, since she was enjoying herself.

Ann was being truthful. She enjoyed spending time with the oversized kid who told her excitedly about his occupation and asked dozens of questions about her. So much so that, when they left, she agreed to his proposal to come over to his place, unable to remember the last time she had been in someone else's home.

She didn't hide her appreciation of the immense house. When he asked what she'd like to do, she responded that she was feeling adventurous. Adam blushed and offered Caesar, the first game in the Roman Empire series, in the way of foreplay. Ann sat down at the computer and giggled each time she tried, unsuccessfully, to break the code behind the premeditated murder of Julius Caesar, totally forgetting the man sitting to her side, who planned his moves with the caution known to him from the secret games of seduction. The nurse, so engrossed in the series of Roman numerals, lost touch with her surroundings, the new relief neutralizing the one waiting in the wings, the one Adam has hung his salvation on, the one his soul thirsts for, the one that would, at long last, wipe away the stain of his perversion and convince the entire world of his true attraction to the little lady whose thin legs did not reach the floor, dangling from the heights of his computer chair, bare to the curve of her round knees, which were stuck together. He watched her flounder as she tried to hinder Brutus, swearing silently that in return for her passion he'd rip up every child's picture in the world and love her and her alone.

"You're so nice to me," he muttered fearfully.

She nodded and sent a secret scroll to Julius.

"You want to play doctor and nurse?"

She giggled and dashed off to one of the palace's secret chambers.

"Don't go there," he warned, "the spies will get you," and she reprimanded him coquettishly, "you're giving it all away."

He put a warm finger on her knee.

She started, calmed, and laughed. "You're tickling me."

Her smile vanished at the sight of the traitors. He laid a whole hand on her knee and slid upwards, slowly, terrified to the core. She trembled but didn't ask him to stop, calling out in a hoarse voice, "I know I can save him if I can find him in this enormous castle."

"Go into the tunnel between Remus and Romulus."

She made it to the tunnel with her legs dazzlingly spread. Adam was beside himself. He got off the chair; Julius Caesar was slain in front of her eyes. "Damn," she said with choked restraint. His head crossed the skirt barrier; in the distance he spied the El Dorado known to no man other than himself. Ann closed her eyes, and with astounding clarity saw the man from the club, the right one, not the suitor; she had no idea what he was doing down there, under the computer table, but she had been transported back to the mysterious and most pleasurable Spot, never had it been more precise, and the warmth of his curious tongue as it probed her depths parted her lips, and as she was about to issue the first cry of pleasure a bloodcurdling shriek was heard, and it took her a moment of reflection to understand that it was emitted from another throat and that it was rooted in terror, not pleasure. She heard Adam from down there. "Don't worry. That's just my brother. He's acting out the part of someone chased by a ghost from the past. It's not real."

"It sounds very real to me," she said, turning her head, with her eyes still closed, toward the source of the ruckus, behind the red door.

"No, my little lady, it's nothing but playacting." The determined head below tried to squirm through the viselike closure of the legs, but the second shriek left no room for doubt. Even Adam recognized that something was wrong in the other end of the house—he'd never heard his brother scream in a woman's voice.

Pulling on her shoes, Ann mistakenly kicked Adam in the head and then called out "I have to see what's going on over there!"

"Please don't," Adam pleaded.

But Ann already took off after the voices, crossing over to the other half of the house. At first she saw nothing. But then she noticed the open front door. She ran outside and saw a man lying on top of a woman on the side of the road, strangling her with all his might, yelling, "You're dead, you're dead, you're dead!"

In a moment of resourcefulness she ran back inside, took a vase off the kitchen table, raced back to the scene of the crime, and smashed the porcelain monstrosity on the attacker's skull. Shahar lost consciousness and collapsed on his victim, blood spewing from the crown of his head onto the forehead of the woman beneath him. Ann only remembered to exhale when the woman coughed and whispered in English, "Help me up . . ."

Once the two managed to roll Shahar over, Ann helped her to her feet, hooked her arm through hers, and stroked her hair. "Don't worry, we're going to the police."

The woman nodded. Only as they passed under the first streetlight did she catch a glimpse of the woman who saved her life. She gasped. The feeling was mutual.

A half hour later, while the two women answered a police officer's questions at the nearby station, Adam put the finishing touches on the bandage around Shahar's head and asked, as he lay sprawled on the couch, how, exactly, he managed to get himself in this predicament.

Shahar answered dreamily, "She's back . . . she came back to haunt me. . . ."

Adam didn't get it. "Who, Shahar, who came back?"

Shahar whispered, his eyes moving in fear. "The woman, the woman with the kids, she came here. . . ."

"Hold on a second. You weren't even supposed to be home. You said you had an interview tonight."

"I was really tired when I got back from the set. I almost canceled the interview, but the producer begged me, said it would be great publicity. So I took a shower, called the reporter, and asked her to meet me at the house."

"That's why the meeting was so late?"

"Yeah, but that's not the point, Adam, not at all. I left the door open for her. She walked in and only after I'd laid the coffee tray down on the table did I see her. Adam, it was her, the woman from the Ferris wheel."

Adam grunted at him. "Don't you think you're taking your new role a bit too far?"

Shahar smacked his leg. "Don't make fun of me! It's all your fault! It was . . ."

"But it's impossible. That woman's dead!" After trying to guess at the thoughts hiding behind his brother's glazed stare, Adam smiled at him and said, "Shahar, maybe she just looked like her. That's all, Shahar, she just resembled her."

"You don't understand," the actor wailed, "it was her. The woman from the Ferris wheel. I'd recognize her anywhere. She's come to haunt me. She's going to haunt me, Adam."

Adam pulled an arm around his brother's quaking shoulders and whispered, "Shhh . . . it's nothing. No one's coming to haunt you. It's just your imagination, Shahar, that's all. That woman is never coming back to bother us."

But Shahar refused to be comforted. It took him two hours to finally fall asleep in his stunned brother's arms, whispering exhaustedly, "She's back for revenge. Back from the dead. That woman. The one I killed on the Ferris wheel."

18

Play

The sharp rapping on the door ended what had been Ben's first sleep in six days. He sighed heavily, wondering who could be bothering him at this hour of the night. Three minutes later, the knocking still intensifying, he gathered the strength to call tiredly, "I'm coming, I'm coming." Stubbing his toe on a round item on the floor, he cursed aloud, flipped on the light, and opened the door with an unwelcoming yawn.

The Charlatan at his door spoke in a hard, forceful voice. "Ben Mendelssohn?"

"Yes," Ben said.

"Pleased to meet you," the silver-haired, mustached man said, shaking his hand. "We've been sent by a woman, name of Marian Mendelssohn."

"What?" Ben said, shedding all traces of drowsiness.

The Charlatan turned around and said, "Get to it. And remember, forty!"

Six blue-uniformed Charlatans poured into the apartment in silence and began picking up the tapes littered all over the place and stuffing them into their jumbo overall pockets.

"Wh . . . what's going on here?" Ben asked, voice rising to a yell.

"The lady said you want to see her," the representative of the living dead said. "In exchange she wants the tapes."

"How do you know her?" Ben asked, watching the years of his life disappear three at a time into their pockets.

"She said you'd like to see her," the Charlatan repeated. "If you come with me, I'll take you to her."

"What about the tapes?" Ben asked. "What are you doing with them?"

"If you choose to hold onto the tapes, then you can't come see the lady. That was her only condition."

"And if I allow them to be taken, then you'll take me straight to Marian?"

"Yes, sir," the Charlatan said, gaining Ben's silent acquiescence before excusing himself and convening the group in the far corner of the room. They huddled briefly and then broke, the six-person crew stomping out of the apartment clumsily, their pockets clicking and clacking with life. Ben watched them go wistfully, rising from his reverie only when the Charlatan lay a guiding hand on his elbow. "Let's go, we're off."

On their way to the multi-wheel, Ben tried to pry information from the chief Charlatan but the man was impenetrable. At the station, the Charlatan turned to leave. "Hey, where you going?" Ben called after him.

"Get on the multi; get off with everyone else," the Charlatan said, fading from view. Bewildered, Ben eyed the somber, late-night passengers surrounding him and realized that there was a dark secret at the heart of this journey and that, as opposed to the smile-filled conversations of daytime travel, this particular voyage resembled a random encounter of people all headed together to the gallows pole, the terror plain on each of their faces. When he turned to the man beside him, he saw a face weathered by grief and wondered whether the Charlatan had taken him to the wrong stop. He would see soon enough, he figured. In the meantime, he tried to rein in his enthusiasm in light of the series of disappointments he had suffered since the day of his death and instead focus on the wonder of the past week—each minute of every day he saw his love living and breathing, permanent and undeniable.

She was there beside him during every twist and turn of life, a ubiquitous presence on screen. At times, he found himself so drawn to the events depicted on screen that he responded audibly, surprised to find that the man on tape acted differently. Nonetheless, he couldn't help smiling for the duration of the six-day marathon, marking mutual milestones in a small spiral notebook, keeping careful records of dates, locations, hours, and occurrences so that in the future he wouldn't have to search at length whenever he wanted, for example, to watch them make love for the first time. The careful dissecting of his life into chapters, paragraphs, passages, and even trivial sentences, made him feel like a clerk wading through the complex clutter of his existence, shelving each nugget of experience in its proper drawer. The meticulous cataloguing pleased him immensely, especially when he happened on long-forgotten episodes. Had the Charlatans not disturbed him, he would have woken up the following morning, after eight dreamless hours of sleep, and started from exactly where he left off, before fatigue bested curiosity. Then he heard the driver's voice say, "That's all folks, we're here."

Ben followed the other passengers who got off the vehicle. Like them, he dispelled the darkness with the bright light of day, eager to find out what waited behind the black steel doors that stood at the end of the sandy path. Walking along, he felt as though he had been swept up in a strange tribal ritual. Fits of crying rippled through the mass of people. Ben, remembering family funerals past, recognized something familiar in the walkers—the terrible yoke of loss hunched their backs and weighted their feet. When the black doors yawned open, Ben stopped in his tracks, blinking at the sight of the strangest cemetery imaginable. A bright white hall stretched before him, its floors marble, its ceiling sky. A black lane ran down its middle, separating innumerable rectangular glass caskets containing naked corpses. The crowd strode between the giant fish tanks and, as they reached the caskets of their loved ones, fell to their knees, conversing in hushed tones. The cooing reminded Ben of soft museum chatter. To his right, a twenty-year-old male corpse lay in a fetal position. To his left, an elderly woman lay flat, spread-eagled on her stomach. Up ahead, a child with his thumb in his mouth, his left leg bent so that it formed a triangle with his straight right one. For the better part of an hour, he toured the grid of coffins, entranced by the variety of tranquil sleep positions. Stifling a smile at the sight of a dark-skinned man who had chosen to die in the classic tanning position, hands behind his head, loins marked by the whiteness of imaginary underwear, as though he died a second after leaving the beach, Ben heard a whisper in his ear. "You see the bald man forty-eight rows in front of you?"

He started, looked around, and then stared ahead, remembering the telefinger. "Yes, I see him."

"Well, then stop flirting with the corpses and go to him," the voice commanded.

Ben stayed riveted to the man, who bowed before the glass coffin just like all of the rest of the visitors. Only when he was a few steps away did he smile. "Samuel?"

"Speak quietly," the Mad Hop whispered, motioning him closer.

Ben bowed beside him and looked at the petite, pretty woman entombed before him. Her body was balled up, her hands tucked under her left cheek.

"Who's that?" he asked.

"My wife, Mildred," the Mad Hop said, looking at him with glassy eyes.

"I had no idea you were married," Ben said, examining her delicate face.

"Five years. First time she died was back in 1985. Lung cancer. Second time was eleven years ago. She got drunk and punched in a seven over three. You know what that means?"

"Eternal sleep," the righter sighed. "So this is where they bring all the permanently dead?"

"There's no way back from here," the Mad Hop intoned miserably.

"I'm so sorry."

The Mad Hop stroked the top of the transparent coffin. "She was my Marian."

Ben turned away from the coffin. "You also killed yourself a year after your wife died?"

"I told you to keep your voice down," the Mad Hop said. "People come here to mourn. And regarding your question: yes, and no. Yes, in that my suicide took a year; no, in that had I not chosen alcohol as the cure for my pain, it's likely that my liver would've held up for a few more years, not that I have any regrets." He looked at Ben out of the corner of his eye and added coldly, "As opposed to you, I reckon."

"Come again?"

"Surely you regret your actions," he said, his voice getting colder with each word. "After all, you didn't commit suicide in order to give up on Marian, did you?"

"What?"

"Look around, Ben. Look at the people who frequent this place. Desperate people, broken people, people who come to grieve for their loved ones. People who would give anything to switch places with you!"

"What are you getting at, Samuel?"

"Is that not clear? I called you here to show you how lucky you are. You haven't yet found Marian, but at least you know she's not here, which means there's still hope."

"That's why you drummed up this whole charade with the Charlatans?" Ben asked, abandoning the code of hushed speech.

The Mad Hop clapped a hand over his mouth and barked, "Shut up, buggerhole, and listen to someone who knows a little more than you do. Last time we met, you said you were going to look up your father and report back to me. It's been a week and I haven't heard a word. I left you twenty-three messages on the telefinger, but you couldn't be bothered to return my calls. Not a single one. Correct me if I'm mistaken, but upon return from your father's or mother's house or wherever the hell you were, you gave in to despair and, rather than contacting all other family members, you did what any weak creature might: You waltzed over to the Vie-deo machine and took out the tapes of your life."

"You have no right to trick me like this," Ben said, shaking with rage. "What right did you have to send them to me?"

"You came to me to help find your wife! That gives me every right in the world to act as I see fit! I warned you before not to go near those tapes. They suck you in, distort your reality. Every day of viewing makes you a bit more certain that you won't see her again. You trap yourself in the gilded cage of memory and forget what's truly important! And what do you make of that, Ben? Exactly what I said at the beginning. You've rendered your suicide pointless! If all you were after is moping, why leave the previous world?"

"Save the sermon; give me back those tapes," Ben insisted.

"No more tapes!" the Mad Hop said, like a parent at the boiling point. "They're off-limits until you're told otherwise."

"You can't do that."

The Mad Hop caught his eye and whispered venomously, "That's it, Ben, it's a done deal. You'll get the tapes back when you find Marian, and not a second sooner."

"Or perhaps," Ben said, his face shining, "I'll simply join you and take them from your apartment."

The Mad Hop shook his head. "You're welcome anytime you like, but you won't find the tapes there." He brought his lips close to Ben's ears. "The Charlatans have taken good care of them. They're far from reach. Ben, save yourself the trouble and concentrate on your wife. You've got a far better chance of finding her than them."

Ben held his head in despair. "You don't get it, Samuel, it's not like you're making it out to be. Those tapes keep me going. They encourage me to look for her, to believe that I'll still find her. Without them I have nothing. Before I took them out, I felt like someone was pulling a rug out from under my feet. My dad lives with a strange woman, my mom doesn't care, the entire world order seems to have been turned on its head. All of a sudden, everything's possible. All of a sudden, the truth has been washed away, leaving nothing behind, as though it were only worth something in the previous world. When I watch the tapes, Samuel, I get stronger. They give me fortitude. I refuse to believe that here, in this world, our love has lost its meaning. I've got no choice. Reality keeps barging in on me, laughing in my face, and I don't have a revolver to silence it with. Everything's messed up. And the worst part is that no one's seen her. No, actually, the worst part is, even if I find her, there's no guarantee that everything will work out."

The Mad Hop laid a hand over his heart and donned an expression of woe. "That was truly moving. 'Reality keeps barging in on me, laughing in my face, and I don't have a revolver to silence it with.' Did you just come up with that on the spot or is that from one of your epilogues?"

Ben stared at him, shaking his head. "So now you're ridiculing my pain?"

"Not your pain. The source of your pain!"

"What's that supposed to mean?"

"Well, it doesn't pain you that you haven't found Marian; it pains you that you *still* haven't found her. You're an epilogist and so it only follows that you'd like to see a well-defined ending to your story. After all, you're incapable of handling the fact that your story may have an open-ended finish. That you don't find your wife, but that you keep on with your death, knowing that perhaps one day . . . That ending is far more tragic than the terrible ending that says you shall never find her, since that option, of course, doesn't exist here in our eternal world. The infinite nature of the story drives you out of your mind, so you throw your hands up in the air and succumb to the tapes, where there's a clear beginning, middle, and end. You'll agree with me that you committed suicide after Marian died with the understanding that in the best-case scenario, you'd find her, and in the worst case, you'd find that death concludes all stories? You didn't take into account a Marian-less afterdeath. You didn't think such a scenario existed. And then, once you'd managed to locate a few family members and learned that they, too, had no information of use, you gave in, turned your full attention to the tapes of life, which proved that you're willing to forgo everything just to secure an ending, pathetic though it may be, to your story. Ben, think of her, just her. She doesn't even know you're here. Think of her reaction when one day, out of the blue, she sees you. She's probably already begun getting used to the idea that you'll never be together again. As far as she's concerned, the story is truly over . . . and then you show up, rocking her world, proving her wrong–the ultimate ending, no?"

Ben smiled through the tears, silently applauding the Mad Hop's speech even as he dared to question him. "What if by the time I meet her we discover it's too late? That she . . ."

"Forget it!" the Mad Hop said, his face weary. "It's never too late for you." He then looked back at the woman entombed in the casket and whispered, "Millicent, my love, only for us is it truly too late." He pressed his lips to the glass, kissed it longingly, and rose.

Ben stayed put, his blue eyes boring into the dead woman.

"You alright?" the investigator asked.

"I thought her name was Mildred," Ben said.

The Mad Hop shrugged. "Millicent was my pet name for her."

Ben looked at him, then back at the corpse and said, "You don't know this woman at all, do you?"

The Mad Hop scratched a phantom itch and smiled. "I haven't the faintest idea who she is."

"Then why did you . . . ?"

He winked. "There was a point to be made, mate, was there not?"

Ben got up and followed him through the hall in silence, the two of them walking together toward the stop, into the awakening dawn.

The Mad Hop cleared his throat. "I lied about her, yeah, but not the rest. My liver condition really was . . ."

"Why'd you choose her?"

"Did you get a look at the other corpses around there? If you're going to lie and say you were married, might as well say you were married to a good-looking woman."

Ben laughed, full throated. "And to think that you're a walking, talking truth machine. Samuel, you're a menace to society."

The Mad Hop smiled proudly. "But I got what I wanted, did I not?"

"What do you mean?"

"Tomorrow morning you'll go try and find some other family members, right?"

"Do I have a choice?"

～

Ben boarded the multi-wheel toward 2001. At the apartment, the missing tapes were too much to bear. He paced the rooms, trying to decide

which family member to look for first, bearing in mind distant uncles
that he hadn't seen in ages, who would probably be of no use.

At last he smiled at the portrait on the wall, smacked his head, and
said, "You see what an idiot I've become since you left? Hours I've been
wracking my brain over who to go see and the answer's sitting right
here. I mean, if there are two people in the whole world who definitely
didn't part, it's Rosanna and Moses. No way! Right, Marian?"

The woman in the portrait didn't change her expression, but Ben
was willing to swear he saw a playful glint in her eye, the same glint
she'd shown each time she met the most outrageous member of the
Mendelssohn clan, Rosanna Horazio Malvina Solpero Mendelssohn,
aka "Grandma Rosie."

19 Last Wish of the People of the Day Before Yesterday

Dear Kobi and Tali,

Please excuse this hackneyed opening line, but by the time you read these words, we'll no longer be among the living. We regret imposing upon you but it would seem you'll have to make another trip to the cemetery and to our lawyer, whose information you can find on the back of this envelope. For a long while we toyed with the idea of cremation, leaving our dusty remains to the two of you, so that you could fulfill our romantic wish of mixing Miriam and Yossef's ashes, ensuring our being together in death as we were in life, but with time we came to abhor the notion that we would then be so distant from our beloved daughter, and so we prefer a more traditional burial, beside her, in a rather morbid imitation of the small happy family we created forty years ago. Here lay a mother, father, and daughter.

Miriam's smiling at me now, urging me to share the secret behind the shady adoption process that has changed the course of our lives forever. And she's right. What use is it to take a secret to the grave? It's better to die a feather weight, to leave this world with the same kind of empty nothingness we possessed when we came into it. We regret burdening you with this, but we'd like you to know, just in case one day, somehow, this information will be of assistance to someone. I always loved Miriam's thoroughness. She'd never leave a Pandora's Box without keys. Okay, I've gone a bit overboard. She's correcting me. She says no Pandora's Box and no keys. Just a short story about two bioengineers who devoted their lives to the study of genetics and found, after five happy years of marriage, that they're infertile as desert rock. We almost allowed ourselves to be lured into all kinds of false beliefs, but before losing our grip on reality, we recognized, with immense sorrow, that we were living through the type of coincidence that nourishes the fantasies of all tabloid journalists on the hunt for human interest stories. During the darkest hours, we blamed the atheism encoded in our nonrecyclable DNA (who else could we blame?), but after a few months we agreed that only the weak seek scapegoats, and decided not to cave under the burden. If nature denied us the chance to bring life to this world, we'd raise a readymade one.

From the onset we knew we wanted a newborn, so that we could keep up the perfect illusion of parents just back from the hospital. We had no idea how much heartache, weariness, and bureaucracy the adoption process would demand. With time, we developed a deep resentment for the powers that be. After two months of trudging from office to office, we realized it would be quite some time before we'd hear a baby's cry between the four walls of our home. Fortunately, we met this character named Arthur. He used to linger outside adoption agencies, waiting for people like us. He knew exactly what he was after. A tall, heavyset fellow, very imposing, he approached us one winter day and gave us his card. Said we should be in touch if we decide we'd like to proceed along unofficial routes. At first we feared getting involved with a man with no respect for the law, but after a week of pondering, we decided we had nothing to lose. We met him in a café and he asked if we wanted to adopt a baby. We said we did, and he told us about an underground organization that handles this type of affair. At the time, we didn't even know there was a black market for such things. He offered little in the way of details. Just took a small pad and asked a series of questions about our financial standing, our health, if we have a gender preference, and if we'd have a problem spending a certain amount. Miriam said, "I don't care. Any amount in the world." He smiled and said we would hear from him shortly. A week went by. Then he called and said he had something for us. He asked that we get the money ready (half then and the other half upon his return), he'd fly abroad (to this day we don't know our daughter's nationality), handle the necessary affairs and return with the baby girl. Only when he said "baby girl" did the fantasy take shape.

We didn't sleep for a full week. Afraid we'd been had by some kind of confidence scheme, we worried about the unknown and, at the same time, worked like mad getting the baby's room ready. On the scheduled day, we waited by the phone for nine hours. Arthur gave us an address in the northern part of the city, a private house, and asked us to meet him there at 7:00 P.M. From that point on, it felt like we were in a dream. Everything happened so fast, so smoothly.

A polite, smiling woman opened the door and asked us for our names. She led us to the living room, excused herself, and went up the stairs. Arthur was in a cheery mood. He shook our hands warmly, asked to see the money in the suitcase, and nodded satisfactorily once he'd counted out the bills. Miriam asked how he set the price for a baby. Arthur grew serious and said the mother named the price, based on her needs and the fact that 20 percent went to the middleman, namely the underground organization. Miriam continued asking questions about the mother. Arthur, smiling, said, "Look, the contract I signed with the mother prevents me from divulging any details about her. All you need to know is that she sold the baby in order to gather enough money to ensure the wellbeing of her other child. She hit rock bottom and, without this, she'd be forced to surrender the care of her other child as well. It's a tragedy, but at least now she knows that Marian is in good hands."

We stared at him, dumbfounded. He tried to cover his discomfort with a sprinkling of humor. "She gave up the girl, but not the name," he said. That was the mother's sole wish, to keep the name given her at birth. We smiled in understanding and rolled the name on our tongues a few times, trying to get used to the fact that the three-hundred-name list we had whittled at for months was for naught. In truth, we were rather pleased that someone else had solved the naming problem for us. Arthur pulled a thin sheath of papers out of his pocket. There was a birth certificate that had us as Marian's biological parents and several other forms filled out by the chief midwife at a Jerusalem hospital, further authorizing that Marian had just recently emerged from Miriam's womb. Arthur looked pleased by the shock on our faces. He pursed his lips and spoke slowly. "In order to avoid any and all unwanted complications we're cautious about covering our tracks. The mother has signed a waiver on her rights to the girl. She has no idea who you are beyond that you're both scientists and are unable to have children. There is no chance she'll ever be able to find you. If in the future you decide to tell your daughter that she's adopted, I suggest you say the mother died. I believe that'll spare all parties undue suffering."

Although we were grabbed by a sudden gloom, it drifted away at the sight of the woman coming down the stairs with the most beautiful thing we had ever seen. Kobi's probably laughing now. Biological parents are always accused of blind love for their offspring, and there we were, two adopting parents, hysterically excited by every sign of life from the most gorgeous, most intelligent, funniest baby, who, obviously, lost none of her charms as she grew up into a fine, impressive young woman. All these years we stayed quiet. We thought there was no reason to confuse our beloved little girl. She had always seen us as parents, so why throw her world out of kilter? And, to be honest, with time we ourselves forgot she wasn't the fruit of our loins. And it wasn't only her that we loved, but also Ben and the rest of the clan.

Ben and Marian were the ultimate couple, and from a pair of old possessives like us that's a lot more than verbiage. Would you think us sycophantic if we said that the two of you also qualify as a match made in heaven? Even if at the very beginning you raised a few suspicions with your monthly trips to your friend's parents' house two hours outside Tel Aviv. But when we learned the reason for the trips, we couldn't stop giggling. Don't worry, friends, we haven't told anyone about your love for restrooms in general, and ours in particular.

In a rare moment of drunkenness, Marian told us how passionate the two of you got by entertaining yourselves in a place not intended for such affairs and that the technical side was no less exciting to the two of you. She told us that you made love in hundreds of bathrooms across the country (sterile, we know), but that ours offered the perfect conditions for your favorite position. Mind you, on one truly surreal night we tried to assess the source of your pleasure in a slightly less than theoretical manner. After one minute of preparation, we realized we were heading toward a spectacular failure and that, if we persisted, our hips would fall prey to our curiosity. Instead, we opted for some old fashioned spooning in our own bed.

And still on that matter, Marian even once informed us in secret that Tom had been conceived in our house. We're quite honored to know that that fabulous kid was made in our bathroom and it would be our pleasure . . . Well, now we're getting ahead of ourselves.

Back to Ben and Marian. If you think we were overjoyed when

they told us they were getting married, you should have seen us when Marian told us she was pregnant. That was exactly five years ago. We felt like we were floating on air. We'd have a grandchild. We'd be a grandma and grandpa. Do we sound pathetic if we say that the notion that Marian carried a life inside her womb filled us with a sense of triumph, as if we managed to defeat our defects through her? What if we admit to the satisfaction we felt at the prospect of sitting the future down on our laps and allowing the amazing, soothing thought to wash over us, that years after our expiry date had passed, we'd continue on in his mind, a sweet remembrance, like that first drop of water he'd see through the microscope or the memory of the first experiments he'd perform with the science kit we'd get him for his fifth birthday?

As you well know, that child never came to be. When Ben called from the hospital, his voice smashed, and told us that Marian had woken up in the middle of the night in a puddle of blood, screaming for help, we knew it was time to pack the science kit and the microscope back into their boxes, but we had no idea that the worst was still ahead. Marian had to have a D and C. Afterwards, the doctors told her she would never be able to have children of her own. We tried everything, spoke to the leading experts in the field, discussed IVF treatments, even proposed surrogate motherhood. Ben wouldn't hear of it. Marian sunk into a deep depression. That was the first and last pregnancy in our home and, believe me, you have never seen a more severe self-flagellation. Marian blamed herself for letting Ben down; Ben blamed the mysterious gene pool of the death-prone Mendelssohns, saying that the fact that he seeded his wife's womb with death only strengthens the Mendelssohn curse; Miriam and I blamed ourselves for somehow transmitting something of our infertile DNA to our adopted daughter, as though the tragedy had leapfrogged the logic of biology.

Two years passed before the plague of martyrdom left our family. We wrestled with our childish and fact-free assertions. And as is often the case with these types of affairs, the recognition that they wouldn't ever hug a child of their own only brought Ben and Marian closer together. After they'd weathered the crisis stage, Marian told us that Ben had suggested adoption, but that she had strongly resisted the idea. We inquired as to why she refused to consider such a stellar idea, and she said she only wanted a child that was the fruit of their own love. We told her that an adopted child could also be the fruit of great love if you care for it from the first moments and take genetics out of the equation. She laughed and said we were bandying hypotheses around. At that moment we realized there was no choice but to tell her the truth. Marian was visibly shocked (obviously we took Arthur's advice and told her that her mother had died two months after she was born), and only after we explained to her that there was no reason to share the inessential truth with her until that moment did she smile and say half sarcastically, "Well, then I guess you're really the best parents in the world if you've managed to hide the truth from me for my entire life."

It took another year for her to come to terms with the idea of adoption. We were the only ones who were in on the couple's intentions. In late 1999 the two of them went to an adoption agency and got the ball rolling. We told them they'd need a lot of patience and that the process could be long and arduous, but in February 2000 they told us that they'd be receiving a baby within two months. We were delighted to find how much smoother the process had become. But yet again, tragedy caught us by the heels, this time worse than ever before. Smack in the middle of our preparations, some two weeks before the much-anticipated adoption date, she was taken from us.

Even now, a year, three months, and nine days since that bedeviled day, we are unable to comprehend the enormity of our loss. Even now, first thing each morning and last thing each night, we think about Marian. We've already spoken volumes with you about her and we've defined her absence in every imaginable way. Of course you've already heard all about the trial, which was no more than an insignificant reprieve to our lives, because when suing the amusement park we were disgusted by those who insinuated that greed stood behind our claims (all the money in the world won't change the fact that we've been impoverished for good by her absence), and we turned to the justice system to let out a fraction of our pent-up anger, to blame someone, to claim a modicum of revenge. They brought their experts and we brought ours. They called her death a "regrettable accident," we called them "negligent murderers." Tempers flared, and when they hinted that she had not died

of natural causes, we responded that it was an unnatural death because, since Icarus, it had been pretty well proven that people were
incapable of flight. We so wanted them to suffer, but we didn't know
who: the Ferris wheel designer, the builder, the manager of the
park—someone. Thus, the trial breathed a combative spirit into us,
and each time we entered the courtroom we faked life. Each time
we left, we verified our own death.

From the moment she died, Ben was unapproachable. He wouldn't
even consider our offer to come stay with us for a while until we all
regained some semblance of ourselves. He showed no interest in the
trial and even managed to totally forget the matter of the adoption,
which had become so inconsequential in the interim. And we won't
lie to you, we were mad at him. Maybe because his mourning was
so absolute, maybe because he truly had ceased living ever since he
holed up in his house, and maybe because in death we became ten
times more possessive of our daughter than in life. We were even
angrier when he threw the birthday party (only in hindsight did we
understand why we were not invited—he apologized in his will and
said he wanted to spare us the gruesome sight) and surprised everyone in his own inimitable way. In her death, his wife had taken the
lion's share of his soul, and in his death Ben took one of the last
chunks of ours, because he was the person closest to her in the
world.

As a skilled righter, even he understood that some stories only
have one specific ending. He didn't try to avoid it, as we did, although maybe he did (we heard that he became addicted to working
out, and we thought it was a joke), but in the end he made the most
important fact of all clear: life need not be clung to at all costs.
Once we realized there was no point in going on, everything became so simple. Call us morbid, but as soon as we decided to put an
end to our lives the color returned to our cheeks and we waited for
the verdict in the trial just in order to tie up all the loose ends of our
plan. When we won, we thanked our lawyer and returned home
quickly in order to write this letter. It's funny, at this very moment
we're listening to the excited tone of your voices on our answering
machine and we're more certain than ever that we're doing the right
thing. Tali tells us she has some good news to share with us. Don't
be upset with us if we don't return your call. At this moment we're

engaged in the last details of our suicide plan and on this day, our last, we reserve the right to total selfishness.

And in that same vein, we'd like to impose upon you, dear friends, to fulfill the last wishes of an old couple who are determined to leave this strange world in the hands of slightly more optimistic generations. If by chance our request reeks of undue gall, feel free to refuse outright. However, if you find a touch of logic in our last wish, then consider it, see if you have the mental wherewithal to carry it out, and remember that we respect your decision even if we have no way of knowing it. At any rate, we're leaving all we have, and you'll be happy to know it rounds out to a neat four million shekels, to your dear children. No, that's not a mistake. We used the plural even though we know you only have one child. We'd be delighted if you could make him a sister or a brother. Surely you've considered it and have put it off for another day. We're the last people to push you and we surely wouldn't want you to interpret the inheritance as a procreation incentive or alternately a bribe. This money is to ensure your offspring's future. Half for Tom and half for the other one. After all, you were always like family and we always said Tom was the grandchild we never had. All we ask is for another grandchild. And the idea of leaving half our money to someone who does not yet exist very much appeals to us.

It's important that you know that we sold the house a month ago and that the tenants are moving in in two weeks. We urge you to use the special room in our house before it becomes nothing more than a memory.

And one more thing, friends. If and when you decide to see our request through, do not give the children either of our names. No Miriam and no Yossef. We'd prefer one of two other names. . . .

Tali, Kobi, time goads us on. For a long while now we have felt like the people of the day before yesterday, the ones for whom the only tomorrow is yesterday, and when you read this letter you'll see that we've already slipped into the past. Not much is left to say. We've parted from Ben and Marian at the cemetery and at present we're facing a curious dilemma. Miriam says poison, I say gas. I'm sure we'll argue for hours. And we haven't even chosen the music.

Loved ones, we leave this world not with sorrow but with great relief. If in the last third of this letter we seemed gripped by a certain confusion and our thoughts began to drift, it must be our great yearning to finish all our worldly affairs and put an end to the fathomless farce we called "life." Send our eternal love to Tom and to the other kid and teach them Shakespeare in your spare time. That's what Marian would've done.

Yours, in death as in life,
Yossef and Miriam Corbin

Tali placed a trembling hand on her stomach and wept.

Kobi hugged her and whispered lovingly, "I know, sweetheart . . . nothing would've made them happier."

Ben couldn't figure out what had happened to his grandma and grandpa. He'd been waiting outside their door for six hours, eager to see the octogenarian duo and to quiz them about Marian. Although the wait was dragging on, he was thankful that at least one pillar of his belief seemed to still be intact. The sign on their door read: ROSANNA AND MOSES MENDELSSOHN LIVE HERE IN MUTUAL UNDERSTANDING.

Rosanna refrained from melodrama when she received word that her love of the past sixty-five years had been run down crossing the street. She asked to see the body, and then gave her husband's corpse a piece of her mind for his obliviousness to the charging bus and, even more so, for not adhering to their agreed-upon schedule. "Now, instead of spending the weekend in Tenerife like two decadent old fogies, I'll have to make drastic changes."

Rosanna had planned her final day sans Moses with startling aplomb. While concerned family members scoured the city for any sign of a runaway old lady, she holed up in a hotel room, a short walk from the cemetery where she had long ago reserved a double plot for herself and Moses and pulled a note from her pocket. She had carried it with her ever since she bought the burial plot. A twisted smile on her face, she dialed the number she'd scribbled on the yellowing note. The man on the other end of the line answered lethargically, and she asked him to please deliver the apparatus to her hotel room. The treadmill arrived at her door at six in the evening. At seven her heart stopped beating.

❧

Ben recalled the sober look on his wife's face when she saw the pair of old people in the double coffin and the way his grandmother, born one day after her husband, died exactly one day after he left this world, calculating their life spans with scientific precision. He remembered how his Uncle David showed up at the funeral with three Adonises in tow and how he'd made an outrageous scene by voicing his displeasure at the way his mother had chosen to leave the world.

On the way home from the cemetery, Marian said to Ben that she envied Rosanna's and Moses's love for one another. Ben smiled. "Don't worry, honey, if, God forbid, anything ever happened to you, I promise not to waste any time. . . ."

"Don't ever say that!" she said, smacking him on the back of the neck, "and don't you dare ask me what I would do in her place. Not all of us are Grandma Rosie."

That's for sure, Ben thought, asking himself for the thousandth time why he waited so long before gathering the courage to follow in his grandmother's footsteps.

"Wimp!" he muttered, tucking his head between his legs, listening to the word echo through his ears. Only the feel of a small, chilly, weathered hand on his shoulder stirred him from his guilt ceremony. "Excuse me, sir?"

He looked up and saw the smiling freckled face of an old bespectacled woman who pointed to the door behind him. "I don't mean to disturb you . . . I just couldn't help but notice you sitting here and I was wondering whether you're looking for Rosanna?"

"Yes," Ben said, rising to his feet and shaking her hand. "Ben Mendelssohn."

"Rosanna Parker," she said proudly. "It's funny, no? Both of us are Rosannas . . . although I'm known as Nosey Parker."

"You mean Rosey Parker," he suggested.

"No, young man, I mean exactly what I said. Nosey Parker. As in busybody."

"I'm sure that's just nastiness on the part of . . . ," he said politely, surprised by the gentle slap on the wrist and the scratchy sound of her voice.

"Not at all. If I wasn't into other people's business, I'd die of boredom . . . I mean, between us, if the grass is always greener on the other side then I'm sure the fertilizer is smellier, too."

Ben cleared his throat thoroughly and pointed at the door. "Rosanna."

"Yeah, son, don't bother waiting. She won't be back for some time."

"She?" he asked, his voice rising, "What do you mean *she*? They're not together?"

"With Moses? Of course they're together. Those two are like Siamese twins. They do everything together. Word is she died a day after him while doing her physiotherapy exercises. Chilling, but romantic."

"Excuse me, Ms. Parker," Ben said, trying to cover his dwindling patience with a smile, "you mentioned that she . . . that they would be gone for a while. Do you have an idea where they might be?"

"Does Nosey Parker have an idea where her own neighbors might be?" she said, setting her hands on her hips and exhaling theatrically. "They set out to find Adam and Eve."

She let perplexity settle in his face and then explained. "Rosanna and Moses are off on a roots trip. They were of the opinion that this world offers a unique opportunity to meet your forebears, so they decided to take a trip through the branches of Moses's family tree. Between us, Ben, if those snobby aliases didn't prohibit us from entering the forests, the two of them would be having a much easier time of it."

"I still don't see what this has to do with Adam and Eve."

A diabolical glint flashed through her smile. "Before heading off on their trip, Rosanna told me she wanted to get to the beginning, and that she wasn't near ready to believe that there was a single pair of people at the root of all humanity. Moses said that if they were feeling lazy they'd just take the multi heading farthest into the past, but he knew that plan wasn't feasible. I've never met anyone who's wandered that far back, mostly because no one knows where the beginning is."

"So there's no chance of seeing them in the near future," Ben said, pouting.

"I'd be happy to give them a message from you, if you'd like," Rosie said.

"Do you have their thumbprints on your telefinger?" Ben asked.

"What do you think? Rosanna's a friend of mine. And anyway, who knows what kind of juicy stuff she might come across on her travels. Even fourteenth-century gossip could be interesting, so long as it's controversial and carries at least a whiff of active loins. . . ."

Ben cut her short. "Sorry. I'm in a rush. I'd really appreciate it if you could call my grandparents and ask them if they've seen Marian."

"Marian?" she said, eyes alight. "Who's she?"

"My wife. She died fifteen months ago and I'm looking for her."

She nodded her understanding. "One of those stories, huh? Okay, let's see here." She fussed with the godget and waited. A few seconds later her face cleared and she called out in a bright tone, "Rosanna, how are you? So, how's the journey going? Really? I'm so glad to hear that. Where are you n . . . 1750? Wow, you've really put some miles on. So, do you have a little something for Nosey Parker? Something good? Sure, sure, I don't want to hold you up. You'll just never guess who's standing here by my side. Heaven forbid, not my husband, may he live forever. No. Your grandson. Yeah, I know how annoying they are with their crazy inventions, instead of a telephone, they have this business with the thumbprint. Anyway, I'm sure you'll talk soon. Yeah, he sends you his love. He looks great, too. Of course, I know he's married. Actually, that's the thing. Seems your grandson has lost his wife . . . fifteen months ago. Relax, Rosie, not everyone's as crazy as you are. Okay, absolute love. Maybe quit waving that flag for just a second. All he wants to know is if you or your husband have seen Marian . . . I see . . . okay, okay honey. Good luck with the others and regards to Moses."

Ben didn't need any further explanations. Head down, he exchanged prints with the gossipmonger, who promised to relay any bit of information from his grandparents regarding Marian, and then left the building.

~

Two hours later he met his mom in a café in December 1999. She handed him a list of all the other family members and their places of residence. He asked whether it wouldn't just be simpler to call them on the telefinger, saving him the trouble of going all around and meeting them face-to-face.

"Benji, sweetheart," she said, "ever since we were touched with the death virus our family's been disintegrating. Everyone's stuck in their own corner of death, and the fact that we're here forever doesn't make matters any better. You know how many times I've seen your uncles since I've been here? Twice, Benji, no more. I'm not complaining, but sometimes I wonder when I'll see any of them again . . . ."

"But Mom, you said you see them now and again, the way you used to do in the previous world," Ben said.

Deborah nodded. "Yes, of course, like in the previous world, just without the holidays, birthdays, anniversaries, funerals, and memorials." After a moment she added, "That doesn't leave much."

Ben glanced at the brief list. "You're right. It doesn't." After a short pause, he added, "Still . . ."

"Oh, alright," his mother sighed. "I'll save you one journey, because I can understand the urgency. And because I've already spoken with him."

"Who?"

"Your uncle."

"David?"

"No. Gad."

A fleeting smile crossed Ben's lips. Uncle Gad. The recluse who preferred animals to humans, and spent the better part of his life with them, saving them from extinction and being one with nature, in his words. Unfortunately, four years ago, after spending the last three years of his life in a wildlife reserve in Africa, he was killed by a leopard, a terrible death albeit not inconceivable under the circumstances.

"What is he up to?"

"You know, same stuff. Works at the Zoombie."

"Pardon me?"

"Zoombie. The biggest habitat in the Other World. Enjoying himself to no end. I'm saving you the trouble of going there since it is very far away, and I wouldn't want you to waste precious time when I know that he hasn't seen Marian."

"He hasn't?"

"Sorry, dear. But promise me you'll go and see your other uncle. I know he'll be ecstatic when he sees you, that's why I haven't said a single word to him. Besides, you two have always been quite close back in the old world."

"I promise."

A brief silence ensued. Looking up, his mother saw a cloud pass over his face. "What is it, Benji?"

"Nothing. Just another anniversary without my wife."

"It's . . . today?" She put a hand out to her son.

"It ought to be," he said bitterly, rejecting her hand. "I took my life on her birthday. Thought it would be a nice surprise. That didn't happen. But I took comfort in the fact that I'd find her a few days later, by our anniversary. Mom, she doesn't even know I'm here. I've been trying to think like her, and if I'm Marian, I'm a woman who died suddenly and left a broken husband behind. I still love him but I know he's no Grandma Rosie. And I also know he's still young. He has a lot more living to do. I'll always be the great love, will always outshine any other woman, but with time I'll go from being a fresh wound to an eternal scar. By the time he makes it to this world, I'll already be a closed door in the halls of his life and who knows, maybe one day, in forty, fifty, a hundred years, we'll bump into each other on the street, smile diffidently, and then carry on. Maybe we'll exchange a few words, but what's clear is that time has staged its own revolution. Turned our love into an interesting anecdote in the ancient history of our existence. Mom, I don't want our love to turn into an anecdote. . . ."

"Ben, honey, there is no chance of that happening. After all . . . you . . . are . . . still . . . already . . . under no circumstances . . . pity . . . she . . . love . . . understood?"

Ben wasn't listening. His attention was turned to the strange goings-on behind his mother's back. A startled woman was arguing with a man who had her by the palm of her hand and refused to let go. Her face spoke of great distress and, suddenly, she reached for a beer bottle on a nearby table and cracked it over his head, taking off before he had a chance to come to his senses. Less than a minute later, the brawny man rubbed the area of impact and set off after the terrified woman, the anger apparent in his stride.

Ben pushed back his own chair, excused himself, and ran outside. He was sure he had misidentified the man, who, realizing the woman had disappeared into an alley, stopped, scanned the scene, caught Ben's eye, and quickened his pace in the opposite direction.

"Can't be," Ben whispered.

His mom followed him outside and asked, "What happened, Ben?"

"Simply unbelievable."

"What?"

Ben answered quietly, "I just saw a paraplegic run like the wind."

21 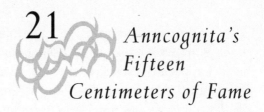 Anncognita's Fifteen Centimeters of Fame

The noise was dreadful. Ann awoke to a feverish cawing of voices, wrapped her head in her two tired arms, and pleaded, "Quiet! Please be quiet!" She couldn't ever remember being this tired. She tried giving sleep another chance, but after ten torturous minutes she realized that the riot outside her door had prevailed. Reluctantly, she dragged herself out of bed and staggered over to the door. Once she opened it, she didn't even have the chance to bend over and scoop up the morning paper; shocked, she froze on her doorstep, and stared into a blitz of flashing bulbs, shielding her face and scurrying indoors with a mighty slam of the door.

"Oh my God, where did all these people come from?" she mumbled, running toward the street-facing window. Pulling back the blinds, she looked out at the dozens of hungry cameramen, who quickly noticed the suspicious movement behind the curtain and brought their lenses to position, eager to capture a shot of the woman who freed the French arts and culture writer from the murderous hands of one of Israel's top actors.

Ann thought Marian was joking when she suggested that she stay indoors until everything quieted down. She couldn't figure out how they had found her house and, more importantly, how she could convince them that she was obliged to keep her promise to the tough detective investigating the case and not reveal any of the details of last night's grisly encounter. Marian also said she wouldn't cooperate with her predatory colleagues in their hunt for the story. Instead, she wanted to delve deeper into the attacker's motive and in good time secure an exclusive interview with her would-be murderer. Ann poured herself a glass of water and then knocked it over at the sound of the telephone ringing.

"Relax," she told herself, picking up the receiver. At first she didn't recognize the man's voice. He was crying and begging her forgiveness. "Who is this?" she snapped. At the sound of Adam's name, she sunk in to the armchair, silent and bewildered.

"Ann," Adam said again, stammering, "Ann, I'll totally understand if you don't want to see m . . . me again, I'm so s . . . sorry about what ha . . . happened yesterday with my brother, but there's a reasonable explanation . . . I'm sure you'll understand. I'd really appreciate it if we could meet one more time, Ann, just to talk it over . . ."

Ann lay the phone back in its cradle. She couldn't speak. An army of thoughts clamored at the fore of her mind: the sublime pleasure of Adam's acrobatic tongue between her thighs filth whore not what she expected the first time to be like his gallantry at the restaurant crazy brother almost killed the wife of the life support patient the hospital tomorrow the suspension ends have to put the white robe back on the hundredth euthanized patient vacation retirement money maybe the Caribbean disconnect the patient or not break it off with the cross-eyed man mistakes she wanted the one next to him he thought she wanted him she's being courted feels good loved it can't be a good idea to get involved with the brother of a murderer it has nothing to do with him it's irrelevant but she's already involved a whole night spent at the police station sworn statement saw him choking Marian it was all supposed to go differently the evening ended suddenly maybe it was a sign she must calm down they're yelling out there what do they want from her planned to leave the house now she can't she's under siege a prisoner eyes watching her seeing her misses her old life must shower emits a familiar scent the Spot the health club where did the man of her dreams go enough facts must be faced he won't be back the earth swallowed him whole and spit her out in front of everyone I'm not scared of closed spaces just of prying eyes the telephone's ringing again not answering maybe it's one of them maybe it's him again poor Adam how could I have treated him like that he's probably hurt rightly so I can't speak to him now enough already stop calling shoot he knows where I live he sent me those flowers God what nerve these people have now they're ringing my bell what could they be thinking maybe I'll hide my face and make it clear that I have no comment that's what I'll do this kind of insanity can't go on I'm putting an end to this!!!

∽

The sight of a young man on her doorstep, looking over his shoulder at the posse of photojournalists and holding a giant bouquet of roses, wiped the decisive look off Ann's face. Her surprise was so great that for an instant she let her guard down, revealing her face and offering the deliveryman a smile. One blinding flash sufficed. She muttered, "Give the bouquet back to whoever sent it," and slammed the door shut. She put her ear to the door and strained to hear what the man was saying to them, picking up fragments of sentences that gave her no new information beyond the journalists' steely resolve to stay put until she showed herself and spoke with them. When she heard the phone ring for the third time, she went into the shower and stood under the stream of water, thinking about her last day on "vacation." Her train of thought was cut off by the repeated clanging of the phone. She toweled off for a while before leaving the warmth of the bathroom and turning on the television. While the cheerful threesome on TV discussed how to prepare a table full of delightful dishes in under twenty minutes, she went to the kitchen, fixed herself some tea, took a bite of an old cookie, and decided to spend the day in the company of the people in the box. She watched a stupid sitcom that didn't elicit so much as a smile, wasted a minute in front of a particularly depressing news broadcast, tested her trivia knowledge with a game show, watched a few bouncy videos on MTV, and then changed her mind, turning off the television and retreating into the bedroom. She dimmed the lights and got into bed, listening intently to the sound of the fading ruckus outside.

Rising, she felt like she'd been asleep for an entire day. The haze still sitting heavily in her mind, she got out of bed and promptly banged into the empty night table by her bed. "Idiot!" she yelled as she appraised the bruise on her ankle, knowing it would soon blacken, serving as a reminder of her clumsy and graceless ways.

"Clumsy and graceless," she said, looking into the mirror, "Retard. If you don't know how to get out of bed maybe you shouldn't go anywhere at all. You are not presentable in public. Now that a miracle's taken place, you are visible. Up until now you were un-everything. That's why no one noticed you. Now you've done something positive and they are all watching you. But don't get carried away. They'll keep on watching you and they'll see you for who you really are. Small, diminutive, an infinitesimal molecule, a grain of sand. They'll see how empty you are inside. And don't even bring up the man from last night. Because that's exactly who he is. The man from last night. Give him a day or two and he'll run away. And don't flatter yourself. So a few pitiful people are clustered outside your house. It's only because of the famous actor. If he wasn't involved, your day would be just as mundane and anonymous as ever . . . Anncognita! They'll lose interest before the ink of today's paper is dry. Just like every news item. Soon you'll go back to being Ann Dolington, the woman who needs to wear fifteen-centimeter heels just so she isn't unwittingly trampled. But for now I'll allow you to bask in the glowing fifteen centimeters of fame, you ridiculous woman!" She lifted an index finger, "I said, for now!"

The phone rang and this time she answered, hesitantly, surprising herself by the about-face in policy. "Hello?"

"Ann?" a female voice asked.

"Yes."

"It's Marian, how are you?"

"Okay," the nurse lied, "and you?"

"Not so great."

"Are you in any type of pa . . . ?"

"No, no, nothing like that. I just don't understand what's going on with you."

"With me?" Ann looked at herself in the mirror, twisting her face into a grimace.

"Yes, I'm getting the impression that you're trying to avoid me."

"I don't understand . . ."

"I've been calling you all day and you haven't answered. At first I thought you might have gone out, but then I remembered the photographers who must be standing outside your door. There's always some bastard who leaks information. But if you're at home, why aren't you answering the phone?"

"It's nothing personal. I just didn't feel like talking."

"And the flowers? Is that also not to be taken personally?"

"Flowers?"

"Yes. I sent you a bouquet, to thank you for last night, but was told that you refused to accept them."

"The flowers . . . were from you?" Ann said, shutting her eyes in self-loathing.

"You thought they were from someone else?"

"Yes, I made a mistake. It's so embarrassing. I'm terribly sorry Ms. . . ."

"I mentioned this yesterday, Ann; please call me by my first name."

"I'm so sorry Marian, I didn't read the note."

"Too bad, because then you'd know that you've been invited to dinner."

"Oh, thank you, but that's really not necessary."

"I know, but I want to, and I'm not going to take no for an answer. Is there any special place you'd like to go to?"

"No, it doesn't really matter to me."

"Great. Are you okay with Indian food?"

"Indian food is great," Ann said, barely able to form a proper giggle.

"Superb. So let's say I'll take a cab and swing by your place at eight?"

A moment after she hung up the phone, she looked back at the mirror and smiled snidely. "Don't let it go to your head!"

Five hours later, Ann opened the door carefully, coaxed her head out, and was pleased to see that the reporters had left the premises. She walked out to the sidewalk and saw a cab coming toward her. When it stopped beside her, she looked in, saw a redheaded woman in the back, and stepped away.

"Are you looking for me?" the familiar voice asked.

The woman with the flame-colored pageboy looked at the nurse through dark glasses that covered half her face.

"Marian?"

Marian motioned her into the car and asked the driver to go. "Every once in a while we all need a little change."

"You're unrecognizable," Ann said, taking in the well-put-together woman in the black suit and red silk scarf.

"You have no idea what kind of day I've had," Marian sighed. "After we left the station, instead of going home to sleep like any normal human being, I went into the first hair salon I could find and asked the guy to do something revolutionary with my hair . . . it took us a while to get to the perfect solution, but I'm now pleased to say I most certainly hate the new look."

"Just because of the press?" Ann asked, her little hands pinching one another gently.

"Yes," she said, motioning her close. "I've got to make sure I don't draw any attention. The last thing I want is to become known because of my involvement in this affair. I hope that by the time someone recognizes me there'll be other developments in the story. By then no one will care who I am and what I look like. They'll all be going crazy about my exclusive interview with the most interesting actor in Israel. It'll be the interview that lays his soul bare. I mean, even when he performed in Europe, like when he had the lead in *FLEA,* he always hid behind the character. I have to interview him. To get to the heart of it. I don't mean the gossipy side of it but the real thing. And in order to get the real thing, I must keep a low profile."

Her laugh contained more than a touch of disdain. "I've been here a week and a half and already I've managed to get myself entangled in an insane mess."

The taxi pulled up to the restaurant, Marian paid the driver, and the two of them got out. Just before they went in, Ann noticed a ponderous look in the reporter's eyes. Staring at the far sidewalk, it seemed to Ann that something sucked the air out of Marian's earlier enthusiasm, but she kept her thoughts to herself.

The maître d' led them to a corner table and opened the menus with unusual ceremony. During the main course, the two rehashed the incident that brought them together. Once they laid down their silverware, an uncomfortable silence hung between them. Ann looked around impatiently, hoping that the Frenchwoman would signal for the check. Instead, her discomfort was elegantly avoided by what seemed to her an innocent question: "How's your husband?"

"My husband?" she asked, her posture rigid, her face suddenly hard.

Ann, not reading the body language, smiled softly. "Yeah, you haven't brought him up once all evening and . . ."

"Well, I had no reason to bring that scum up . . ."

Ann cut her short. "That scum is lying helplessly in a hospital bed, attached to life support."

The cold look that had been trained on the nurse's face turned playful. "Oh, God, you're talking about Yonatan . . ."

"Your husband," Ann agreed, feeling stupider by the second.

"No, honey," Marian said, laying an explanatory hand on Ann's sweaty one, "You've got it turned around. Yonatan's not my husband. He's my virtual lover."

An hour sailed by. Ann listened to the story of the two Salman Rushdie fans with dreamy contentment. When Marian reached the end of the tale, she cleared her throat and lit a cigarette. "I'm sorry I jumped all over you before when you brought up my husband. It's just no one likes to be taken down failure lane, especially when the memories are from the not-so-distant past."

"So you're not together?"

"Not at all," Marian said victoriously. "I cut all ties with that idiot. Spent too much time with him as it is. Invested too much energy in pathetic attempts to convince myself that the two of us were destined to be together. You meet tens, maybe hundreds of men in your life, and you think that based on the bad experiences you've amassed over the years you'll know how to recognize something good when it comes along. At least that's what I thought when I was with him. I didn't give marriage a second thought, didn't even think in those terms, but when he asked me to marry him, I had this feeling that we'd be immune to what the stats had to say about the institution of marriage. I was sure we were different, special, two intelligent self-aware people who knew exactly what they were getting themselves into. Turns out self aware-ness and love have little in common. We started out over the moon and ended up ass over teakettle."

Her voice became sweet and childish, her face placid. "With Ormus it will be a totally different story. He won't break my heart. He'll know when to end it, if God forbid . . ."

"Don't be so pessimistic."

"On the contrary, Ann. The mere recognition that every story has a beginning, middle, and end has a calming effect on me. I think that's the lesson I learned during my years with the bastard. Instead of stretching things well beyond their natural lifespan, a common couples' mistake, I now know when to put a full stop at the end of a relationship. But enough about me," Marian said, pointing at Ann. "I've been gush-ing for hours, but what about you? Do you have someone in your life?"

Ann shook her head quickly, trying to bat the idea away before it stuck.

"And the actor's brother . . . ?"

"We're friends."

"Just friends?"

"Hmm . . ."

Marian, sensing Ann's unease, decided to ease off the subject. Much to Ann's surprise, Marian smiled and pounded the table once for effect. "Okay, the blab session's over. I have a little something for you."

Ann's eyes widened at the sight of the small square box wrapped in shiny purple paper.

"Well, are you going to open it?" Marian asked.

"You shouldn't have . . . ," Ann murmured, her cheeks flushed.

"Yeah, yeah," Marian said, waving away her awkwardness, "it's the least I could do. I really hope you like it. You can always exchange it if you don't. There's a receipt in the box."

Ann tore the paper daintily, trying to hide her excitement. She hadn't received a present from anyone since the old lady had bequeathed her the house. Ann peered at the black velvet box, immobile, and would have continued to stare had Marian not urged her along. Hesitantly, she pried open the box and emitted a partially muffled shriek.

"Take it out," Marian whispered.

Ann picked up the thin gold chain with the diamond-shaped ruby, holding it loosely, between thumb and forefinger, as though it belonged to someone else.

"You hate it," Marian said.

Ann didn't say a thing, still examining the most beautiful piece of jewelry she'd ever seen, trying to cast aside the inexplicable feelings of guilt the present had aroused.

"Well, say something. If you don't like it, you can always exchange it. The store is on . . ."

"I'm sorry," Ann said, swirling the chain back into the box and pushing it toward Marian, "I can't accept this. It's too much."

Marian gave her a baiting smile. "My life isn't worth the price of a small necklace?" Ann was tempted to say that *her* life wasn't worth the price of the necklace, but instead explained that she didn't accept gifts, particularly not ones of value.

"Well, this time make an exception. You earned this," Marian said, her voice rising.

"I'm sorry," Ann said, "I can't."

"You aren't being offered a choice," Marian said, giggling over her consternation and pushing the gift back in Ann's direction.

"I'm not going to change my mind," Ann said, making a show of pushing the box back across the table.

"Ann, you're starting to act really weird," Marian said. "It's not some fourteen-carat rock. It's a simple token of my appreciation. It will never change the fact that I will always feel indebted to you."

"You don't owe me a thing!" Ann said, pounding the table, rattling the glassware and drawing the attention of the other diners.

Marian, looking hurt, rose to her feet, fished through her wallet, pulled out three one-hundred-shekel bills, smacked them down on the table, and signaled for the waiter.

"What are you doing?" Ann asked.

"None of your business!" Marian said, shouldering her pocketbook. She took the jewelry box, lodged it in the nurse's lap, and made for the exit.

It took Ann a long moment to react. By the time she caught up to the reporter, she was on the sidewalk, hailing an approaching taxi. Ann reached her, panting and upset, and tried to shove the little black box back into Marian's bag.

"What the hell do you think you're doing?" Marian shouted, snatching back her bag. The violence of the movement ripped the thin shoulder strap and sent the contents of her pocketbook tumbling onto the sidewalk.

"Now look what you've done," Marian muttered as she gathered her things, pushing away Ann's hand as she made a last-gasp attempt to get rid of the gift. Hugging her bag to her chest, Marian got into the cab and slammed the door. Ann, not wanting to meet the reporter's eyes, kept her gaze on the sidewalk, where she found a small makeup kit. As she picked it up, she noticed another item that had dropped from the bag. She picked up the facedown picture, looked at it indifferently, and felt shock descend on her like a drug. Still staring at the picture, she felt her legs fold under her and, seated on the sidewalk, she started to whimper.

A cop on foot patrol asked her if she was okay, finally snapping her out of her shock. She nodded, picked herself up off the curb, and started to stumble down the avenue, ignoring the wispy chain that slipped through her fingers and into the outstretched hand of a weary homeless person, who could not believe his luck when he awoke.

22

Gaymorrah

On the twelfth day of his death, Ben woke up from dreamless sleep to a morning comprised of equal parts fear and excitement. He was happy to meet up with the most flamboyant of the Mendelssohns, whom he missed sorely since the latter had succumbed to the terrible disease. Ben recalled Uncle David saying that he always knew the untamable workings of his sexual appetite would ruin him, but never, in his wildest dreams, did he imagine that a woman would snuff out the eternal flame of his erotic escapades.

Amidst a stormy sex life of daily conquests, David dared go without protection a single time, and that was because he didn't think that the strange and foreign gender, which never aroused him before, could pose a danger. One night, during a wild vacation in Ibiza, inebriated and snubbed earlier by a Spanish hedonist, the man-slayer felt an unnatural excitement in his loins when the beautiful Finnish tourist laid a hand on him. The pill that she slipped under his tongue before dragging him off to her bed didn't hurt either, and he, in a daze, went at it till his consciousness waned.

Two months after the last of his friends' rolling laughter had died down, once they'd finished asking him to retell of the peculiar encounter at every get-together, David opened the paper and spotted a picture of the Finnish prostitute. The article detailed how the HIV-positive hooker went on a rampage, determined to punish the stronger sex collectively, instead of settling the score with the one who "gave" it to her. The headline, "Cold-blooded Killer," took on a chilling new meaning, and David swore off the fruit of life for an entire month. The test results were unequivocal and brought with them the realization that the party was over, or at least restricted to a small segment of the population, since, despite his soaring libido, David had a black-and-white conscience and was unwilling to endanger the healthy. David kept up an active, albeit limited sex life and began to tell his confidantes that he thought perhaps it was high time to find his long-lost Jonathan. The search for a soul mate stood in direct contrast with one of the central pillars of his outlook on life: that men, of all stripes, sizes, and colors, were to be enjoyed equally. Consequently, seeking out a single lover drained him of his ardor for the sexual act. A few months before the disease surprisingly raided his body and developed into a life-claiming case of pneumonia, he told his nephew, Ben, that, merciless virus notwithstanding, it was clear to him that he was next in line. "The Mendelssohn curse, you know." When he died, on a glorious fall day, his friends carried out his final wish and conducted a funeral procession that passed by the six sports apparel stores he owned. His close friend, Doron, spoke in a wavering voice and said that David's last words before leaving this world were "Back to the closet."

But Ben was well aware of the implications of going to seek out his wild uncle. David Mendelssohn was the last close family member on his list. Having grown familiar with failure, Ben knew the chance of finding any valuable clues about Marian's whereabouts was negligible, especially as David lived in a county of men who preferred their own kind. His mother encouraged him not to lose hope, saying that if there was one place where a woman would certainly stick out, it was there.

Traveling to Gaymorrah was discomforting. The onslaught of offers he received from the fleet of hungry eyes made him squirm in his seat. It only got worse once he turned around and told one of his potential suitors that he was sorry but he went for women. Three dead ringers for Jimmy Somerville shattered the silence on the multi by bursting into a rousing rendition of "Woman In Love," sweeping up the rest of the passengers, who rocked the vehicle with their ridicule-laced pathos.

Fortunately, the journey came to a close before they finished their torturous falsetto rendition of the tales of the romantic lady. Ben surveyed his surroundings in complete shock. The multi's last stop was on the summit of a mountain, beneath which stretched a wide-shouldered, colorful valley brimming with activity. Ben gave silent thanks for the change in surroundings and fell in line with the rest of the people traipsing down the clover-colored hill. A few moments later, Ben's enthusiasm for the view died down, and he opened his eyes wide at the sight of the simple pink closet, in the center of the vast lawn. Ben got up on his tiptoes to try and see why guys were waiting in line to go through a door guarded by two fiercely muscular men when it was clear that the pastoral valley continued on well beyond the threshold. Within an hour he reached the front of the line and the hulk on the right was addressing him. He spit out a confused "What?' and listened to the bored voice say, "Welcome to Gaymorrah. It's my pleasure to announce that you're on the doorstep of the largest gay county in the Other World. Not far behind you, you'll find the Sexually Baffled Arena, where you can hang out with groups of still-undecided guys and have a go at your first male-male sexual experience, in the event that you did not have a normal adolescence. If you want into the closet, let me have your left wrist please."

Ben offered up his left hand and then looked closely at the navy blue XY that the guard had stamped on the inside of his arm. As the doors opened, the guard gave Ben a gentle tug and pulled him inside, into the immense darkness, not giving him a moment to get his bearings. Ben saw the doors close behind him, realized he was by himself in the closet, but couldn't figure out where all those ahead of him in line had gone. Totally confounded, Ben felt a slight shudder in his leg and, as the floor dropped beneath him, he screamed, understanding, only midway through the freefall, that the closet was actually an elevator.

After a three-minute plunge through terra incognita, the lift came to a stop. Before Ben's eyes had a chance to adjust to the dark, the ground beneath him opened again, only this time he felt a strange pushing motion, moving him, like a suitcase on a vigorous conveyor belt, into another, parallel elevator shaft. He sailed up through the dark, came to a stop, and walked out of another pink door. His exit was applauded by his fellow passengers, who were waiting for their procrastinating friends.

Ben overcame his initial embarrassment and stared half amused, half bewildered at the line of identical circles that continued on to the horizon of the populous city. He spent two long minutes blinking at the erect stone phallus at the center of the nearest circle as it sprayed a fine mist of water from its open end onto the nearby citizens, who were engaged in animated conversations at the foot of the long-nosed totem pole, their upper bodies sprinkled with aqua as they worshiped the sun, courtesy of their godgets. An older man walking in the opposite direction fixed Ben with an unequivocal stare and said, "You've got nothing to be ashamed of, sweetie."

In response, Ben asked him if he could direct him someplace.

"Sure, where do you need to go?"

"To the *Gaily Male*," he said.

"Oh, that's simple," the old man said, sucking his finger and pointing down the long avenue of phallic symbols that cut across the line of the imaginary horizon. "Keep going straight till you hit the third fountain. Make a left and you'll see it."

Ben made it to the right building in a matter of minutes. He passed on the elevators, preferring the enlivening jaunt up the stairs, at the end of which he found a wholly ordinary newsroom. Hardworking types typed away furiously on their obedient laptops, while some hollered into their telefingers, and others raced between the towering stacks of paper on the desks, yelling like brokers on the commodity market floor, flinging bits of information into the densely packed room, items ranging from blatant gossip about celebrity hookups and breakups to sorrow-filled announcements about those who died a second time over, by accident, suicide, or murder.

Ben tried to avoid any unwarranted attention, crossing the room quickly, seeking out the desk manned by his uncle. Finally, he caught sight of the tall man with the closely cropped black hair, the slanted green eyes, the long thin nose, and the square jaw beneath the thick lips that were the focus of plenty of jokes. Judging by the singsong in his voice and the pandering of his smile as he spoke on his telefinger, he was on his way to yet another conquest. Only once Ben stood right in front of him and smiled warmly, did David notice him.

"Eddie, Eddie, please excuse me . . . you have no idea who's standing here in front of me. . . . Eddie, I'll talk to you a bit later," he said and threw his arms around Ben, eliciting loud cheers from the reporters.

"Perverts!" David yelled playfully. "He's my nephew!"

"Now who's the pervert?" one of them called out, setting off a ripple of laughter.

David, much impressed with the brawniness of his formerly rail-thin nephew, said that, momentary shock aside, he wasn't surprised to see Ben in this world. Ben picked up on his reference to the "curse" and, trying to put off the question he had come to ask, spent hours chatting with his beloved uncle, who told him, among other things, about his job as a sportswriter for the paper, specializing in track and field, a discipline he'd already grown to love in the previous world. Smiling

slyly, he added, "When you showed up, I was just in the middle of setting up a meeting with a sprinter from Trinidad that's built like a black
God."

"So, I see you're back to your old ways," Ben said, joining his uncle
on a tour of the flashy city.

"Back to my old ways?" David said, blushing and bowing his head
as they passed an acquaintance from a forgettable night. "Ben, a renais-
sance is what I've had since I arrived here. One can sleep with the whole
world—well, half of it anyway—and no longer has to worry. Thanks to
that Finnish whore, I rediscovered the joy of sex, and if I come across
her one day I'll slap her on one cheek for the suffering of the previous
world and kiss her on the other for the pleasures of this one."

Ben laughed and hung on his uncle's every word. "That massive
structure over there is the Gay-ser, a building built with a nod to the
ancient Roman baths, which serves as a spa favored by all those lovers
of amphibian activities. Behind the acropolis-like façade are springs
with supposedly unusual healing powers, and in fact the volcanic waters are intended to still the stormy souls of the insane, to quote my old
pal Hesse. You know how it goes, *in corpora sano, mens sana.* But between
us, some pretty sane swimmers have long ago flippered their way over
to the Gay-ser and taken over the territorial waters of the lunatics. Even
I sinned and took a rather pleasant dip with a Russian gymnast . . . oh,
Dimitri, Dimitri."

David continued to point out the eye-catching sights. There was
Gayhinnom, the city's largest sauna, a Gothic building with ornate chimneys that pumped fake smoke up and over the blackened roof, in order
to give the building the appearance of being aflame, and, to its left, the
strange pagoda that housed one of a few dozen sadomasochist temples,
run by a disciplined group of male gayshas, who enjoyed catering to
the needs of the queens.

"What's the tall building at the end of the street?" Ben asked, pointing to the bluish structure ahead.

"The Gay Schläfchen, a hotel for straight people who come to visit
gay friends and relatives. Maybe you'll find it interesting, considering
that every gay man has at least one good girl friend and most of them
stay there. Some men stay there, too, but most of the rooms are occu-
pied by women who prefer not to impose on their gay friends."

Ben tried to remember if his wife had such a friend and, without giving it a second thought, asked his uncle if he'd like to get a cup of coffee in the lobby of that establishment. David shrugged. "Oh, hell yes. I'm happy to see you're on the mend."

~

A gaggle of smiling women approached Ben on the way to the hotel's main entrance, unabashedly bumping into him under the guise of drunkenness. David chortled in appreciation of their brash forwardness. Ben smiled peevishly, without a flash of interest.

David cracked, "Hon, in Rome, you know, but don't get carried away with the interpretations."

"Excuse me?" Ben asked groggily, still stuck on the sentence about being on the mend.

They walked into the clamorous lobby and sat in a far corner. From there Ben could survey the women as they crossed the blue carpet on their way in and out of the unimpressive building, which very much resembled scores of uninspired hotels the world over, save the array of sleep-inducing blues: the ceiling, the chandeliers, the tables, the cutlery, the doors, and the long front desk were all stroked with different touches of indigo. Slightly disturbed, he looked into the cup of coffee that his uncle had brought him.

"Would you please stop staring into your cup like some coffeeholic and start paying attention to the world around you?" David said, turning his attention to the three sweetly smiling women seated nearby.

Ben brought his cup to his lips, his eyes fixed on a new group of women striding into the hotel. David followed his gaze. "What's going on, Ben? Why are you ignoring their invitations? Wasn't that why you wanted to come here? These women are drooling all over you and you're doing your best imitation of a eunuch."

"I'm a bit surprised by how eager you are to get me to respond to these women's come-ons when you know full well that there's only one woman in the world for me."

"Oh," David groaned, shaking his head, "you're talking about the lovely Marian."

"Yes, I'm talking about her," Ben said, "of course I'm talking about her. Who the hell else could I be talking about?"

"All the others," David said, nodding in the direction of the threesome, which had just grown into a sextet, all of them engaged in unspoken competition for his graces. "I thought you were over the whole Marian thing."

"That's what you meant when you said that shit about being on the mend?"

"Of course. Your mom told me that Marian died a while ago. I didn't think that a year and a half after her death you'd still be . . ."

"In love, David, same as I was on the day we met," Ben said.

"How can you be in love with a ghost? Too much time's gone by. I'm sure she's over losing you."

Seeing the wounded animal rise in his nephew's eyes, David diluted his statement. "I don't mean to come off as cruel, it's just that I can't see someone as wonderful as Marian living like some old, forlorn woman. It's got nothing to do with how she feels about you. She proclaimed her love for you from just about every mountaintop, but she got here way before you. What do you expect her to do? Sit with her hands in her lap and wait for her knight from the land of the living?"

"That's why I came to see you. I wanted to know if you'd heard from her. If she'd visited you . . ."

David smiled sympathetically. "Sorry, darling. Till I heard from Deborah, I had no idea she was dead."

Ben nodded, mumbling, "That's what I thought."

David tried to think of some appropriate gestures of sympathy, but they all felt strained, especially as he watched Ben spring out of his seat, his face reduced to a convulsing muscle and his eyes casting terror in the direction of the coiled pack of women.

"You alright?" David asked, pondering the fast-moving clouds traveling across Ben's face.

Ben marched over to a nearby table and barked at the six smiling women, "What the fuck are you looking at? What do you want?!"

David couldn't believe the way the women continued to track him, utterly undeterred by the attractive man's display of bubbling rage, when it dawned on him that all the temptresses in the indigo room were ogling his nephew with glossy eyes and incontrovertible poses, weaving unseen webs around their recalcitrant prey. Ben looked around to make sure his eyes were not leading him astray. Fifty women were employing all of their God-given wiles. Perhaps it was the black hole that glared in Marian's absence, a void that couldn't be filled by fifty blue orifices, the poignant unfairness dictated by the vast supply and the monogamist's meager demand; or it could have been the foreseen frustration provoked by his uncle's laconic response, which starkly stated that he had almost reached the end of his search; either way the result was the same. Before his uncle had the chance to restrain him, Ben opened his eyes wide and, with the kind of impulsiveness that characterized his dashing epilogues, forgetting that, in art, an act of madness draws rave reviews, but in life the same act elicits derision, he roared and flipped over the nearest table, then ran to the one just beyond that and sent it cartwheeling across the lobby. Pleased by the panic-filled room that had been rendered devoid of women within a matter of seconds, the one-man mob—and a single uncle, who was transfixed by the rampage of his gentle peace-seeking nephew—roused the *schläfchen* from sleep, breaking lamps, tossing chairs across the room, flinging plates, smashing vases, and ignoring the staff, who would not accept such behavior even from a heartbroken man and managed to get a hold of him, not letting go even as he thrashed at them as though they alone were responsible for his current state, until they carried him away from the scene of his tantrum, holding his head still and photographing him, placing his Polaroid in an album alongside other undesirables and marking him with an X, which, for the rest of his days as a dead man, will bar him from entering the peaceful hotel.

Once the undercover security staff forcefully calmed him and made sure that he understood he was persona non grata, David ran toward his nephew, who stood on the sidewalk like a fire-breathing warrior, and screamed at him to cease and desist from his insane behavior.

Ben buried his head in his hands. "God, I'm so sorry. I don't know what came over me in there. I've never done anything like that. Like some kind of thug . . . but did you see the way they were ogling me?"

"I saw it all, not that that justifies your behavior. I'm not sure Marian would be too pleased to hear that you turned a hotel lobby upside down like some rock star in the throes of an infantile rage."

"If she was with me . . ."

"You can't use that excuse forever."

"I can use it till I find her," Ben retorted, looking back at the scene of destruction, still unable to believe what he had done.

"I've got a stupid question, but it's one I need to ask," David said. "When was the last time you've been with a woman?"

"Our last night together," Ben said. "It was . . ."

"I don't want to hear what it was like," David said, hardly concealing the dread in his voice. "What you're telling me is that you haven't had sex in fifteen months? Nothing?"

"Mm-hmm," Ben affirmed.

"And yet you're surprised that you're ripping apart lobbies with no advance warning? Fucking-A, you're a terrorist dressed up as a romantic. Ben, what happened in there is the tip of the iceberg. Believe me, I know what I'm talking about. When I came here I had five months of abstinence under my belt and soon enough I realized that if I kept on starving myself I'd lose the point and would be going to the Gay-ser on a daily basis. Ben, what happens if you only meet her ten years down the road? You're prepared to wait for a decade?"

"Alright! Enough already with the lectures," Ben yelled, moving away from his uncle. "You've got one mechanism for solving problems and I've got a different one. At this point, do me a favor and give my sex life a rest."

"What would you prefer to discuss?"

"Don't worry about me, okay? I'm going to be fine," Ben said, eking out a smile. "I think I'm going to head back to my apartment."

"So soon? We haven't even had a chance to do anything . . ."

"Don't worry, next time I'll be much better company." Ben hugged his uncle, exchanged thumbprints with him, and whispered in his ear, "And please let's just keep the madman-in-the-café incident between us."

David nodded, caressing his nephew's head. "Promise me you'll take care of yourself, okay?"

Ben forced himself to smile again and then set off for the faraway pink closet, his thoughts muffled as he trudged on, sights, smells, and voices mingling of their own volition, like a bustling marketplace.

Four hours later he mistakenly got off the multi-wheel at April 2001, and walked, his body slack, his mood bluer than before, toward the skyscraper that would have been his had he committed suicide two months earlier. Focusing on the uninteresting lay of the land beneath him, he tried to forget it all, to walk just for the sake of walking, like his grandmother on her final jaunt, with no destination in sight.

An unexpected jostle woke him from his melancholy trance. He mumbled an apology and carried on as though he hadn't touched anyone.

"Can't you see where you're going?" the woman said, grabbing her arm.

The next three steps proved unnecessary. Something in him brought the walking motion to a halt. That voice, that familiar voice. And not just the voice, the entire situation. Years ago, in a faraway and different world, under a driving rain, he met a woman with that honey-coated voice. He turned around and surveyed the bustling scene around him. So did she. Their eyes met.

23

Tom's Friend

Kobi and Tali took the "friends" approach to parenthood. They provided for their only son but tried to avoid any and all doctrine that smacked of typically parental behavior. His peers were madly jealous of the way Tom was able to discuss any topic under the sun with his parents and of the way he was given their true and undivided attention. Tom was the best student in his class, but he was in no way one of those kids who were all brains and no friends. His popularity skyrocketed when he vowed never to cut his hair. Boys and girls whispered whenever the ten-year-old breezed past, his long honey-blond hair accentuating his every movement. The skinny, inquisitive child was every parent's dream: sharp, funny, polite, modest, and kind. Tali once confided in her husband that she worried that in the future some kind of hidden flaw would materialize. Kobi laughed and nodded. "We're either raising a psychopathic killer or a Nobel Peace Prize winner."

When told about Tali's pregnancy, the boy hugged his mother and said, "Finally I'll have a little brother to share some of your attention with."

Kobi made a face. "Does our attention bother you?"

Tom winked at his mother. "All I'm saying is, brace yourselves for some pretty terrible fits of jealousy. It'll sure be interesting."

Kobi laughed. "Tali, who did he get his sarcasm from?"

Tali got all serious and then spelled out the name of the old neighbor. "It was when you were away on business. I was lonely and . . ."

Kobi flung a pillow right at her head. It hit its mark and bounced back onto the couch. Tom laughed and was about to pounce on top of his father and tickle him all over, when the phone rang and his mother called him. "It's for you, honey."

Tom took the phone from his mother's hand, an amused expression still spread across his face. "Hello?"

His face got serious instantly. "Why?"

The response didn't appease him and he asked again, louder this time, "But why?"

Kobi watched his son intently. He'd never seen him go so pale.

"Then when?" Tom asked, shifting his weight from foot to foot, "Tomorrow? The day after? In three days? When?"

Kobi looked on as his son stared at the receiver. "Who was that?"

"Tommy, is everything alright?" his mother asked, approaching him, about to stroke his cheek.

The child squirmed away from her touch, smiled, and mumbled, "Sorry I yelled. That was the instructor from the computer course. He called to say the class was canceled today." Without waiting for any follow-up questions, he turned on his heel and headed upstairs, slamming the door to his room behind him. Tali considered following him but decided to accept her husband's advice and leave the kid alone. "He needs to learn that the world doesn't run like a Swiss watch," Kobi said.

"But did you see his reaction?" she asked.

"You know how much he likes that group. He hasn't missed it once in fifteen months. I'm surprised it didn't happen beforehand."

"What didn't?"

"A cancellation. It's not that strange."

"I don't know," Tali said, looking at the phone, "his reaction was a bit overboard."

"He's a kid, that's how kids react."

"God," she said, sitting on the love seat, "if that's how he reacts when one of his extracurricular classes is canceled, what's he going to do when we tell him about the old couple?"

Kobi got down on his knees and took her hands in his. "Tali, not yet. We need to wait for the right time. I don't want to confuse him too much. Your pregnancy, their death. It's too much for him."

"We're not going to tell him the whole truth," she said, a tear sliding toward her mouth.

"Sweetheart," he mopped a trail of tears with his finger, "as far as the kid is concerned, they died in their sleep."

She nodded and wrapped her arms around him tight, smiling at their reflection on the face of the dark television screen.

∽

They were both startled by the bell. Ronny, Tom's good friend and class-mate, stood at the entryway. He asked if Tom was around.

"Yeah, he's up in his room" Tali smiled, asking him if he'd like to eat or drink anything.

"Coke," said the hefty kid, "and maybe some of those chocolate and raisin cookies you make."

"How did you know that I just baked a few trays of them yesterday?"

"The smell," Ronny said, touching his nose and rubbing circles around his protruding belly.

Kobi, drawn to the kid's sense of self parody, said, "Pretty lucky the instructor canceled the class today, otherwise you would've missed out on Tali's cookies."

Ronny looked at Tali as she poured some of the cookies into a bowl. "The instructor?"

"From the computer course."

The light in the kid's eyes went out as soon as Tali stopped pouring and snapped the lid back on the cookie jar. Watching her put it back on the shelf, he reissued Kobi's words. "From the computer course?"

"Are you even listening to me?" Kobi asked, still smiling.

"Yeah, yeah . . ." He turned toward Kobi but still kept an eye on Tali's movements. "You were asking about the instructor . . ."

"Did he call you, too, to let you know the class was canceled today?"

Tali opened a drawer and pulled out a bag that crinkled. Ronny turned back toward her and stared at her back, trying to guess what else she was adding to the bowl. Softly, he said, "No one called me."

"Then how did you know that Tom is home? And how did you know there was no class today? I mean, don't you guys always meet at the class?" Kobi pried.

It took about thirty seconds, but the kid's face finally registered some kind of understanding. "Oh sure . . . the class . . . Tom told me . . . he called me and told me the instructor called today to cancel . . ."

Tali pounced. "Ronny . . . Tom didn't call you . . . he just got the message a few minutes ago . . . we would have seen him use the phone."

"He used his cell," the kid beamed.

This time Kobi answered. "Ronny, his cell's broken."

"I'm sorry, Ronny," Tali said, approaching him with an outstretched bowl. "We don't mean to cross-examine you. It's just that I've never seen Tom react the way he did to that call." She handed him the bowl. "Go ahead, sweetie."

The sudden calm he felt at the first taste of the cookies subsided when Tali asked whether he had "any idea why Tom acting so strangely?"

"No. He must have been very disappointed. He just really likes . . . going over there . . . really likes it . . . ," Ronny said, wiping a sweaty bead off his forehead.

"Oh, sure, we know," Tali said, stirring the contents of the bowl, reminding him to partake. Ronny, huffing, turned around and said, "I just remembered . . . I . . . have to go . . . I've got things to do . . ."

"You don't want to see Tom?" they asked in unison.

"I'll catch him in school tomorrow," he said, mumbling a good-bye and storming out.

"What a funny kid," Kobi said.

Tali went back into the kitchen, put the cookies back in the jar, and said, "No, Kobi, he's not funny at all; he's just a kid who doesn't know how to lie."

"Whatever, so Tom lied about the phone, no need to make a big deal out of it," Kobi said, sinking back into the couch.

"Sure," she said, "but still something's going on here. Something's off between those two kids and I'm going to find out what it is."

"Good luck then, Miss Marple," Kobi said, clicking the television to life.

Tali knew that, to her husband, her behavior served as further proof that women love to pick and pry at the placid surface of things, fishing for drama and then panfrying fiction into reality. But when she woke from her afternoon nap, ready to discard her plan, she couldn't help but notice the rumbling silence emanating from Tom's room. Most of the time he spent the early evening hours in front of his computer, yelling at the screen, maneuvering the joystick with his whole body, trying to kill his enemies while some of the most awful strains of teen pop streamed out of the stereo he'd gotten for his tenth birthday. She knocked on the door and heard nothing. Opening it quietly, she saw Tom in his bed, face buried in the pillow, faking sleep.

Two hours later, while she was making dinner, the phone rang. Tom

bolted out of his room and raced down the stairs. Chopping and stirring, she noted happily that Kobi had fallen asleep on the couch. Her
son, she hoped, would be equally unattuned to her heightened state of
alertness. Once he answered, she moved to a more deliberate, less riotous pace of chopping. He was speaking with Ronny, chewing him out
in a harsh whisper. The gravity of the situation was readily apparent.
Tom's voice shook with rage.

"You fat idiot. You couldn't think of something that made more
sense? Now they're going to be suspicious. How could you forget, you
fool? Look, I can't talk now. No, they can't hear me, but I'll talk to you
in school tomorrow." And then, just before the conversation ended, he
added, "He said he wants to keep a low profile, so I can't see him again
till he says so."

Just before setting the table, she woke Kobi and asked him not to
bother Tom about what had happened earlier. He yawned, sighed, and
said, "You're still thinking about that?"

After they'd had dinner and Tom had left the table, she peeked at
her watch.

Kobi chuckled. "What, your period's a little late?"

Tali pointed to the dishes. "Be a good husband and try not to make
any noise while you clear the table."

Kobi laughed and wrapped his arms around her middle. "God,
you're sexy when you're scheming."

"No idea what you're talking about."

"She's dying to know what the two kids are up to," he whispered.
"Perhaps they've killed a helpless old woman and hid the body, perhaps
they've gotten their hands on the math test, even though there are only
three days left till summer vacation, or perhaps they're just hiding their
love for one another from us, even though I don't think Tom-Tom is
into the big boys . . ."

"Let go of me, you maniac," she giggled, swimming out of his arms,
"I've got something important to do."

"Tali's scheme," he said, rubbing his hands together and kissing her
ear. "Good luck."

"What are you talking about? I'm just going to pee."

"And this is how you forsake your loving husband, instead of being
the perfect wife and asking him to come along?"

"Not today." She kissed his lips and started up the stairs. In her bedroom, with the door closed, she rummaged through her drawers till she found the folded piece of paper. She flattened it out with her hand and scrolled down her son's class list till she found Ronny Ma-or's name. A thin, congested voice answered on the third ring. "Ma-ors' residence, good evening."

"Good evening," she said, thinking how strange it was that she'd never met her son's best friend's parents. Ronny's mother seemed eager to be liked and went out of her way to compliment Tom, hardly allowing the concerned mom a second to get a word in edgewise, pausing only to sneeze. Tali seized the opportunity. "I just wanted to ask you a quick question. Do you know if Ronny's computer course instructor called today to cancel his class?"

Ronny's mother sneezed again and asked, "Which course?"

"Ronny and Tom's computer course; you know, the one at four on Wednesdays."

Mrs. Ma-or blew her nose. "Huh? Ronny watches his brother on Wednesday afternoons."

"But he was at our house today at four."

"Yeah, he was lucky, his mother has a cold and didn't go to work today. I've explained to him a thousand times . . ."

"Excuse me," Tali said, cutting her short, "but what about the computer course?"

"I'm sorry, but I think you have Ronny confused with another kid. He's never said a thing about a computer course."

"I see," Tali said, hastening to bring the conversation to a close.

The next day she called the travel agency and said she wouldn't be able to make it into work due to a loss in the family. For most of the day, she busied herself trying to find a less devious plan; for naught. Tom's words a few hours after the instructor had canceled the course lingered. When the door opened in the early afternoon, she beamed at Tom, and the boy, as was his habit, tossed his knapsack in the middle of the living room and poured himself a glass of Coke. She asked about his day. He said it had been good and avoided her eyes as he turned toward the stairs. She watched him disappear up the staircase and, just as he was near the top, she called up to him and said, "Oh, sweetie, your instructor called today."

The kid stopped in his tracks, turned, and asked, "My instructor?"

"Yeah sweetie, from the computer course. He said to tell you that the class would be meeting at four o'clock today."

For a moment the child's face remained perfectly still, and only when his mother smiled at him did he enthusiastically return the favor. "Thanks, Mom!"

An hour later, he came down the stairs and, his face alight, said he'd be back in the evening. Tali nodded, kissed his face lightly, and wished him a good time. A minute later, she donned dark sunglasses, put on a wide-brimmed hat, and left the house. Feeling ridiculous as she recalled similar scenes from detective movies, she made sure to stay a safe distance behind her son as he picked up his pace, crossing familiar streets turned ominous. Twenty minutes later, slipping into a speed walk, she was certain he was trotting toward the park, but before entering he turned into a quiet street nearby, slowed to a walk, and knocked on the tall door of a stately home. Tali's heart thumped in her chest as she ducked behind a parked car.

She tried to see who opened the door but couldn't make out anything beyond her son, who took a step backwards and gesticulated angrily with his hand. For a short while he was quiet, listening to the person who had opened the door, but then he started to scream, his long hair flailing all over the place, "You can't do this. You're my friend!"

At that moment, Tali's heart skipped a beat at the sight of the tall skinny man with the black glasses who, like a rat, poked his head out of his hole for a brief, brave moment, bowed and gently shook the boy's shoulders, raising his voice plaintively. "Don't you see this has nothing to do with you? There's a lot of things you don't know about me and my brother. It's too complicated to explain. But for now I can't be in touch with you. Try and understand, Tom. You know how much I like playing with you, but this time I have no choice. I'm sorry."

Tom burst out crying and the man embraced him for a long while, stroking his hair and calming him. Tali's body started to tremble as she watched this strange man with his hands around her son, but she stayed put until the man had gone back inside the house and her son had turned away from the door with an expression that was hard to mistake. Only when she was sure the coast was clear did she straighten up, stretch, cross the street, take off her shoes, and tiptoe to the front door of the house. She wrote down the resident's name on the palm of her hand and left at a run, slowing down as she spotted her son's back farther down the sidewalk. For a second or two, she considered keeping up her undercover routine, but then came to her senses, striding toward her stooped son and placing a hand on his back.

Tom swung around and looked at her in a disbelief that, in an instant, melted into understanding. In a crushed voice he asked, "Mom, what are you doing here?"

Before she could find the right words, his full lips formed a crater of shock. "You followed me, right? You lied to me when you said that . . ."

"Adam called," she said, putting a steadying hand on his shaking shoulders.

Tom took a step back. "Did you talk to him?" he asked in a threatening tone.

"No, Tom, I didn't talk to him. I preferred to ask you."

"What do you want to ask me?"

She pointed at a nearby café. "Let's not have this conversation right here."

The mother and son walked to the café in silence. They sat at a corner table. Tali ordered both of them her son's favorite, a strawberry banana milkshake. They said nothing until the waitress set their drinks before them. Tali asked if he was hungry and he said no. When she turned away from the table, Tom glared at his mother and said, "I know what you're trying to do, Mom."

"Excuse me?"

"You're trying to get on my good side so I'll tell you about my friend," he said, taking a smooth pull from his shake.

"Honey," Tali said, "you apparently have no idea what you've done. Tom, for the last fifteen months your father and I thought you were going to an extracurricular computer course. I just found out that that course doesn't exist."

"If you're worried about the money, you can relax," he said. "I didn't spend a shekel of it. It's all in my piggy bank."

"I don't care about the money. I want to know how you met this man"—she prayed he didn't feel the shudder in her leg—"and how, for God's sake, you weren't afraid that . . ."

"That what? That he'd hurt me? Do something bad to me?" He sneered. "I knew that the second you found out I had an adult friend you'd go nuts and start dreaming up all kinds of crazy things."

Had they been at home, Tali thought, he would have heard her raise her voice for the first time, but as she pondered that notion, he amazed her by voicing genuine disappointment. "You're just like that friend of yours . . . what's her name? The one that fell . . ."

This time she didn't hold herself back, rasping, "How dare you mention Marian like that?"

The kid smiled indifferently. "It's cause of her that I met Adam."

Tali stared at her son for a long moment before asking in a frail voice, "What the hell are you talking about?"

"If you promise not to be mad, I'll tell you."

"If you don't tell me, I promise to be mad."

It was obvious he was choosing his words with care, and when he spoke there was a new wrinkle in his brow and a false calm in his voice. "I know you and Dad think I'm a good boy. And you're right. But even good boys sometimes do bad things. Well, things that aren't good. Anyway, don't think I planned this or anything. It was just a really beautiful day and class was super boring. Our history teacher was going over the same stuff for like the millionth time. I put my hand up and asked if this was what people meant when they said that history repeats itself. Everyone laughed but she threw me out of class. While I was walking down the hall, I already knew where I was going to go."

"Where?"

"To the amusement park. I was dying to go there."

"Where did you get money for that?"

"Dad gave me my weekly allowance that morning and I borrowed twenty more shekels from Ronny."

"Ronny went with you?"

"No, I waited for him till recess and asked him if he wanted to come. He said he did but that he was too scared."

"Of what?"

"He thought someone might see him there and tell his parents. I told him there was no chance, but he still chickened out. Anyway, I went alone. And, ironically, as Dad likes to say, just what he was afraid of happened to me."

"Oh my God . . . you met Marian on that dreadful day."

"Yes," Tom said, biting his lower lip. "On line I saw a big group of kids go in two minutes before me. I was really happy because I thought an entire class had skipped out of school or something, but then I saw two women walk back from the ticket booth and hand everyone tickets. Like a total moron I stood next to the group of kids and one of the teachers handed me a ticket. I gave it back to her and told her she was wrong. She looked at me and laughed. . . . Marian heard her laugh and turned toward me. I froze. She was really surprised and asked what I was doing there. When I didn't answer she got it all by herself. She also laughed and said that next time I cut school I should bring a friend or two along."

"That's what Marian said?" Tali asked.

"Yeah. She said those places were unsafe, and then turned around and pointed to a guy sitting by the ice cream stand. It was Adam. He looked like a blind businessman. He had on dark glasses and a suit and carried a briefcase. He kept moving his head from side to side like he was looking for something. She told me to watch out for that guy and that he looked really sketchy, but I wasn't listening to her."

"What? Why not?"

"Because Adam bent down and pulled out a new game that I'd never seen."

"Marian didn't notice you weren't paying attention?"

"She lost her concentration. It was kind of funny."

"What was funny?"

"She asked me something and then she started to stare at this old beggar under a tree. And the beggar was looking real hard at Adam. I think she felt bad for the beggar because she asked me to wait a second and then she went over to him and asked if he wanted to join her group of consulate kids."

"What did the beggar do?"

"I think he must have been, like, high or something, because it took him a long time to smile. He was so ugly. His teeth were all black and his beard was really dirty."

"That's the beggar who sat next to her when she was on the Ferris wheel and then disappeared! Did you see . . . what happened . . . ?"

"No, no, I wasn't there when it happened."

"I don't get it."

"I asked Marian not to tell you guys that she saw me at the amusement park, and she said it would be our little secret."

"You didn't tell us that you saw Marian on the day she died because you were scared we'd know you'd cut school . . . ," Tali said in a low voice, "That's so remarkably stupid."

The kid, trying to look away from his mother, examined the coffee rings on the table.

"Well, what are you waiting for," Tali said, "what happened after that?"

Still focusing on the stains on the table, the child tried to sound cool, but before long he got too excited and his sentences tumbled out. "She took the beggar and the class to the Ferris wheel. And I was looking at Adam, who took out this other game that I had never seen either. I was really curious. Then he opened his bag on the grass and I couldn't believe it. He had like ten brand new games there that I'd never seen. He pulled them out and started to arrange them. Every couple of minutes he looked up and smiled at me. I smiled back, and then he made a sign for me to come to him. So I walked over. He introduced himself and asked if I like computer games. I said it was the thing I liked most in the world. He asked if I knew the Cryptograph series. I said I didn't, and then he asked if I wanted to play with him. At first I was thinking about what Marian had said, but then he chuckled and showed me the name of the inventor of the game, and it was him! I thought I was going to pass out. Mom, Adam *invents* all of these games! That's his job! I asked him what he was doing at the amusement park, and he said he was looking for guinea pigs for his new game. Eight- to twelve-year-olds who would try it out and tell him what they thought. He said it would help him improve his product. In exchange for helping him, they'd get to take free games home."

"I don't know if I can go on listening," Tali said.

Tom leaned toward her. "Stop it, Mom! I know what you're thinking, and that's totally disgusting. All he did was take me back to his house, explain the rules of the game, and watch me play. I was having such a good time I didn't want to leave, and he said he was also but that I should get going so that my parents wouldn't worry. He gave me two games, and when I asked if I could come back and visit again, he said that he had no problem with that. By the third time I went over there, I realized that if you or Dad knew I was meeting with Adam, who is like old enough to be my dad, you'd go nuts and start imagining all kinds of crazy stuff. So we thought up the idea of the computer course together and then printed up the application and then, so that it wouldn't seem weird, I asked Ronny to go along with it and say he was also doing the course."

Tom sipped his milkshake and looked up at his mom. She sighed heavily. "You've been going to Adam's house for fifteen months every single Wednesday and you're telling me all you did was sit around and play computer games?"

The kid licked his long-stemmed spoon. "Sometimes we also ate pizza."

"I imagine he isn't a married man, this guy?"

"No. He lives with his brother. But I never got to see him because he's always at work."

Tali glared at her son. "You realize that I forbid you from ever going near this man again?"

Tom nodded sullenly. "It doesn't matter. He said he doesn't want to meet again anyway."

Just as the waitress came past to ask if she could get them anything else, the two started to sob. The child asked his mother haltingly, "What . . . are . . . you . . . going to do . . . to me?"

Tali brought her napkin to her face, daubed her tears, and whispered, "The question is not what I'm going to do to you, but what I'm going to do to him . . . ."

"To who?" the kid asked anxiously.

"To the man who made me lose my faith in the person I cherish most in this world." Tali put the napkin in the ashtray and signaled for the check.

24

Anntarctica on Fire

"Something's wrong with Annplugged," one of the nurses said, huddling with her coworkers, surveying the sudden change in the diminutive woman, who'd tried to cover up the emotional storm she'd weathered with ill-applied cosmetics. The thick makeup theatrically laid over the white face did little to hide the puffy eyes; in fact, it lent her a Gothic quality, as though she'd come to work straight from a Transylvanian ball of horrors. Moreover, the smeared eye shadow, the clumped mascara, and the cementlike layer of concealer made it all too clear that the woman had sobbed for hours and, judging by the state of her concealment efforts, the tears were still flowing when she began to work on her face.

"She looks terrible," one of the nurses whispered.

"I think she's sick," another said.

"She must've been through some kind of treatment during this past week," a third surmised.

"And it failed," a fourth concluded.

The hospital director's request that Ann see him in his office lit the other nurses' eyes. They rejoiced at her return, not least because after years of nothing but boredom from Ann, the crew had grown to resent their distant superior, their imagination whisking them away to the day when she'd fall sick and then, at the mercy of her replacement, wait unknowingly to be disconnected from life support, a termination of her existence between these walls, for beyond them she never dared to live. But that morning the nurses learned that the cheeky little nurse had a life elsewhere, too.

The nurses were not alone. After Ann closed the door to his office, the hospital director looked her over for a long moment before greeting her and apologizing for the chagrin the week of suspension may have caused. She said that the only thing that mattered was that he believed in her innocence. He restated his earlier conviction and offered her a cup of tea, trying to buy enough time to satisfy his curiosity about her strange appearance. She declined his offer with a miserly smile, wished him a good day, and left the office.

Only after the door closed, did he realize that the detail that had caught his eye had nothing to do with the garish carnival from the lips up. It was the way she stood. The stoop in her back, as always, threatened to throw her off balance; her left hand, as always, hung frozen by her side; but her right hand was stuffed into the pocket of her white uniform, furrowing in its depths, unaware of its jarring effects. He'd never seen her walk that way, with one hand in sync and the other hidden from view. Five minutes later, on his way to a class he was teaching at the university, he turned around and saw her speaking with the replacement nurse, leaning over Yonatan's bed, her right hand still jingling inside the pocket, a separate being from the rest of her body, as though she were operating on two different axes.

Briefed on Yonatan's situation, she thanked her replacement and addressed the paperwork that had been waiting for the past week. The letters moved in front of her eyes like marching battalions of black bugs, and she found herself doodling on the corners of the pages, wondering who the hell cared about the amount of medicine in the closet when she had the most sensational news ever languishing in her pocket. She ran her fingers over the surface of the photo, barely holding back another stream of tears. She got out of her chair, brought the papers into an orderly stack, and decided to come back to them later on. It was shocking to her that she couldn't handle this simple task. A week ago she could have banged out the forms while discussing the health of one of her patients. Catching yet another glance from one of her colleagues, she summoned the proper tone and gave them all something to do, scattering them across the ward merely to avoid their inquisitive glances. She checked her watch and decided to break for lunch. Instead of eating the usual sandwich, she spent her fifteen minutes staring at the rear parking lot, aware that no one would come bother her in this little nook in the wall.

All night long she'd been running through the paces of her next meeting with the mystery woman, desperately seeking a smooth path over the moat that divided them ever since the miserable end of their otherwise amicable dinner. An apology was mandatory, same for an offering of thanks, perhaps a bit of small talk, a dose or two of compassion for Yonatan, some hope-inducing talk about his chances, then the natural bond and the careful interrogation.

When she got back to Yonatan's room, Marian was in the midst of another one of her "wall" conversations with the expressionless man. The nurse had no doubt who she was referring to when she lowered her voice and told her virtual lover that "she's really weird."

Ann drew in a long breath, felt around in her pockets, and belted out, "Good afternoon, Marian!"

Marian didn't even bother turning around. "Whatever," she said, her voice dark and distant.

"Would you like me to leave?" Ann asked.

"I thought you already had," Marian said, caressing Yonatan's smooth bald head.

"Actually, before I go"—Ann stopped in front of the door, her eyes locked on the statuesque back—"I wanted to say something."

"I'm not taking it back!"

"I don't want you to," Ann said. "On the contrary, I just want to thank you for the beautiful chain and apologize for last night. I acted like a complete idiot."

"Well, I can't argue with that," Marian said, her voice softening. She turned toward Ann and a giggle sprang from her mouth. "What in God's name did you do to yourself?"

"Excuse me?"

"The makeup. It looks like you're auditioning for Frankenstein's bride. . . ."

"I'm not used to putting on makeup."

"Clearly. But we can't let you walk around like a roving advertisement for domestic violence. . . . Come here, before Yonatan wakes up and goes back down for another week."

Pleased by the unexpected development, Ann dutifully followed the reporter into the bathroom. Marian asked her to shut the door, pulled a few tissues out of her light green leather bag, touched them to the running water, and wiped away the bashful nurse's war paint. Marian's attention was too intimate for Ann. It reminded her of the altercation near the cab the night before, and she turned her head away when she felt the sweetened warmth of Marian's breath on her face, inhaling her French perfume despite herself and focusing her gaze on the tiles on the far wall.

"Stop fidgeting," Marian said, holding her face steady and wiping away the last remnants of the makeup. When she was through, she asked the nurse to wash her face and mentioned the name of a certain face emulsion that could inspire her haggard skin.

"I've made a fool of myself with all this makeup," Ann said.

"Not at all," Marian chuckled. "If you'd like I could give you some tips."

"I'd love that," Ann said, nodding, "and by the way, yesterday, when your bag . . ."

"Just a second," Marian said, raising her index finger as her cell phone started to vibrate. "Yes? I see. Okay, no problem." She stuffed the phone back in her bag, checked herself in the mirror, and said, "I'm really sorry, Ann, I have to run. I have to be at the airport sooner than I thought. We'll speak some other time."

"Where are you off to?" Ann asked.

"Paris. Please keep an eye on Yonatan and tell him I'll be back in three days."

Ann watched Marian breeze through the doors, and then turned her attention back to the mirror. "Silly woman," she whispered, "you should be glad. In three more days you'll know where he has gone."

The next three days were devoted to meticulous preparations for Marian's much awaited return from France. Ann decided to invite her over to her home in a well-coordinated attempt to strengthen their ties. For two consecutive days, she'd been glued to the television, watching cooking shows that showcased maximum creativity with minimum work, trying to upgrade her reasonable proficiency in the kitchen, pleased by her passable replicas of the delectable dishes laid out by The Naked Chef. With a confident bounce to her step, Ann spent the third day shopping for jewelry, covering her face in shock at the many digits on the small price tags, till she found a chain, just like the one she'd lost, in the window of a small store that specialized in high-quality knockoffs. Ann bought the chain and, still thriving on the success of her mission, decided to improvise with her next errand, surfing the wave of adrenaline to an almost-fashionable shoe store, where she tried on black high-heeled shoes made for women with unusually arched feet, and asked the saleswoman to wrap them for her. On the way home, she bought two bottles of wine and a host of other supplies for the impending meal.

She rose early the next morning, ran the vacuum cleaner over all the rugs, scrubbed every corner and, before leaving for work, found time to buy a bouquet of purple roses, put them in a glass vase on the window-sill, and exited the house uplifted. Walking past the health club, she smiled to herself—Adam hadn't been there the past three evenings, a blessed fact that saved her the trouble of staying out of range of his watchful dark lenses. Yet again she felt flooded with the warmth of good fortune. Yet again she told herself that nothing would go wrong.

But she was mistaken. Everything went decidedly wrong. Three days had passed since Marian was due to come home. Ann had left ten messages on her machine, had called Ben Gurion International Airport to see whether "her friend" was in fact on one of the incoming flights, and even drove to her apartment on three separate occasions. And still nothing. Six days after their hurried parting, all of her preparations seemed to belong to a different reality. There was no choice but to face facts—at the worst possible moment, the earth seemed to have swal-lowed Marian, leaving behind a woman who experienced a lifetime in a week, a woman smashed to a thousand smithereens of hope and dis-appointment, a woman who looked in the mirror and wondered where the hell everyone was disappearing to just when she was becoming vis-ible.

25

On the Wings of Imagination

"Ben," she called, marching in his direction, panting.

"Keren," he said, surprised, striding toward her.

They stopped next to each other, taking in the overarching changes. Keren simultaneously admired and scoffed at the sight of his new body; Ben noted her new curves with a throb of pleasure and a twinge of regret. Each noticed the deadened eyes of the other. They smiled in mutual embarrassment.

"I don't know what to say," she said.

"Yeah. I wasn't really expecting to see you here either."

"It's crazy. I mean it's been fifteen years since we . . ."

"Broke up. It's okay, you can say it."

"Since we broke up, and I hadn't seen you once in our little village of a country, and then I come here and in this colossal place, just walking down the street, I literally bump into you, just like . . ."

"Like the way we met the first time, Keren."

"Only it was pouring then and both of us were down in the dumps, if I remember correctly."

"Well, we can arrange a downpour in a second with the godget if you want an exact replay."

"And what about our moods?"

"As far as I can tell we won't be needing any technological assistance."

"It's that obvious?"

"It's that obvious."

They fell silent, their words echoing faintly, like long-lost history. Beyond them, an unresponsive multi-wheel ran down three old men. A young woman in a winter state of mind glided past, a cold, private cloud hanging over her head.

"Did you come here a long time ago?"

"About a year ago. What about you?"

"Two weeks."

"Two weeks? Straight off the boat, huh?"

"How did you wind up here, Keren?"

"Car accident."

"Sorry to hear that."

"Don't be. I was on my way to the pharmacy to buy enough sleeping pills to put me down forever, but before I got the chance an angry truck driver rammed into me and crushed my VW Bug."

"You were killed on your way to commit suicide?"

"What do you think, Ben, is that story-worthy or what?"

"Truth is, I really did end a story once in a similar way. A guy with a gun in his hand sees the light at the last possible moment, decides to call off the suicide and then, while handling the gun, mistakenly pulls the trigger."

"Only difference is, I had no intention of changing my plans."

"You have no way of knowing. You were spared the last moments, when the decision's really made."

"That has the ring of firsthand knowledge."

"It is. I pulled the trigger."

Keren widened her mournful eyes and shook her head back and forth, her wavy hair flying across her face. "You committed suicide? Ben, you're the last person in the world . . ."

"No, Keren, please, not the cliché about two kinds of people, those prone to suicide and those immune to it. Who better than you to attest to the falsehood of that?"

"You aren't familiar with the circumstances."

"I imagine life wasn't smiling down on you."

"Funny hearing that from you."

"Why?"

"Because you were the first guy to break up with me."

"We were kids, Keren. Two clueless Hebrew Lit students. You remember how much we fought toward the end?"

"The first year was a dream."

"The second a nightmare."

"And yet we had our good days."

"True, but as you remember, I didn't only leave *you*."

"Yeah, I remember, you bailed before graduating. You were thirsting for action, couldn't stand the academic gibberish. Pretty bold move, especially when one considers that you went into what must be the strangest profession in the world."

"You know, I never planned to be an epilogist. I guess it was just luck that I ran into that desperate screenwriter at the local bar. Sinking into a glass of whiskey, he told me how he'd woven this web of a plot but couldn't fight his way out of it, couldn't get it right at the end. I asked him to lay it out for me, and once he told me the whole story, I suggested a possible ending. He started hooting and hollering, called me a genius. I laughed and went back to my beer, but he took down my number and called back two weeks later, inviting me to the studio. My life changed. They offered me a job as a screenwriter, but I said I didn't have enough patience to write a full story. The only part that was really interesting to me was the ending. For some reason, they loved the idea and signed me to a contract on the spot. That's where it all started."

"And I, dreaming my whole life of being a writer, ended up a much-glorified book critic, and it stung each time people praised my work and said I was born to write reviews."

"You even wrote about me once, you know."

"About you? You never published a book. . . ."

"Not me personally. You reviewed a book that I wrote the ending for after a well-known author totally lost his bearings some thirty pages from the end."

"Really? Who?"

"I can't say. That's my little morsel of revenge."

"Was I brutal?"

"If words could kill I would've been here long ago."

"I guess an apology at this stage would be ridiculous."

"Well, only if you apologized to me. You directed your fury at the poor author."

"That is bizarre."

"Not as bizarre as us bumping into each other in the street."

"Maybe we were meant to bump into each other, right here, right now."

"Pretty soon you're going to start talking about circles closing, and we'll both raise an eyebrow."

"Hey, don't be nasty. You're the one who seeded the fear of abandonment in your first love."

"I'm starting to feel like abandonment is more than a recurring theme in this conversation."

"Rightfully. I told you, you were the first. After you there were six more. All told, seven men left me."

"Wow, Keren, I'm so sorry to hear that."

"I doubt that. And you know what, I spent a year with the last guy. I was sure it wouldn't happen again. We had a really gentle, beautiful love. And on our one-year anniversary he went out to get cigarettes and never came back. The next day the coward left me a message on my machine: 'Keren, I'm sorry but I just had to go.' I thought I was going to lose my mind. I'd sworn I'd never let that happen to me again. And then the rest is history."

"I really am sorry, Keren."

"You should be. You're the one who started this and it's because of you that I drove all the other ones crazy with my paranoia, till they really did get fed up and leave."

"But if you remember right, even then, before I bailed, you were always worried I'd leave you, and I warned you about how dangerous your dependence issues were."

"My psychologist said that in a dependent relationship the independent individual cultivates the other side's dependence to the same extent that the latter does."

"She would know, considering her hourly rate."

"Don't be crude."

"Judging by what you say, I've been a lot worse than that."

"True, but like it or not, you'll always be the legendary ex."

"Me?"

"Yes, you. You know damn well what you're worth, and I'm sure you won't be the least bit surprised to find out that all your successors were just pale imitations of the real thing."

"And yet a pale imitation drove you to suicide."

"The last straw."

"With all due respect, in my current state the last thing I need is to stand trial for long-term emotional abuse before the first woman I ever loved."

"I'm not putting you on trial for anything, just tying up loose ends and trying to gauge if I made a mistake by going to the pharmacy."

"Luckily you get the benefit of the doubt."

"But had I not been involved in the accident . . ."

"And had the last one not left . . ."

"You're right. Reality's twisted enough as it is. It doesn't need layers of guesswork heaped on top of it all. So, give it to me straight from the horse's mouth: What made Ben Mendlessohn kill himself?"

"His beloved wife died mysteriously and he was unable to go on without her."

"How long were you married?"

"Eleven years. Happy ones."

"And your wife dying mysteriously?"

"She fell off a Ferris wheel."

"What?"

"Yeah, I know how it sounds."

"Kids?"

"No."

"What did she do?"

"Marian was an English teacher."

"How did you meet?"

"Why are you asking all these questions?"

"I'm curious about the woman who won your heart . . . so much so that you killed yourself for her."

"You remember Kobi?"

"Your friend with the bathroom fetish?"

"That's the one. I met her at his wedding. I was with the groom, she with the bride."

"How convenient."

"Yeah, but it wasn't like that. No one introduced us and they invited so many people to the wedding that I'm pretty sure we wouldn't have noticed each other without the incident."

"The incident?"

"I'd been working like crazy that day and realized only on the way to the wedding that I hadn't eaten since the day before. I was starving. Anyway, just as I was about to greet the bride and groom, a waitress floated past with a tray of *bourekas*. I took the biggest one I could find and crammed as much of it as possible into my mouth. Before I could swallow, I started to choke. It was terrifying. Everyone was laughing and dancing and I was in the corner choking to death. Luckily, Marian was standing behind me. Later, she told me I had started to convulse.

She wrapped her hands around me and pulled off a perfect Heimlich Maneuver. The flaky chunk of *bourekas* came flying out. It was mortifying. I turned around to thank her. She introduced herself and I just stared at her like a fool. I'd never seen such an intelligent face. Then I asked to take her out. Just like that. I needed to wipe away the first impression. She smiled and asked if I thought I could handle a full meal. I laughed and promised to take my time swallowing in the future. She agreed."

"Then you started going out, and I take it it was clear cut from the very beginning."

"Not at all. We argued nonstop on our first date. About books, records, movies, politics. Everything under the sun."

"And the second date?"

"Kept on arguing. About things that would seem stupid to others."

"Like . . . ?"

"We tried to guess the names of the songs on Morrissey's next album."

"What?"

"I knew you wouldn't get it. And I don't mean that condescendingly. We just realized that we inhabited the same mental realms but that our opinions clashed. Right from the start we both had the feeling that we knew each other. There was no initial tension."

"So how did you fall in love?"

"I don't know. I think we skipped straight over that part. We loved each other from the start. As though the falling in love part was a minor detail in the past. And we knew we were fascinated by one another. We just didn't waste time with games and stuff."

"And what about the thrill that you have at the beginning of a relationship?"

"Oh, believe me we felt it. Marian thrilled me with the crossword puzzles she crafted especially for me, and I returned the favor with endings I wrote just for her, inserting them in the books she was reading. We were thrilled when we met other couples whose conversations had run dry and we were still arguing incessantly, we were thrilled when we didn't notice the time pass and we were the last ones left in a restaurant, we were thrilled when we went for walks and got lost, we were thrilled each time we got into bed and each time we got out of it. And we were thrilled most of all when we realized there was no sense in living apart."

"But how did you know she was the one?"

"Did you have an imaginary friend when you were a kid?"

"Yes."

"Right, so did I, but at some point around puberty he disappeared. Then around a month after I met Marian I felt like he had come back to me in female form. That feeling you get that someone's watching you, when you're shocked, when you're happy, when you're mad, when you're put down, that feeling that someone's always with you even when you're alone, that's Marian."

"I'm dying to meet her."

"I died to meet her, and it still hasn't happened. Marian's disappeared. I've been looking for her for two weeks and . . ."

"Is it possible she doesn't want to be found?"

"What do you mean?"

"I have no idea what was going on between the two of you, but women don't just go flying off Ferris wheels. If anything, they plunge to their deaths."

"There's no way in hell Marian committed suicide. The notion is absurd."

"What about if you just rest your wounded ego for a second and think logically: Couldn't there be some things you didn't know about?"

"You don't even know her."

"So what. I'm way too familiar with the feeling of loss and shock that comes with sudden abandonment, and I'm terribly familiar with people's unwillingness to accept hard facts."

"Who're we talking about here?"

"You, Ben, you. You look like a modern day Job, pawing uselessly at your wounds."

"You're starting to sound like some kind of mad preacher."

"Cynicism isn't going to save you here. Maybe it's just hard for you to handle the awful fact that you committed suicide in vain."

"The fact that I can't find her does not mean that she feels differently about me."

"I think you have blind faith in the love of a woman who's left you."

"Why are you doing this?"

"Doing what?"

"Pricking and prying, trying to pull the rug out from under me."

"Because you mean so much to me."

"If I mean so much to you, I'd expect you to show some support. Not that it matters much anyway."

"That's insulting."

"I didn't say a thing."

"But you were going to."

"True. I was going to say that when one's been through the trials of abandonment as many times as you have, one might find it rather enjoyable to project their own emotional baggage on the man who first hexed one's relationship karma."

"Now you're just being a kid, trying on words for size."

"Aren't the parallels you keep reaching for a bit childish? Might it not feel a little too good to learn that the wife of the man you first loved left him and then you met him and showed him the light? I guess for you it would be the perfect closure for the story that had never come full circle."

"God, you've grown so arrogant with age if you think I'm using this to further my own agenda."

"Keren, do us both a favor and give the saint routine a rest. It doesn't take superhuman insight to see that you're pretty damn pleased with the way things have played themselves out."

"Understanding your current predicament, I'll ignore your insults for now and just ask you a question: Why do you think we met?"

"Because we thought we'd be bettered by a higher education, I guess."

"Not back then. Why do you think we met again in the Other World, and why in a manner so similar . . . ?"

"Come on, Keren, you know contrived symbolism makes me sick."

"Contrived?"

"It might work for a Hollywood flick, but thankfully reality is more independent and low budget. Only the really far-gone cling to coincidence and assign meaning to whatever suits their needs at the time. That's why they're called coincidences, don't you think? As far as I'm concerned, the fact that you and I crossed paths is exactly as significant as the fact that Marian and I haven't."

"But if the two of you were just walking down the street and happened to bump into each other and then got back together, you'd have a good time telling everyone that fate brought you back into each other's arms."

"Not fate, but the unavoidable necessity of being together."

"I won't split hairs with you. It's abundantly clear to both of us that you're in a state of deep denial."

"That's it! This is too weird for me. I'm arguing with my ex about my chances of finding my wife in tones that are already doing a pretty good job of reminding me why we broke up in the first place. . . ."

"I apologize if I got carried away, Ben. I guess I just had a lot to get off my chest. You have no idea how truly happy I am to see you."

"And I to see you."

Looking around, Ben realized they'd covered a lot of ground while arguing and that he had no idea where he was.

Keren pointed at the skyscraper to his left. "Come."

"Not sure that's a good idea . . . ," he said, holding his tongue at the touch of her soft finger on his lips and the sight of her still-beautiful face.

"Don't worry," she said.

The string quartet welcomed them with a smile and, as the elevator doors closed, the slow pour of music began. Ben tried to tame the thoughts that came to his mind, but the years truly had been kind to his first real girlfriend, and he found himself unable to keep his eyes off her smooth body, rounded and shaped by time. Watching her graceful movements, he tried to push back the creeping calculations about when last he had been with a woman, while, at the same time, scenes from his university days flashed through his mind and he recollected how they had gotten wrapped up in the distinct joys of sexual discovery, and that, he reminded himself glumly, was back when the body by his side was angular and inexperienced. He contemplated the peaks of pleasure she was capable of now that she had matured into full-fledged womanhood. A dangerous tiredness descended on him, threatening to eat away all that remained of the tenacious resistance he had exhibited hours earlier. He exchanged a limp half smile with Keren's bothersome reflection.

Ben hesitated before stepping out of the elevator, surprised to find that they had come to a stop on the expansive rooftop and not at Keren's apartment. He smiled questioningly, and she nodded in understanding, ambling over to the edge.

"What are you doing?" he asked.

She held out her hand for him and waited patiently while he gathered the courage, taking her hand lightly, their fingertips grazing each other. Standing next to her on the edge, he felt his head start to swim and he tightened his grip. At the sight of the city spread beneath his feet, Ben locked his knees and asked to retreat.

Keren held his hand tightly and brought her warm lips to his ear. "Don't be afraid, my darling," she whispered. But Ben's fear had advanced from near paralysis to organ-shaking shudders. She brought him in close. Ben shut his eyes and inhaled the sweet warmth of her body, rubbing her back as the rise and fall of his chest merged with the swell of her breasts, burying his head in her fragrant neck, traveling up and down the artery of life, pausing by her locked lips, glancing against them and reveling as they opened, revealing a gleaming cavern, her thirsty tongue flitting against his lips, a serpentine seduction, teasing his tongue into a lover's game, which, when answered, was cut short as his excitement mounted. He pulled away from the comforting body, shaking his head. "I'm sorry, Keren, I can't . . ."

Keren, looking like she'd been awakened from an enchanted dream, looked at him crossly and moaned, "Can't you be untrue to her just this once?"

"It's myself I'd be cheating on," Ben said.

Keren nodded, her eyes welling up. "Have I already told you that you're every woman's dream?"

A colossal tremor went through the building.

"What was that? Don't tell me they have earthquakes in this place, too."

"No, darling, what they've got are monstrous elevators that sometimes get stuck."

"The elevator's stuck?" he asked.

"I didn't know you were in a hurry . . . ?"

"Well, when there's no choice . . . ," Ben said, shrugging.

She burst out laughing as he headed toward the door. "You're not seriously thinking about walking down twenty-four flights of stairs," she said.

"Like I said, when there's no choice . . ."

"But there is a choice."

"I'm not . . . ," he said before he understood her meaning and then added, "You don't mean . . ."

"Trust me, you don't know what you're missing. I do it at least twice a week. The perfect catharsis for a miserable day." Looking at his incredulous expression, she added, "And if that's not enough, just think of it as an opportunity to relive Marian's last moments, as much as possible."

"As much as possible?"

"If you wanted the really authentic version of events, I guess you'd have to introduce terror into the equation."

"Oh, there's plenty of terror."

"Well, that's just because you're newly dead. Believe me, as soon as you get used to this place you'll forget what fear is. You have to learn to utilize the upside of death."

"Like jumping off a twenty-four-story building?"

"Here, watch," she said, pointing to three nearby buildings, each capped with a waving teenage boy about to take the plunge.

Keren walked right up to the edge of the roof, spread her arms sideways like wings, and called into the wind, "Just don't look down."

Ben approached the edge cautiously, Kolanski's trembling stance on the cloud foremost in his mind. He took a step back, imagined Marian's last moments, readdressed the edge, closed his eyes, and jumped a split second after Keren, her laugh still trailing behind her.

The initial dread that seized him when he dared open his eyes turned hypnotically tranquil when he realized he was hovering between the sky and the ground. A silence enveloped him during his virgin flight, and he saw nothing through his slit eyes but the image of his missing wife, his body drifting down, weightless, an irrational smile plastered across his face, finally understanding what Keren meant when she said it was the ultimate catharsis. The events of the past few days receded into the spreading quiet. The freedom was incomparable. His soul was liberated of everything beyond the soothing thought that if man can fly, he is truly all-capable. Prompted by untethered optimism, he bellowed Marian's name. Even when the call went unanswered, he persisted, certain that though they were flying through separate skies, one way or another their paths would cross. The free fall continued for an additional minute before the black blotches on the ground sprang to life, and Ben realized that the flight was about to end when he was able to discern male from female. As they made their way to and from their modern dens, they didn't bother to look up at the man rocketing down among them till he shrieked, flailed with his arms and legs, and impacted with a dull thud in the midfield of a soccer pitch, much to the chagrin of both teams.

Opening his eyes, Ben, encircled by kids, couldn't understand why he heard a woman's voice in his ear. "Ben? Ben Mendelssohn?"

He remembered the telefinger when one of the kids pointed at the glowing red light on his godget. "Yes, that's me."

"Of course it's you," the woman replied, "I called you. Listen, it's Marilyn."

"Marilyn?" he said, scattering the kids with a brusque series of hand movements, "Oh, oh, Ms. Monroe?"

"Yes, hon. I'm sorry to be so direct but I'm late for a show and there's an old couple here holding me up. They're looking for Maria."

"Marian?" he shouted.

"Yeah, Marian. I can't explain everything to them right now but they're dying to see you."

"Wait a second, who?"

"They say they're her parents."

"Tell them I'll meet them at my place in an hour . . . I live in June 2001, Circle twenty-one, Building M, Floor twenty-four, Apartment seven."

∽

Reinvigorated, Ben trotted off the field and headed toward the nearest multi-wheel. Then he suddenly stopped, looked up at the darkening sky and clapped himself on the forehead. He searched around for Keren. After a while he spotted a leg sticking out of a bush on the far periphery of the park. He ran toward her. She was flat on her back, eyes half open, full blown befuddlement all over her tired face, and a frail, hallucinative smile hanging from her lips.

"Keren, you alright?" he asked, leaning over her.

"One more time and I'm there," she said in a drowsy voice.

"What are you talking about?" he asked, bringing his head close to her moving lips.

"There . . . it's better . . . darling . . ."

He noticed that she was clasping the godget in her hands. "Hey, you can't do that!" he barked, prying her surprisingly strong fingers off the button that would send her to the kingdom of eternal sleep. Only when her hands went slack and rested daintily on his, did he relax. Just as he was sure she had sunk into a deep sleep, he felt her nails ripping at the back of his hand. He yelled and jumped back.

"Good luck with what's-her-name," she said, pushing the button for the seventh time and closing her eyes.

"I'm sorry," he whispered, kissing her smiling lips and carrying her in his arms, consoling himself with the knowledge that at least this time he had decided to stay and accompany her on this, her final journey.

26

Trunkation

To: Halfabillion, Director of the Forest of Family Trees
From: Abillionandaquarter

I'd like to call your attention to the corpse atop my table at this moment. As you know, I try not to bother you with the autopsy reports of uprooted trees, unless, of course, there's cause for suspicion. In this particular case I can categorically say that, based on my years of experience as a tree pathologist, I have never seen a more clearcut case of arboreal abuse. The fact of the matter is that someone has, time and again, been committing a crime that must be answered for immediately. It goes without saying that I will stand by any decision you make, even though I am sure that once you see the evidence, you will share my opinion that those who perpetrated this murderous scandal must be relieved of their jobs and punished, as you see fit.

Following are eight basic facts that have come to light during the autopsy of the Mendelssohn family tree, situated in plot 2,605,327 until 6/21/01 at 23:07.

1) The tree's roots are strong and stable, aside from some mild rot (nothing that a routine root canal couldn't solve)–conclusively indicating that the tree had many fruitful years left and that it was uprooted before its time.
2) The tree's bark is new, fresh, and vibrantly brown in color. Scruff patches, caused by pointy-toed shoes, are visible at the eighty centimeter mark. The perpetrator kicked the trunk, leaving bruise marks all along its lower section. As opposed to truly aged trunks, which often exhibit "acne" all along their length, this specimen shows wounds only at the points cited above, additional proof of deliberate harm.

3) Over the last ten years, the crown has shown no signs of foliar renewal. In essence the tree has suffered an imposed autumn. With your permission I'll quote Sevenmillion's seminal work *On Leaves and Branches:* "When a tree loses its leaves and they do not prove to be self-regenerating, it is a strong indication of severe autumnal trauma, hinting at the beginning of a gradual decline. If disease is not a factor (the usual culprit is tri-seasonal jaundice, presenting itself in the form of yellow, lackluster leaves) then one must conclude that the culprit is external influence–unusually fast balding is a means a tree uses to signal to its surroundings that it is in distress, induced by violence."

4) The sap marks alongside the origin of the last eight branches have faded and are almost illegible–a common sight among old growth hardwood. Radiometric dating indicates that the Mendelssohns had been around for 2,609 years, thereby discrediting the age theory. Therefore, the smudging of the sap marks must be the result of the other known factor, fear. The oversecretion of sap points to grave existential concern (see: *When the Tree Trembles: The World Wars and Their Effect on Families with Boys).* This is heightened during storms in the Family Tree Forest, storms that are both a hysterical and credible reflection of particularly violent periods. What did the tree fear? And why did it only start to fear during the last few years?

5) The smooth hollow marks typical of natural branch stubs stop at 02.01.94 (Menachem Mendelssohn). From that point on, all eight branch stubs are fibrous and pointy. In other words, they were cruelly removed from their spots, and the perpetrator of this crime did not clean up after himself. Moreover, the angle at which the branches were severed is identical in all eight cases–a forty-five degree pull to the right, a thirty-five degree pull to the left, a twist and an *intentional* dismembering. There are also clear signs of struggle. A very weak branch readily succumbs to physical strength; in this case the perpetrator was forced to employ a twisting motion, indicating, to my dismay, the branch's temporary resistance to this abhorrent attack. That is to say, there's no reason to believe that the branch had been naturally weakened to the point of falling, which yet again indicates wrongdoing.

6) Further thoughts on the dismembering–despite the similarities in the manner in which the branches were torn from the trunk, there are distinct signs of improvement in the technique of the assailant. The first two stubs show a clumsy method of attack, requiring *nine* counterclockwise twists to separate the branches from the trunk, but the next four show far more efficient form and the final two are downright expert (a mere three twists, executed while pulling).

7) The murders were committed by hand, without the aid of tools or implements. Had the crimes been committed with some type of sawing tool, we'd see no evidence of this type of "sloppy" result, hinting at one of three scenarios: The murders were not premeditated; they were premeditated but the perpetrator has tried to stage it so that it looks otherwise; the perpetrator is a scatterbrained, illogical character.

8) Once the outer layers of bark were peeled away, the heartwood was revealed–tall, smooth and robust. Heartwood that promises a tree many more fruitful years. Its crown is not intertwined, its branches are well spaced and symmetric, its trunk shows no unusual bulges or knots. In summation, it is one of the more aesthetic specimens I've seen.

Fraternally,
Abillionandaquarter

PS: If you require any help at all drafting a psychological profile of the perpetrator, please don't hesitate to get in touch. I recommend two primary courses of investigation–a mysterious hatred for said family (perhaps there's a connection between the criminal alias and the Mendelssohn family, if you know what I mean) or a severe psychological disorder that prompted the perpetrator to act like a merciless psychopath each time he came near the tree, may it rest in peace.

PPS: If I may, I'll conclude on a personal note and congratulate you on your new love.

Best of luck.

Halfabillion folded the letter and slipped it back into the envelope. Nodding, he began thinking of his next schnapps with Billion. He decided to call the two main suspects to his office the next day and demand answers. It was high time this episode was brought to an end.

27

"Adam," Shahar called out in a childish voice, his fists monotonically pounding the tabletop between them.

Adam approached his brother's chair slowly, his red eyes riveted on the sore sight before him. Eyes wide, hair disheveled, shoulders stooped, stubble sprouting across his face, Shahar grinned luridly as he watched his brother draw near.

"I'm so happy to see you," the actor whispered hoarsely.

"Your throat," Adam said, sitting down, "clear your throat."

"I haven't spoken for three days," Shahar said.

Adam nodded. "I know. They told me you didn't say a word to anyone, not even the lawyer."

"What took you so long?" Shahar asked. "I told them you were the only one I was willing to talk to."

"They wouldn't release me," Adam said, looking down at the dirty floor.

"What do you mean?" Shahar asked, gazing at him curiously.

"I'm here with a police escort. They arrested me yesterday."

"What are you talking about, Adam? The police arrested you? Because of me?"

"No, Shahar, nothing to do with you," Adam said, struggling to keep his voice calm. "They came by yesterday morning. There was a complaint. To a sex crimes unit or something. I told them it was nothing. That it was all platonic. But just as they were getting ready to leave, this policewoman asked to use the bathroom. When she got back, I realized something awful had happened. While I was talking to the other two, she walked into the room 'by mistake.'"

Looking at the confusion on his brother's face, he repeated. "The Room."

Shahar shook his head in disbelief. "I always say lock the door. I'm always saying . . ."

"You're right," Adam said, placing an unsteady hand on Shahar's agitated one. "I acted irresponsibly. This is what you get when a police-woman opens the door to a room and sees a wall of naked children. They marched me straight to the back of the patrol car. Read me my rights. And since then I haven't had a moment's rest. They took all of the pictures and made me give them the names of each one of the kids. Then they put me up on the national list of pedophiles and said they wouldn't let me go until each and every one of those kids had been spoken to and had convinced them that they hadn't been touched."

"Oh God, this isn't really happening," Shahar said, rolling his eyes back. "Who filed the complaint?" he asked after a brief pause.

"Tom's mother," Adam said, twisting his lips in derision.

"That annoying kid again?" Shahar said, kicking the table leg. "Will he ever leave us alone?"

"It's not him, Shahar, it's his mother."

"Oh, please. And last time? In the amusement park it was his moth-er's friend. I told you then and there that kid is trouble."

"Shhh," Adam hissed, "they're listening to every word."

"What are you talking about? There's no one here," Shahar said, pointing to the glass window.

"Don't point," Adam grunted. "They're sitting behind the glass. It's like on TV. What do you think, that they let me meet you out of the goodness of their hearts? Shahar, they know it's the only way to get you to talk."

"Adam, about her . . ."

"Don't say anything about her, Shahar, they're listening to every word."

"I have to," Shahar said, clenching his teeth. "If they do what they said they're going to, I won't have a choice. I'll have to tell the whole story."

"What? Shahar, what's going on? You're shaking like a leaf."

"I'm scared shitless, Adam."

"You can't let them get to you."

"I don't give a fuck about them. She's the one who scares me. They said they were going to bring her in for a confrontation."

"What's keeping them?"

"She flew out of the country and they're waiting for her to get back. . . ."

"Okay, confront her, what's the big deal?"

"Are you out of your mind?" Shahar yelled, eyes popping. "I can't be in the same room with that woman. Every time I close my eyes I see her chasing me. The one time I managed to go to sleep I saw her chasing me on one of those old turn-of-the-century unicycle-type things. Wheels, Adam, that's all I'm able to see . . . wheels, circles, spheres. . . ." And then without another word he spun around in his chair, examined the cracked wall, and began to trace circles in the air.

"Shahar, enough," Adam said, swatting his drawing finger out of the air. "Look at me. Listen. No one is chasing you!"

"Easy for you to say," Shahar protested, "your little brother did it all for you. Well, I got news for you. Turns out big brother doesn't see everything. In your case, all he sees is half the picture."

"What do you want?" Adam asked. "You sound like a lunatic. Shahar, buddy, let's agree on one simple fact: The reporter who came to our house, the one you attacked, was flesh and blood, not a ghost, right?"

"I don't know what she was," Shahar said.

"No, no, no, Shahar, that's not good enough. You're getting confused with that damned script. The woman from the movie, the fictitious one, she's haunting you. Her! The reporter who showed up, at the worst time, looks exactly like . . ."

"No," Shahar cut him off. "She doesn't look like her; she is her!"

"That's impossible," Adam said. "If she died, and you're responsible for her death, how could she show up on your doorstep one year after the fact. Unless, of course, she miraculously survived the fall, which would clear you of any guilt. You can't be held responsible for the death of a living woman. That's why you went so crazy three nights ago. You wanted to finish it off."

"I can't listen to your idiotic explanations any longer," Shahar said, pushing the table away and abruptly rising. "You keep trying to distort the truth because of them." To Adam's amazement, he turned to the glass, yelling, "I killed her in her previous incarnation! Yes, friends, you waited three days to hear me open my mouth, well then, here's the director's cut."

"Shahar, please, calm down. You're out of control. You're spewing nonsense."

"Pay no mind to the crybaby behind me. Adam is a tortured pedophile. A moral one. It doesn't matter. The two go hand in hand, no? Torture and morality. That's Adam: most guys hit and run—not my brother, he runs the kids off and then hits it alone in his room. Who's the wiseass who lit a cigarette and asked smugly, 'Am I my brother's keeper?'"

"I'm begging you, Shahar," Adam said, rising from his chair, approaching his brother deliberately and directing his cries at the one-way glass window. "You are responsible for the mental health of the incarcerated. He needs a psychiatric evaluation. Did you see him drawing circles in the air like some kind of psycho? He's not . . ."

"Enough already, idiot," Shahar said, pushing Adam strongly as he tried to pull him away from the window. "Come near me again and you'll be sorry." He turned back to his invisible audience and giggled. "You see how I must constantly restrain him? Watch that he doesn't cross the line? Like that other morning, when I saw the look in his eye and knew that hunting season was on. He seemed more stressed than usual and I had a good idea as to why. Three months he'd made do with the pictures, didn't lure a single kid to the house. Tried to kick the habit. You got to give him credit for his powers of denial. On the night that I attacked that ghost bitch he even had a woman over at the house. But on that critical morning, it was clear that the twelve-step program to kick the kid-addiction had gone down the drain. He was burning up inside. Barely finished his morning toast. His leg was bouncing like a sewing machine. I asked him if I could tag along. As you see, even pedophiles need nannies. He said there was no need. I saw that my instinct was correct and said we'd meet at the amusement park. I showed up an hour later, dressed as a beggar. You remember *From Hand to Mouth*? The one that won me the prize? Back then I used to go around like a beggar, to try and get used to the feeling of nothingness. I'd come home once a day, in the mornings, for breakfast with my brother. That's it.

"Anyway, I showed up that day to make sure he didn't do anything stupid. We stayed in eye contact and everything was working just fine till she showed up—a school teacher who was there with her students and another teacher. I didn't know what she wanted from me. Turned out she was offering me a ride on the Ferris wheel as a way of raising my spirits. You know who I mean. She was all over the papers. Her parents sued the park's management and won just a few days ago. Amazing what lawyers can do. At any rate, I accepted her offer. To be honest, I was a bit proud. Everyone was sure I was a real homeless man. We got onto a rather empty section of the wheel. She said she wanted to hear me and with all the noise around . . .

"You already know where this is going. She asked me about my life and I served up some of the character's back story. As soon as the wheel started to spin, everything changed. Everything. She started talking about the hypocrisy of our society, a society that scorns people like me and ignores truly dangerous characters, who, thanks to their sheep's clothing, walk around freely, unmolested. I tried not to laugh till she pointed at the businessman with the fancy attaché case, standing near the hotdog stand. She said he didn't fool her for a second. I asked what she meant, and she said she knew that behind those dark glasses was a pair of predatory eyes. From that moment on, everything sped up. I didn't even have time to think. She looked down to point Adam out, but he was in the middle of a conversation with some kid, and all of a sudden she started to go crazy—'Oh my God, I can't believe it!'—then she started to yell the kid's name. Who can hear a woman shouting at an amusement park, you ask. And you're right. But at that moment it seemed possible. Especially when they started to leave, Adam and the kid, and my idiot of a brother put his long arm around the kid's shoulders in an innocent hug that drove the teacher mad. When she realized there was no way anyone was hearing her, she stood up, tried to draw attention. I didn't know how to stop her when she started waving her arms. I had no choice. I couldn't bear the thought that my brother would be tried for seducing a minor. Before she found her voice, I grabbed her legs, lifted a little, and pushed. It all happened in a matter of seconds. I couldn't believe how easily her weight relented and, more so, how no one seemed to notice. Only about a second before she landed did people become aware of what was happening. Then all hell broke loose. The wheel stopped at the perfect time, though. I hopped off and flew the hell out of the park.

"You want to hear the great irony? Half an hour after I got home, the two of them walked in, giggling, on their way to the computer, while I scraped the makeup off my face as fast as I could, not believing that over the course of the last hour I'd gone from an innocent man to a murderer and, worst of all, the motive for the crime was sitting in the next room totally unperturbed! I could go deep into my state of mind at that time, but I have a feeling it doesn't interest you one bit. So that's it, end of story. I've spared you the need for evidence and witnesses. The perfect confession, no? I thank you for listening."

Still standing in front of the glass, he bowed deeply, till the applause in his ears subsided. A weary grin hung off his face. He turned toward Adam and sighed. "Believe you me, Adam, this kind of relief is worth murdering for."

For the first time since he had assumed a fetal position on the floor, Adam looked up. "You're a sick man, Shahar."

Shahar put a hand out to him. "Get up, Adam, the show's over. They're going to come in here any second, and you don't want to give them the satisfaction of seeing you like this."

Adam got up unassisted and plodded back to his chair. He sat down and stared at the wall. Shahar mimicked him.

Ten minutes later, the door opened and the investigating officer strode in, accompanied by five yawning policemen. The brothers wondered what had detained them. As soon as the investigator opened his mouth, it became clear. The stern-faced ranking officer turned to Shahar and asked him, in a tone that hid years of fandom, "Well, Shahar, now that we've let you see your brother, you ready to talk?"

Shahar exchanged a surprised look with Adam and then donned a weighty expression. His voice measured, he said, "Sure, but I haven't got much to say. I attacked that woman for no reason. I have no idea what made me act that way."

The officer glared at him, remained silent for a minute, and snuffed a cigarette out on the floor. "Take him away," he told two of the uniforms. As they pulled Adam to his feet and out of the room, the investigator asked, "You sure she didn't do anything? Maybe say something that pissed you off?"

Shahar shook his head. "She didn't get the chance."

"Maybe you knew her from somewhere else?"

Shahar shrugged. "Sorry, but I've never seen her before."

The investigator caught the shard of a smile on the actor's lips as Shahar looked over his shoulder, but by the time he turned his head, he had missed the one that passed across Adam's face, already on the other side of the door.

28

Four Undertakers, a Client, and a Liar's Chair

Two friendly undertakers laid Keren to eternal rest in a glass sarcophagus. When they were through, Ben thanked them for taking his tight schedule into account and allowing him to go to the front of the line. The undertakers produced angelic smiles and, before turning to the next body, winked at him, saying there was no need to get too down, for she was now in a far better place.

Ben took the miniature key from the golden-haired undertaker and turned the lock on the sarcophagus three times, as asked. The bald undertaker took it back from him, placed it on his tongue and, throwing his head back, swallowed, convulsing slightly.

Looking at Ben's expression, the golden-haired one clarified. "Just another safety precaution against tomb raiders, necrophiliacs, and postmodern artists."

Ben thanked them again and headed out, a faint smile on his face as he thought about the last time he'd visited the strange cemetery. His smile faded, though, when he considered the investigator's likely response to his current condition. He had gone to see all of his close family members and come up empty. The little man would offer a heartfelt apology and say he had done everything in his power to locate the missing woman, but even an old hand such as himself had never seen a missing-person file go as cold as this one. Ben would look at him, eyes glazed, and thank him for all the hard work. A few more hollow sentences would pass through their lips, followed by a firm handshake and a final farewell. Then loneliness. Then the futility of searching for a needle in a haystack, fighting windmills. His brain would comb through an inventory of clichés. With time, his fierce determination to find his wife would become more and more self involved and . . .

A bitter cry echoed through the hall, violating the deathly silence. Turning around, Ben saw a woman lying flat on top of a young man's body, probably her son, pounding his chest and slapping his face in a desperate attempt to resuscitate him. The man by her side, perhaps her husband, looked around and begged her to stop. She refused to be calmed and began flailing at him, alternating between weeping and laughing, unintentionally providing rather amusing entertainment to the other visitors, who dealt with their loved ones' second deaths as a simple but brutal fact, an attitude the anguished mother was reluctant to adopt.

Ben nodded at her sympathetically, and rather than stare at the distraught family like everyone else, he looked back at the undertakers one final time before leaving. The image that caught his eye was far more intriguing. Farther down along the hall, he spotted one of the undertakers talking to a man who had his back to Ben. He was wheelchair bound, and as Ben strode in his direction, he wondered who this particular athletic paraplegic was burying.

The bald one handed the key to Robert, pointed to the lock, and mumbled a few words of explanation. Ben didn't know why he felt himself go weak at the sight of the distant dead man, and only as Robert swiveled the key a third time and handed it back to the undertaker did Ben get close enough to the proceedings to feel the sweat stream down his back and the hammer stroke of his pulse throb mercilessly in his temples—the undertaker took the key, opened his mouth, and lost his balance as Ben tackled him to the marble floor, grabbed the key out of his hand, and stood up, looking down in amazement at the Mad Hop, strewn on his back, frozen in a position of sweet sleep, his mouth slightly open like a child waiting for a surprise with his eyes closed, his hands tranquilly folded over his belly, his bearing, chillingly euphoric.

"What's going on here?" Robert called out, his tone going from annoyance to surprise when he recognized the man standing over him and the equal measure of surprise on his face.

"I was just about to ask you the same thing," Ben said.

The golden-haired undertaker helped his stunned colleague to his feet. "Why'd you do that?" he asked.

"That's my friend there," Ben said, pointing at the Mad Hop, "and there's no way he opted for eternal sleep."

"You'd be surprised to hear how many people find that option a viable one," the golden-haired one exclaimed. "Everyone can choose their own escape to . . ."

"Oh shut up already!" Ben snapped. "The guy lying in that coffin did not opt for eternal sleep. No way. Anyone takes a step in the direction of that sarcophagus and we have ourselves a big problem."

"Ben, why make such a scene," Robert asked in a soft voice, "when we both know there's nothing that can be done? I feel your pain and your anger, but what choice do we have but to accept the frustrated investigator's fate?"

"Frustrated? Samuel wasn't frustrated."

"Not as a man, my friend, but as an investigator. By the way, was he able to track down your wife?"

"No, but what's that got to do with anything?"

Robert laid a hand on his star. "I'm sorry to put things so bluntly, especially when I'm the one responsible for your acquaintance, but the Mad Hop hasn't solved a single case in the last ten years. Not one. And in the end, his stubbornness has exacted a very steep price."

"What? So why did you go out of your way to glorify him when we met?"

"Because I, too, was lured by blind faith and a general belief in the goodness of mankind. Not for a second did I think that he was a crook. . . ."

"Samuel? A crook?" Ben pushed aside thoughts of the lie detector's strange tactics and his use of trickery and deceit.

"One of the biggest," Robert said, sighing and leaning back in his chair, "one of the biggest."

"You brought him here?"

Robert nodded. "I couldn't just leave him in the state he was in. Even crooks deserve a proper burial."

"How do you know he punched in a seven over three?"

"Samuel called me and asked me to come over to his house as soon as possible. I thought maybe he had some new information regarding Catherine. When I got there, the door was open. I found him lying on the floor. I bent down and tried to pick him up but he was unresponsive. Much like you, Ben, I couldn't believe that the Mad Hop had opted out in this way, but the note he'd left on the table was conclusive."

"Note?" Ben asked, looking at the investigator's still body.

"He apologized to all those whose trust he'd betrayed. He admitted that he wanted more than anything else to be a superior private eye in this world but that desire turned into an obsession, which clouded his judgment. Hence the dizzying string of failures. Hence the feeling of worthlessness. Hence the decision to put an end to the tragic farce."

The doleful effect of Robert's words did not stop Ben from barking "Forget it!" when the golden-haired undertaker took a step forward and put out his palm for the key.

"Why won't you give back the key?" Robert asked.

"Because then he'll swallow it and I won't have any way of getting Samuel out."

"What do you mean 'getting Samuel out'?" the bald undertaker asked.

"I'll explain in a second," Ben said, "but first tell me: what happens if someone who never pushed the magic numbers is buried in a sarcophagus of eternal sleep?"

"There's no such thing. It's unthinkable that we would force someone . . ."

"No, I don't mean you guys. I'm just wondering if there's a way to prove that someone actually chose the option of ultimate sleep."

"Of course," the baldheaded one guffawed, "you see if he wakes up."

"But if he wakes up after you've swallowed the key?"

The golden-haired one giggled. "Take it easy. Once they've been put in their eternal beds, they don't wake up."

Ben nodded, walked over to the sarcophagus, shoved the key in place, and flipped the lock three times.

"What are you doing?" the undertakers yelled in unison.

Ben smiled and extended his hand to Robert. "Come. Out of the chair. Let me put Samuel in there. It'll save us all a lot of time."

"Are you out of your mind or have you just forgotten that I'm a cripple and can't go anywhere without my wheelchair?"

"Oh, but I've seen your form in the hundred meters," Ben said.

Before Robert had the chance to respond, Ben apologized and cracked him on the back of the head, breaking his neck and pulling him out of the chair. On the ground, Ben flipped the Belgian onto his back and used Robert's thumb to press 3 once on his godget, ending the dead man's moaning. Within moments, his eyelids were fluttering and he had dropped into a deep sleep.

The undertakers looked on in shock. "Don't you get it?" Ben asked. "I did that just to demonstrate that it's entirely possible that you've been locking innocently sleeping people in these sarcophagi."

"Like Robert," he added, still not seeing comprehension in their eyes. "What would happen if I put him as is in a sarcophagus and locked it up? Pushing three once assures eight hours of dreamless sleep, right? What happens when those are up?"

"He'd keep on sleeping," the golden-haired one mumbled, exchanging bashful looks with his friend.

"In other words, if I wanted to do away with Robert, not only would it be easily done, but I'd also have your help. In the previous world, you'd be seen as accomplices to a murder. And I think that's a little worse than pummeling a phony cripple—a fact you'll be able to verify quite easily in a few hours when he wakes up."

Ben lifted the coffin's heavy lid, took hold of the Mad Hop's warm body, and folded him into the empty wheelchair.

"But . . . ," the bald one began.

"I'm sorry," Ben said, "this isn't up for discussion. I'm taking him with me. If I've made a mistake, I assure you I'll return. In the meantime, I recommend you start thinking about ways of verifying eternal sleep . . ."

"On one condition . . . ," the golden-haired one said.

⁓

The reunion with Yossef and Miriam was moving, even though the two kept sneaking surreptitious glances at the dead man in the wheelchair, who was flanked by four suspicious undertakers. Ben could hardly hold back the tears as he listened to the story of their departure from the previous world and the gift they'd left for Kobi and Tali. When he told them about his exhaustive efforts to track down their daughter and the assistance he had received from the inanimate man in the chair, they promised to do all they could to help him. Ben realized that the old scientists had a hard time coming to terms with the new world. When Yossef asked if he had an explanation for their current reality, Ben said their new existence would make sense soon enough, even under their scientific scrutiny, but that in the meanwhile they should just be thankful that they arrived together.

The couple exchanged thumbprints with Ben, asked him to keep them up to date with even the smallest development, and warned him not to drift away as he had during their long mourning period in the previous world.

After they had left, Ben leaned against the door. Yossef and Miriam had aged a decade since the tragedy. And if that wasn't enough, he'd left them with the insincere notion that they were sure to run into Marian at some point soon.

Losing himself once again in one of the desolate cars on the train of thought, he wasn't able to decipher the words spoken by the cranky voice in his ear and turned toward the speaker, asking, "What did you say?"

The youngest undertaker nodded in the direction of the Mad Hop, who stretched his short limbs to full capacity, yawned, looked around, and said, "Bloody hell, this is one ugly apartment."

The four flabbergasted undertakers crowded around him. "What do you want?" he asked, jumping back.

Seeing Ben approach him, he stomped his right foot. "This is my seven over three? Four undertakers, a client, and a liar's wheelchair? No ladies? Nothing to drink? No city? Something small . . . chimneys . . . God, it isn't supposed to be like this . . . this is one fucked-up kind of internal wor . . ."

"Samuel, you alright?" Ben asked, getting on his knees and taking him in his arms.

The little man, lost in Ben's arms, said, "That's all I needed, the blooming of a latent homosexuality . . . bloody hell . . ."

One of the undertakers burst out laughing. "Sorry, sir, but you're mistaken. You're still in the Other World and we've made a grave error."

Turning to Ben, his head bowed, he said, "I believe we owe you a profound apology. We shouldn't have doubted you."

Ben waved off the apology. "Don't worry about it. The important thing is that Samuel's awake . . . I'm sure you have a ton of work and I wouldn't want to keep you."

Once they'd gone, Ben turned back to the investigator. "What happened to you, Samuel? I know you didn't opt for a seven over three."

"I didn't even opt for a one over three."

"So what then?"

"Robert."

Ben laughed unwillingly. "Huh?"

"Lose the clownish expression. The man's a pathological liar."

"You mean the business with the wheelchair?"

"That, too. Since you brought me here in his wheelchair, I assume you realize he's not in need of it. He just uses it as a ploy for sympathy."

"It did strike me as odd, considering he's the only physically disabled person I've seen in the Other World."

"The only person posing as physically disabled. There are no handicapped people in the Other World."

"You say the wheelchair is a ploy for sympathy?"

"Absolutely. He wants to convince as many people as possible that he was wronged in the previous world. Don't think he chose you because of your uniquely keen listening skills. I assure you there are hundreds like you, random people who have heard the tragic life story of the pathetic creature who's incapable of forgiving himself and therefore seeks out the sympathy of all and sundry. . . ."

"Well, now I see why you kept avoiding the matter, but how can you be so sure he's that big of a liar?"

"He brutally raped that poor girl."

"What about the whole thing with the sleepwalking?"

"Bollocks. He made a copy of her key and snuck into her room at night."

"And you know this, because . . . ?"

"Robert came to me and asked me to find out as much as possible about Catherine and to alert him when she came to the Other World. Before agreeing, I asked him to relate the story of his life. When he got to the part about the rape, which he of course described as her romantic initiative, I couldn't hold the laughter back. I told him I suffered a rare nervous system disorder that triggered sudden paroxysms of laughter. Inside, I despised the bastard. I asked him to bring me the video documentation of that night, but he claimed all of his tapes had mysteriously disappeared from his apartment. My jaw hurt for days, but I agreed to help him."

"Why? You . . ."

"Ben, sometimes you're as naïve as an alias."

"Samuel, sometimes you're as foggy as a patch of London sky."

"I agreed to take on his case knowing that I'd do everything in my power to ensure that he never met up with her again."

"You lied to him."

"I couldn't bear the thought that that poor woman would be persecuted in death as in life. I found several articles about the story. It was clear the man was a beast who had taken advantage of a young woman preparing to devote herself to God. Her life was ruined in one fell stroke. Even though I knew it was a lie, I felt compelled to make this case mine."

"What did you do?"

"You mean what didn't I do? I sure as hell didn't tell him when she came here a little over a year ago."

"How did he miss her? I mean, he sits there in that chair all the time."

"I guess she was lucky. Maybe he was off to Narcotica, buying one of those hideous cigars."

"Unbelievable."

"Well, that's not the half of it. Right after I made his acquaintance, I contacted the White Room Directory and asked for a daily report of the newly dead. When her name eventually came up, I tracked her down, warned her about him, and found her a new place to live. Once I sat down with her and heard the true version of events, I was mad enough to kill him. Ben, the man's mental. He's obsessed with the woman. After so many conquests, he couldn't handle her rejection, so he decided to take matters into his own hands."

"So you think he doesn't really love her?"

"I couldn't care less. What's important is that she doesn't love him and that, as far as she's concerned, he is the devil incarnate."

"Aren't you getting a little carried away? According to the old truism, to err is human but to forgive . . ."

"Never have I been more proud of my humanity and lack of divinity."

"I meant Catherine."

"She can't forgive him. And besides, for her, this business isn't even part of the past. Her nightmare continues."

"Because when she shot him she thought she was putting an end to it."

"And then she comes here and discovers that not only is this loathsome creature still hunting her, but his determination had increased tenfold."

"But as long as he never finds her . . ."

"He already has. In a café. She lashed out at him and ran away."

"I know! Oh my God, I know! I was there with my mother. I saw the whole thing. That's how I found out he isn't crippled."

"Right. So she managed to get away, leaving the bastard feeling degraded and betrayed. He came straight to my place and started howling about my inadequacies, saying he'd trusted me all these years and, had I not made all these false statements, he would have met her ages ago. I smiled and said that since he's in an accusatory state of mind, perhaps he'd like to discuss some fraudulent statements of his own. . . ."

"You told him the truth?"

"Ben, any good liar knows that the lowest lie is meant to serve an even lower truth. The spectacle was a true pleasure. His face went white, a catatonic tremor went through his limbs, and his countenance took on the hysteria of a man who realizes he's lied to a far more gifted liar. And then . . ."

"He came for you?"

"Surprising how much strength the man has. He lunged at me, and before I had the chance to fight back, he got his hands around my neck and started to bellow like crazy. Then he took my thumb and forced it down on the button, sentencing me to a sleep I wasn't supposed to rise from."

"I don't get it. If he planned on sending you to the kingdom of eternal sleep, why'd he only force you to push the button once?"

"He forced me to push the button seven times."

Ben smiled limply. "Okay Samuel, would you do me a favor and tell me what the hell you're talking about? Because what you've just said makes no sense whatsoever."

"Well, it does if you've had the button 'fixed' years ago," the Mad Hop said, taking the godget off his neck and pointing at the sleep button. "I'll demonstrate with my pinkie, since the godget only responds to the thumb. If you use your pinkie to push the sleep button seven times, what will happen?"

Using his pinkie cautiously, Ben pushed the button seven times. "Okay, nothing."

"Good," the Mad Hop said, pushing the button once.

Ben stared at his godget. "Your button stays depressed. It doesn't bounce back."

"No, it doesn't. And it doesn't matter if you push it seven times or seven hundred times. It will only respond to the first one."

"Eight hours of dreamless sleep."

"That's right," the Mad Hop said, putting the godget back around his neck. "I asked the manufacturers to disable all of the other sleep options."

"But the undertakers told me that . . ."

"True. Which is why I'm so grateful to you. Had you not extracted me from that ridiculous aquarium I would've been down for a whole lot longer than eight hours. That Belgian may be out of his mind, but he is a thorough bastard. He realized what I'd done, so he dragged me all the way to the cemetery to bury me before I woke up."

"So, in this world's vernacular, you could say I saved your death."

The Mad Hop groaned and got out of the wheelchair. "Well, at least you got yourself a piece of vintage furniture in the deal."

"Which reminds me, what are we going to do with Robert?"

"We won't be hearing from him anytime soon. As far as Catherine is concerned, no need to worry. She lives far away. The only reason he bumped into her is because she came to see a friend." After a brief silence, he continued, "In the interim, I understand you've hit a dead end."

"Couldn't have put it better myself," Ben said. "No one's seen her, no one's heard from her, no one's . . ."

"Okay, I get it," the Mad Hop said. "The easy part of looking for this missing person has come to a close. Nonetheless, I must say this case is getting more intriguing by the minute—on the one hand, your wife went missing in the Other World, an easily accomplished task, the dream of any escaped criminal, a place that grows in size every day like a geometric progression gone haywire, but, on the other hand, your entire family is here and over the past fifteen months not one of them has heard a word from her."

Ben nodded, eyeing the portrait on the wall as though it might reveal another clue.

The Mad Hop watched him. "Rather like the Mona Lisa, eh? Says nothing, looks at you with the wisp of a smile, knows something you don't, and yet manages to look so innocent, as though the mysteriousness she exudes is a mere figment of the spectator's imagination."

"Wish she could talk."

"If she could, she'd probably beg for a frame."

"Sorry?"

The Mad Hop took the canvas painting off the wall and tucked it under his arm. "Ben, the artist did a great job, but it's not enough. This needs to be framed."

"I meant to do that but . . ."

"It's alright. Just a little something in return for all you've had to endure."

"Wait up, I'll join you."

"No need. Take my generosity and go to sleep. By the time you wake up the enigmatic lady will be framed and perhaps that will get us on the right track."

"What do you mean?"

"Truly, I haven't the faintest idea. I'm just trying to cheer you up with my supercilious banter. As a matter of fact, I'd be pleased if we could start plotting a new strategy upon my return."

29

The Exorcist

"Yonatan, you're starting to worry me. I was gone for a week and you still show no signs of recuperation. Maybe you got used to having my voice around and thought I'd abandoned you. No way, my dear, not a chance. I'm really sorry I was gone for so long. It wasn't planned. Not remotely. I was supposed to catch a flight, have an operation, and come back three days later. You remember which operation, right? I should have taken care of it years ago, but each time I got anywhere near the hospital I thought of my mom's terrible story. In the end, I decided to conquer my fears. After all, the place is known as the world leader in treatment for remov– Merde, it's impossible to have a private conversation in this place. . . . It seems like the nursing staff seizes every spare moment they have to eavesdrop. Anyway, I hope you won't mind if I whisper till they're gone. I guess you'll be pretty surprised to hear that I didn't go through with the surgery after all. You're not going to believe what happened. I went to the hospital, and when everything was ready to go, just as the surgeon walked into the room for prep, I started to think about what had happened in that very same place years ago and realized there was no way I'd ever be able to do it. It's just too much.

"You probably think I'm a wimp. I flew out of that place and decided I was going to keep it as is. It's always been part of me anyway. I'd be someone different without it. I know these are just excuses, weak rationalizations for my cold feet, but what can I say, I'm a lot less brave and a lot less tough than I thought. Impulsive, perhaps, but brave? I was thinking of what you'd write me if you heard that at the moment of truth I succumbed to my old demons, allowing them another victory. My mother would've been upset if she had heard I hadn't gone through with it, but she would've also understood. All along, when she was still alive, I think I detected a hint of opposition to the surgery. Like she preferred I let the whole thing go. The only reason she would've been upset was because the trauma still had such a hold on me. As though the creep had gotten over once more.

"I know I sound confused, but I have my reasons. It's not for nothing that I found you, the mate I've looked for my entire life, someone who can help me escape to faraway worlds. Oh, Yonatan, how I miss our little games. I don't sound too weird, do I? When you wake up, we can pick up right where we left off. You have to wake up, Ormus. I refuse to accept that by the time I found you this all turned out to be make-believe, that by the time I found you, my love, you were in a coma. Everything's ready for you. I left it all behind me, all the nastiness. Nothing's left in France. My mother is dead, my husband is a relic of the past, and I decided to skip the operation altogether. Who cares if the little scar stays as a keepsake? That's what I decided on my final trip to De Gaulle. Despite its charm, I'm done with France. That's what held me up, honey. I had to say my final good-byes. Take a last minute tour through the stations of my life. Before I start anew.

"I know the timing is strange. After all, I left France two weeks ago. I guess I needed to be here to realize that I had to go back there one last time. It's a matter of perspective, I suppose. It took me a while to come to terms with everything. To understand that I was really starting afresh in Israel, that I didn't care that everyone thought I was cuckoo for moving to such a crazy place. The job I got here turned out to be the best possible gift. Only thanks to that was I able to gather the courage to end all my affairs in France. And I haven't even mentioned you yet, Yonatan. The only person who's ever managed to get me. At long last I've shaken free of my private history and embraced a brighter future with you, darling. Some might say I didn't dare battle my demons when I upped and left. Whatever. If they had any idea how awful the past year has been. It's all thanks to you that I was able to crawl out from under the burdens of the past and be reborn. Only thanks to your support was I able to chase the demons away. Amazing how much sustenance you can get from someone in a coma, ah?

"And you know what the funniest part is? This will probably sound morbid but, when that actor assaulted me, during the scariest moment I've ever known, right then I realized how happy I am to be here. The thoughts going through my head were so strange. People in life-threatening situations always say they saw their lives flash in front of their eyes, but I saw all the things that would happen after my death. The funeral, the friends from work, the actor's career cut to a sudden end, the media frenzy. Then I thought about you and realized I had to save myself any way I could. I mean, imagine if you'd woken up and they'd told you I'd been murdered. That would be too much.

"But you've got nothing to worry about. I'm here and I'm not going anywhere. Oh, and the actor? I changed my mind about him. At first I thought I'd dig around and then interview him. The assaulted interviews the assaulter. A great exclusive. This past week in France helped underscore just how uninterested I am in that, though. It's just another demon to chase away. According to the cops, it's no secret that he's a bit off. I'm sure that if it wasn't me, it would've been someone else. In a profession like his, where you're always cloaking your true self, a nervous breakdown comes with the territory. And the truth is, I'll pass on the dubious pleasure of listening to him explain away the attack with all kinds of creative process crap. I've been there already. It's boring. I don't want to offer him a platform for his lies. Mandatory psychiatric assistance in a closed ward? A few years behind bars? Hallelujah. I'm not going to waste my time with that stuff. Luckily, this is an open-and-shut case, with a witness who saved my life. . . . Well, you know the details.

"What you don't know has to do with the little woman who's taking care of you, a friendly and opaque sort. Ann. I don't know why, but I get the feeling that's she's trying to get close to me. I know it sounds ugly, maybe even inhuman, but if someone saves your life, does that mean you're forever indebted to them, even if they don't interest you in the least? God, I don't want you to think I'm an awful person, but really I have more important things to do than bond with that weird woman. So? Am I unspeakably despicable? I wish it were the other way around. I wish I would have saved her life. Then at least I wouldn't be the one with the debt. I feel so bad. Yonatan—she left me ten messages on my machine saying I should contact her as soon as I got back from my trip. I was sure something had happened. I took a taxi straight here. Turns out, she wants to invite me to her house for dinner. Ten messages, Yonatan! For dinner. You should have seen her face, too. She was beaming. She ran up to me, pulsating with energy. I asked if there had been some kind of change in your condition. She just stared at me, and only after I repeated the question did she wake up from God knows what kind of dream and say no, not yet. I'm sorry, sweetheart, but there's something scary about her. She's so unpredictable. Maybe I'm going a bit overboard. At any rate, I couldn't disappoint her. I'm going over to her place tonight. I just hope she doesn't turn it into a habit. Well, speaking of the . . . she just walked in the room. You should see how she's looking at me. Like she wants something. Watching me with those tiny eyes. Then disappearing again behind one of the curtains. Yonatan, I could swear she's snooping. What the hell does she think she's doing?

"Okay, enough honey, I don't want to wear you down with all this talk. Obviously I'm a bit impatient these days. Which reminds me—I think you'll go wild when you hear this: One of the writers from our book review just told me that Rushdie's coming out with a new book in September. I think it'll be called *Fury*. Well, what do you think about that? You think you're going to let yourself sleep while all of the midnight children party? It's due out in only two months, but don't expect me to read it to you if you're still in this bed. Honey, you're going to read me the new Rushdie, otherwise it's going to be my fury you'll have to deal with. And on another note, think what an awesome present we're getting. A new book from Rushdie to celebrate our union. And this time we'll read it together, in real time, like we always dreamed . . . Yonatan, don't be cruel . . . Who will I talk about the book with, if . . . ? No, no need to get carried away. No way you'll still be asleep then . . . right?"

30

The Partial Mirror

The Mad Hop's face did not bear good news. Ben's initial reading showed anger and disappointment in equal measure. He walked into the apartment too quickly, head bowed, and offered a subdued "hey." Ben noted the way the investigator attempted to avoid his gaze, and more troubling, his empty hands.

The Mad Hop snapped open his lighter, lit a cigarette, and sat down in the wheelchair.

"Where's the portrait?"

The Mad Hop squinted, examining the cigarette from close range. "I'm not sure you want to know."

"Samuel," Ben said, "you went to frame a picture three hours ago. What could have happened in three hours?"

The Mad Hop engaged in some serious sighing. Looking at Ben, his eyes revealed a newfound, melancholic glaze. "Ben, I have to ask you a strange question. Please try to be objective. Is it possible," he asked without a trace of drama, "that Marian is still alive?"

Ben burst out laughing. "So this is the new direction we're taking in the investigation? We can't find her, so we deduce that she must be in the previous world?"

"I remind you that I asked you to be objective."

"Objective?" Ben said, his nostrils swelling with disdain. "How could I be anything else when we're dealing with such cold hard facts?"

"Regarding the facts," the Mad Hop said, "I suggest we both use caution. I remember you said it was impossible to recognize the face of the woman who fell off the Ferris wheel."

"Yes, but I told you about the other marks that allowed me to identify her: the beauty mark between her big toe and . . ."

"I remember," the Mad Hop said, "I'm simply trying to raise another possibility. Perhaps Marian fell off the Ferris wheel, but the body you saw wasn't hers."

"Have you lost it completely?" Ben cried. "That's the weirdest theory I've ever heard. If the body I looked at in the morgue wasn't my wife's, then where the hell is she?"

"France."

"Excuse me?"

"I have reason to believe that your wife moved to France after her 'death' and only moved back to Israel some fifteen months later. Rather conveniently timed, don't you think?"

"Hold on, I just want to get this straight. You're implying that Marian staged her death just to get me out of her life? Could you come up with something a little more convoluted?" Ben asked, laughing.

"At this point, might your brimming self-confidence not be the biggest obstacle in our way? I've already met plenty of couples whose refusal to look their spouse's betrayal in the eye, whose utter reliance on the enduring strength of the vows of love, as though they were unbreakable, as though people never change, has led them astray, but don't misconstrue my meaning here. I don't insist on betrayal. I'll settle for a form of weariness."

"Weariness?" Ben said, the repulsion plain on his face.

"Yes, Ben, as in fed up. As in, maybe she got tired of you and decided to put an end to the whole thing—in an albeit sickeningly original manner, but I'm not here to find answers to the ways in which a withering heart responds to an expiring marriage. It's difficult for someone to realize that his mate has grown weary of him, that all the channels of communication have run dry, and that their spouse had just upped and gone. Mate, how much fortitude will it take for you to just imagine—not accept, mind you, just imagine—that Marian grew weary of you for unknown reasons? Did the Epilogist in you prepare for such a cruel end?"

"No," Ben called out triumphantly, "because that ending is the epitome of refutable endings. Marian and I loved each other fiercely to her dying day, and I assure you that she hasn't grown weary of me."

"How unfortunate that all I get is one side of the story," the Mad Hop said, chewing a half-detached fingernail. "After all, there's no chance you'll even consider the possibility that makes the end of your life a complete travesty. . . . I reckon if this were one of the stories you'd been asked to end, you'd pounce on this wicked development and rightfully reap the rewards of your agile imagination, but when it comes to reality you prefer to curl up in the warm den of denial, willing to accept nothing but the conventional ending. After all, when you committed suicide you were as certain of her love as you were of yours, but you placed a partial mirror opposite your own feelings without for a moment considering the slight chance that . . ."

"A partial mirror?"

"One of romance's most common maladies. The certainty that your partner's feelings are identical to your own, the desire for an artificial symmetry, the reach for equilibrium between lovers, all the while ignoring the fact that, when dealing with a pair, the absolute peak is harmony, not symmetry."

"Another moronic fortune cookie?" Ben asked, his voice growing hoarse. "Our relationship was incredible. I never tried to impose an artificial symmetry between us. You, on the other hand, are imposing on me the sensibilities of a twelve-year-old girl and not those of a man who knows that the woman by his side is the exact opposite of his own reflection and because of that loved her so fully. Don't think for a second that it was all chocolates and roses—we were a normal couple, fought on occasion, didn't speak to each other every once in a while, but that's all beside the point. We always knew we'd make up in the end, and that we wouldn't let the bacteria of everyday life infect us more than necessary . . . a sneeze here, a cold there, even an occasional flu, but never enough to chill our love."

"And what about a terrible case of pneumonia? A fatal case of tuberculosis? No, don't answer me. You've been looking in that tricky mirror for too long. For a newly dead person such as yourself, the fact that someone you thought was dead is actually alive is just as shocking as learning that someone close to you has died when you're alive. Maybe even more so, because from here there's no way out. If she's alive, only she can decide to come to you. Unfortunately, reality has once again defeated the fond symmetry."

"What do you want from me?" Ben said, leaping out of his chair, pacing across the room in loping strides. "Samuel, what the hell's happening here? How did you come up with this? How is it that in your mind I'm now starring in the role of the rejected husband in a plot cooked up by my weary wife? Where did you get this load of horseshit from?"

The Mad Hop pointed to his chair. "Sit, Ben, I don't think this is going to sound too melodic."

Ben gritted his teeth and sat down, listening to the investigator speak in a tone masquerading as peaceful. "My plan was simply to frame the picture, as a means of expressing my gratitude. I could have gone to a thousand different places, but I chose the Borderer's shop. He's an eighty-year-old Chinese bloke known for his perfect eye. I knew that by going to Chu Ming-tun I'd be killing two birds with one stone. The wicked octogenarian has a knack for finding the missing by touching the lines of their faces."

"Why didn't you go see him earlier?"

"He's one of those who believe that a picture of a person captures the soul; surely you've heard of such things in the past. And that's our problem, because we don't have a picture, we have a portrait. I didn't know if it would work. The second reason I resisted going is my instinctual repulsion of all things mystical. I've got no patience for clairvoyants, especially dead ones."

"And . . . ?" Ben said between clenched lips.

"I asked him to frame the portrait. When I inquired whether he could tell me where I might find this woman, he responded with alacrity, said there was no such person. It took me a moment to understand what he meant, but then I put my finger on the beauty mark and kept it hidden from view. He closed his eyes and let his fingers traverse her face. His fingers went around her eyes, nose, mouth, and ears. Finally he opened his eyes and smiled mysteriously. 'She's here but she's there, it's hard to say in which world.' I was obviously pissed off and asked if Chinese wisdom is by definition enigmatic, he laughed and said he was sorry, he couldn't help me find the woman, but that he did have a few hundred picture frames that could work well for the particular portrait I was holding. While he was working on the mahogany, I sat down on a stool in a corner of the room and tried to make sense of his logic-proof sentence. I repeated it a few times like a mantra, and suddenly it all became clear. As he brought the hammer down for the final time, I jumped up out of the stool. Ming-tun looked at me and smiled as though he knew that I had finally got it."

"I'd be ever so grateful to you, oh wise inspector, if you could share this understanding with me," Ben said, "as I'm sure you are able to discern I am not at the moment yelling eureka."

"Ben, think about it, if she's here but there and it's hard to say which world she inhabits, then there's really only one solution. Ben, who are the only people who inhabit both worlds?"

Ben distorted his face like an upset child. "She's a Charlatan? That's what you're telling me?"

"Is that not logical?" the Mad Hop asked, caressing the skin around his smooth round chin. "Maybe something happened to her and she's on life support in some out-of-the-way hospital?"

"And how does that sit with the story you were telling me a few minutes ago, the one that had her pulling the wool over my eyes and leaving the country? Seems it's either-or."

"You're not following me, Ben. When I said something may have happened to her, I wasn't referring to the Ferris wheel. I meant something else. An ordinary accident or something."

"And the basis for this fantasy is a sentence by some inscrutable old Chinese picture framer?"

"No, it's a little more complicated than that. When Ming-tun was through, I took the portrait and went to Ambrosia, you know, where the Charlatans like to hang out. I just wanted to ask around a bit, see if anyone had seen the lady."

"And those zombies probably sold you stories that made the tales of the Grimm Brothers seem like neorealist manifestos."

"No. No one, and I mean no one, out of thousands of people, had seen her."

"Ok-aay," Ben said, not hiding his impatience. "So you left there empty-handed and, as I know you, you took the next multi to Ambrosia 2000, a far more sensible destination if we lend your fantasies some credibility."

"I didn't make it there, Ben," the Mad Hop said, trying to fish a final cigarette out of an empty pack. His voice low and cold, he continued. "On my way to the multi I walked by a bookstore and looked at the window, kind of hoping Ms. Christie had come back to her senses and started writing again. Looking in, I saw something else—the reflection of a man pretending to be window-shopping but actually watching me. I carried on; he followed. As I walked I could feel his shadow behind me and, in his case, it was a thick shadow indeed, because he was clearly a Charlatan. When he got too close, I spun around and told him the obvious, that one always trails a person from the opposite side of the street. He smiled, a nice smile, and to be frank it was hard not to notice a certain likeness between the two of us. He was also bald and chubby and just a few inches taller than me. He didn't even contest my charge. He just stared at the portrait. I asked him if he knows the woman in the frame and he, with great sadness, said that the hair was a little off and that the beauty mark seemed out of place, even though he'd only seen her from afar. I was going to carry on, but then he looked at me with these accusing eyes and asked, 'How do you know Marian?'"

"Marian? He said Marian?" Ben yelled.

"And a lot more. He told me an interesting tale about how they met. On a fan site for Salman Rushdie."

"Rushdie?" Ben asked, knitting his eyebrows. "Marian liked him, but it's more like her to spend her time on a site devoted to the Bard."

"Let me remind you that you're talking about the Marian *you* knew. The Charlatan made no mention of Shakespeare. Maybe the new Marian has different tastes. But what's abundantly clear is that this man is head over heels in love with her and, much as I'm in your corner, it's hard not to want the best for him."

"Excuse me?"

"Well," the Mad Hop said smiling, "they never had the chance to meet face-to-face. After a torrid online correspondence, she from France and he from Israel . . ."

"He's Israeli?" Ben asked, wide-eyed.

"Yes. After a long period of correspondence, she told him that she'd gotten a job in Tel Aviv and that it was about time she met the man she'd fallen for. That night, our Charlatan got out of a taxi opposite the restaurant, saw her from across the street, and had a heart attack."

"The man she'd fallen for? Did you tell him that she has a husband who . . ."

"I tried to be frugal with the details. I did ask, though, if she ever mentioned a husband or a partner, and he screwed his face up into a ball of disgust and said she had divorced her awful husband a little over a year ago."

"That is impossible," Ben said, squeezing his head between his palms. "This whole thing. . . . There must be some profound mistake here. . . . Please don't tell me you think this is my Marian. . . ."

The look on the Mad Hop's face made him yell. "What? Why the hell are you looking at me like it's all over? Maybe that idiot you just met got her confused with another woman? Maybe he's lying. . . ."

"Ben, I didn't so much as giggle during my conversation with him.

I don't even think I smiled. The man was speaking the truth. And in all honesty, I think we both know he was talking about your Marian, the same one we've been looking for for naught in the wrong world."

"But a minute ago you said you thought she was a Charlatan."

The Mad Hop stiffened his lips victoriously. "How awful to want the death of your love."

Ben shook his head stubbornly. "Agh. Stop. Just stop presenting everything as though it's a done deal."

"Ben, you simply can't ignore these developments. The Charlatan swore to me that just two weeks ago he was supposed to meet your wife in Tel Aviv, and that closes off most of our options. And as for Mingtun . . ."

"I don't give a fuck about that Chinese nincompoop!" Ben yelled. Staring at the floor, flipping through dozens of scenarios, Ben looked up suddenly and asked, "What happened to the portrait?"

The Mad Hop cleared his throat several times. "He, ah . . . he asked me to leave it with him . . . he practically begged. . . . I told him that I couldn't, but I did offer to take him out of his misery. . . ."

"Samuel, don't tell me you gave him the portrait. Please, for the love of God, tell me you booted his ass back to the other world."

"Ben, we are in the Other World, and no, he refused to go back there. He didn't trust me, said he thought it wiser to wait. I told him there was no reason to wait around in this world, but he just snatched the picture and took off."

"And what did you do?"

"What did I do? I ran after him. But just as I was about to catch him, a multi slammed into me. By the time I woke up, I'd lost both the Charlatan and the portrait."

Ben chuckled and looked with dim eyes at the portrait's old spot on the wall. "I was looking for my wife, now I'm looking for her portrait, next I'll search the dead for a voice that sounds like hers. . . . Is that the hell that awaits me, Samuel?"

"It'll be much worse than that if you keep up this level of self pity." The hard-edged words came out of the Mad Hop's mouth despite his desire to sound soothing.

Ben trapped the stream of profanity fighting for freedom from within and mumbled, "She wasn't that kind of woman . . . she didn't have a

single devious bone in her body . . . she loved me with all her heart . . .
Marian was brave . . . only a coward could weave that kind of a plan to
lose their lover . . . not Marian . . . it's unfeasible . . ."

The Mad Hop made his way to the door, stopped only by Ben's cold
voice. "Where do you think you're going?"

The investigator, hoarse and obviously speaking through a bulge in
his throat, said, "home," and opened the door.

"If you leave now, don't bother coming back," Ben said. "Just make
sure you send the tapes to me ASAP."

The Mad Hop's response rocked the bitter righter back on his heels.
The short man with the tearstained face marched back into the apartment, slammed the door, and hollered, "What do you want? What do
you want from me? How do you expect me to leave? You think seeing
you crushed slips right off my back? You think my worn-down conscience isn't going to sting a few months down the road when I hear
that you punched in a seven over three because you realized she'd
never be yours? You think it was easy coming here to tell you about the
lovesick Charlatan? That I didn't consider the repercussions? You need
to understand, Ben, I'm not built for weathering these tragedies day in,
day out. In death, I thought I'd solve all kinds of fun and rewarding
cases. No one told me it would be tearjerker central. What do I know
about what went on in your charlatan of a wife's mind, and I use the
word conventionally, when she decided to disappear and send you off
with a one-way ticket to hell? Like all the lovers I've known, she also
seemed to be well endowed with selfishness and, like her, you too exer-
cised some first-rate egoism when you chose not to tell me about the
rest of your family members, and the more I fiddled with the integrals
of the formula of your insane relationship, the more certain I became
that what I had on my hands was a case of two hopelessly selfish people
who raised their love to the heights of a holy ideal—otherwise, how else
can you explain that in eleven years of marriage you never thought to
bring a child into this world, as if you'd be devastated by the need to
share your sacred and controversial love with another human being?
Do you have an answer for me, something that can explain away your
towering selfishness and prove that the mirror is not, in fact, partial?
Do you, Ben?"

Ben sighed long and hard. "You have no idea how badly we
wanted a child, Samuel."

"Which part of the copulation did you not get?"

"The carrying-to-term part. Marian conceives, we're both as happy as can be, but then she wakes up in the middle of the night in a pool of blood and discovers she can never carry a child again. . . ."

The Mad Hop apologized and said he'd be back in another minute. He ran outside, knocked on three different doors, got the cigarette he needed, came back to Ben's apartment, lit it and said, "Now tell me this again–Marian was pregnant with your child?"

Ben nodded.

"And she had a miscarriage?" The Mad Hop didn't need Ben's confirmation. He put the cigarette between his lips, pulled hard, and kept the smoke down for as long as he could. Staring at the floor as he exhaled, he said, "I wish I was Superman and I could turn the world back in time to the moment we met and refuse to work for you. . . . I'd like to drill through your skull just so I could see which of the lobes they removed from there and what, exactly, they had left behind. . . . I'd like to know why you never told me that your wife was once pregnant and had a miscarriage, but I don't dare, because, as always, you'd play dumb and say, you didn't ask so I didn't tell. . . . I'd like for you instead to walk over to that door and wait patiently while I regulate all the smoke between my two choking lungs . . . and most importantly I'd like you to have a few glasses of water because in a few hours you're going to meet your lost child . . ."

31

Pandemonium

In an instant everything collapsed.

Ann prepared for the evening as though it were a matter of life and death. Having once read that a hostess's success is measured by the guest's ease, she set to the task with unwavering sincerity, determined not to miss a single opportunity to ingratiate herself with the woman, who was sure to provide answers. The ideal setting for her cross-examination, she concluded knowingly, was one in which everything operated according to the adage about wine and secrets. And even if wine failed to free the chained tongue of the well-versed Frenchwoman, she would still not allow panic to take hold. Her theory held true for food as well, although it did demand a great amount of preparation from the hostess. She knew she would have to serve such a variety of dishes that, despite the Frenchwoman's likely forte in this regard, she would slide back in her chair, rub her stomach, and grow as pliable as a well-fed cat. And even if extreme satiety failed to generate the desired results, it was always possible to stick with the topic that interested her guest the most, and, with parasitic expertise, to question, peruse, dig, investigate, and examine every possible angle, to give her that warm familial feeling you get when speaking about something dear to your heart, to neutralize all fears and suspicions and indulge her rambling till the last remnants of her resistance have been ground down, and then, once the walls have fallen and the path to the target is laid bare, to steer the conversation to the proper spot and ask, with supreme tact, the question.

And no less important, Ann reminded herself as she ushered Marian into her home, is to keep her smile beaming at all times. A gentle spirit seems to have descended on the house and the guest cannot be allowed to speculate how much work went into this mass production of an evening. All she knows is that she's come for dinner. Nothing special is going on. All is ordinary. And with a half smile on her face, the excited nurse thought, just like me, my ordinariness is my believability.

So how did the ordinary become a colossal catastrophe? Ann wondered as she washed the thin coat of makeup from her frightened face. The fragrant scent of cooking still hung in the kitchen, the dining room table still bore the memory of the feast, and the bedroom still housed the guest. She looked down at the sullied water in the sink, jealous of its powers of erasure. She then raised her scoured face to the mirror and examined its ridiculous contours from up close.

"I have no regrets . . . ," she whispered. She noticed the chain around her neck, a perfect copy of the lost original. A secret muscle clenched on the left side of her lower lip as she remembered the fond look in Marian's eye as she sat down to the table. "I'm glad you decided to exchange the necklace. At least now I know you're happy with it."

God, she thought, how was she able to tell the difference? A deceitful smile on her face, she nodded, eager to do away with the unnecessary diversion. "Yes, I'm very happy with it."

Then she sat down. The hostess noted the pleasure on the guest's face when she saw the new ashtray laid out for her, an invitation to smoke as much as she pleased, yet another step on the path to the much anticipated conversation. Walking unsteadily, the nurse left the bathroom and walked to the edge of the dining room table. She picked up the ashtray. One, two, three, seven butts. No doubt she had felt comfortable. The nurse spilled the contents of the ashtray into the garbage can and laid a restraining finger on her pulsating lower lip. She could not lose control. Simply could not.

She laughed in desperation and recalled how she'd feigned rapture after asking the reporter for a rundown of recent cultural events, and how the Frenchwoman had gone on to tell her about Rushdie's upcoming book, and how the licking torches in her eyes conveyed her ravenous interest, and how, only when the enthused speaker slowed, did she spur her on with another question about Rushdie, trying to figure out what it was in *The Satanic Verses* that so infuriated the Iranians, and why, she wondered, did they commute his death sentence, and, by the way, did his own personal distress ever come through on the pages of his later books, and, if she were to start reading him, which book would be best at welcoming her into his complex world; the questioner yawned inwardly and nodded outwardly while the questioned showed yet another side of her winning character as she proved not just beautiful and clever but also well read and analytically adept, perfectly capable of splitting the books wide open without once straying into academic jargon, relying instead on pure curiosity, and so, the nervous nurse listened, enchanted, to learned explanations about the Indian Anthology edited by the renowned author, and a little more about the writing, and the wordplays, and even the book covers, and how the picture on the front cover of the *The Moor's Last Sigh* encapsulates the entire novel, and please do not confuse the Moor and the matter of spices in his family with a different book, also written by an Indian author, where she, too, plunges headlong into the mystical qualities of spices, and, in general, how authors from that part of the world tend to season their writing with strong lively flavors, so much so . . .

Ann lost her as she delved into the sensory assault she'd experienced while reading *The God of Small Things* and, just as she was starting to praise the literary feats of Vikram Seth, Ann caught hold of the string she needed, entangled though it was between a web of words, poured her guest a seventh glass of wine, seized the abrupt silence of drinking, and smiled gaily. "But with all due respect to the others, you love Rushdie the best. . . ."

Marian nodded, her eyes misty, her smile widening as her host announced, "I think I'll start with the one about the artist. What's it called again?"

"*The Moor's Last . . .*"

"*Sigh,*" Ann said, like an attentive pupil. "The one with the interesting cover."

"The picture drawn by . . ." Marian said, smiling and not finishing her sentence.

"Oh God, I'm such a scatterbrain. . . ." Ann giggled, her fingers fidgeting with the chain. "You mentioned that picture and I just realized that I have something of yours. . . ."

"Really?"

"Hm-mmm . . ." Ann said, trying to sound mellow as she bounded out of her seat, returning a few seconds later from the bedroom with the picture between her fingers. "That night outside the restaurant, when we were arguing, this fell out of your bag."

Marian glanced at the picture and shrugged. "It's okay, you can throw it away. It's not mine."

"I don't understand."

"I don't know the people in the picture," Marian said, intent on getting back to Rushdie but unable to disregard the shade change on Ann's face.

Placing a hand on her arm, she asked, "Are you alright? You're pale as a ghost."

Ann pulled her hand back, looked long and hard at the photo, and asked, "What do you mean you don't know the people in the picture?"

"Two days after getting to Israel, I was riding the bus, on the way to my new office, and my mind was elsewhere, I think you know where. It was before we'd met and I really wanted to surprise him. This woman and her son sat down opposite me, and I think, although I'm not sure, that they were staring at me and arguing, because eventually the woman took the picture away and gave it to me. She must have thought I was someone else. I glanced at the thing and put it in my bag. I haven't thought about it at all since then. It was just an honest mistake."

"You don't seriously expect me to take that story at face value, do you?"

"You can take it however you want. I'd just appreciate it if we could drop it altogether because, in all honesty, I have nothing more to add on the matter."

"I just want to understand," Ann said, "if this picture is so irrelevant to you, why didn't you toss it?"

"I told you, I completely forgot about it. The fact is, I didn't even know it had fallen out of my bag."

"And really, in all honesty, you have no idea why the woman on the bus handed you this photo?"

"I realized that apparently she found some similarities between the woman in the picture and . . ."

"Some similarities? Please," Ann said, "you'd have to be blind to not realize that you two are the same person."

"Very interesting," Marian said, lighting her seventh cigarette as she scanned the photograph. "I admit she looks a lot like me, but her style is not exactly my cup of tea, and the world is full of similar-looking people . . . and anyway, both of us know how they say that every person has a double."

Ending a brief silence, Marian said, "Can we please talk about something else?"

"Is there any special reason why you so don't want to talk about the picture?"

"Is there any special reason why you so *do* want to talk about it?"

The tension that had been accompanying Ann since her first waking moment was no longer exclusively hers. A delicate hostility hovered between the two tired women. Neither could figure out what the other one wanted, and the free exchange of giggles did not deceive either of them; a foul wind swept through the room, turning even an innocent giggle into a ruse of delay, and when the guest showed her first signs of boredom, yawning and rubbing her eyes, the hostess grew vigilant and scratched her knees under the table. "I know why you want to change the topic," she said.

The tolerant expression on Marian's face didn't baffle the small frightened woman before her. "You just don't want to recall the good days you had with him."

"With whom?"

"Your husband."

"My husband?"

"The two of you look very happy together in the picture."

"This is not the first time you're confusing that scum with other men. First it was Yonatan and now it's this guy who I don't even know."

"I understand why you'd want to keep him to yourself."

"Who?"

"Your husband."

"Darling, if I could I'd take his face and shove it in a hungry lion's mouth . . ."

"I find it hard to believe, especially when you continue to ignore the photographic evidence."

"And for me it's hard to believe that we're still talking about this silly photograph as though it has something to do with me."

"What's his name?"

"Who?"

"Your ex."

"Jacques."

"And where does he live?"

"Jacques? I don't know, I guess in our old apartment in Paris."

"How long has he been living there?"

"Seven years."

"Impossible."

"Excuse me?"

"I've seen him working out at the health club at the end of the block for an entire year."

"We didn't even have a health club on our street."

"Here, Marian, at the end of this street."

"In Tel Aviv? Jacques? He can't stand this country."

"And yet he spent the last year here, up until two weeks ago when he disappeared."

"Ann, you're making a big mistake. Jacques never . . ."

"Do you still love him?"

"Are you deaf?"

"Then why won't you help me find him?"

"I told you exactly where he is. If he hasn't moved, then he's in Paris, in the . . ."

"I couldn't care less about Paris."

"But for some reason you care a great deal about Jacques. Why do you want to find him?"

"I can't say."

"Okay. But I can tell you aren't looking for the SOB for the right reasons."

"As far as you're concerned."

"What do you want from me?"

"That you leave Jacques alone and help me get in contact with him."

"I left him alone a long time ago. And I'm more than happy to give you his address."

"In Tel Aviv?"

"No, Ann, not in Tel Aviv. He has no address in Tel Aviv."

"Why did you go to Paris?"

"Excuse me?"

"To Paris. That urgent trip you took. It had to do with him, right?"

"No, not in the slightest."

"I'm starting to get the impression that you're living a double life."

"And I'm starting to get the impression you've gone too far."

"Yonatan is your virtual lover, to quote you, and Jacques is your real lover. One in Tel Aviv, one in Paris . . ."

"That's ridiculous!"

"Marian, stop, I'm not judging you. I'm just trying to understand why you'd lie about Jacques."

"I have no reason whatsoever to lie about the scum!"

"Then why did you go to Paris?"

"It's personal."

"I rest my case."

"Don't be ridiculous . . . I went to France . . . Wait a second, why should I have to explain myself?"

"So I can know if I have any chance of getting to Jacques or if you're just taunting me."

"There's no reason for me to taunt the woman who saved my life."

"So save hers in return and tell me the whole truth about the man in the picture."

"God, we're back to that damn picture. Ann, how many times do I have to tell you I don't know a thing about it?!" Marian grabbed the picture from Ann and ripped it as many times as she could. "Here you go. You want proof that I have nothing to do with this thing, well here you are! Now there's nothing left of it. Same as the rest of this idiotic evening!"

Ann watched as Marian left her seat and walked to the coat hanger. She ran after her and called piteously. "I'm sorry, Marian, please stay a little longer."

Marian slipped into her jacket. "It's late already."

"I'm asking you, please, don't go yet. I didn't mean to badger you. I will hate myself if you leave now because of what I've said. And I really wouldn't want to totally ruin this idiotic evening." With a rare display of nerve, she began to help her sour-faced guest out of her coat, hanging it back up, and leading her by the arm toward the living room, where she sat her on the couch, opposite the TV, right near the glass table she'd gotten when it had become clear that little kids would never enter this home, and with the smile she saved for obstinate patients on artificial respiration, she asked, "Coffee or tea?"

Marian smiled. "Tea, no sugar."

Ann nodded and pointed to the remote control. "In the meantime you can watch . . ."

"I'm fine," Marian said.

"If the vase is in your way . . ."

"I said I'm fine."

∽

In an instant everything collapsed.

Then came the improvised Plan B. The thrill Ann felt when she decided not to let the information channel known as Marian slip away called for decisive action. A vision of the man from the health club haunted her as she filled the kettle and pulled two tea bags from the silver box, forcing her to admit that if she harbored hopes of ever seeing him again, then she simply had to struggle against the crude obstacle in her way. That woman is the embodiment of evil, she thought, as she slipped into the washroom and snatched a bottle of sleeping pills she'd taken from the hospital during the week when Jacques had kept her up at nights. Back in the kitchen, she stared at the bottle of pills with a kind of playful terror.

She could not relent!—she washed the dishes. She could not relent!—she threw away the scraps of food. She could not relent!—she blew out the candles. Once she had mended the photo, sticking all twelve pieces together, she nodded enthusiastically. "I must not relent," she mouthed, and went out to the old shed, returning with a length of coarse rope. On the way to the bedroom she eyed the mirror and asked, "Are you sure this is what you want to do?"

The reflection answered laconically. "Got a better idea?"

She pondered that for moment and shook her head.

"So then what, exactly, are you waiting for?" the reflection nudged.

Ann looked away from it, coiled the rope, took a deep breath, and walked into the room. "It's going to be a long weekend," she heard the mirror at her back giggle.

Ann fulfilled her obligation with utmost tenderness. Once she was sure that only supernatural powers would suffice to extricate Marian, she turned off the light, dragged a chair over to the side of the bed, and sat down to watch her, both threatened and threatening. The dizzying thought that she could do with her as she pleased brought a smile to her lips, a smile that receded after eight hours of dreamless sleep. She awoke from her painful sleep and recoiled at the sight of the woman bound to her bed. It took a few seconds, but the events of the previous night came back swiftly. The morning light made it all seem as though she had gone well beyond the pale.

It's still not too late. It can still be undone. She ran to the kitchen and pulled the chopping knife out of the dishwasher. Then she froze. The scream from the bedroom parted the silence that hung in the house. Striding somberly, she made for the room, forgetting the glinting knife in her sweaty palm and forcing herself not to make eye contact with the mirror.

But the mirror was mum and the guest fell silent at the sight of the armed hostess. The terror in her eyes melted away, and she smiled at Ann. "Oh, Ann, you have no idea how happy I am to see you."

Ann looked her over, trying to decide what Marian was up to, wondering if this was some kind of wily feminine trick, as the Frenchwoman called her close with a sideways nod of the head and asked in a whisper, "Did you get rid of them?"

"Of whom?" Her grip on the knife loosened.

"I don't know; the burglars or whoever it was. . . ."

"Burglars?"

"I'm tied to the bed and you're walking around with a butcher knife in your hand. So I assume . . . ?"

"Marian, I think that you're . . ."

"Shhh . . ." Marian silenced her. "Maybe they're still here. Let me go and we'll call the police." Not hearing a response, she bit down on her lower lip. "I hope they haven't done anything. You look like you're in shock and I, I don't even know how I got here. God, they must have given me Rohypnol or whatever the hell it's called . . ."

"What are you talking about?"

"That drug they use to make rape victims forget everything."

"I know what Rohypnol is!" Ann said.

"So, don't you think . . . ?"

"Will you just shut up already, you idiot!" Ann barked, waving the knife, amazed at the effect of the words she'd never before spoken.

Marian's eyes widened. She waited obediently for an explanation.

"I, Marian, am the reason you are where you are. I tied you up. And the knife I'm holding was meant to untie you."

"Why would you tie me up?" Marian asked, and then, face brightening, she continued in a amazed tone, "Oh, Ann, why didn't you just tell me straight away? God, what a diversion. You spent half the night driving me crazy with questions about my ex just so you could cover up what you were really after."

Ann thought she was dreaming. "You're crazy . . . totally crazy . . ."

"It's okay, Ann, I have no problem with that kind of thing even though you should know that as far as sexual orientation goes I'm as average as most."

"Oh, do me a favor and stop complimenting yourself. I tied you up for a different reason. Then I changed my mind."

"So why don't I see you working on the rope? My entire body aches and I can't believe I spent the entire night like this."

"I can't," Ann said, looking down.

"What can't you do?"

"Untie you."

"But a second ago you said you reconsidered and came here to untie me."

"I reconsidered again."

"Look at me when I talk to you!" Marian yelled.

"How dare you yell at me!" Ann yelled back.

Marian burst out in awestruck laughter. "Excuse me?! I don't think you understand what you've gotten yourself into here. I'm not sure what you're thinking, and it's starting to seem like you've seen *Misery* one time too many, or maybe you've been helping yourself too liberally to the hospital medicine cabinet. All I know is that if you don't let me go this instant I'll scream so loud the whole world will be at your door and then you'll really have some reconsidering to do."

Looking at the woman writhe against her restraints, Ann came to her senses. "Okay, I promise to let you go. Just tell me where he is. That's all I ask."

"Who's he?" Marian asked.

"Jacques."

Marian shut her eyes. "Holy mother of God, why are you obsessed with that jerk?"

"You want me to let you go, or not?" Ann asked.

"I already told you where he is," Marian groaned.

"You didn't give me the Tel Aviv address."

"There is no Tel Aviv address!" Marian shrieked. "I told you already, you got it all wrong."

"No, Marian, you've got it all wrong if you think I'm going to let you go without giving me a straight answer," Ann hissed. She left the room and returned a few seconds later. She sat down beside Marian, brought a whiskey-soaked sock to her lips, forced her defiant mouth open, and shoved the bunched sock down her throat, wiping a traitorous tear from her face and shaking all over. "Now you've got no choice but to shut up and think about whether you want to keep playing games with me. I'm going to make some breakfast. If you behave, I'll come back, take the sock out, and feed you some. But I swear to you, Marian, if you don't tell me where the man in the picture is, I won't hesitate. And as I'm sure you've already gathered, I don't usually provide advance warning on my threats."

Before even beating the eggs, she handled the concerned neighbor who thought he might have heard screaming from within the house. She smiled and apologized. "Sometimes you're so in the movie you totally forget yourself. I'll be sure to turn the volume down next time."

"Oh, that's okay, I just wanted to make sure everyone was alright," the old man said before leaving.

She locked the door, returned to the kitchen, made some tea, and dropped a pat of butter in the pan. The faraway cough, a constant intrusion, made her crack the eggs over the warm pan rather than in a bowl for an omelet. Upset, she turned on the radio and pretended to listen to a culture and entertainment show hosted by an authoritative, almost militant announcer, who somberly reported the passing of Rafael Kolanski, the noted artist, of a stroke in the wee hours of the morning. Ann nodded. "He should have been the hundredth one."

While the announcer praised the artist's extraordinary body of work and acquainted the listeners with his life story, Ann appraised the tray of food, pleased with herself indeed. True, the guest was bound and gagged, but the breakfast she prepared, to the elegiac tune of the grandiloquent announcer, was chock-full of all the necessary food groups and, were the Evil One to complain about the hard knocks she had received, she would certainly not be able to find fault with the hostess's nutritional pampering.

The phone cracked the tranquility of the moment. She decided to ignore it, wondering who was calling her early on what was supposed to be an obligation-free weekend. She hit the blinking PLAY button on her machine and heard the hospital director's serious voice. "Ann, good morning. I'd appreciate it if you could come in to the hospital as soon as possible. Thanks."

"What terrible timing," she muttered, lifting the tray and placing a motherly smile on her face, walking with surprising confidence to the silent bedroom.

The bedroom is silent—the reflection wrinkled her forehead in contagious suspicion.

The bedroom is silent—the walls responded in an ominous echo.

The bedroom is silent—the tray trembled.

"Hope you're hungry," Ann said, using her most heartfelt voice. But the position she found Marian in was not the kind one prone to noticing the finer points of hospitality might choose. Ann bent over and laid the tray on the floor, giggling in dread. "Stop, Marian, don't you know I'm a nurse and that I can spot an impersonator from afar?"

Marian did not respond. She lay frozen, as though Ann had nailed her to the bed, arms and legs sprawled, much as they were before she'd awoken, only her chest did not rise or fall and the front of her shirt was stained with the whiskey that still dripped from the sock stuck deep in her mouth.

"Stop playing games," Ann said, keeping her smile intact, hoping, childishly, that her loutish grin would somehow breathe life into the still woman, who did not respond even after Ann slapped her face three times, each stroke slightly more vigorous than the last. "I know you're faking it," Ann said, circling the bed, keeping an eye on the fraudulent body, waiting for an unintentional sign of life. "Marian, don't you realize I'm not going to let you go till I figure out what happened to the one and only? The more you fight over him, the more you'll lose your hold on him, because the two of you are not made for one another. Even in that picture, the two of you are in the midst of falling. Falling, Marian, falling, shuddering, convulsing, perishing. Acknowledge it, just acknowledge it."

Her gentle fingers rested on the woman's lively pulse. As she thought, alive, but something about her position was worrying. She could ill afford any unnecessary risks and, if something happened to her, she'd be unable to pry from her mouth the secret she so jealously guarded. She pulled the sock out of Marian's mouth and raced to the kitchen, looking for the butcher's knife. There it was, right where she left it, just like the guest, only the latter surprised Ann, and when she came back to the room she was already in the throes of a seizure, rattling her ropes, her hands and feet convulsing in a singular way, the jig of epilepsy. The end of the seizure was as abrupt as its beginning, and the bed lay silent beneath the still patient, who had not revealed her condition nor left the terrified hostess any options. Ann made quick work of the rope and dropped it on the floor, along with the knife, looking at her arms fall beside her taut body and placing a hand on Marian's face, when a searing pain coursed through her.

Marian's teeth dug into the hand like a dog clamping down on some appealing prey, and before Ann managed to react, the livid guest opened her eyes and whispered in contempt, "Thank you for the idea." Ann felt herself go woozy as soon as the pretend patient got both her hands around her neck and squeezed the shocked jugular vein. The murderous look in Marian's eyes paralyzed Ann; however, the lack of oxygen streamlined her thoughts, and she realized that if she didn't defend herself and get the wheezing animal who kept yelling "Bitch!" off of her, she'd be done for.

The two struggled, largely in silence, for a long while, intent on choking the life out of one another, the only sound an occasional, smothered moan of exertion, and, in unison, the two of them remembered the weapon by the side of the bed, each keeping their hold fixed with one hand and groping blindly with the other, ten fingers fighting for a single blade, and whenever one seemed to have gotten a hold of it, the other made a quick foiling move, until they lost their balance and tumbled to the floor, falling into a chaotic ball of limbs, scratching, pulling, kicking, slapping, punching. And throughout, it was clear to the two of them that the battle would go on for hours unless one of them managed to land an ingenious blow, ending the exhausting contest once and for all. And when that blow came, in the form of a hardcover book crashing down on Ann's head, she cursed and looked wide-eyed at Marian, who grabbed an end of the rope and raised it, back arched, eyes seething. But Ann scrambled out of the war room and gained the living room, temporarily free of Marian's wrath. She came after her, though, deaf to her pleas for a ceasefire, and only when the rope finally thumped flush across her back did Ann, red-eyed and drunk with pain, turn to Marian and look her in the face, as the latter yelled, "You're insane! I hate you!" and, like an old cowhand, she whipped the hefty, lasso side of the rope straight into Ann's face, the blow falling with stunning force.

Ann recognized the metallic taste in her mouth and forgot all she
had ever known, the hypnotic burn all across the side of her face making clear that she had been right, the meeting between the two of them
was truly a matter of life and death. She dropped to her knees and
begged Marian to stop. Marian threw the rope to the floor and limped
to the door as though their battle were already a thing of the past.

Beaten and afflicted, Ann watched the woman walk away, knowing
that if she turned the key in the lock, she would never find the man who
had rescued her from her own skin and dispossessed her of her inhibi-
tions. Marian, unprepared for another burst of violence, laid a hand on
the doorknob. Fingers on the key, her ears picked up the sound of fitful
breathing, and she managed to turn around and see the heavy candlestick arcing toward her head, pulling her yet again back into the mal-
adroit fray. She disarmed Ann with a quick movement and tossed the
candlestick away, pushing the small woman, who had yet to finish tor-
turing her, against the opposite wall.

Three minutes had elapsed since Ann writhed out of her grip and
pounced on Marian, and two minutes since Marian broke three nails as
she raked a hand across Ann's face, and a minute since Ann blocked
her mind and kicked the crouching woman in her loins, and a half minute since Marian managed to shake the pain and forced herself to concentrate on the blood and sweat and animal madness that had come
over the hostess, and twenty seconds since the crumpled woman on the
floor made it to the low glass table, took the big clay vase and aimed at
Ann, and fifteen seconds since she turned her head toward the kitchen,
drawn by an undefined curiosity, and ten seconds since Ann had taken
advantage of the distraction, snatched the vase from her hand and
smashed it down on her head.

The bloodied shards scattered everywhere, lending the puritanical
living room the ambiance of an archaeological dig turned rowdy pub.
Ann sucked on a finger that had been cut by an errant shard, staring at
the wounded woman by her feet, transfixed by the silence that super-
seded the sense-smothering cacophony of battle. She remained motion-
less for a long time, soothing the queasiness in her stomach. Marian's
hair and face were colored by the pond of blood, her static body surrounded by an improvised puddle that meandered ever so slowly toward
Ann's shoes, which were cemented in shock; forced from immobility by
the advancing blood, she took a step to the next tile over. Too late. In a

Just after boarding the multi to Aliastown '96, Ben sat down and muttered, "I feel like a complete idiot."

The Mad Hop sat opposite him, smiling silently. Ben continued, "Samuel, I just want you to know I do not for a second believe that I'm about to meet . . ."

"Your child," he said, finishing for him.

"I don't have, nor have I ever had, a child," Ben said, eying the last of the stunned parents to arrive.

"I understand you, Ben. A nameless, unidentified entity, previously defined only by its absence, has all of a sudden bloomed into existence. I know it must sound sick. The child never existed for you and now you are on your way to meet him."

The multi started to move as the Mad Hop continued. "If we all arrive here in death, why shouldn't a fetus, who died before . . . ?"

"Please, stop!" Ben said. "You don't really expect me to believe that a miniscule being, that never drew a single breath, now lives somewhere in a city at the end of this line? What exactly am I going to see, Samuel? A pseudo-human mutation in a jar of formaldehyde that's going to say *da-da* and make me feel like Frankenstein at the peak of his powers?"

"No, Ben, I expect you to imagine seeing a perfectly normal five-year-old child who has never seen his parents. Unlike us, they don't stop aging at the time of their death. Instead, they continue to grow until they decide to halt the advance of the years . . . after all, that's their privilege as people who never had the chance to live."

A spark of understanding rose in Ben's eyes and he whispered, "God, now I get it all. Those who didn't have the chance to live as humans, all the fetuses that didn't make it to the outside world, they're the aliases . . . they're the ones who run the Other World . . . that's why they're called that . . . they came here without names, they use pseudonyms."

"Serial numbers, Ben, not pseudonyms, based on the order of arrival."

"And that's the only difference between them and us," Ben said. "They never came to our world but we brought them into this one. That's why they don't like to talk about differences between us . . . we created them, and they help us through the rest of our existence . . ."

"Glad to see you back to form," the Mad Hop said, clapping him on the back.

Ben's speech became rapid and disjointed. "But what happens to the babies who lived a few months and then died, I mean they lived already, no? They're not aliases. Who takes care of them? And what about all the women who died while pregnant? Does that mean they stay uncomfortably pregnant for all eternity? And what about . . . ?"

"Why don't you just keep your eyes on the prize," the Mad Hop laughed. "Perhaps first I should tell you a bit about the place we're going to. Every year in the Other World has its city of aliases, populated by fetuses and babies that passed away before, during, or immediately after birth. They're cared for by 'surrogates,' in other words, replacement mothers and fathers, that is to say aliases looking for respite from their infertility by raising young aliases. The newborns spend their first year in a 'greenhouse,' much like hospital nurseries in the previous world, where all of their physical and mental needs are met. At the end of that year, the nursery graduates are transferred into the custody of either their 'surrogates' or one of their biological parents or grandparents, if they arrive in time. Only six people are granted immediate custody over the young alias—the mother, the father, the mother's parents, the father's parents. Even if the biological parents are late and the alias was given to a 'surrogate,' that person is easily located because, as you might imagine, careful records are kept. There are no cases of missing or lost aliases. Moreover, the Association for the Wellbeing of the Aliases stays in touch with the children and makes sure they're being properly cared for. And just one more statistical fact that should wipe the interrogative expression off your face—only twenty percent choose to freeze their age in childhood. Thirty percent opt for adolescence, and the remaining fifty percent choose their early twenties, with twenty being the single most popular age for freezing the life cycle. You have no idea how many elderly twenty-five-year-olds roam these towns."

"The issue of age doesn't really concern me," Ben said, biting his thumb. "Samuel, this whole thing seems contrived to me. Totally contrived. I'm supposed to be excited, moved to the marrow, going out of my mind, something, anything that'll prove I'm human, but aside from the initial shock, I'd say all is as usual. Maybe because I buried my dreams of fatherhood long ago. Maybe because death has rendered me a cold, emotionless man."

"That's the absolutely last thing I'd say about you," the Mad Hop said, pointing to the other, stone-faced passengers. "Look around. Everyone here looks like you. Strangers on their way to meet other strangers who just happen to be their offspring. In an instant some irrelevant tot becomes the most relevant thing in the world. In an instant he undergoes a metamorphosis from a kid to *your* kid. Just an hour ago you were telling me how much you wanted to have one."

"An hour ago I knew nothing at all."

"And in another hour, who knows?" the Mad Hop smiled mysteriously.

In another hour, Ben knew that the aliases had a very strange sense of humor. The maze at the entrance to Aliastown 96, The Labyrinth of the Tied Fallopian Tubes, forced visitors through a circular network of hedges, with hundreds of paths ending at an ivy covered wall or some other impassable barrier of foliage. While plodding through the maze, the excited parents were surrounded by the gleeful shrieks and pealing laughter of unseen children. Luckily for Ben, the Mad Hop made quick work of the logic behind the botanical maze. After forty minutes of walking in circles, he covered his ears, drowned out the children, and heard the calm voice of an older girl explaining how to choose the proper path. She directed them to a towering wall of wild grass and asked them to push. Putting their weight behind it, the wall swiveled on its hinges and opened up to a hall full of running children. Ben scanned the kids fearfully, wondering if he would spot the lost fruit of his loins.

The Mad Hop, a few feet ahead of him, turned around and said, "Ben, come on, the kid is not in this hall."

"How do you know?" Ben asked, scrutinizing a group of five-year-olds playing tag.

"They're ignoring you . . ." the Mad Hop said, signaling him toward the ninth door on the left. A drawing of a panda bear decorated the middle of the door, just beneath the word SEPTEMBER.

"Of course they're ignoring me, they have no idea I could be one of their fathers."

"They do . . ." the Mad Hop said, groaning and looking up toward the ceiling. "I can't imagine why they don't hand out a guide right after the orientation, a Lonely Planet for the Other World. . . ."

"What should I know that I don't?" Ben asked. "Samuel, how do these kids know that I'm not their . . ."

"Genetic composition."

"And for laymen?"

"Every alias genetically recognizes any of their six biological relatives. I say genetic, but in truth I also could have said magnetic. Whenever an alias is near one of the six, he or she feels an inexplicable gravitational tug. As if he were face-to-face with a magnetic field and not a human."

"And what about the biological six? Can they sense the offspring when they're nearby?"

"No. That's another one of the aliases' unique privileges. They are the barometers of irrefutable truth. Better than a DNA test, don't you think?"

"So the fact that not one of these kids is the slightest bit interested in me is basically scientific proof that none of them are mine?"

"Putting it mildly."

Ben caught the Mad Hop's smile. "Meaning?"

"They have a very interesting way of expressing their sudden welling up of love."

"When you say an interesting way, you mean that all the aliases react the exact same way when they meet one of the parents or grandparents?"

The Mad Hop, his face brimming with glee, said, "I know it sounds robotic, but to me it's brilliant. I've seen it happen dozens of times and each time I've been struck by the aliases' stunning innocence at the hair-raising moment of revelation. The relatives' startled reactions have been no less amusing, as the toddlers clung to their legs, didn't let go, and uttered a cry of admiration as if they've come across a treasure like no other."

He fell silent at the sight of his travel partner leaning against the wall, staring down at the floor, his lower lip trembling.

"Christ, Ben, what's wrong?"

"I . . . met . . . him . . ." Ben managed to whisper.

"Who?" The words froze on the Mad Hop's lips. "The kid?"

"Yes." Ben's shoulders fell. "He was playing with a ball and then he just latched onto my leg. Exactly as you said . . . and I rejected him, pushed him away because I didn't know what he wanted from me, but he really did keep on coming. It was so strange. . . . Samuel, I chased away my own son when he . . ."

"Ben, please don't," the Mad Hop said forcefully, "you had no idea who he was and it makes perfect sense that an adult wouldn't want some strange kid hanging onto his leg for no apparent reason. But if you don't mind me ruining this poignant moment, would you please tell me where this encounter took place?"

Ben said, "When I went looking for Marian. In the labs. I mean outside of them. Near some park."

"Well that's not much help," the Mad Hop said, pointing at the door. "And our answer's in here anyway."

Ben nodded and followed a few paces behind the investigator, who rapped on the door. The gentle voice that asked them to come in belonged to a dark-skinned girl, who smiled at them sweetly and gestured for them to be seated at the desk, behind which she sat reading a book.

The Mad Hop cleared his throat and began. "Hello love, my name's Samuel Sutton and this here is my friend . . ."

"Thumb, please," she ordered politely, laying a red ink pad and a white silk handkerchief on the desk. Ben pushed his thumb down on the cushiony pad, made an imprint on the handkerchief, and handed it back to the girl. She looked him over and said, "The pad is for identification; the handkerchief for tears."

The Mad Hop made a show of presenting him with the handkerchief, but Ben was transfixed by the alias. She took the identification pad and held it to the center of the computer screen before her, waited three minutes, wrote the relevant data on a slip of paper, slid it across the desk, wished them "good luck," and returned to her book.

Ben thanked her and the two men left the room, the Mad Hop reading over his friend's shoulder, his voice projecting, "Alias 9562300483371, male, born 9.21.1996, father, Ben Mendelssohn, mother, Marian Corbin, placed in the custody of alias 57438291108 and alias 88888888 on 9.30.1997, returned to the nursery on account of incompatibility with 'surrogates,' placed in the care of aliases 74321555 and 74321556 on 12.4.1998, returned to the nursery on 2.17.2000 after decision of both 'surrogates' to simultaneously punch in a mutual seven over three, and given, on 6.5.2000, to legal female biological guardian."

"That's it? That's all the information they provide?" Ben asked, looking back at the door.

"You still don't get it?" the Mad Hop asked. "You're not as smart as I thought."

"What don't I get?"

"Ben, think for a second. The kid's with a legal biological guardian. What do you deduce from that? Don't you get it? A few hours ago I told you why I thought your wife had played a trick on you and that she was still alive. But now I've got no choice but to concede that I'm as confused as I've been in years. The kid's legal female guardians are either the grandmother from the mother's side, the grandmother from the father's side, or Marian, and since you've met with the first two options, that leaves us with our answer."

"You think Marian came and took the kid?" Ben asked.

"Well, at least you now have some hard proof that the woman is really dead."

"It was never in doubt," Ben said looking down at his feet.

"Okay, don't be cross, but I have to ask, are you an idiot, a masochist, a schizophrenic, or all three rolled up in one?!"

"This isn't rock solid proof to my wife's passing anyway, Samuel, because, aside from my mother, there's another legal guardian."

"You mean Miriam Corbin, the one who died yesterday."

"I mean Marian's biological mother, not her adoptive one."

The Mad Hop's eyes narrowed to threatening slits. "Have I told you yet today that I hate you?"

"I know you always say I'm absentminded," Ben said, trailing behind, "but you never asked if Marian was adopted and I didn't have any reason to think it was relevant and, before you ask, I'll just say that, no, Marian never tried to find out who her mother was."

"I'll tell you who her mother is. Her mother's the total stranger who's raising your son! The total stranger who decided to take advantage of her rights in this world and is soothing her conscience by raising her grandson."

"But there's no way of knowing whether it's the grandmother or Marian who's raising the kid."

"There is," the Mad Hop said, pounding him on the shoulder and guiding him toward the entrance to the hall with renewed vigor. "Come. We're going to the Family Tree Administration offices. They'll give us the name and address of the woman; we get off the multi, go to her apartment, and I guarantee you that by the end of the day, you've met your little son."

Doubt ridden, Ben nodded, and was about to join the light-footed detective, when an old woman's voice came alive in his ear. "Ben? Ben Mendelssohn?"

Ben looked at the godget and saw the blinking telefinger. "Yes, Mrs. Parker. How are you?"

"Nosey, sweetheart, Nosey. There's only one Mrs. Parker and, much to my disappointment, I never wrote any poetry."

"I understand. I guess you're contacting me because you've heard word from my grandparents."

"Yes, they asked me to let you know that they have some vital information about your wife."

"What do they know?"

"I'm not sure. They sounded pretty confused, but Moses was adamant about seeing you as soon as possible."

"Why didn't he just tell you what he knew? That would've saved us so much time."

"You know I asked. But he just kept saying how important it was that you meet them where they're staying."

"Where did you say they were? At 1700 and something, no?"

"No, they made it farther than that. They're at 1616 now."

"Do you have any idea how long it will take me to get there?"

"Well, if you take an express to the seventeenth century, you should be in transit all night."

"Hmm . . . do you have their address by any chance?"

"They're at the Stopped Watch Tavern."

"Tavern? Why aren't they at a hotel or . . . ?"

"Oh, you know, they seek authentic experiences. About fifty years ago, the Hundred Year Project was finally completed, upgrading the living spaces in all of the centuries A.D. So don't be surprised if the seventeenth century looks a lot like the twentieth century, at least as far as architecture goes."

Ben couldn't help himself. "What was before? I mean, during the upgrade period. Where did the dead from the seventeenth century used to live?"

"At the end of the nineteenth century, of course. Some of them were even put in the early twentieth."

"What?! That's impossible?"

"Oh, the naïveté, the naïveté. Ben, do you really believe these skyscrapers just grow out of the ground? I suppose you know about the aliases . . ."

"You mean the fetuses."

"Yes. And since they more or less run this funny world, they also take pains to punish all the louses that were mean to aliases and/or other children. Instead of incarceration, they get hard labor—and if I tell you that according to the most recent reports, no living man, up to at least the year 2500, will have to worry about becoming homeless, will you get the system?"

"So, the criminals build the living spaces of the future?"

"An outrageous and enticing social concept, you must admit. Especially if we bear in mind the contractors are the only ones with access to the future, and those aliases, like some of the toughest law enforcers in the previous world, are extremely nervous beings who channel all of their childish cruelty into overseeing the prisoners."

"But you said they weren't prisoners."

"Semantics, my friend. Let's say the contractors take them to 2312. They work all day and are free to roam the ghost town at night. In principle they're not prisoners. There are no steel bars, no chains, no cuffs. But they also have no way out of 2312, because only the contractors have the keys to the white rooms, which you need to go through to get to and from the future. And these aren't the kind of keys that can be stolen, if you know what I mean. . . ."

"The prisoners are stuck in the future?"

"The safest jail imaginable, if you want to make sure they learn their lesson. I mean the perverts are one thing, they pay their debt to society for an exact period of time, but what about all those who sinned

against humanity in their lives. Most of them can't have even a semblance of a normal death with all of humanity breathing down their
necks, seeking revenge. Some of them join up with the prisoners just to
make sure no one comes after them."

"Because no one can make it to the future besides the prisoners and
the contractors?"

"Exactly. I guess you won't be surprised to hear that the mad Aus-
trian has spent the past fifty-odd years mixing cement in the early
twenty-sixth century and that he has yet to give up his dream about the
Ubermensch, at least according to *Mein Kampf II*, where he goes on and
on about what a revolting species Holocaust deniers are, seeing as they
rob him of his greatest achievement. Nice paradox, no?

"Oh, and before you start asking me why they don't just push seven
over three and get it over with, I'll remind you that the prisoners'
godgets are confiscated before entering the future cities, which I guess
explains the rumors about the mustached madman who sings *Tristan
and Isolde* every night as he ties a noose around his neck and leaps off
the scaffolding in a hopeless attempt to change the ways of the Other
World and die again."

"Nosey, I must say you are a fountain of knowledge."

"And I must say you are a fountain of curiosity. Promise me that one
day you'll come over to my place and we'll have a long and digressive
conversation like the one we just had now."

"I promise, and thanks for taking the time."

"Enough with the niceties. Tell me what you dig up and have a good
journey."

Ben turned to the nodding Mad Hop.

"You have to go to the seventeenth century and hear what your
grandfather has to say. That's what I gather."

"He is so annoying sometimes," Ben sighed, following the Mad
Hop, who asked for silence, cupped his hands over his ears, and led
them out of the labyrinth as quickly as possible. With the gold gates
shutting behind them, the Mad Hop shrugged expansively. "Don't look
at me as if I'm going to dissuade you. Both of us know what I think of
your chances of finding her in this world. But when word comes your
way, you might as well follow it. If I were you, I'd go."

"Where do I get an express to the seventeenth century?"

"You go to the 1996 central station, it's just two blocks away, and you take a ride to 1900. Unfortunately, the express lines only leave from the beginning of each century."

"Are you going to the Family Tree Administration?"

"Yes, and lose the hangdog expression. You didn't see the kid for five years; two or three more days won't make a difference."

~

Three hours later, Ben found the multi-wheel he needed, hopped on confidently, and asked a twentysomething if the seat next to him was available. The guy nodded coolly, slouched farther back in his seat and, with his eyes shut, mumbled a few unclear words, intoning them like a mantra in the midst of a meditation. For a long while, Ben replayed the events of the past day, thinking excitedly about the child he'd soon meet, so long as they were able to find his legal guardian. Deep inside, he knew that the paternal fantasy he was weaving was far removed from reality, and he preferred to sequester himself in the alluring den of dreams. Still, a persistent doubt arose: at first a pinprick, then a puncture, then a slash, till a great hole had been opened in the vista of his imagination. Even after he had finished speaking with Nosey and was on the way to the station, he was acting instinctively, without thinking, a gloomy reflex of bereavement that preceded its acknowledgment. Some would say he traveled far in full faith that he would find his love. He will neither refute nor authorize, and only in the confessional booth in the back of the mind will he bow his head and admit that he acted as he did out of faithlessness; the pilot inside of him had not left his passengers alone, he had simply nodded off. Command was passed to the autopilot, which obeyed an internal order; every time the name Marian is heard it responds, M a r i a n will fly, M a r i a n will soar, M a r i a n will glide, M a r i a n will land, M a r i a n will crash, and the flight aviation officials will find the black box, and in it there'll be a one-sentence summation, "died in the name of . . ." And in the same breath, the grounded righter will admit that the kid is a fresh and blessed diversion; a future scenario creeps in: thirty years down the road, my son and I go looking for his biological mother, the tale of a voyage that only the future can complete, and for once I find no pleasure or majesty in the open-ended tale; it's like a pit of possibilities, none of which have been used, and those willing to reach, welcome it, and those willing to reach further, curse it, because, like him, they've learned that a story is nothing more than a stretch of road between two points, a mileage of plot and character and the space between them, and suddenly he is hit by logic that has just awoken from a long slumber and with merciful malice encourages Don't worry sir, at any moment you can end the story and whatever doesn't happen soon enough will happen later. Ben jousts with his thoughts and wonders, how can I end it when both of us know where the end point lies? No no no, both of us know where the d e s i r e d end point lies, but if you use me you'll realize that where logic doesn't help, time does, and just as the opening of every story is arbitrary, in so far as its placement in the plot goes, so, too, is the ending, if you know what I mean. You're implying I should forgo the desired ending . . . Dear sir, if you aren't convinced, agree at least to consider that the path from one point to another changes the destination in most cases and you suddenly realize that the end of the story had been different all along. Why am I even having this sketchy conversation with you? Because you know we mustn't give ourselves to only one aspect of our existence. What are you talking about? You're talking about romance, and not just romance but the rigid, fierce, hardcore Anna Karenina kind that goes all the way or, in your case, somewhere close to all the way. What do you want? That you remind yourself there's a lot more to life and death besides romance. My love for Marian is a whole lot more than romance. I don't doubt your love, but rather the direction it has taken you; after all, if there was no Marian, there'd be someone else, or maybe even no one. No one? Love, when all is said and done, fills a void that could be filled by other things as well, and as I've said before, if you don't get that at this point in your story, you'll get it later. How can you be so certain? Your rippling despair tells me so; at any moment you can place a period at the end of the story and decide you lost her, that she's alive, that she'll die of natural circumstances forty years down the road, that despite the eternity you have at your disposal there's no sense spending decades fighting a futile battle, close the book, put a full stop, prepare for suffering but also for freedom, call it a tragedy, call it whatever you want, but know that in the end the plot has been unraveled, so there's no happy end, so it hurts, but termination, completion, epilogue, and you'll be on the outside looking in. At what? At the story that anguished you so much, you'll look at it from the outside in like an eighty-year-old man flipping through his biography, remembering moments, feeling a pinch, but putting the book back on the shelf, and what remains for him? The rest of his life, the margins of the story, and the shorter the story, the wider the margins. Stop philosophizing. It's not me, it's you; we both know no one

"We're talking about the seventeenth century, right?" Ben verified with apparent trepidation.

The young man choked back a laugh. "Dude, are you for real? Did you, like, fall straight from the moon onto this multi? Or are you maybe on the wrong ride. I thought you wanted to get to 1616."

"Yeah, that's where I'm headed," Ben said.

"Well, then it's just a funny coincidence. A guy's going to 1616 and doesn't know a thing about the most important audition in the history of theater. First the thing with the Announcer, and now you say you don't know a thing about the audition."

"The Announcer?"

"You didn't notice that just when you started going through those nonsensical lines of yours the Announcer called her name? You were repeating her name like a broken record and the Announcer joined you exactly on cue," and then the actor shocked Ben by sitting straight in his chair and, moving his lips robotically, spitting out the three syllables in a chillingly metallic tone: "Marian Marian." Returning to his slouched position, he looked at Ben and grew serious. "Why're you looking at me like I've gone crazy? Or actually like you have?"

"Are you sure you heard right?"

"Yeah, but I don't remember the family name. I'm used to that grating voice in the background. I don't usually pay it much mind. If you hadn't repeated her name like that . . ."

Ben didn't hear his last sentence. He sprang out of his seat and turned around, surprised at the feel of the actor's rough hand on his goose-bumped elbow. "Where you going?"

"I have to get off the multi. I have to get back."

"You can't. This is an express. It only stops at the seventeenth century."

"But I have to get to the white room," Ben cried hysterically.

"I think you should just calm down," the young man said in a soothing tone, motioning him back to the seat. "Even if you did get off here, you'd still not make it back in time. We're somewhere around 1810, and I guess even a space cadet like you knows that the doors open two hours after the Announcer goes on air."

Ben's pupils raced back and forth like a trapped animal's during the awful realization of its fate, and he grabbed the godget with two hands, searching for the Mad Hop's print.

"Not worth the effort," his seatmate said, "the telefinger doesn't work on the express lines. There's no reception."

Ben tried to bring the godget to life and realized the actor was right. "So what do I do? I have to let someone know that she's come. . . . I have to . . ."

"But I didn't even hear her last name. . . . You do know that in terms of statistics and probability . . . ?"

"No!" Ben insisted. "You're right, but I know it's her."

"How do you know it's her?" the actor asked, looking at him curiously.

"Because it's the plot twist that's waited for its diabolical moment, it's the end I never considered; she died and arrived in this world while I'm stuck in a charging multi with no way to get out, and by the time I reach the seventeenth century and get back to the beginning of the twenty-first, I'll find that she's changed her address for some reason or another and I'll keep looking for her for years, knowing that she's here and that I have no way of getting in contact with her."

"But with all due respect to your very convincing show of panic, you're forgetting a small, encouraging detail."

"What?" Ben snapped. "What detail am I forgetting?"

"That if it really is the woman you're so intent on finding, doesn't it follow that she'll be equally intent on finding you?"

Ben looked past him to the window, a desolate expression on his face. "Nothing makes sense anymore," he said.

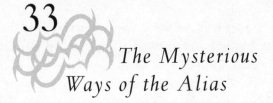

33

The Mysterious Ways of the Alias

"Dear aliases, I wish we were convened here today in this forest clearing for far less distressing reasons; however, to my dismay, that is not the case. The first strokes of dawn have just appeared, and I'm sure you would all prefer to have another hour of precious sleep rather than gather here on such short notice. I do beg your pardon. As forest director I saw no other alternative. You're looking at me with unbridled curiosity and wondering why the ado and the dramatic tone. I salute your aliastic innocence and request that you steer your concentration toward one specific alias. Noble tree uprooters, if you look around, you'll notice the glaring absence of 57438291108, a worker in plot 2,605,327 for the past fourteen years. He always seemed an excellent uprooter and never drew any kind of undesirable suspicion. Unfortunately, the absent alias managed to pull the wool over his work partner's eyes and vent his rage in the most heinous manner, one that every previous forest director had warned against time and again. Needless to mention, we have taken every precaution to avoid this type of scenario—patrols through the plots, a pair of sentinels at the entrances, and a battalion of guards around the forest. Each and every one of you here in this clearing is well aware of the chilling implications of a lowly act of revenge, and who among us has not conjured the ghastly sight of a human sneaking into the forest and settling old scores with the slightest tug of a branch? My predecessors certainly did well by forming the legion of loyal guards devoted to safekeeping the trees, but they failed to fathom that the danger could well up from within.

"We must not ignore the fact that we, too, are the products of mortal loins, and the full panoply of human frailties flows through our veins, as well. Of course we've been granted a comfortable existence, far more wonderful than that offered to the dwellers of their world, where colossal moral rectitude is needed to properly deal with the unpredictable shadows lurking beneath their innate survival instinct, a world complex and susceptible to corruptive capriciousness. I've also heard of cases where aliases have grown deeply forlorn after an encounter with a mortal. Innocently, I thought we were immune to such lethal bitterness, until I came across the uprooting dossier of the Mendelssohn family. Over the course of the last decade, the final eight offspring have come to our world with an eyebrow-raising rate of expiration, a fact that spurred me to consult with Billion, the former director of the forest. Billion asserted that from time to time regrettable mishaps do occur, and when I raised the issue of possible malice, he dismissed it with great certainty, allaying my fears.

"And now is the time to share an intimate detail that, under different circumstances, I would spare you. As many of you know, I met a woman ten days ago and we have fallen in love. A woman, not an alias. Sandrine Montesquieu. My partner shocked me when she asked me to clarify the inexplicable suddenness of her death. Much like you, I figured it was just another one of those accidents that happen when an uprooter breaks off a branch inadvertently. I examined the relevant tree and couldn't ignore the unequivocal signs. In addition, I noted the strange coincidence—the tree was in the same plot as the Mendelssohns'. Still, I did not act. I knew that only when the pathology report landed on my desk could it verify or dispel my suspicions.

"Yesterday, late in the evening, the report arrived. I won't bore you with the details; I'll merely state that the evidence of repeated criminal acts was irrefutable. The poor family's tree suffered shocking abuse, systematic and intentional! I decided that my first task of the morning would be to confront the uprooter with the facts. I figured I'd be faced with vociferous resistance, overarching denial, or at the very least a great feigning of innocence. But I had no idea what would transpire before the first glint of dawn.

"Once again I must share a personal anecdote with you. Today, after not having seen each other for a year, my partner is to meet her best friend. They were to have met yesterday, but a certain hitch delayed the meeting and my partner had to wait on pins and needles until I could pull her friend's faraway address from the central thumb directory. Last night, Sandrine couldn't get to sleep and said she'd like to go out and clear her head. I asked where she'd like to go, and she giggled and said she'd been yearning to see her family tree, voicing a deep desire to witness her sap mark, where the branch had been severed. I explained that the rules forbid humans from entering and that even non-staff aliases are prohibited from going into the forest, but she had a hard time understanding me. At the end of a long argument, she convinced me to break the rules. 'After all, you're the forest director and you'll be by my side,' she said.

"And so it was. We reached the forest in the dead of night. Sandrine insisted that I tell her as much as possible—about the death crackles of the drooping branches, the fine threads strung by the Weavers, linking the crowns of the trees so that the binds of marriage could be accurately marked, and even about the gentle breeze that whistles slyly through the leaves. She was utterly enchanted by the forest and questioned me incessantly as I urged her toward the plot. I wanted to show her the mark and return home.

"When at long last we crossed into the desired plot and approached her family's tree, Sandrine stopped me, said she thought there was someone there. We approached the tree with caution and could not believe our eyes. The criminal was in the midst of a wild attack, hanging at the two-point-oh-five-meter mark and ripping at branches as he spewed insults and invective. He didn't notice us, and when I ordered him to cease and desist from his crazed behavior, he looked at me surprised and kept at it. Not left with much of a choice, I asked my partner to call the guards and I climbed after him, easily recognizing the criminal on the basis of his tattered boots, the footwear of an uprooter who spent much of his time brutally bashing the Mendelssohn trunk, as Billionandaquarter stated in his report. I grabbed his legs and pulled him down with all my might. He dropped wordlessly and, much to my surprise, passively. When I demanded an explanation for his actions, he started to warn me about my love: 'You'll see,' he said, 'she'll do just what my alias did. She's already made you violate the law.' He got down on his knees and burst into tears. He told me that his beloved had left him again, that she had already left him twelve times, and that after each breakup he'd come to the plot to release his rage on the branches. This was the thirteenth and final time! He disclosed the whole truth as pertains to the Mendelssohns—seven detachments. As far as the tree's final branch is concerned, he swears he was uninvolved. And in fact, an inspection of the dossier revealed a story of a meticulously planned suicide characteristic of natural withering, not malice. I asked him who the other four branches had been, and he said that three of them had fallen victim to the first three breakups. Turns out that as the uprooter's modus operandi grew methodical, his confidence rose to levels that all of us combined would have a hard time attaining. The first three were ripped from random multi-limbed trees, but in the aftermath of the fourth breakup he focused, with parasitic criminality, on the afore-mentioned family. He explained that from the moment he happened upon their tree, the matter of choosing had been put to rest. An almost naked trunk, sporting eight final branches, a dynasty on the cusp of extinction. He didn't grasp the paradox—on the contrary, he was sure that in this way he spared random branches and focused on one single tree, as though he were doing right by the rest of the plot when attack-ing the chosen tree. Once their tree was uprooted, a fresh victim in the form of my beloved's tree was found, and in the aftermath of the twelfth breakup, he viciously severed the branch that brought her to my bo-som. Surely the morbid and macabre interpretation of these events is that I should thank the murderer for his twelfth crime, but I refuse to accept that. The perpetrator of these crimes used his own lack of re-straint and, instead of addressing his worsening problem, chose to draw malevolent strength from his "unpremeditated" murders. He claimed that he felt euphoric after the acts, as though his twisted soul had found solace.

"My partner lost control when she realized that he was responsible for her death and the wholly unnecessary deaths of two other family members, and she pounced on him, whipping his face with the gener-ous help of the two downed branches. The task of disentangling them was not simple, especially considering that rather than express re-morse, the idiot ranted about merely moving people from one world to another and that the latter was considered far superior anyway. I asked Sandrine to relax as I tried to convey to him the severity of his deeds. I explained that he had murdered fourteen innocent mortals, with only the abstract of motives. Much to the guards' astonishment, he laughed and said he had no idea what all the fuss was about. In the end, all branches are severed. A moment before he was taken by the guards, he smiled and asked, 'When a man raises a gun and shoots another man, and at exactly that same second an uprooter breaks off the victim's branch, who is responsible? The one who pulled the trigger or the one who pulled the branch?'

"I wasn't tripped up by his question, and I requested that he quit trying to avoid taking responsibility for his offenses. He glared at me with a pair of fossilized eyes and repeated the question in a toying voice. This time I didn't relent and I said, 'The one responsible for the death is the one who's taken the life, and in the case you've described, there seems to be a random collaboration.' 'But how can I collaborate with someone I don't even know?' he asked, playing innocent. 'The same way you can kill them,' I responded, unwilling to listen to another word.

"Two hours later, in accordance with the Code of Unusual Criminal Offenses, I called the five former forest directors to my office in order to sentence the tree uprooter. The six of us unanimously decided that he was responsible for the deaths of fourteen innocent mortal beings, seven of them from the same family, and therefore will be punished with the utmost severity, with no extenuating circumstances. We brought the accused into the room and informed him we'd reached a decision. He thought, wrongly, that we'd suffice with ceremonial banishment from the forest and a request for him to return his uprooter's boots. At that point I realized how right we were in our judgment, not least for his lack of contrition and comprehension. Billion asked to elucidate the linkage between the severing of branches and death.

"Allow me to quote from the protocol of Unusual Criminal Trials, 2001: 'For those living in the previous world, death has no meaning beyond the negation of their existence. Many of them are albeit involved in the development of different and strange theories that help them contend with the fear of the unknown, but until they reach the Other World their anxiety is alive and well. They cling to their lives with all their might, resisting the end. Imagine, 57438291108, that one day you ceased to exist. Are you even able to envision such a terrifying notion? After all, even a seven over three pales in comparison to their understanding of the black hole that awaits them. Now that we've established the fear, let us turn to the element of danger. For the living human being, danger lurks at all times, in all places. He can cross the street and find himself under the wheels of a moving vehicle, he can frolic in a body of water and find himself pulled to the depths by a whirlpool, he can stand on a mountaintop in the middle of a summer hike and fall into an abyss, and he can, of course, fall victim to his own traitorous body. We are absolutely forbidden from intervening in any way! We are merely responsible for the documentation of the trees' development, providing them with the best possible care. And not for naught do we guard the forest of family trees with such stridency. We, too, much like our friends from that other world, wish to protect them as much as possible from the many dangers that existence holds, and we, too, bow our heads in anguish when humanity brings awful calamities down upon itself or when nature strikes an unexpected blow. The devoted care we provide the trees is our effort to afford them a tranquil, storm-free existence, in the hope that in death the formerly living will arrive here with as light a load as possible. The uprooter's job is to pick up the fallen branches and uproot the naked trees. When an uprooter takes the law into his own hands and maliciously tears branches away, he does not merely transfer an individual from one world to the other. With his own hands he uproots the living's ability to survive in their danger-filled universe and seeds indescribable suffering among the loved ones left behind. Such a person hastens the end! I looked long and hard at the Mendelssohn family dossier and I am forced to conclude with frightful grief that each and every one of those eight family members fell prey to the type of circumstance that only strengthens my argument regarding the diversity of existential dangers.

"'Several hours ago you asked the forest director who he thought was responsible for the death of a shooting victim. I would like for you to ask yourself the following questions: Why, despite the well-documented slackening syndrome, did you have to pull the branch to and fro several times before it gave way? Why did you encounter such stout resistance from the branch when all that was holding it to the tree were a few thin, virtually invisible fibrous strands? And what the hell do you think happens down there when you're battling a branch up here? Not when you sever it, but when you twist it and turn it, when the soul understands the danger that awaits it and tries to overcome the dizzying distress but, to its dismay, there lives an alias in a faraway world who's squeezing the life out of it, draining it of its powers of resistance, its last reserves of strength, its survival instinct? The alias launches a surprise attack and the soul surrenders with devilish haste. The person facing the drawn weapon, succumbs, not because he lacks any choices but because they've been denied him. In the first instance, he has the option of struggling and winning, wounded, but alive. In the latter one, he has no chance. In the heat of that awful moment the wretched victim loses all hope. In no way is it similar to a light severing blow, which is equivalent to split-second accidents, instantaneous death, because, in the case before us, the victim is not spared the final anguish of submission, the spasms of the soul, the fearful realization that he is leaving the only known world forever! I'm not sure you're smart enough to grasp the finer points of branch dislocation and their direct impact on the victim because it seems clear you never fully understood the significance of the trees of life, and therefore,' he turned to me and waited for me to finish his sentence."

⁓

" 'We sentence you to life!' "

⁓

"Dear aliases, this is one of the few times in the history of the Other World that we have meted out the stiffest sentence of all. The alias who uprooted life will be uprooted from his world without further delay, and as we speak the guards are dragging the criminal, whose screams echo in your ears, the screams of a fearful creature who will land in the truly other world in no more than twenty-four hours, without any memory, without any knowledge of where he came from or where he's going, adrift, without roots. He will be forced to deal with life as though he were born into it.

"And regarding the question that interests you all. As far as we're concerned, that alias stopped being an alias the moment he denigrated the existence of others. His death was denied him. Believe me, there is no harsher punishment. I ask that you remember his story and never forget how it ended. It will make you better aliases.

"And one last confession before adjourning. I apologize from the depths of my heart for abusing your trust and allowing my human partner into the restricted areas of the forest. I violated the oath of the forest directors and am unworthy of continuing in my position. I hereby announce my immediate dismissal and the appointment of Billionandthreequarters as my successor. I've always hated good-byes, so I will not continue to tire you with my words. I wish all of us a good day and a brighter future. Thank you."

34

A Comedy of Terrors

A thick, stubborn fog dampened the small murderess's ability to think, hovering as it did from compartment to compartment in the rooms of her brain, refusing to part even when she squeezed her eyes shut and concentrated. No ray of light pierced through the cloud that bound her to her spot, planted in a chair alongside the kitchen table. When she tried to move, to rage against the cruelty of her fate, she felt stricken by a gust of dizziness, which turned the entire room into a colorful melting pot of blurry particles. She sat back down. Her eyes waded around the obstacles of several dull objects that inhabited the living room, freezing, finally, on the central object. A body drained of life, sprawled across the floor. The body of a foreign woman. In death, Marian had become that much more foreign. Or at least so thought Ann, peering at her through the mysterious fog, which intensified the fear about what she might discover when it parted. If it parted. And if she was afraid. She wasn't. She found the murderer's survival instinct, the urge to detach herself from her victim, funny. "Truly, Ann, truly," she chastised herself, "survival is what got you into this mess in the first place."

She nodded without so much as moving her head, verifying what she knew long ago, that the man of her dreams was nothing more than bait meant to keep her alive, something to clutch at just before drowning. She was a small fish begging to be eaten, a little minnow who forgot that its presence slipped under the radar of the predators as they whooshed past with an ambitious fluttering of their fins. False hope encouraged her to carry on, to drift toward the glint of the enticing hook. How uncalculating she had been when she failed to think the story through in her limited imagination: Even if the unknown creature had reeled her out of the water, did she really believe he would wrap her in his brawny arms and carry her to the promised land? What could bind her and him? Oceans languished between them.

Ann blanched when she resolved the twisted trickery of survival. Even the body by her side was of no use. In death she had denied her his acquaintance. In death she put an end to the subterfuge. The intoxicating contradiction carved a thin smile through her parted lips. In order to survive, she murdered the woman whose survival she depended on, only to discover, in the end, that survival itself is an unconvincing pretext. How distorted—she marveled at her understanding, mesmerized by the raucous discoveries that continued to shine through the foggy screen—under one set of circumstances, she had saved the woman's life, under another, she had taken it. Her eyes drifted over the lingering fog and examined the full length of the body, passionately studying the newly revealed irony: the pottery shards around the body. She had saved her life with one vase, and with another . . . Was it structured, planned, or mere chance?

A dull noise from the back of the house reached her ears. She didn't bother checking. Must be the prying neighbor's grandkids over for a visit again, playing with a ball. The sweetish stinging in her eyes accentuated her tiredness. She launched an exhibitionistic yawn into the stifled space of the room, leaned forward, placed her head on the table, and shut her eyes, hoping not to wake. In her dream she saw a spirited pair of swordfish dueling on the bottom of a worm-infested aquarium. The two lashed at each other in remarkable silence, the tiny organs torn from their bodies floating all around, mingling with the worms on the sides of the tank, when a pair of manicured female hands lifted the aquarium into the air and smashed it on the ground. Forest. Helicopters hovering in the sky, casting purple beams of light from three different directions all aimed at the small male figure, working out. Deserted beach. A manicured feminine hand digs in the sand. Someone's laughing in the background, a mirthless laugh. The hand draws a dead eel from the deep hole. Then it produces a dead sea horse. A dead baby crocodile. A dead baby shark. An octopus. Dead. The laugh dies, too. A cheap lightbulb hangs from the sky above the sea; a latex-gloved hand stretches toward it, revealing in its advance a forearm clothed in a white doctor's cloak; the fingers wrap themselves around the scorching bulb and twist slowly. Absolute darkness.

Ann barely managed to open her eyes, begging for a little more sleep. Her exhaustion rewarded her with ten additional minutes. She rose from the chair without feeling dizzy. The mists melted away. She looked down at the body and said lethargically, "You're still here?" and, dragging her feet toward her, looking her over apathetically, a serious smile on her lips, "Now you and I are one and the same." With a sure hand she picked a burgundy shard from the dead woman's auburn hair. The doorbell rang with deterrent immediacy. The shard fell out of her hand and skittered across the floor, stopping near the door. She crawled to the rectangular slab of wood that stood between her and the world. The silences between the ringing of the bell grew shorter until the visitor decided to drive her out of her mind and leaned his hand on the doorbell, flooding the entire house with an infuriatingly trite *ding-dong,* forcing the deafened homeowner to turn the key in the lock and open the door.

He hid behind a pretentiously large bouquet of Sweet Williams, a Magritte-ian character in an elegant suit, three-quarters man and one-quarter floral arrangement, awaiting the response of the battered woman, who exposed nothing more than her head. She accepted the flowers and muttered into the bouquet, "Another small fish . . ."

"What did you say?" Adam smiled hesitantly.

"Thanks for the roses," she said, burying her head in the petals.

"They're Sweet Williams, Ann."

"Does it matter?"

"If I had wanted to bring roses . . ."

"You would have brought roses."

"I'm sorry I didn't ring."

"You rang like a madman."

"I mean on the phone. I wanted to surprise you."

"You have."

"Are you upset that I came by unannounced?"

"No."

"I wanted to come earlier, but unfortunately I was out of town on business. I just got back this morning. I had to see you, so, right after visiting my brother, I went to the flower store and came here."

"Your brother?"

"Shahar. He had a nervous breakdown. He's been institutionalized . . ."

"I thought he was arrested."

"He had a breakdown at the police station. We all hope he'll come out of it soon."

"Hmm . . ."

"Ann, why are you hiding behind the . . . ?"

"Adam, I'm sorry, but I can't see you anymore."

The lavishly fragrant man took off his glasses and looked at her forlornly. "You never let me explain what happened that night."

"It has nothing to do with you," she whispered feebly. "I must ask you to leave."

"If you'd just let me in . . ."

"I'm afraid not," she said, returning the bouquet, revealing her battered face.

"Oh my God, what happened to you?" he asked, putting down the bouquet and extending a hand to caress the long scratch marks along her plum-colored cheek. "Who did this to you?" he yelled, gently pushing the door open.

The sound of the phone perked up her tense shoulders and she moved ghostlike toward the sound of the noise, answering sluggishly, "Yes?"

The hospital director began in a panicky flow, "Ann, why didn't you return my call? Did you hear the message I left you? I asked you to come in to the . . ."

Ann lay the receiver back in place and pulled the cord from the socket in one swift, indifferent motion. Hearing the door slam behind her, she turned around, annoyed. "Didn't anyone teach you to close the door like a civilized person?"

Adam emitted a muffled shriek when he saw the body, recoiled, moved toward it fearfully and recoiled again, shifting his weight from foot to foot in an amusing dance of horror until his body was willing to stride forward again, his head straining onward, his body remaining behind.

"Dear God," he muttered softly, "isn't that . . . ?"

Ann sunk into an old wooden chair by the kitchen table, smiling sweetly. "I told you not to come in."

"What happened here?!"

"Want some tea, Adam?" Ann asked, rising out of her chair and floating toward the kettle.

"I asked you a question!"

"We argued," Ann retorted dryly.

"You argued?" he said, holding her spindly shoulders in his large hands. "You have a dead woman in your living room!"

"They can't hear you downtown," she said, pushing him away and looking at the kettle. "Do you take sugar?"

"How can you be talking about tea?!"

"Do you think that if we abstain from tea she'll come back to life?"

She grabbed two mugs from the sink, washed them, and pulled the silver box toward her, fished out two teabags, placed them at the bottom of the mugs, and shot the kettle an impatient look. "You still haven't told me if you take sugar?"

Adam ignored her question, grabbed the garbage can from the corner of the kitchen, and ran back to the living room.

"What are you doing?" she asked, staring at him in surprise.

"What do you think I'm doing?" he carped, and leaned over Marian, careful to keep his knees away from the pool of blood that ringed the body as he sifted through her hair for shards. After gathering all of the pieces of the vase, he rose and began pacing, his palms pressed hard against his temples in thought.

"Stop thinking about it," came the lifeless voice from the kitchen. "She's dead already. Nothing matters anymore."

"Ann, I want to understand something. What would you have done had I not come?"

"Take a long shower. After that I suppose I'd have gone to sleep. You have no idea how tired I am."

"At some point you would've had to do something about the corpse in the middle of your living room."

"I imagine at some point I would've done something."

"What kind of something?"

"Well, I guess I would've tried to get rid of it."

"Yes, that's obvious, but how?"

"Do me a favor, Adam, I'd rather not deal with the details."

"But, Ann, that's exactly what counts. The details. Even the slightest mistake could send you to life behind bars, and please excuse my ignorance of all that has transpired here, but . . ."

"There's not much to understand. She was married to the guy from the health club."

"What?"

"You heard me. They were divorced and she wouldn't give me the necessary information. You know, in case I wanted to find him."

"And would you want to?"

"I told you, I don't want anything anymore. Jacques wouldn't notice me anyway."

"Jacques?"

"The guy from the health club."

"But still you wouldn't want to spend the rest of your days behind bars."

"You meet a man twice and already he's an expert on all your wants and desires."

"Ann, maybe you should go shower. I think you need to unwind."

He sat opposite her, held his mug of lukewarm tea in a remarkably steady hand, and sipped long and slow.

"What?" Ann said, moving uncomfortably in her chair.

"Will you come with me to the Caribbean?" He put the mug down and took her hand in his.

"What?" she asked again, looking from the corner of her small eye at her captive hand, held in his big damp one.

"I think we both need a change of atmosphere. What do you say?"

His grip tightened and her childish hand was swallowed by his five demanding fingers.

"If I say no, will you crush my hand?"

He eased his grip and smiled apologetically. "I just think it wouldn't hurt either of us if we kept a low profile, at least till we know we have no problem coming back."

Ann's laughter did little to disguise her shock. "You sound as though everything was planned out in advance and all we have to do now is follow your perfect plan."

"Nothing was planned in advance, but I think our best chance right now is to make her disappear and then disappear ourselves. Imagine if by tomorrow we were far away from this place, lying on some divine beach, inhaling tropical air."

"I've never done anything like that."

"Nor have you ever done anything like that," he said, pointing at the body and smiling peacefully. "I hope your passport's valid."

"Yes," she said, rubbing her calf against the leg of the table, relishing the touch of something cold and metallic.

"Excellent. All we have to do now is work out the details and, in my opinion, if we're careful and clearheaded, there's no reason for us to fail. I hope you're not expecting any visitors today."

"No," she said, trying not to laugh, contemplating the outcome of her one and only attempt at hospitality.

"Great. I see all the windows are closed and the blinds are drawn. Leave them that way. Don't open the door for anyone and don't answer the phone."

"That won't be a problem," Ann said, wondering if her way of life had been a punctilious preparation for the perfect murder.

Adam nodded alertly. "Wonderful. I'm going to go get us tickets, hopefully on the first flight out of here tomorrow morning. Afterwards, I'll go home, pack a bag, and wait patiently for darkness. Then I'll come back here with Shahar's cello case."

"His cello case?"

"A few years back, Shahar took some cello lessons for one of his roles. It's a long story, but what's important is that the case is long and wide, and this woman here is short and thin. We'll be able to get her out of here without raising any suspicion. In the meanwhile, scrub the floors, don't leave a drop of blood anywhere, get things back to the way they were, and pack a bag. Don't forget a bathing suit. And no matter what you do, don't touch her."

"If it's fingerprints you're worried about, I'm sure her whole body . . ."

"Okay, okay, let's think a second . . ."

"I have an idea, Adam, but it sounds a bit cruel."

"Cruel to whom?"

Ann curled her lips and whispered, "Acid."

"You don't need to whisper. Acid is not a bad idea at all. It meets all of our requirements, distorts evidence, destroys the body, and points to a real motive on the part of the murderer. An acid burn and a cracked skull is exactly the kind of combination that confuses the cops, especially if we go overboard."

"How do you mean?"

"We'll embellish the crime. They do it all the time in movies. We'll cut off a finger. Maybe two. And a toe."

"But what will we do after . . . ?"

"We'll bury her."

"Where?"

"We have a few more hours, my dear. We'll think about it and by nightfall I'm sure we'll be able to agree on the ideal burial spot."

Adam leaned in toward her, pressed two fleshy lips to her forehead, and whispered, "You'll see how happy I'll make you."

Ann breathed in his fragrance, afraid that if he continued to stand in such close proximity, she would lose control. The joyous feeling continued to accompany her as he distanced himself, walked toward the door, turned, smiled apologetically, returned to the kitchen, bundled the garbage can in his brawny arms and left, signaling her to lock the door behind him. Ann chuckled and flipped the lock. "The small fish got a whiff of blood and turned into a shark." She knew it was all a dream, and that only within its delicate frame did she take the wet floor rag, get down on her knees, and diligently scrub the disgusting stain, gazing at the fading blood marks through the delicate gossamer of mist. Ann smiled. The frame cracked. She prostrated herself beside the placid corpse, nestled up to her, and combed a few strands of hair away from her ear, laying her lips on the lobe and whispering calmly, "Hey, Marian, remember me? What do you have to say for yourself now? All the Jacques and Rushdies in the world didn't do you much good, did they? But nonetheless I feel like I owe you an apology. After all, both of us know that I'm not a violent woman, and certainly not a murderer. That's why I'm sorry that you were such a selfish bitch and that you forced me to act like an animal. But surely you witnessed what happened here a few minutes ago? Did you ever have a man who was willing to put himself at risk in that kind of way? Have you ever known that kind of love? So what if I'm dreaming and he'll never be back. At least I have a life that lets me dream, sober up, and dream again like a true moron. And you? You'll sleep forever. That's the big difference, isn't it? Did you hear that? Listen. He's knocking. Adam's back. He's come to take me to the Caribbean. Is it possible I was wrong and it isn't a dream? He said he'd only be back in the evening. I'm going to open the door. Listen to the urgency in his knocking, as though he hadn't just seen me less than an hour ago. I hope you're dying of jealousy, Marian."

A second prior to touching the handle, she heard a stern female voice from the other side of the door, "Open the door, I know you're in there."

Ann drew back from the door. For a moment she feared that the lady might knock the door off its beaten hinges and bring it down with a victorious blow. "Ann, it's Bessie. Bessie Kolanski, Rafael's wife. I need to ask you something." The voice softened: "I don't know if you happened to hear, but my Rafael passed away. He died early this morning." The sorrowful tone did not fool Ann. "Listen, I can't afford to waste any time, tomorrow's the funeral and I'm sure you know all too well why I've come calling on such a feverish day. So please, open your door."

Ann's cold eyes roamed across the kitchen, scanning the cabinets, the sink, the table and chairs in amazement before returning to the orphaned mug in the middle of the table. Before she had the chance to recall where the other mug had disappeared to, the annoyed old lady delivered another, even more clamorous volley of knocks, yelling in a wavering voice, "Listen, you fool, I have no patience for your games. I hear you panting behind that door. I'm not here to argue with you. Believe me, on the darkest day of my life I'd rather focus on the dear man I lost and not on some small strange nurse holed up in her house."

Her feet rising and falling like a blind woman's, Ann felt her way to the kitchen, halting at the entrance, her eyes caught by the garbage can, rimmed by a glistening bloody shard. In the distance she heard an old woman's agitated voice tell of a high-spirited husband who thoroughly enjoyed the nurse's tasteless trick and refused to wash the ink off his palm, even avoiding getting any soap on the area. To the new widow's great distress, the mortician informed her that the strange substance could not be washed off at all, even after countless attempts with the most efficient of cleaners.

"I refuse to bury Rafael with the mark of disgrace you've left on his hand!" fumed the old woman, kicking the silent nurse's door as Ann entrenched herself next to the garbage can and tried to rage against its nefarious presence.

"I'm begging you, Ann, if you have even a modicum of human respect for the dead, tell me what kind of ink you used so that we can figure out how to erase it. That's all I'm asking of you, Ann. It doesn't compute, inerasable ink, there's no such thing."

In the hands of a murderer an innocent pottery shard becomes a weapon of destruction. Leaning against the kitchen wall, immersed in the deliberative carving of the four uplifting words into her palm, she ogled the blood as it flowed from the life line to the indifferent wrist, stalled alongside a sleepy vein, and dripped to the floor. A minute later, the nurse critically examined the first word she'd managed to squeeze between the intellect line and the life line, shocked to find that her small hand did not offer a wide enough parchment for the whole sentence and angered by the unnecessary whim that had brought her to this childish position, legs spread apart, bleeding, heedless and wild, reality askew and dreams dashed. A moment before she fell asleep for the umpteenth time, she drew the garbage can toward her with her uninjured hand, pulled out a few pieces of the shattered vase, and aimed at the corpse, missing and trying again, and each time she managed to land a shard on the body, she called out, "Yes! Yes!" until no more. At last she was asleep, dreamless, sealed off from within and without.

Devoid of consciousness, her body was laid out like abandoned furniture, cuddled and tucked away in a slumber of sweet oblivion. And when her eyelids implored her to return to the circle of life, she was sure she'd happened on a scene in which she had no part, not knowing what all the police officers were doing in her house, how they got in, and who's the person lying next to Marian, oh God, another body, this time a man, and who's the old woman clad in black calmly chatting with a smiling policewoman, and will someone please turn off those sirens, and is it possible they don't notice her, how many of them are there, at least ten, and wow, how much attention they're devoting to Marian, strutting around her like a herd of blind suitors, photographing, documenting, noting, hanging around her as though she'd repay them with some great insight, and the same goes for the dead stranger, another inexplicable focal point, she can't identify him, has no idea how a naked stranger had managed to sneak into her house or how he had died. Suddenly the young woman in the police uniform turned her head, stared at her, and called out to one of her fellow officers, "Yaron, she's wounded. Got to bandage her up before we take her."

She recoiled, trembling frightfully as the tall man bent down to her and asked to bandage her immobilized hand. He took no special notice of her behavior, simply doing his job. And then she ambled over and stood over Ann. The black widow. Her eyes daggers, her lips a long dark slit. Her voice rose from a hidden cave in the depths of her throat. "You should have opened the door."

Ann shrunk and whispered, "I share your pain."

"I wish I could say the same thing." Bessie exchanged a knowing look with the policewoman. "From the first moment I knew something was wrong with you. That thirst for the kill. That glint in your eyes when you convinced me to sign the paperwork for Rafael. But at no point did I imagine that you take your work home with you. Don't think I don't recognize that poor woman lying there lifelessly. I remember her from her visits to the hospital. The man no, but what does it matter. Just another number on the merciful nurse's list, eh?"

Ann craned her neck in curiosity. "I have no idea who that man is. I've never seen him before."

"It's not nice to lie. Even though in your case you didn't leave yourself much of a choice. . . ."

"What do you mean?"

Bessie shrugged. "Who ever heard of a murderer that tosses a victim out to the backyard? What were you thinking, that no one would notice him because of the hedges between you and your neighbor's property? If you had even a touch of intelligence, you would have dragged him to the little shed in the back rather than leaving him for all to . . ."

"I have no idea what you're talking about."

"Yes, well, I didn't know about any of this either when you refused to open the door and I went looking for a back entrance into the house and, instead of finding a door, I found a naked body on the grass." Bessie sneered.

"So you called the police because of him?" Ann asked in horror.

"Of course. I didn't entertain the notion that you were building yourself a little morgue here, hiding bodies all around." The old woman leaned toward her and lowered her tone. "Listen to me. I really don't care about your private life. All I want to know is what kind of ink you used."

"I didn't use any kind of ink!" the nurse cut her short with a shout. "I already made that clear in the hospital. I had nothing to do with the mysterious writing on your husband's hand."

Bessie shut her eyes hard, straining to rein in her reaction, when she heard a cry of surprise from the heart of the living room, "Jesus Christ! He's alive! He opened his eyes!"

The attention was immediately turned toward the young man, who threw the sheet off of himself in fright and rubbed his eyes in consternation at the sight of the blue-uniformed crowd around him. He moved his lips and mumbled three inexplicable syllables, and when the police doctor put his own hand on his heart, the man burst into silent sobs that lasted no longer than a minute. The policewoman who had bonded with the artist's wife suggested that everyone wait till he calmed down and that she'd talk with him face-to-face back in the station.

"In the meantime we need to get him some clothes," she said, directing her words to a junior colleague. "Dov, you live close by, right? Go home and get him something to wear."

"I'm telling you, this is really strange," said the nearly delirious cop, who had been an eyewitness to the awakening and refused to calm down. "Ten years I been doing this and I've never seen a guy without a pulse come back to life after we've signed off on his death."

From her lair, Ann saw the strange man rising slowly, teetering toward the window, drawing the blind and looking out.

"Are you looking for something?" the policewoman asked.

He turned his face toward her and asked quietly, "You . . . speak Hebrew?"

"Of course," she smiled, pointing toward her colleagues, "we all speak Hebrew."

"Why?"

"What language would you choose to speak in Israel?"

His forehead creased with confusion. "Israel?"

"Where did you think you were?"

He looked out without responding, his eyes riveted on the lonesome cluster of clouds that hung in the sky.

Dov didn't invest much effort in choosing the clothes that would cover the nakedness of the unknown man and hurried back to the house, holding brown corduroy pants and a green T-shirt, both draped over uneven hangers and both having known better days. The male slacker collection was filled out with boxers with small holes in the rear, gray wool socks, and a pair of battered sneakers. The naked man looked at him uncomprehendingly when asked to get dressed, and when he was handed the underwear he didn't think twice before flicking them on his head.

"Oh shit," Dov muttered under his mustache, asking the man to accompany him to the bedroom and summoning two other cops, who stopped their giggling as soon as they were chosen as part of the dressing team. For several long minutes, the three panting officers of the law battled the man's clumsy limbs until they were able to fit the proper arm and leg in the appropriate encasing, and when they led him out of the house, the others present restrained themselves from laughing at the sight of him and exchanged looks of wonder at the thin smile that crossed his lips when he hesitated by the row of hedges and plucked a few stray leaves.

The only one who released a bashfully childish giggle was the small woman in the kitchen, suspected of murder, who listened only half intently when she was read her rights, considering the slew of rights she had denied the woman being carried out on a stretcher, such as the right to see Yonatan one final time or the right to read Rushdie's next book. She didn't stop chuckling even once the door of her house was closed behind her and she was led with utmost delicacy to the waiting patrol car, holding her head high in the face of dozens of neighbors' eyes, who had crowded around the front of her house. People who passed her by, day in day out, and never bothered to find out who she was. She happily parted with the hated street, saying never again to the loathsome route between the two rows of sycamore trees, the identical houses, and the sleepy convenience store.

Looking through the streaked windows of the patrol car, she spied a frustrated old woman in black stomping furiously, and she continued to smile, the mists having parted, the thoughts beaten into obedience; it had been a long time since she'd encountered such fine humor, and in another minute the patrol car would pass by the famous bend in the road, and with a quick head motion she shifted her narrowed eyes toward the front of the health club and saw a blind man working out with fantastic concentration on one of the machines, unaware of the buffoonery of his movements as he bent over onto his stomach and lifted a pair of weights with his ankles, and when he raised his head with extreme exertion and every muscle in his face convulsed in shock, she knew that he saw, and she burst out in unbridled laughter.

"Why are you laughing?" Dov asked, detesting the low and disturbing voice gurgling from her throat.

"Nothing, just thought of someone," she said, as though desultory, and turned from the window.

35 The Hundredth Dead Woman and the Flickering Man

Marian was sure she was a Charlatan. Even though she didn't know the term's current meaning. She had no doubt whatsoever that the battle she'd waged with the murderous nurse had ended in the hospital and that she was hooked up to the machines, much like her love. Marian, confusedly, based her judgment on the familiar tales of many people who, with confident and placid expressions, told of the notorious white hallways and, despite her disdain for clichés, she had to admit that there was a grain of truth to their testimony, even if, as opposed to all their descriptions, the room, and not the hallway, was both vast and obnoxiously full.

Apparently a lot of people get cracked in the head with vases, she thought, grinning timidly and laying a hand on the back of her head, feeling for remnants of the struggle and explaining away her blood-free hands as part of the authenticity of the experience, since surely she wasn't really in an enormous hall surrounded by tens of thousands of curious nudists thirsting for an explanation, and therefore there was no need to insist on terrestrial details like the gaping wound she must have had in her head. Marian paid no attention to the screen and the beautiful orientation lecturer's speech that was broadcast on it, preferring to spend the little time she had at her disposal considering her dire condition. Since she'd landed in Israel she had twice been brutally attacked. And if those violent episodes weren't enough, her new love had suffered a heart attack before revealing himself to her. She was filled with excitement at the prospect that he, too, could be somewhere in the same strange room.

She strained her eyes by the glow of the screen, trying to locate him among the sea of heads. When the light was turned back on and the room was flooded with fluorescent whiteness, she rubbed her eyes at length and quickly got to her feet, looking for him alertly, distractedly fingering the strange device that hung from her neck, careful not to miss a single face, as surreal and asinine as it may look. To her surprise, she spotted Kolanski, the famous Israeli painter, on the far end of the room, jumping up and down like a kid, completely ignoring the leering group around him that called him "crazy," and plowed toward him, but the stern-faced old man, who continuously leaped and called out "It's impossible! It's impossible!" didn't so much as blink in her direction until she tapped his shoulder.

He spun around and addressed her with typical rudeness. "What do you want?"

"I know you don't know me but I wanted to congratulate you on the medical miracle."

Rafael planned on smiling but responded instead with a restrained nod and pointed at his jittery feet. "You see that? You know how many years it's been since I stood on them?"

"Yes," she answered winningly, and repeated after a brief pause, "You don't know me, but . . ."

"Of course I know you. Your husband's ridiculous friends asked that I draw a portrait of you, which I obviously refused to do. Kolanski doesn't do portraits."

"My husband's ridiculous friends?" she asked with an innocent smile. "You must be mistaken, Mr. Kolanski. You don't know me because I only got to know you when you were in the hospital in a coma. Maybe you noticed me on the day they let you go home."

"Enough with the nonsense. I know exactly who you are. Even though it's a little funny to see you here after all this time. I thought we were the newly dead and here I am talking to someone who died over a year ago."

"No, no, no, Rafael, you've got this all wrong. I'm just like you, deep in a coma. You had another stroke. I read about it in the paper."

"And you didn't read that I didn't make it through that last stroke?"

"No, not at all, you're still lying in the hospital bed and sweet Bessie is sitting beside you waiting for you to wake up."

"Bessie's probably burying me as we speak, you lovely imbecile. My poor Bessie, what troubles she has waiting for her. But that's nothing compared to what awaits me when she shows up here one of these days. The flower's profound optimism beat the thorn's shallow prickliness. Unlike me, she always believed that death was just a word."

Marian very nearly took up the chant of the leering group around Kolanski but changed her mind at the sight of the opening doors. Certain she was right, she didn't join the curious mass as they stormed the doors, waiting listlessly till the last of them left. Rafael was swept away by the mass, carried against his will toward the exit, and despite his forceful cries, the galloping dead did not spring him free, forcing on him an enjoyment he had already managed to forget in his fifty years of crippled existence. Marian, pressing herself against the wall, stifled a laugh as she avoided the flowing mass of people, and even from the far corner in which she hid, she could make out the hotheaded old man raising his legs and kicking away with supreme delight.

Marian chose to revel in the blessed time-out and was the last to leave, a childish wish pulsating inside her that perhaps she will not be thrust back to that violent world too soon, and that she'd get a week or two of reprieve. She turned her head slowly to look at the closing doors before she caught sight of the monstrous vehicles on the far end of the vast lawn, giant streetcars that swallowed up the tens of thousands of people and reversed with terminal velocity until they morphed into black dots and vanished into the horizon.

Marian tried to remember if in the tales of those who came back from the dead, something had been said about multi-wheeled streetcars or the silly electronic toy dangling around her neck or even the chilling voice that was broadcast over a hidden loudspeaker until the doors opened. Her thoughts were disrupted by the sight at the far end of the path, about eight hundred yards away, of a bluish, rather rotund figure that did not take his eyes off her. Without understanding what it was that drew her toward him, she ran in his direction, seized by excitement, and with each stride the spark of recognition intensified and she hastened toward him, eager to ensure that her eyes did not deceive her, because, three hundred yards away, the unassailable figure of Yonatan was turning into an apparition; he extended a hand toward her and smiled happily, she smiled back, incredulous at her good fortune, a match made in heaven, a pair of temporarily dead people in a semi-blind date. One moment he was here and the next he was gone. Marian called his name passionately but was not answered. It seemed as though the fading man one hundred and fifty yards ahead of her was yearning to respond—his lips moved helplessly, his other hand extended as well, and his smile was blurry—when suddenly he lost some of his clarity, like an actor in a color movie who bleeds into black and white and ever so slowly melts away. Marian closed and opened her eyes; his being waxed and waned, and then he was back again, strong and sturdy, moving toward her—and then froze again—and she was not willing to give in, spreading her arms wide to hug him—his overalls vanishing and reappearing—in four steps she and he would be one. And then he expired. Marian hugged air. The flickering man had extinguished. Marian didn't lose her calm. Over the course of the last minute, he had managed to dissipate and be restored dozens of times, like a light that refuses to die, and she continued watching, fully confident of his reappearance, not relenting even after two uneventful minutes, certain that the invisible man was merely testing her emotional endurance. Forgetting her surroundings entirely, she stood alone, detached, in the heart of a lane devoid of people, until her ear picked up a low and gentle voice on her left.

Marian smiled, turned victoriously toward the voice, and awarded the gnome a withering look. The pale man called her by name again, this time with a stridency that underscored that he would not allow her to ignore him, and she responded, "Leave me alone and stop distracting me, jackass."

Rather than granting her her wish, he called out sadly, "I'm sorry, Marian, but you could stay here for hours and he still won't come."

"Butt out and quit ruining the moment." She shut her eyes and stamped her foot. "Come on, Yonatan, please, don't make me get upset."

"No, love, doesn't work that way," the low and congenial voice said, "that moment's done. It's over; he woke up. But if you open your eyes and look down, you'll see he left you a memento."

Despite herself, she obeyed the strange man and bent down to pick up the portrait of the woman who bore a sickeningly close resemblance to her, aside from the redundant beauty mark and the straight black hair. She shouted, "This woman again? First the little scumbag tried to kill me because of her and now even Yonatan leaves me her portrait? To hell with her!"

Before he had the chance to restrain her, she smashed the portrait against a nearby tree and called out in a threatening voice, "Where is he? Where's Yonatan?"

"I told you. He's come out of his coma."

"I also want to come out of my coma!" she demanded, sprinting toward the doors of the white room, disregarding his calls to halt, fleeing from his wheezing approach. Finding no knob on the doors, she knocked with her feet, kicking and screaming in panic, "Open the doors! Open them! I need to get in! I need to snap out of it! You must help me get back! I've heard of people living on in a vegetative state for years and I can't afford to waste all that time! Yonatan's awake! I have to wake up, too! I have to meet him! Make me flicker! Make me flicker!"

"It's impossible, dear," the man said softly, after finally closing the gap between himself and the sobbing woman. "You'll never be able to go back there."

"Why not?"

"Because, as opposed to what you think, you're not in a coma. You're well beyond that."

"How do you know?"

"You're naked, you've got a godget around your neck, and the Announcer called your name. That's the reason I'm here and that's also why Yonatan was here." At the end of a long silence, he smiled and said, "Welcome to the Other World, or, in simpler terms, the world of the dead."

Marian turned around gradually, her pupils filling her eyes, both hands covering her lips. "What did you say?"

This time he was the astonished one. He recoiled as though he'd received an electric shock, his eyes fixed on the small birthmark on her left breast that had only now been revealed. "Oh my God, it's so simple! When I got to the Family Tree Administration and they told me who your mother was, I thought it was nothing but a brilliant coincidence, but now . . . now I understand it all . . ."

"What are you talking about?"

"The birthmark on your chest . . . the star . . ."

"I was supposed to get rid of it a few days ago, but in the end I decided against the surgery."

"Because it reminded you of the last time, right? When your mother went with you to the clinic, and there you met the only man in the world who has the exact same mark, the man your mother killed in a fit of rage, the Belgian bastard who ruined her life."

Marian whispered in terror, "How do you know all that? And who the hell are you?"

He hung his head modestly. "I'm the Mad Hop, private investigator by trade, but you can call me Samuel, and I'd be obliged if you'd join me for a fascinating journey."

"Journey?" she asked, looking back at the doors.

"The sooner you accept the fact of your death, the better it'll be for you. Marian, quite a few people are waiting for you in this world, quite a few of them will be happy to see you."

"But what will I do about Yonatan?" she asked in desperation. A harsh animosity crept into her face and she seethed, "The little bitch murdered me. She eliminated me and took me away from him before he woke up. God, he'll think I abandoned him. He'll think . . ."

"Okay, Marian, okay," the Mad Hop said, laying a warm palm on her shoulder. "You have to let that story go and hope that you'll meet again one of these days. After all, he wasn't a particularly healthy person, judging by what he told me, and at the risk of sounding macabre, you surely know that sooner or later his heart will give out, and then I have no doubt that the two midnight children will give thanks to the twists of fate that separated them and brought them together in the same world. Maybe you'll even laugh about your dramatic entrance into the Other World and the strangest request I've ever heard . . ."

"Which request?"

"Make me flicker . . ." The Mad Hop smiled, offering her a cigarette.

36
The Chronicles
of a Death Foretold?

The residents of 1616 could not recall such a strong flow of people to their city. Even though they were accustomed to pilgrimages large and small, this current wave was of an almost ungraspable proportion, as hundreds of express multies pulled into town and spun back around in order to transport the legions of dreamers that waited dozens, even hundreds, of years for the critical moment, and now that it had arrived, were simply unwilling to be left behind. Nearly four hundred years passed before the greatest of playwrights saw fit to release a new play, his thirty-eighth, which he had worked on for a considerable period of time, perhaps as long as a decade, if the rumors were to be believed. On the first day of auditions, thousands of nervous, overwrought actors stormed the theater doors, since the word was that, aside from a stern crew of casting personnel, the man responsible for the whole ado would be in the theater, personally supervising the selection process.

Those who'd had the opportunity to audition reported, frustratingly, about a large dark hall, a floodlit stage, and a soft voice in the dark asking them to read two segments, as they liked it. The brief auditions had been going on for four weeks with no end in sight, as a stream of daunted actors washed through the city, some waiting for the telefinger to ring and others compulsively rehearsing for their audience with the incomparable Bard. The unbearable congestion on the streets and the neurotic behavior of the actors (fits of rage, anxiety attacks, hysterical crying, and desperate giggling from every nook and cranny), who treated the audition with pristine reverence, embarrassing all those in their company, especially when they decided to collaborate and bring entire scenes to life, and at times entire acts, in the middle of the street, emphasized the sense of distorted reality for those who wanted to die in peace and happened on dramatic events on their way to their humdrum existences—like the woman who craved some ice cream and, on the way to the stand, passed thirty-three indecisive Hamlets, until the last of them stepped in her way, grabbed her head in a viselike grip, and asked *the* question, or the poor kid who found himself witnessing a brutal murder courtesy of *Titus Andronicus*; Shakespeare mania gripped every corner of the tranquil city and the harried residents nodded sullenly, all too aware that this was but the beginning.

For one man, though, it was the end. Utterly detached from the boisterous festivities, Ben spent more than an hour traipsing through dozens of theatrical scenes that, at some other less apathetic period, he would undoubtedly have recognized. In a moment of resourcefulness, he tried to call the Mad Hop, but all that came over the line was a disturbing silence. He smiled and nodded in full understanding. Only someone who had devoted his life to writing endings knew how to detect the end with near scientific certainty—it's the weighty feeling of enormous unburdening from the shoulders of the protagonist and the teller alike.

He swerved away from the Caliban-lined street and turned into a quiet narrow alley, where he leaned against a high stone wall and breathed in the hush. He had once asked Marian what he should do if he lost her. She laughed and said, "Find someone else." "But she'd be someone else," he snickered back, and she chuckled and, growing reflective, said, "That's the essence of loss. Someone once asked me what I find in you. I thought about it and answered—things I never knew I'd lost."

Ben sorted through his options: one, to return to 2001 and renew his useless search, but then he'd surely be the recipient of unsatisfying explanations—if she felt the need to deceive him to the point of staging her own death, then surely she did not seek his company; two, to meet his grandparents and pretend he was interested in the information for which he'd come all the way to this frenzied city; and three, by far the most appealing—to destroy it all with the flick of a finger. Without delay. The only valid alternative for an existence sans Marian. He was experienced. He'd taken the risk before, abandoned his life without any qualms, clinging to an innocent and optimistic faith in the happy end his death would bequeath him. And even now, in the face of a reality so squalid it left no room for faith, he knew he would do it again.

He stroked the steel boxes of his stomach and sighed. "How insipid my moral reckoning has been since the day you died, Marian. How insipid I've become. Bereft of my senses, I wandered through cities and among people in my futile search for you, whereas you decided not to reveal yourself. Maybe already back then, in our good old days, you detected a worrying fissure in your lover's composition and, in your infinite wisdom, you knew that leaving would lay waste to the man by your side? Maybe you decided to teach me a lesson, to break me down into my elements and let me deal with the consequences? But I, a silly and inane lover, did not pass the test. Uncle David thought I had begun to put the pieces back together, but he has no sense of the enormity of the destruction you left in your wake. Why can't I, like most people who have lost a significant other, manage, in the end, to get my head back up above water? Why did I need this kind of drama? And maybe if you're my significant other, I'm the other without significance? Is it possible that love is the loftiest reason to live—and its loss, to die? It's the worst end, Marian, the most bitter, thorny, disappointing, dark and defective of them all. You shouldn't give your all in love, because it demands tenfold in return. Not just what a person is willing to give, but his very being. A dark tunnel where the light at its end is inverted and inside out. The end is the beginning, otherwise how would one even get there? He needs a thin beam of light to take his first steps.

"On his way where? Into the infinite darkness? Like birth, my love? A passing glimpse of light shines through and then . . . bam! Blackout. Forever. That's the promising beginning, misleading sparks of light? The day we met, the day my first ending was published, the day you told me you were pregnant, each and every one of those days ends too early because I no longer know you, because I no longer care to write a word, because our son is an alias, and he's better off without his ridiculous father. For the love of God, a single flicker of light and off we go, throwing ourselves into the diabolical tunnel of life. Albeit without a choice, but still. How programmed we've been to believe that the redemptive light also exists at the end of the tunnel. And what a large role I played in propagating that fallacious tradition. True, I wrote willfully provocative endings, open endings, sad endings. People don't fear death, Marian, they fear a bad ending, where the illusion of the chandelier at the end of the road shatters in their faces, darkening their world. Marian, there's no other ending. There's no other ending. I'm not interested in trudging through this fucking tunnel that refuses to end. I'm not interested in fooling myself with the thought that at some point it will happen. As far as I'm concerned, the choice is not between to be or not to be but between not to be now and not to be later, and, in all honesty, I see no point in procrastination. I think the time has come to put an end to the story, and if I'm wrong, I do hope you'll never know. . . ."

Ben took the godget in both hands and placed his thumb on button number three with utmost care, when he heard a dry cough behind him. "If you think punching in a seven over three is going to make you forget about her, you're fooling yourself."

Ben turned around and looked at the oldest man he'd ever seen. The stooped character, wrinkled as a paper bag that had been reused endlessly, cleared his throat. "Please excuse the rude intrusion but I thought it would only be right to tell you something before you shut the light."

"How long have you been standing here?" Ben shuddered.

The tattered character wheezed back, "Since 'I've wandered through cities.' About there. I don't ordinarily eavesdrop on others, it's just that you invaded my alley, my refuge from all the irritating actors. I thought you were an actor, too, and was about to ask you to go find a different stage, till the matter of the godget . . ."

"Unfortunately I am going to have to ask *you* to find another refuge. You're in my way!"

"I'm sorry, but a seven over three will not grant you a pass from the fears you just voiced." The old man approached listlessly.

"What do you know about seven over three?"

"That if a person no longer wants to be, seven over three is the worst option for him."

"What's so bad about eternal sleep?"

"You can't wake up from it."

"Fantastic!" Ben called out with tempered enthusiasm, unsure if he wanted to hear more.

"That's where you're mistaken." A surprising urgency slipped into the old man's cautious voice. "When the first stage of your life came to a close, the prologue that, judging by your looks, was about forty years long, you must not have expected to find this type of world."

"True." Ben nodded in spite of himself. "That's why I'm tempted by the thought . . ."

"Yes, yes"—the old man barged in with a cough—"I'm about to get to that. Desperation, depression, boredom, curiosity—doesn't matter why, you decided you've had enough. The option offered by the godget sounds enticing—eternal sleep in seven pushes of a button. The perfect epilogue. The End! Or maybe not."

"What do you mean?"

"It's simple, son. This world is the proof that there's no such thing as nonexistence. Not being. It's all about 'geographical' differences."

"Huh?"

"You're able to not exist only in a certain world. Just as you're able to exist only in a certain world. In your current state, you're able to not exist in the world in which you were born, and, in your former life, as a mortal, you couldn't exist in this world, and from that we are forced to deduce that if you punch in a seven over three you will experience a different kind of existence, an existence you couldn't have experienced in either of your other two worlds."

"But it's just sleep."

"Which may turn out to be feverish and fitful. Who can say? After all, for your loved ones that remained behind when you died, if there were any such, you're in eternal sleep now. They don't know a thing about our cockamamie world. Wooden casket, glass sarcophagus, what's the difference? And if I still haven't managed to convince you, think of the big hint. Eternal sleep. Must we analyze the term to death or are you capable of unwrapping it yourself?"

"You mean dreams," Ben said in astonishment. "Do you really think that eternal sleep is to be eternally dreaming?"

"Far more dangerous than that," he said, a sly smile flickering across his creased face, reclaiming Ben's attention.

"Okay, talk to me."

"When a man dies, what do the living say about him?"

"The living?"

"Yes, where do they say he's gone?"

"Well, where I come from, they say *halach l'olamo*, went to his world."

"And is this world your world?"

"Not really."

"And was the previous world your world? Did you ask to be born into it?"

"No."

"And if you hit seven over three, then that could be the first time in your existence that you come to a third world of your own volition."

"But I came to this world of my own volition, too. No one else is responsible for my death."

"The aliases must be taken into consideration, don't you think?"

"What?"

"If this third world is a world that belongs to you, only to you, your world, it must be comprised of something, right? Impressions, tastes, loves, hates, traits, colors, senses, wants, fears, inclinations, thoughts, dreams. All of that is based on your life, otherwise how could you ever determine for yourself who you are and in what alternate manner you could have amassed the entire array of existential experiences?"

"But if I will eventually pass into my world, why must I go through this world first? Why can't I just skip over it?"

"I don't pretend to have all the answers, but two things are clear to me—if you were an alias and you died before being born, what world exactly would you arrive at? How could you go to your world if you didn't have the chance to experience anything? This world has to exist for those to whom the other world remains beyond the realm of their experience. The second fact is no less important—everyone knows that particularly advanced aliases developed the godget, without which you can't get to any other world . . ."

"In other words, in any case, there must be an intermediary world between that world and . . ."

"I think it would be best to compromise on the term intermediary world between the external world and the internal world."

Ben closed his eyes and called out excitedly, "The godget. The simulation of freedom, allowing us to choose our preferred terms of existence, practically without restrictions. The transition from an arbitrary world devoid of choice to a world where we are not asked to confront the hardships of the body, the difficulties of communication, and the woes of economics. An ostensible utopia, which readies you for the true utopia—the internal world. A world where the topography of the soul reigns. Ben *halach l'olamo.* The world of Ben Mendelssohn—a religion of the self. With a quick turn of the mind, the sparse Israeli landscape can be exchanged for the ruins of a monastery in Portugal, the colors of spring can be made ever present, Schubert, Costello, Woody Allen, one cat or two, hypnotic tranquility, I'm going back to writing, I'm painting because all of a sudden I can, I'm encircled by Marians. No need to search for her, she's everywhere, like the sky and the earth, she's an element of nature, with her rolling laugh, she's there just like me, in the dream, a permanent resident in my castle, which looks out over the great sea, and every morning we'll swim, and make love on the beach, and he . . . he'll be with us, too, our little alias . . . maybe even more than one. I always wanted two, brother and sister . . . mother and father, the perfect familial idyll. Well, what's preventing you from seeing the vision through?" He opened his eyes and recoiled in dread. The old man had disappeared and in his place stood the most beautiful woman in the world.

Ben came close to her and laid a hand on her exposed shoulder. "Are you real?"

She smiled her famous smile and hooked her arms behind her back, accentuating the full curve of her hips and her impeccable posture, wearing the blue velvet dress he loved most.

"Where did you get the dress from?" Ben wondered.

"From the closet." The most famous voice in the world squeezed his heart like the last notes of a melody.

"Where's the closet?"

"In the bedroom, silly," she giggled warmly, twisting the skin on his elbow between her two fingers as she always did whenever he asked a stupid question.

"Where's the bedroom?"

"At home."

"In the house in Tel Aviv?"

"Do you know any other?"

"And when did you stop in there?"

"You tell me."

"I don't know. It's so far away and there's no way you've been hanging out here for the past fifteen months in a blue velvet dress when everyone knows that this is a clothes-free zone."

"Who's everyone?"

"Everyone."

"Benji, there's no one here but us. And what's this nonsense about no clothes? What are your jeans made out of, air?"

Ben stared at the well-worn denim longingly. "But where did everyone go?"

"Where did you go?"

"I didn't go anywhere. You're the one who left."

"But here I am. Right here. In front of you. At an arm's length."

"So, why can't I touch you? And why is this meeting so cold? Marian, it's not supposed to be like this."

"Benji, honey, what do you want from me? You make the rules, you can break them, too. For some reason you decided that I'd be icy and unapproachable, and that doesn't leave me a lot of options. Maybe you should turn up the temperature of this meeting."

"I can't. I'm stuck on tepid."

"Then for now we'll have to work with tepid."

"Marian, I didn't come all this way to do tepid."

"So do something about it."

"What can I do? And what are we doing in this alley anyway?"

"Do you want to go home?"

"To Tel Aviv?"

"Or to Saint Madera Sanctus."

"What's that?"

"A small ruined monastery north of Lisbon."

"Why there of all places?"

"I don't know . . ."

"But before you said we only had one home."

"We do have only one home."

"So why would we go to the ruins of a monastery north of Lisbon?"

"You like those kinds of places."

"Marian, what is this? What's the meaning of this conversation? Why can't I get through to you?"

"Maybe it has to do with that thing. . . ."

"What thing?"

"With the aliases' funny little toy. I have one of those, too."

"An alias?"

"No, a godget. But you're far braver than I am."

"I'm not brave at all."

"You're right. You're a coward. First the gun, then the button, and now we have a problem."

"I pressed the button?"

"You were never very good at dealing. Instead of finding someone else, you went off and committed suicide. . . ."

"In order to be with you, Marian. I can't believe that it's hard for you to understand that I shot myself in order to be with you."

"Then why didn't you listen to the old man?"

"I didn't?"

"He warned you and you still opted for seven over three and now you'll never be with me."

"But that's impossible. You're here."

"Only because you called me. You remember what the Chinese man said?"

"The Chinese . . . ?"

"She's here but she's there, and it's hard to say in which world. So, are you satisfied now?"

"Wait, but what does that mean? Marian, what does that mean? You're part of my world. Where are you going? You can't leave. . . ."

"I'm not going." She drifted out of the alley, leaving a smiling Marian in a velvet blue dress in her place.

Ben looked agape at the human inheritance opposite him, the painfully familiar compound of tissue, tendons, and skin devoid of the soul that filled it with essence, and extended a hand to the statuesque nape of her neck. In his fury, wishing to wring the smooth neck that only masqueraded as the one belonging to his love, he noticed her lips move without voice. He strained to decipher her words: "Cowards die many times before their deaths; the valiant never taste of death but once."

Animated as a child, he called out, "I know where that's from, Marian. *Julius Caesar*! *Julius Caesar*!"

The duplicated Marian smiled at him, as if confirming that he had passed the test, brought her lips to his ear, and whispered, "Next time be careful when your finger touches the button. Now get up and do what you must."

Ben woke from his unexpected nap more vivacious than he had been in months, knowing that he had been blessed with a second chance. He bounded out of the alley and onto the city's main streets, passing three foul-tempered witches, three troubled kings, six Rosencrantzes and Guildensterns, five savvy merchants, and a complex prince putting on a juggling show with three skulls, before he recognized the big sign at the end of a side street, advertising the establishment beneath it, in moving neon letters, as the place for spirits and socializing. Aside from the amusing sign and the upbeat music, which even from afar was obviously high-quality digital, the wooden tavern with the rotting thatch roof and the knobby door made clear that time had stood still here for hundreds of years.

The first thought that crossed his mind when he walked inside was that if the clock stopped at a certain time, then it must have been at happy hour. The splendid display of inebriation included off-key ballads accompanied by hiccups and belches and other sounds emitted from who knows where, giddy sliding competitions through a soupy puddle of ale, friendly wrestling matches that got out of hand, and several couples who failed the test of self restraint and carried out their affairs for all to see. Apprehensively, he sought out his grandparents, and between declining an offer from a drunk woman who was rude in body and soul and dodging the upper half of a bottle flying over his head, he weaved his way to a single table, alongside which, radiant as ever, sat his straight-backed grandmother, immersed in unpleasant thoughts, judging by the deterring gravity on her face as she sipped methodically from the archaic glass of wine.

Ben didn't wait for an invitation, coming toward her with his arms spread wide. "Grandma Rosie! Grandma Rosie!"

The old woman turned her veiled look toward him, smiled warmly, rose from the rotted wooden bench, and embraced him. "Oh my dear, you've been so sorely missed. We've been pining for you . . ."

She planted a fragrant kiss on his cheek and then scrutinized him at length. "Let me look at you. God, Nosey wasn't exaggerating at all, you've really developed quite the physique over the years. . . ."

"You haven't done too bad either. You're as beautiful as ever. Tell me, how's your journey going? You must be enjoying every second of it. . . ."

She sat down and clasped his arm with surprising force. "Absolutely, honey, one of the most fascinating adventures we've ever had. Your perspective changes entirely and you learn more about family genetics than all the books about Mendel and his pea plants combined. Did you know, for instance, that your grandfather and his grandfather are identical as two drops of water? Not to mention your great-great-grandfather's mother. Totally nuts. Buried three husbands before getting pregnant. Two of them are still in love with her and prefer to ignore her fondness for poison. And now this incredible city. What timing we had, it's just unbelievable. But I'm sure you already noticed that."

"You mean the actors swarming all over this place?" All of a sudden he froze and mumbled, "How did I miss that? I've been so wrapped in nonsense that I didn't put two and two together . . . it's 1616 . . . and the city's alive with actors . . . on the multi an actor told me everyone was headed to the most important audition in history . . . He lives here, right? I mean he died in . . . and he must have written something new, otherwise I wouldn't be witnessing all of this Shakespearemania." He bit his finger in thought.

"What are you thinking about, Benji?" She caressed his hand. "Why do you look so disturbed?"

"I just had a thought. You know who was crazy about him, and Nosey told me you had some information about her."

"Let's leave this revolting bacchanalia and go talk somewhere else," she ordered. She got up quickly, stomping across the squawking room and slamming the door on the way out.

Ben caught up with her, a concerned look on his face. "Grandma, what's wrong? Why are you . . . ?

She shook her head from side to side, sighed for a long while, hooked her arm through his, and commanded in a whisper, "Come!"

Ben complied silently and, to his surprise, he found that she was leading him back to the alley that he'd left a little over an hour ago. "Grandma, what are we doing here?"

"This is one of the few quiet spots in this entire city. Here we can talk in peace."

Ben nodded and the two walked in silence until they reached the two familiar walls. "Well?" he spurred her. "What did you find? What kind of news did you come across?"

Rosie looked up and caressed his questioning face. "Ben, I just want you to always remember that you're a lucky man. I haven't known many people who have shared such love with someone else."

"I know, Grandma. And in all honesty this preface doesn't bode well, does it? Don't answer me. I know the answer to that, too."

"What do you know?" she asked, her forehead folded in suspicion.

"I know Marian's not here."

"How do you know?"

"I heard the Announcer call her name while I was on the express, and that, along with a few other reasons that I shouldn't go into now, paint a pretty full picture, so don't worry about telling me whatever you came across. I didn't for a second believe that I'd find her in this city, despite the unavoidable conclusion—Shakespeare . . . Marian . . ."

"Yes," Rosie smiled mournfully, "you're right." Several seconds later a bitter smile flitted across her face and she mumbled tartly, "The unavoidable conclusion, I couldn't have put it better myself."

"Grandma, what are you talking about?"

She accosted him in a loud voice, "Why did you wait, Ben? Why did you have to wait so long?"

The stunned grandchild remained speechless for several minutes. "Grandma, why are you asking me this kind of question? By now it's clear that you were mistaken when you told Nosey that you had information about her. She just died tonight. I have no idea what happened, but . . ."

"Ben, Ben, you have no idea what you're talking about . . . you don't know . . ." Her voice cracked.

"So then maybe tell me what you're talking about? I came all the way here for a scrap of information about my wife and now you're playing home theater with me. What did you find out? Tell me so that I can carry on."

"Okay," she said, looking him in the eye. "Just remember it was your grandfather's idea. We deliberated for a long time about whether to tell you and in the end he threw his weight down hard on the side of divulging. He said you'd never forgive us if you found out some other way."

She exhaled long and slow and placed her tender hand on his head, her delicate fingers massaging his scalp. "It's not so simple, my dear, not in the slightest. We're very much alike, Benji, much more so than most people think. Both of us took the reins into our own hands, only one of us managed to stop the carriage while the other lost control. Through no fault of his own. Through no one's fault . . ."

"Grandma, would you please lay the metaphors aside for a second and tell me why you were thinking of not telling me whatever it is you know? Or is that answer self-evident? You wanted to shield me from the pain of knowing?"

"We weren't sure what was preferable, to hide the truth and leave your hope intact or . . ."

"She's with someone else. She's in love with someone else?" he guessed in a frosted voice.

"Don't be ridiculous, honey," she laughed hoarsely, "she's not with anyone else. Not at all. Except for the mother."

"The mother? You mean her biological mother? They met?" His eyes showed reinvigorated hope.

"Yes. We bumped into her by accident. Day before yesterday."

"You saw Marian?" Ben screeched.

"No, no, not Marian. Her mother. Not far from the theater where they're doing the auditions. We were curious to see why so many people were milling around the entrance, and we spoke with a few of them. She walked by with some shopping bags, apparently on the way back from the grocery store, and just as we turned to leave, she walked toward us, and within a few seconds it was clear we had piqued her interest. She froze, stared at us, and once she recomposed herself she came over and said she knew who we were. She recognized us from the tapes, Marian's tapes. She literally begged us for information about you. Said if we know anything we should make contact, even if it's years down the road. We said that actually we did have information and that you were here, in the Other World. At first she had trouble believing it, but then she broke down crying and begged us to tell you that she had to see you. She must have repeated the sentence five times: 'Tell him I have to see him.' We promised we'd tell you as soon as possible, and Moses asked if we could go see Marian. She said she didn't think it was a good idea, and then she told us where she was."

"Grandma, where's Marian? Where the hell is she?"

"I'm sorry, Ben. I think it's best that you hear it from her, the mother. She knows exactly what happened, she's involved in this more than anyone else, and she's waiting for you. She specifically asked us not to tell you a thing about Marian's whereabouts before you come and speak to her, and we think she's right on insisting on that."

"Listen to what your grandmother says, she's a smart woman," a warm voice proclaimed behind him. Ben turned around and disappeared between the lanky arms of his grandfather. "Sorry I got held up, Benji, I had to say good-bye to a few people before we hit the road again."

Ben buried his face in his grandfather's shoulder and was willing to die in that consoling stance, without any future complications, the forthcoming sorrow, the responsibility inherent in loving a person by choice. He'd never before seen his grandmother writhe like that through the thickets of her emotions, picking her words with care, fishing with unusual fastidiousness for the most tactful terms, clarifying with every painstaking phrase that the worst was yet to come. Never before had he heard his grandfather so silent, as though he'd purposely come late as a pretence for an apology, something small, laconically delivered, after which he could fall silent and exchange desolate glances with his knowing wife. Never before had he witnessed such a frightful show of com-

37

The Unavoidable Conclusion

Two hours. No more. That's the amount of time that passed from the moment the overwrought righter arrived on the doorstep of the woman with the answers till he left her apartment, pale and shaken. Two hours is also all it took to travel to Marian's residence. All the missing tiles of the mysterious mosaic of disappearance had been drawn out of hiding, hovering in the air in the form of spliced sentences before finally touching down and merging into a cohesive picture. Half-formed questions, quarters of answers, jumps in time, appalled interruptions, onerous silences, tears aplenty. And this is another way to describe the most loaded conversation he'd ever had: so much information in so little time. He had never before guessed how dense the truth was, and at the same time, how horrifyingly simple. He marshaled all of his powers as a storyteller when, sitting on the surging multi, he retold the tale to himself on the way to 1700.

A clear and continuous chronology. That's the secret. Along with a grain of logic. Because were he to connect two simple facts, the emptiness that filled his wife upon death and her admiration for the greatest of playwrights, he would have deduced that she had moved at quite an early stage to the faraway city that her platonic lover and his adoring fans called home—an unavoidable conclusion. That, alongside other, far less obvious conclusions, ones that cunningly escaped his attention on account of their improbability, such as the identity of the biological mother. When she opened the door, smiled, and said she'd waited for him, he felt a slight queasiness. He expected to meet a complete stranger, a woman who just happened to have birthed his wife. Soon enough he discovered that her short stature and the soft dreaminess that radiated from her face were merely a trap laid by first impression for the casual gazer. The moment he cleared the angelic hurdle of the glazed turquoise eyes, the naturally plush red lips, the high cheekbones, the lofty forehead, the velvety golden mane that framed the refined beauty, he succeeded in finding countless little cracks in her demeanor that spoke to the very opposite: During the course of their conversation, she will bow her head on more than one occasion and suddenly her eyes will rise up and peek at him in panicky suspicion, bordering on paranoia, and when she will hush and listen to him speak, an anxious nerve pulsating near her ear will mar her polite countenance with angst, and she will slump her lips into an expression of disappointment or commiseration even when neither is necessary, and she will stroke her concave chin with her stubby fingernails until her skin is raw and red.

Even before being exposed to her body language, he tried distancing himself from the clammy feeling her looks evoked, as though he knew the woman. He was sure he had seen her over the course of the past two weeks, certain that it was only in this world that he had come across her. She shook his hand and put an end to his ignorance with four syllables. He felt blessed relief when he understood that he hadn't been wrong, she was the woman he'd seen in the park outside the multilingual labs on the day he went looking for Marian, the woman into whose arms his child returned after he failed in his attempt to cling to his father, the woman he had seen outside the café, breaking a bottle over the head of the lying Belgian, and if he was unable to see the invisible line that connected the two formerly disjointed points, then the queasiness in his stomach was only churned by the sound of her name, Catherine Dumas. Hidden blades poked at his diaphragm when he smiled at her amiably and said he was pleased to meet her. A second unavoidable conclusion flashed, disappeared, and reemerged behind one of the creaking doors in his mind. Was it possible that Robert was . . . and then she commanded his straying train of thought, saying matter-of-factly, "Marian was right. He does look like a little you. No doubt the boy inherited the inquisitive eyes from his father."

He almost yelled at her not to talk about the child right now; soon, but not right now. He wanted to get the facts in order, the chain of events that brought him to the apartment of the ex-con who had filled her nemesis with lead, but she had already brought up the kid. The Mad Hop was right. A small syllogism that proves her exclusive identity—had she not been the legal guardian, she would not have gotten custody of . . . but where was he? He sought out the last of the Mendelssohn offspring, perking up his ears and listening for childlike rustling behind one of the far doors of the apartment, perhaps a jubilant sparkle of laughter or even an irate wail, piercing the counterfeit calm imposed by John Ward's madrigals warbling in the background.

"Henri's at a friend's house. He'll be back in the evening," she cooed in her effeminate voice.

"Henri?" he asked, clearing his throat, finding it difficult to hide his dissatisfaction with the name.

"In my opinion it's better than 9562300483371, no?" She bit her lip hesitantly and the possessive anger that had surged inside of him at the sound of the name was replaced by gratitude. All the grit and grime she labored to conceal behind the softness and the calm evaporated at the mention of the child's name, and he understood that the fetus Marian had lost five years ago had become Catherine's only solace. He figured that the grandmother and the grandson had come to 1616 on the heels of the lost mother, even though he had no idea how Catherine had managed to find her new address.

Catherine laughed and corrected him. "How could I have come looking for my daughter if I didn't even know she was dead? When I learned about the aliases and the right to adopt close kin, had there been such, I took my chance, and when I found out I had a grandson I proceeded with the understanding that it would be years before she . . . after all, she's so young . . ."

Then she told him about the meeting. The one that took place far from Shakespeare's hometown.

Three months after adopting the child, she brought him in for an interview in Aliastown 1996—a common practice put in place in order to assess the child's satisfaction with his or her legal guardian. After passing the evaluation, Catherine decided to treat her grandson to a spur-of-the-moment trip to March 2000 to visit one of his best friends from their "greenhouse" days, a child who was also being raised by his grandmother. The kids played for hours while the grandmothers chatted, till Catherine peeked at her godget and said it was time to go. Henri's protestations got him another hour of play with his redheaded alias friend. When they left, Catherine promised they would come back again soon.

On their way to the multi-wheel that would take them home, they passed a long line of people waiting for the Vie-deo machine, and the curious child lagged, looking them over as his grandmother urged him to carry on. Catherine took his hand and marched quickly in the direction of the multi stop, when all of a sudden the child turned his head, released his grip without any warning, and sprinted madly toward the line, disregarding her calls, and, like a creature in a trance, galloped toward the only woman who didn't notice him and fell upon her heedlessly, clinging to her leg with devout longing. The woman was so startled by the intensity of the surprise attack, that for the first few seconds she merely stared at the child without opening her mouth to speak. Catherine was far more shaken when she recognized the genetic attraction her grandchild had experienced when she first met him. Only the child, who didn't understand a thing, showed no signs of alarm, emitting a long cry of admiration that brought bashful smiles to the agitated faces of those waiting in line. The woman looked around helplessly, trying, in vain, to delicately pry the child away. The boy wrapped both his hands around her leg and pressed his smiling face to her side. Catherine was sure she was headed toward another heart attack, more severe than the one that sent her to the Other World, when she asked Henri to behave like a good boy and tried to get him to relinquish his grip on her astonished daughter's leg.

Then their eyes met. The ignorant daughter and the knowing mother. Catherine couldn't control the urge to caress her daughter's cheek, and when her trembling fingers almost touched her daughter's face, Marian withdrew and pushed the child away with all her might, finally free of the passionate touches of the two strangers who looked at her with open wonder. Feeling cornered by their stares, Marian left her place in line and began walking away, not daring to turn back and face the strange pair's inscrutable demands. Only once Catherine regained her composure and called her daughter by name three times did she slow to a halt. The two trotted toward her, the grandmother trying to quell the child's ardor with her tenacious grip and the grandson doing his best to wiggle free, not understanding why she insisted on denying him this inexplicable pleasure, as Marian fixed them with the frightened stare of a woman on the run.

The silence could have gone on for hours had Catherine not shaken her hand and identified herself. "Hello, Marian. I'm Catherine Dumas, your mother, and this is Henri, your son."

Ben believed Catherine when she said that Marian burst out laughing a few seconds after the dramatic announcement, certain that he wouldn't have acted any differently had he been in her shoes. Marian asked the woman what weird soap opera she'd stepped out of, and when Catherine repeated her earlier statement, this time in a more forceful voice, her daughter said she was "demented" and asked that she stop bothering her. Catherine maintained her composure, pointed at the long line in front of the Vie-deo machine, and said in an even tone, "I guess we barged in on you just as you were about to take out the tapes of your life. I'm sorry. Go back to your spot on line. We won't bother you anymore. Just do the two . . . the three of us a favor and watch the first tape, the one that begins with your birth. Remember my face. Imprint it on your mind. And if you want, call me."

Marian did not voice any resistance when her mother took her godget and pressed her thumbprint into its memory. Catherine looked her full in the face and in a crushed voice added, "Please, don't disappear. I lost you once already . . ."

Ben noted, "Were it not for Henri you could have passed her right by on the street without knowing she was your daughter."

Catherine shook her head vigorously, every muscle in her face revolting against his comment. "Absolutely not. As I said, there's no way I would have let her go a second time."

"But how would you have known . . . ?" He fell silent at the sight of her burning turquoise irises. Now and again she sipped from the tall glass of water on the edge of the table, unfurling for him the story of the young theology student in the sixties in Paris, just a few years before the uprising, in which she did not take part on account of the disastrous turn life had handed her. Robert. Her heinous roommate. The failed actor who cut and pasted freely from the truth, threading a false string through its entire length. Like the fact that he never made it on time to auditions because he used to party till the wee hours and that, when he did make it, he was always ushered out the door unceremoniously on account of his poor skills. Like the fact that he used to drink himself into a stupor and then crawl to her room and beg until she'd prod him away from the door with a broomstick and swear she'd rent elsewhere if he did not leave. Like the fact that when they met, he swore up and down that he loved men, convincing her to move in with him, taking advantage of the innocence of the young woman who had run away from her drunken father's house. Like the fact that one time, when she was cramming for a final, she forgot the key to her room outside the door and only remembered it late at night, unaware that the charming scoundrel had already seized the opportunity and made a copy for himself. Like the fact that, several days later, Robert came home one evening drunk as a sailor and decided it was high time to demand his due, broke into her room while she was in the shower, and hid behind her drapes, pouncing on her like a man possessed not long after she'd fallen asleep. By the time she woke up and managed to get her bearings, it was too late. Like the fact that she carried the results of the brutal rape in her womb for nine awful months, during the course of which she lost her job caring for an old sickly priest, no longer able to hide her pregnancy. Robert was sent to jail, and she swore never to reveal to him what he had done. He had no knowledge whatsoever of the twins she bore in the late days of her final innocent spring. The girl who was vehemently opposed to abortions was not examined once during her gestation period and was accordingly shocked when she found herself lying on the delivery room bed, sweaty and in pain, listening to the midwife tell her with a wink and a whisper, "We've got another one on the way out. . . ." Her initial shock turned to a muffled shriek when one of the nurses put the twins in her arms and she noticed the tiny mark on her firstborn's chest, the unmistakable perfect star, the badge of dishonor Robert had bequeathed to his daughter.

Catherine knew she would not be able to shoulder the financial burden of raising two daughters and so, during the first month of the girls' lives, she sold all she had, hoping to make the impossible happen, praying day and night for divine intervention in her predicament. The miracle refused to materialize, and when she went to see her only kin, her fanatical father chased her off his property, calling her a whore.

Catherine poured herself a fresh glass of water, gulped it down thirstily, and continued, this time at a quicker pace. She grew impatient when telling of the hardest decision of her life—separating the twins so that she could raise one of them. As soon as she had decided to give one of the girls up, she knew she would keep the one bearing the telltale mark as an act of self-flagellation. Each time she looked at the mark she would be reminded of her terrible deed. The lump sum of money she received went toward ensuring some financial security for the "marked" one. The random meeting in the park with the strange man who answered to the name Arthur was, as far as she was concerned, a sign from above, and she insisted on one single rule—that the adopting parents not change the child's name, even though the transparent nature of her own deceit was readily apparent to her: If both babies answered to the same name and were outwardly identical, perhaps then, with time, she would come to believe she had birthed but a single child. Deep in her heart, she hoped the two sisters would never meet, and cried for weeks on end after the deal was done. And maybe her insistence was merely the result of her desire to leave her small mark on the two-month-old baby girl who was taken from her in the middle of a glorious, sun-dappled day. Six months later she found a job and took the baby along to the apartments she cleaned sixteen hours a day, but by eighteen months she enrolled her in day care, preferring to keep the glowing baby out of the filthy apartments. When one of the apartment owners grew overly interested in her, she knew she had no choice, that she'd never let history repeat itself, and so, in a back alley deal, she acquired a gun, disgusted by the thought that she carried a weapon in her bag and, doubly so, by the reason she was forced to carry it. Over the years she vigorously rebuffed the advances of many men who were not indifferent to her beauty and, to her dying day, she kept herself apart from them.

When her daughter asked about her father, her mother said he had died many years before, nipping in the bud any talk of her private nightmare. She spent her best years raising the sole ray of light in her life, who grew up to be a blinding sun—Marian surpassed all expectations: an exemplary daughter, a brilliant student, a journalist, and an independent woman. With the loving daughter's encouragement, the proud mother went back to school in her mid-forties, stooped yet curious and determined to complete what she had started years ago, refusing to allow life to foil her plans again. Upon receiving her masters, seven years later, the dean of the department called her to his office and said he had read her thesis, "The Individual's Relationship with God: The Most Perilous Love Story Of All," and that he had found it fascinating. He suggested that she expand it into a book, so that she would be able to continue what she had begun with her modest work—telling the life story of a simple person, from the perspective of God. At first she was startled by the pretentious smell wafting off such a vexing undertaking, but after further consideration and with the help of the old professor she came to the conclusion that as a believer she could not afford to pass up the opportunity to examine her life from the divine perspective.

Three years later, when her daughter informed her that she intended to surgically remove the birthmark on her chest, Catherine asked to accompany her, eager to witness her daughter "change" into the daughter she'd never known and to pretend that she was meeting her for the first time, pushing from her mind the stupid fear that without the birthmark her daughter would lose her identity as the Marian she had known and loved. The last man she ever dreamed of seeing in the small clinic was the one who dominated her mind ever since she had helped wheel her daughter into the OR. And when he opened the door, without thinking of who might be behind it, she lost the power of clear thought. His eyes filled with wonder as his lips stretched into a smile. The repulsive grin pushed her hand into her bag. She drew the gun, took aim, and squeezed the trigger. Robotically. With no feeling whatsoever. Afterwards, when her stunned daughter questioned her motives, she told her a half truth. Sometimes that's enough. Only her cellmate, dear Sandrine, knew the whole truth, and on her deathbed, Catherine made her swear she would find her lost daughter and bring the two sisters together. When Ben asked her why she waited till her final moments to reveal her secret, she shrugged and looked at the floor gloomily, and when he asked about the book, she managed a partial smile and said, "Forget that, it's just meaningless nonsense."

The unavoidable conclusion. The Charlatan who met the Mad Hop is in love with a different Marian, the one who's living unperturbed in a faraway world. Ben couldn't comprehend the notion of two Marians. One of them was a world in and of itself, and now he discovered there was a second, an assuredly fascinating alternative. He toyed with the idea of a different Marian, her expressions foreign, her personality different, the Marian he never met, and perhaps he was mistaken and the similarity between the two was far greater than he suspected.

"I'm guessing that at some point you heard from her . . . my Marian . . ."

"Yes. A month after the incident at the Vie-deo machine. She wanted to meet. In her hometown. 1616. I didn't need to mull it over. I took the little one and set out. She lived six blocks from here, on King Lear Boulevard."

"Lived?" he asked with mounting fright, feeling the nausea creep back into his belly. "In other words, she left that apartment, too? Moved somewhere else?"

"Marian left her apartment two months ago. You must understand, Ben, things have happened . . . in effect, I was the one who convinced her to leave . . . there was no other choice. . . ."

"What are you talking about? Why did you convince her to leave?"

For the first time since the beginning of their conversation, tears pooled in her eyes and the stoic façade she tried to maintain between herself and the events that had shaped her death dissolved fast. Her steady voice lost its clarity, and the clenching feeling that crept into her throat truncated some of her words. "You can surely imagine how difficult it was for her to meet her mother and son . . . she had watched the first tape . . . she recognized me . . . and maybe it was the shock that prevented her from noticing the likeness between Henri and his father, back then, by the Vie-deo machine. . . . It was not an easy meeting . . . not easy at all . . . I wanted to embrace her, to touch her, to make her understand that I'm here forever, but I didn't dare . . . she was distant . . . cold . . . I don't blame her, I know . . . but she hardly showed any warmth even toward the kid . . . again, I thought it had to do with the shock . . . she shook his hand and smiled a bit, but nothing more than that, as though she were on guard . . . even a month later, when I let her know we were moving there, in other words, here, to 1616, in order to be close to her, she reacted strangely. . . . I thought she'd be happy . . . after all, from what I'd gathered we were the only family members she'd met . . . and you know how hard it is to find alternate apartments in the Other World . . . but Marian didn't seem excited in the least . . . she mumbled something like 'welcome' and went back to her affairs . . . I tried to gain her trust by any means . . . I was willing to do anything for her to forgive me, and in fact we began to meet more often, but only later did I realize that I don't really interest her . . . nor does Henri. . . ."

"The child didn't interest her?" Ben asked in wonder.

"You, Ben, you were all that interested her. Even Shakespeare lost most of his appeal when she wasn't chosen to be part of the casting team for his new play. And that was in the beginning. Before we really got to know each other."

"But you said that she said that he has my eyes . . . that didn't . . . ?"

"To the contrary, Ben, to the contrary. The few times she looked him in the eye she shivered and burst out crying. She said it was too much, that she simply couldn't deal with those eyes. When I asked if she'd like to watch the child for a day or two, she looked at me like I was out of my mind. . . . Later on, we'd come by her place once a week in order to get her out of the apartment, but it was impossible . . . she preferred to stay indoors and watch the tapes. . . . Sometimes I joined her and watched some snippets of your life together . . . I thought I'd get to know her better that way, but she made it very clear that my presence only bothered her. I wasn't upset with her, but I admit it was rather hard to understand her . . . up until that terrible afternoon two months ago . . ."

"What happened two months ago?"

"Henri did something a little bit . . ."

The doorbell rang twice. Catherine leapt out of her chair, ran to the door, and opened it with a giggle. The woman on the other side of the door wrapped her in a tight hug and the two swayed back and forth, laughing, crying, and laughing again. Catherine took her friend's hand and introduced her. "Ben, I'd like you to meet Sandrine Montesquieu, the friend I was telling you about. . . ."

Sandrine came over to him and shook his hand warmly, exchanging amused glances with her beaming friend. Ben was astounded by the sudden swing in Catherine's mood, as though new life were breathed into her as soon as the visitor arrived. He assumed that the two must share something so significant that it dwarfed all he had heard up until now. The two of them sat on the couch and held hands, blabbing away, as though all of the world's sorrow had been muted, as though the room were their old cell, as though they weren't sitting opposite an appalled son-in-law waiting for the most important response of all. But it was slow in coming. For many a minute he sat there and listened as they relived the old days together, speaking in their own indecipherable code, bringing up pearls from the ocean of grief the two of them had crossed, oblivious to their surroundings. Ben was envious of their remarkable ability to shut him out, and it brought to mind all the times he had done much the same with his wife, until they were brought back to the here and now with a barbed remark.

"I know you have a lot to talk about . . . and I don't want to disturb you, if you could just, please, give me the address . . . ," he stammered.

Catherine looked at him with a silly grin and apologized. "I am so sorry. I totally forgot myself there for a moment. I'd offer to invite you for dinner . . ."

"That's alright. I'm sure we'll be seeing each other soon enough."

"I'm sure we will," she said, ripping the corner off a newspaper he hadn't noticed. She jotted down a few words, handed him the note, and whispered, "Be patient, please. And I beg you, do not give up. You've come this far, you can't lose hope."

Ben nodded and looked at the slip of paper only once they had exchanged thumbprints and parted ways. Since then his lips had rehearsed what had been written hundreds of times, much like the actor who sat next to him on the express multi: "October 1700. First right from the central station, second left, then second right—Worldly Rest."

38

In the Dark

PMD—Post-Mortem Depression. That's what the alias in charge of the Incurable Disease ward called Marian's condition. Three consonants that encompassed the full measure of her postmortem decline: the initial shock, which almost all of the deceased experience upon arrival in the Other World; the illusory acclimatization stage; the primary shock stage; the denial stage; the sinking stage; the frozen stage. Or, in other words, as the alias put it as he smoothed his frizzy beard, the inability to come to terms with the withdrawal from the previous world and the trenchant refusal to accept the new world as the only framework of existence, or, even, as *a* framework for existence. "Ironically," 270 added, smiling generously, "the two population groups most susceptible to this worrying mental illness are diametrically opposed:

"The larger group is comprised of those who suffered their entire lives and mistakenly believed that death would put an end to their existence, and so, they cannot deal with the fact that the Other World extends onward toward eternity, and rather than rejoice at the second chance they've been given, they defiantly reject that reality, treating it like an inexplicable but certainly malicious plan designed to compound their disgust at their existence. Since they so abhor the misleading state of their being, they embark on a silent campaign against the 'puppeteers' behind the deceitful existential conspiracy, are ensnared in it, and thereby avoid the final, seemingly inexorable measure. They feel cheated and betrayed, left to dangle against their will between the uselessness of their current situation and the uselessness inherent in an act that will not produce the desired results. On the fringes of that group is an especially strange subgroup of frighteningly realistic folks who simply refuse to believe in the existence of the Other World and all of its fantastic elements, insisting instead on trying to convince everyone who crosses their path of its overwhelming inconceivability. Most of the time, these folks come to Worldly Rest after they've compulsively destroyed several stolen godgets and attempted, in vain, to print currency bills in order to 'get some reality flowing through the veins of this grotesque universe.'

"The second group, which, statistically speaking, represents only one percent of the larger group, is comprised of people who experienced great joy in their lifetimes and in death have come to realize the good with which they were endowed, and subsequently, have trouble divorcing themselves from the past. The transition to a new world is, from their point of view, an unwanted new beginning and, consequently, they show nothing but a keen contempt for the forced grappling with death, which stripped them of their joie de vivre. These patients claw through their personal biographies and sanctify the masterpiece that began with their birth and ended with their infinitesimal death. As opposed to the Disappointed-By-Death patients, who suffer from active depression as a result of their paranoid frame of mind, the Formerly Joyous patients sink into a passive depression that prevents them from extricating themselves from the imprisoning trance of their memories. That being said, one should exercise caution around them, as they are the most dangerous and can react in an extreme manner if they feel threatened." The expert added sympathetically, "This latter group is the one to which you wife belongs."

Ben smiled. "Marian would never react as extremely as you say. She's not a violent or dangerous woman. She is the most . . ."

The expert cut him short. "Marian almost killed her own child."

"Liar."

The alias grinned. "I wish. In another world this story would have ended terribly."

"What story?"

"Your wife, Mr. Mendelssohn, is addicted to the tapes of her life. She steps away for a moment, goes to the kitchen, the child stays by himself in the living room and looks for something to amuse himself with. He plays with the buttons on the Vie-deo machine. He erases a week. He erases the wedding and the honeymoon. That's what the kind grandmother told me. Marian returns to the living room and discovers what the child has done. She loses it. Goes wild. A week of her life, and not just any week, has been stolen from her. She pounces on him and starts to strangle him with all her might. The grandmother finds the daughter in an indisputable position. She understands that the woman needs help. Marian does not make a scene when we send a special multi-wheel to her house, along with four orderlies who ask that she come with them. 'The tapes'–that's all she says, that's all she cares about. She takes them with her; she doesn't mind moving to Worldly Rest. After all, everything that happens after death isn't really happening."

"And how does she explain the week she's lost from the tape?" Ben asked, shocked at his own equanimity just a moment after learning about Marian's sickening metamorphosis.

The alias played with his facial hair again, this time tugging on his beard with a gentle, tranquil motion. "A technical glitch. On the other hand, she remembers what happened in a distant part of her memory. The experience is rather tricky, Mr. Mendelssohn. She didn't forget that she strangled the child, but the fact was insignificant as far as she was concerned. As I said, anything that does not pertain to the past is rendered superfluous and worthless to her. The fact that she met her biological mother in our world, the fact that she found her only son in our world, the fact that he erased the week and the fact that she reacted with fury, all these facts are immaterial, relegated to the far reaches of her brain and even there are doubtlessly buried under mountains of exhaustively chewed-over information. A colleague of mine once described this phenomenon as Regurgitating. And that, in essence, is what all passive PMD patients do. Introspection, followed by conclusions, is not why they watch their lives. They simply live their lives anew, as spectators."

"And that's why this ward goes by that awful name? Do you really think Marian's depression is incurable?"

"Post-Mortem Depression is like no other depression. Unfortunately, none of the fashionable potions psychiatrists prescribe these days work on the human body in our world."

"So what exactly are you doing here?" Ben snapped. "In what way are you and the other members of your staff helping her out of this terrible depression?"

"We let her be."

"Excuse me?"

"As opposed to other mental illnesses, which can be cured or alleviated with games, discussions, drills, and a whole host of other therapeutic means, PMD is best not tampered with, and believe me when I say I speak from experience. Aside from the futility of struggling frantically to make conversation with patients who are divorced from reality, even if they manage to break free from the prison of their memories for a short while, they will view any violation of their privacy as an impingement and will only crawl deeper into their warm shell of estrangement. History has taught us that the best way to deal with them is to simply let them be, and, to my delight, I can report that some seventy-five percent of patients from the second group show a full recovery."

"When you say recovery . . ."

"I mean accepting this world and coming to terms with the final separation from the former one. I mean being born again, and pardon my contradiction in terms."

"Why then is the ward called 'incurable diseases'?"

"Because we do not take any invasive measures. From our perspective, as a medical institution, we do not offer any cures, aside from the necessary solitude."

"But how does one get better if the sum total of the treatment you offer is zero? I'm sorry, but I'm just having a hard time understanding what prevents a depressed individual from merely wallowing in his misery. I mean, isn't that one of the great and infamous temptations of those with suicidal or self-pitying tendencies, and don't for a second think that my wife fits into either of those pigeonholes, but . . ."

"I know, Mr. Mendelssohn. On one of the few times I happened to visit her in her room, I saw a few scenes of the two of you together, and it's all too clear to me that she was an energetic and altogether impressive woman—further evidence of how dangerous this disease is. And still, there is no better way to treat those afflicted by it. For all intents and purposes, the dying space we give them is unlimited. You want to rot in front of the TV screen for forty years? Go right ahead. And regarding your question about curing patients, I know how ludicrous this might sound, but, in the end, they just get sick of it. They get sick of their existence in the bubble they've so meticulously cultivated and they just pop it and go free. We had an eighty-nine-year-old PMD patient here who sat like a sloth in front of the TV for seventy-four years . . . seventy-four years she refused to move, and then, one fine morning, she just got up and left."

"Maybe she went somewhere else to punch in a seven over three?"

The alias smiled compassionately. "If there's one thing PMD patients don't believe in, it's death."

Ben nodded in understanding. "The worst figure relates to the time that passes from the diagnosis till recovery. Can you say why it takes so long?"

"Of course. In most cases they're so enchanted by their ability to watch their cherished lives, that during the first two years or so they skip through the tapes and watch particularly moving moments, the milestones, if you will, of their existence. Once they've seen the special moments enough times, they sink into a painstakingly detailed documentation of their lives, watching it all in real time."

"In real time?"

"Yes. You lived forty years, then you spend four decades of your death w–"

"Have you ever considered destroying the tapes? Just putting an unflinching wall in their face?"

"Mr. Mendelssohn, you've been in this room for ten minutes. We've been living here generations. Any idea that comes to your mind has already been tested, evaluated, and reevaluated. For your information, the destruction of the tapes is a crime if perpetrated by anyone other than the owner of the tapes, and the temporary confiscation of said tapes for healing purposes has led to nothing more than the aggravation of the divorce between the patient and their surroundings."

"And what about me?"

"Excuse me?"

"I'm sure I could help heal Marian. After all, I know her better than anyone else."

"You know the former Marian better than anyone. As for the new incarnation, allow me to be skeptical about the depth of your knowledge and utility of your meeting her."

"I don't believe she's changed so profoundly."

"Because, like her, conceptually, you're still stuck in the previous world."

"I think you're mistaken."

"Mr. Mendelssohn, we both know you have nothing but the best intentions. Let's just hope you were wise enough to prepare for the worst. . . ."

"The worst is already behind me. From here on out things can only get better."

"You insist on seeing her, then?"

"Did you think otherwise?"

"I thought I might deter you from making this mistake."

"Mistake? What's mistaken about truly wanting to see your wife?"

"The refusal. The stubbornness. The childishness. The lack of comprehension. The ignorance. The woman you will see is not your wife. As far as she is concerned, death has rendered you absolute strangers."

"And you're trying to protect me from the chilling confrontation with the naked truth?"

"That's somewhat parabolically put, but not too far off the mark. If you want my advice, I say go back whence you've come and try to understand that there's no use in this romantic nonsense. I have full respect for your surging martyrdom but it is fundamentally gratuitous. You are absolutely unaware of the dimensions of the ensuing disappointment, and that's leaving aside the cliché about a hundred years being like a drop in the sea of eternity. Do you really expect that if and when she recovers she will leave this place and come running straight into your arms, weeping with heartbreaking longing? Do yourself a favor and imagine your reaction when she looks you over coldly and says you are part of the past, like the tapes she destroyed, like this place. The damage you will bring on yourself will be immeasurably greater. All I ask is that you take a clear-eyed look at the whole picture."

"You don't have such a great view of the whole picture yourself. After all, you base your entire prognosis on other stories and are dangerously close to a criminally crude generalization when you ask me to leave without having seen my wife."

270 sighed with learned desperation. "People always make the same mistake. They convince themselves that their story is different, unique, special. Good luck."

Ben trailed behind him, head down, eyes examining the gleaming floor. He tried to forget everything he had heard from the moment he set foot in the cursed hospital, if it was possible to so label this serene hotel, with its expansive views of empty, manicured lawns and its ghostly tenants in their noisy rooms. From behind each door came the sounds of vitality, bubbling conversations, intimate quarrels, lovers' moans, dozens of horrifyingly accurate sound bites from scenes shot in one take, no rehearsal, no help from a prompter, pure improvisation, unpolished by screenwriter or director, a stylized fantasy, because behind the doors there wasn't an iota of life, behind them life was being recycled with the diligence only death can deliver.

The firm partition the sick placed between the two worlds enraged him; all of a sudden everyone had become a righter and decided to end their stories where they saw fit without seeking the advice of an expert; all of a sudden everyone had seized the fine excuse offered by death and shut the book with limp hands, unwilling to write another word, sitting in their sofas and reading the dead words ardently in a pathetic imitation of a conclusion. Marian, too, was among the righters. She, too, had sunk into the depths of the couch, tossed away her writing instruments, and brought about a premature end. His task was complex and difficult. He had to emancipate his love from the talons of the past and show her that their future lay before them. He had to prove to her that he, of all people, who used to jangle a chain of keys and lock stories up for others, could cut an ingenious key of his own, which would open the glorious horizon for her, would ever so carefully unlock the firmly sealed ending. . . .

Before he had a chance to fully unravel the thought, his tour guide stopped suddenly, offered a second "good luck," and turned on his heels. Ben examined the orange door. At first he had no idea how the alias knew Marian's door from all the others, since there was no name, number, lock, or any other identifying sign on it. Only when he looked up and down the hall and saw at least twenty doors, each in a different shade, did he understand that each patient had been given their own color, and thought to himself how intentional it was that the woman who so hated orange had been put in this specific room. He decided not to dawdle, fixed his hair with four jittery fingers, closed his eyes, and put his ear to the door, straining to hear what part of life his wife was listening to at the moment, as though his timing vis-a-vis her viewing would influence the nature of the meeting. There was not so much as a murmur within the room. Maybe she's watching us sleep, he thought, and knocked on the door. Answered only by a deep silence, he put a sweaty palm on the door and pushed gently. The submissive panel of wood opened with a soft sigh and he entered the absolute darkness. He called her name hesitantly and then again, confidently.

"Benji?" The tired voice stripped the darkness away.

He turned his head toward the source of the familiar voice and answered, "Yes."

The long silence that greeted him did not leave him bewildered, and he asked pragmatically, cloaking the tremble that went up and down his body, "Where's the switch?"

"Leave the light off," she suggested coyly, giggling.

Ben smiled as he felt his way through the darkness until his nostrils were flooded with the bittersweet smell of perfumed skin and he bent down and patted the open space longingly. His wandering hand stopped when it recognized her small, upturned nose. He took a long moment to reacquaint himself with her welcoming face, and in the midst of the most luminescent blindness he'd ever known, a soft dainty hand took his and led it with deliberate leisure to her belly button. His hand glided around her belly button in circles, sending forth ripples of pleasure, Marian's signature sign of desire, one of many secrets from their bedroom lore, and an unmistakable one at that. She pulled him toward her with sure hands, her body rising to meet him, bewitched and bewitching, a mound of flesh and blood craving to rub up against a longed-for skyline, to realize the only remaining dream, the impossible, the inexplicable. He was shocked by the purifying warmth that spread beneath his skin, the feeling of a man who has come home after a long time away, and even if the house is cloaked in darkness he is still able to pick out its scents, the trapped air in the closed rooms, the history smiling possessively from every corner, lying in wait and appearing suddenly, the house which is a detailed map of every movement and meditation. An instant after he opened the door and dared to enter, Ben already found himself wandering through the rooms, verifying that absolutely nothing had changed during his fifteen months away, opening one door and slamming another, pulling up blinds and drawing the drapes, straightening chairs, realigning the furniture, clearing away obstacles, making lanes, and, surprisingly, she did not reject him like a miffed dwelling, she accepted him with the passion of longing, and the moment was invincible, an unmatchable summit meeting between the home and the dweller, especially when her fingers sensed the sinewy tissue on his body, the slenderness she was so fond of that had been coated with unimaginable brawn. He could not have fathomed a warmer welcome, storming the contents of the house with impressive greed, leaving his mark on every object, shaking the walls, oozing with pleasure at the moaning roof held captive between his lips, huddling in the fissures between the damp tiles and skillfully skipping between every goose-bumped brick.

Finally, when Marian announced her satisfaction with a satiated moan, her ecstatic husband sighed and caressed her hair, thinking she'd say something, and yet she was unassailably mute. Even his whispered, "I missed you . . ." did not earn a reply. He gazed at her for a long while, seeing only what the darkness allowed, little fragments of Marian that his imagination fleshed out. The annoying alias's words pecked at his mind, sounding like a baseless theory in the moments after their rational lovemaking in the bed where they were returned to the days of yore. A hint at what the future held—his lips spread in an optimistic smile. The alias had overstated the effects of the illness. *I would have done the same exact thing had I died first. She did not stray from the normal. She simply broke down. That's all.*

It was the hushed voice that woke him from his rumination, the internal voice that managed to sneak away and settle near the base of her throat, the voice no one is supposed to hear but the speaker, whispering surreptitiously, expecting no answer. "That was so real you're here next to me behind me in front of me above me underneath me this time I managed to feel you even to hear you you asked where the switch was and I asked that you not turn on the light because even though I was dreaming I was scared that if you turned on the light I'd wake up and understand and I really wanted you to stay really didn't want you to go because only in the dark do I see you only in the dark do I feel you only in the dark do I know you're here and that nothing will change the fact that you're here not even the other patients in the other rooms I hope you're not one of them there already was one who claimed he was Ben but he didn't know what to do with my belly button so I chased him away and I shut the light and I went to sleep just like I do every day there's nothing new under the sun so what use is there in turning on the light it's not real not tangible definitely not like the way you were today I couldn't believe it I still can't believe that you made it and that you made me think you were real like in the movie I finally managed to bring you to me all thanks to the dark my love it did it all it kept the fire going I'm the only one who can see the spark I can smell you even now and hear those short breaths of yours but that will be our little se-

cret I promise not to tell anyone if you keep on coming to visit me
while I'm sleeping sweeten this nightmare flood me with promises
we'll keep it between us just like now Marian met Benji Marian was
right and that idiotic alias was wrong he said I would never find you
in this room between these walls outside the tapes and lo and behold
you came and I'm not upset that you left because I'm sure you'll be
back tomorrow I know you have things to do probably another story
to finish I'm busy too I still haven't found the missing week like a
black hole sometimes it confuses me where have seven days disappeared to I'm not sure I'll find them but I'll keep on looking and you
keep trying to sneak into my room oh how I love you sweet Benji trying to find the perfect ending and I'm just here hanging out well not
really because my ending was written long ago and now I'm just
blabbing . . . ."

Stunned, Ben lay by his prattling wife's side for two more hours, scared
of the moment when she would decide to get out of bed, turn on the light,
and see the fruit of her imagination that, under the cover of darkness,
grew flesh and blood, both believing and disbelieving what his ears
reported. When she hushed, he thought he'd seize the moment and slip
out, but she didn't give him enough time to act. She moved through the
dark with precision and Ben, paralyzed, heard the familiar sound of the
switch being raised. The sickly light that spread over the room, a foul
mixture of pale beige and rotten mustard, forced him to blink twice before his eyes rested on his wife. To his amazement, she didn't notice him
at first, as her eyes were racing among the tapes scattered on the floor,
and only when she got down on hands and knees to retrieve a tape she'd
inadvertently kicked under the bed, did she look up, see him, and smile.

Ben's smile congealed on his lips. Her smile was not the smile of
mutual understanding, the sarcastic smile, the offended smile, the seduc-
tive smile, the flattering smile, the dry humor smile, the dirty joke smile,
the praised intellect smile, the deliberating smile, the derisive smile, the
orgasmic smile, the confused smile, the perfunctory smile, the doubtful
smile, the white lie smile, the idiotic smile, the frightened smile, the
capricious smile, the sly smile, the morning smile, the generous smile,
the wild smile, or the wonderment smile.

It was the smile of a complete stranger.

39

In the Realm of Dreams

Some twenty-seven months after Marian lost her life under bizarre aeronautical circumstances, she woke up in the dead of night to the sound of suspicious movements near the door, crawled over to the switch, and flipped on the light. She exhaled in relief when she saw that the room did not contain the mysterious intruder who had fueled her fears, but then her eyes fell on the TV screen. A rectangular white envelope was taped to it, bearing her name, in script she recognized from a different world. She pulled the envelope away from its unusual spot, sat on the bed, removed a sheath of papers, written in the same familiar scrawl, and strained to still the tremble in her hands. Her eyes focused on the jaunty lines of words and she forced her lips to speak them aloud, afraid that if she read in silence, the tremor would sift entire lines from her field of vision.

Dearest Marian,

This is no dream. The pages you are holding in your hand contain words written by your loving husband, and this letter is the first and last one you will receive. That's in order to ensure that you don't destroy it in a moment of rage or think that it is one more detail in the wild fantasy your mind has concocted. I don't know if these words are able to touch you at all and reach into the depths of your fortressed soul, I have no idea whether you'll read this letter and be able to see beyond your four walls. This endeavor may be utterly ridiculous. You may not understand what I want, you may toss this whole thing into the trash. But remember, there won't be another letter. Not today, not tomorrow, not in another hundred years. I have no doubt you'll recognize the handwriting just as you will the hand that produced it. The same hand that squeezed the trigger and brought me to you.

Yes. I, like you, found no point in soldiering on once you were cruelly uprooted from my life. I also shut the blinds, locked the

doors, and enclosed myself behind the wall of the end. I wanted to
believe that I would find the fortitude to overcome the loss and I
craved that noble moment when I'd scale the wall and cross over to
the other side, and when I started going to the health club in order
to finally work on the body you'd yearned for, I lied to myself, hoping that by returning to the company of humans I would soon have
my life back, rather than the lowly and remote version that felt like
a bland memory from a happy childhood. Soon enough I understood the essence of the lie—a dead person cannot socialize with
living, breathing beings. I felt like an unskilled spy, a mole that had
lost his sanity, a double agent betraying both worlds at once. I was
disgusted by the helplessness. If you are so pained, there's a great
way to put yourself out of your misery, I told myself. But make no
mistake about my intentions, Marian—I wanted to break down the
wall; at times I sought to forget you, to wipe the memory of you
from my life, to master the immense power you had over me, but I
never managed to stop laughing. I swear to you I was laughing. In
jest. In rebuke. In the knowledge that it was all in vain. I asked myself, why were others able to handle their bereavement and I remained
such a miserable failure? What the hell made my loss different, unique,
special?

Alas, I never found an answer. It's simplistic to say that we had
something no other couples had. That's obvious. And what other couples had was not ours. And still, I rejected every rational explanation
in favor of survival in a world devoid of my beloved. The days passed
in intoxicating stillness, and the only consolation was to be had in
the strange worship of the body. In death you left me an unfulfilled
aspiration, a small wish that served as a temporary lifesaver. Every
night I looked into the mirror through your eyes, wondering if my
body had swelled to the dimensions that would delight your tickled
desires, and stitch by stitch the plan started to come together. I admit that I never realized that this is how the Other World would
look, but as opposed to many others, I believed in its existence. I
knew that if you left, you had surely gone somewhere. Even if that
place was no-where, I preferred to wind up there and be with you
rather than spend my time in a no-where where every breath of mine
was staged, every opening of my eyes, a fraud. I thought that all
other pain would be dwarfed by the pain I experienced there, in our

house, which turned, in an instant, into my house, singular, a meaningless ownership, hell.

I was wrong.

No, I don't have the slightest twinge of regret. Well, maybe about the wretched waiting. Maybe had I come earlier, we could have bridged the gap. The time gap. Who's the idiot who said time heals? If anything, it debilitates. The fact is, you're there and I'm here. And we're both in the same world. How ironic. When I was in the previous world and you were here, we were, mentally, in parallel universes, if you'll excuse the worn phrase. And then here, of all places, we were forced apart. And that's where I dropped the ball, because even in my wildest dreams and worst nightmares I did not foresee the odd possibility that while I march, determined, toward my future with you, you stagnate and retreat toward the past, which ended with your death. You see, I feared that by the time I reached you, I'd realize that you had continued on without me to an unknown future. Like any efficient epilogist, I wanted the past over and done with, even though it spurred me into action and dictated my steps. I don't fault you for the far-reaching changes you've undergone from the day you died to the chimerical present, even though I must admit I was surprised.

The first time we met, you asked that I not turn on the light, and we made love like in the good old days. Naïvely, I thought all our woes had been salved and that we would pick up again from where we had left off. The head of the department and all of his ominous forecasts could go to hell. I refused to accept the dictates which he handed down with such certainty, and I detested his chilly demeanor, as though he knew you better than me. I scorned him and his outrageous diagnoses and, above all else, I despised his assertion that in death you had become a different woman. And then you turned on the light. And smiled at me in a way I had never seen. Like you were surprised to see the man who just a second before had made love to you, like you were shocked by his very presence in your room, like someone amused and abashed by the sight of her lover who dared slip out of her dreams.

Marian, there's nothing more frightening than a new and foreign expression on a loved one's face, it's like listening to a piece of comforting music you know well only to find that it's been tweaked with discordant notes. We looked at each other for over an hour, I tried to convince you that I had come back to you from the world of the living, I shook you with all my might, yelled in your ear, even tried to slap that obtuse expression off your face, that same frozen expression that followed me for the next six months each time you turned on the light after our daily act of love. I thought that if I fulfilled my lover's murky whim, then, with time, the woman with whom I had fallen in love would return to my arms, and every night, when walking out through the gates of the building, I felt satisfaction and disgust course through me as one, aware that for as long as I continued to visit you, your belief in the awful lie would grow, the same exasperating lie that had turned me into a ghost. For six months, the ghost's body served your desire in the hot darkness of your room, and the steel bonds that tied our souls together rusted and cracked, leaving not so much as a single strand to hold on to, nothing. Six months, and we didn't manage a single meaningful word to one another. I'm not willing to continue to make do with our tenebrific intercourse, Marian. Not anymore. More than anything else I desire your mind, which you've cordoned off with coils of barbed wire. Even from yourself. I have no place in your world. How could I possibly join you, when I know how wondrous you are in your being and how hurtful you are in your cessation.

It's not you I fell in love with, but who you were. When you were.

It's not me I detest, but the man you ask me to be, the fraud who comes in the dark, fulfills your dusky desires, and leaves with nightfall.

Marian, do you remember the difference between past and present?

Can you discern between the two?

The last time we met, exactly five months and one week ago, I came to part with you, without telling you. I thought something might change that day, that maybe the fact that I had already decided on leaving would somehow alert you to what was going on. Long ago, in simpler times, you would just look me in the eyes and understand. But that day you outdid yourself and the moment we finished our lustful act you turned back to the screen and asked me to move out of the way. "You're blocking me," you snorted, waving me aside. I looked at the screen and I saw us making love. The real Ben interfered with your viewing of the taped Ben. The reality that was half fantasy stepped aside for memory. And still I tried my luck. I scooped a handful of tapes off the floor and made to leave. The smile faded. You looked at me like a dangerous animal protecting its young and before I was able to open the door you pounced on me and attacked me with a ferocity I didn't know you possessed. When you pummeled me and pried the tapes free, I realized that if I didn't remove myself from view, I would worsen your situation immeasurably. Do you remember what happened after I threatened to rob you of your past and the subsequent outburst of violence? Do you remember how you hugged the tapes to your chest lovingly and continued smiling your foreign smile as you sat back down in front of the TV as though nothing had happened?

Recognition came to me late. Nothing happened. The conclusive evidence of my existence didn't so much as scratch your skin. You wouldn't let anyone, not even me, crawl into your carefully framed world and ruin it. You didn't want anyone "blocking" you. You were always stubborn, but in death you've become downright indomitable.

And again I want to be clear that I do not have any regrets about finding you. I would have lost my mind had you remained in the realm of dreams. Today, I can safely say that having met you turned you into a dream alright. My own personal nightmare. A Marian who does not recognize me outside the borderlines of her private fantasy, a Marian who refuses to talk reasonably with me, a Marian who loses all interest in me a moment after she mouths my name in passion. On the other hand, I still dream about you as though I had not found you between the walls of the ancient building. About the Marian I knew. About the Marian you see every day on your screen. My mask-free love. My naked love.

I thought I would break down again when I came to the decision not to return to the room. I thought the anguish over my betrayal by abandonment would rip me to pieces. I thought and I thought. Too much. Sometimes you just need to let thoughts race around till they get tired and subside on their own. Sometimes you need to go to sleep and wake up and find that it was all a dream: The thought that you'd be waiting for me with open arms and that we'd pick up from where we left off. The natural continuation of our harmonic relationship without any difficulties. The charmed eternity of lovebirds.

I admit, this wasn't the end I'd hoped for. Its lack of clarity is so strange. And again it entails waiting. Less anxiously, more bindingly. Along with that, though, I've discovered a freedom I'd already managed to forget. There's not a day when I don't see you in my mind's eye, there's not a night when I don't envision your form, there's not a morning when I don't wake up and seek you out with my fingers. Force of habit. But I'm free of the depression that had seized me early on. The bitter sadness that had seeped into my bones was blotted out as though it had never existed. And when the sadness lifted the cool fresh breeze of a new beginning began to blow. I started to understand that our existence side by side is not a dictate of reality. To understand that if memory is your way of loving me, I must respect and remember you in my own manner. To cherish your memory. I needed every step of this journey in order to let go of you. I needed this whole journey to lose you and find you again inside of me. Funny, eh? I committed suicide in order to come to terms with your death. People less prone to the extreme could have traveled this rocky path from their living room couches, and yet your husband needed all the drama. What won't a righter do in order to find the period at the end of the story . . .

And still, it is over but not done with. Almost. You know why. Or perhaps not. Maybe you had the chance to forget about the meaning of time when you buried the present. Allow me to remind you. Today, forty-one years ago, you came into the previous world. Today, one year ago, I left that same world. And today, just a few hours ago, we finished celebrating the birthday of the woman who bears your exact likeness and name. Everyone came to the park in 2001. Everyone, Marian, even some people I didn't know. Mom, Dad, Catherine, Henri, Uncle David and his new boyfriend, Uncle Gad, Yossef and Miriam, Grandpa Moses and Grandma Rosie, Sandrine and her partner, and even "the Norwegian hussy," as Mom calls Dad's girlfriend. And Samuel, my good friend, who helped me with my search. In the end, your charming sister managed to get over her embarrassment and thank the family that had adopted her, said she knew who she owed the really big thanks to, and looked teary-eyed straight at the empty chair at the head of the table, raised a glass of wine, and drank to your recuperation. We all stood up and offered birthday wishes to both Marians, the present and the absent, and we expressed the hope that next year perhaps you'd be willing to join us. You'll be happy to hear that the idea of the empty chair was Henri's.

Marian, each day that passes without you in our midst pains me, not least because of the pure magic we unknowingly brought into this world. I am simply in love with him and have gotten used to the annoying name Grandma Catherine gave him. The kid fills my days with smiles and, in all honesty, I admit that he made a great deal when he had himself "born" into the extinct Mendelssohn clan. He gets love from all over. Catherine moved in to Marian's apartment, ten minutes from here, and they come over to visit every chance they get. Sandrine, your biological mother's best friend, sewed him wings so that he can get more hang time when he basejumps off the roof. Yossef and Miriam take him traveling all over the Other World. David made him a mini multi-wheel and he drives it around the special paths in the park, and that's not the half of it. As far as the kid is concerned, life may not have been a picnic, but death . . .

I'm laughing again. Last time I laughed because in a flash of sincerity Henri asked if I could be Aunt Marian's boyfriend. "They look almost exactly alike and they already have the same name," he gushed. Kids. I wish it were so simple. And then today I laughed again when I served Marian her birthday cake. Our eyes met and for a moment a shiver went up my spine. For a fraction of a second the amazing likeness paralyzed me. Seems I wasn't the only one who noticed the innocent exchange of glances. The whole clan hushed and stared, trying to interpret what was happening. It's not the first time our eyes have locked like that. She thinks of the poor nurse who murdered her when she looks at me and I . . . well, you know what I think of. And in these miniscule icebergs of time, where consciousness slips away in freezing drops, there I understand almost all of it. How our private associations rear their heads without warning and shake our logic, seeking to confront us with indelible historical snapshots of happiness or darkness, to pull us down to dangerous depths at the spur of the moment, and freeze us. Why'd I laugh? Because her eyes don't tell what yours once did, when they still had the knack. Because her pupils reveal much, but not of you. And then I see that only the very discerning can tell the twins apart. And in that tumultuous moment of identifying the difference, I grin like an idiot, pass the slice of cake, and sit down to chat with Samuel, embarrassed by the artificial intimacy imposed by imagination.

Even when Catherine first proposed a meeting between the two of you, when you refused to leave the room and left the television on, the differences were clear to me. When you stood one beside the other, I knew I'd never be able to find you in her. Even though today, after ten months of acquaintance, I can definitively say that the two of you would have made great friends. Both of you know a ton about modern art and, more to the point, you both love it wholeheartedly, and I have no doubt that you would have spent days and nights at the movies, the bookstores, the concert halls, the open air stadiums . . .

Marian and Samuel supported me no end during the first two months after I stopped coming to Worldly Rest. They ripped out the degrading, selfish feeling that had taken root inside me and encouraged me to get back to writing. Marian got back to her arts and literature reporting (over the course of the past six months she's landed two interviews with Orson Welles about two different films he's working on as part of his plan of ousting *Citizen Kane* from the top of the all-time list) and Samuel continues to investigate strange mysteries even as he works on his masterpiece *A Guide for the Deceased Detective.* . . . You see, sometimes I forget that you're not interested in all the tiresome details and I find myself communicating like in the old days, back when you would have done anything to get a ticket to an unknown Orson Welles movie and worked the name of an actor or a character from it into one of your smashing crossword successes. Marian, have you forgotten the down-and-across joys you loved to craft? Will you really ignore Shakespeare's new play? Will you embrace the ignorance your solitary cell provides you and turn your back on the cornucopia offered by the universe outside? Will you, like the faithless and the low-browed, refrain from looking beyond the keyhole? Will you, like them, experience conventional, stultifying, cold, monochromatic, rotten death? Will you turn into a lazy, stone-necked corpse that only gazes in one direction—back—a woman without the will to walk on, a goddess of intellect who ceased using her intelligence?

I still don't believe it. Don't believe in the forced separation. Don't believe we lost the power to communicate. But I believe in you, otherwise I wouldn't have snuck into your room while you were asleep and left you this letter and a birthday present. I have no use for it anymore. Let's hope it can help you. And just before you get to the last lines and press play on the Vie-deo machine, I'll have you know that two weeks ago I wrote a prologue. If you were back at your best you'd laugh and call me a liar. But I swear, darling, a prologue. The beginning of a story. It takes place here. In the Other World. The potential for storytelling in this world is simply endless. I won't reveal the details but I will confess that I have no idea how it's going to end. For the first time since I ever took up a pen and started to write, I don't care about the end. It's meaningless to me. After all, who says that every journey, whether real or fictional, has to have a destination point? Sometimes we just long for the journey and nothing more. And actually, now that I think about it, the starting point is the decisive one, no? That's what has sent us off on out adventuresome, aimless wandering, just like life, my love. I believe it's high time we looked into the beginning of things, and before that the introduction, to discover the roots of the motives and why the teller decided to embark at one point and not another.

You'll find my address on the back of the tape, if and when . . .

Yours,
Ben.

Marian turned on the TV, pressed PLAY, and leaned forward with interest. The figure of her husband, in the purple silk shirt and brown corduroy pants she'd bought for him with her shop-aholic friend Tali, filled the screen. In the background loud, unfamiliar blasts could be heard, accompanied by shouts of encouragement and hoots of happiness from an unseen crowd. The ruckus did not distract the righter, who held a gun in his right hand and pulled a note from his pants pocket, gripping it firmly in his left. The table by his side was laden with snacks and the ceiling just above him was decorated with a colorful strand of balloons.

He wiped the sweat from his brow with the back of his left hand, scanned the room in terror, opened his trembling lips, and shoved the gun deep down his throat. His eyes closed, his unsteady finger caressed the trigger three times before finally squeezing it all the way back. The sharp tenor of the shot was muffled by the deafening explosions of fireworks; the TV screen went dark, the Vie-deo machine, with a slight beep, announced that the tape was over and, in the partial darkness, Marian recognized the reflection on the screen of a woman crying softly, her smile lost and gone.